SEE WHAT I MEAN?

WORKS BY LEWIS BROWNE

NOVELS

All Things Are Possible
Oh, Say, Can You See!
See What I Mean?

HISTORIES, ETC.

Stranger Than Fiction
This Believing World
The Graphic Bible
Since Calvary
How Odd of God
Something Went Wrong

BIOGRAPHIES

That Man Heine
Blesséd Spinoz~

See What I Mean?

A NOVEL
By LEWIS BROWNE

Random House New York

FOURTH PRINTING

This is in a literal sense a work of fiction, and no character in it is intended to be identified with any real person now either under arrest, at large, or dead.

L. B.

COPYRIGHT, 1943, BY LEWIS BROWNE

PUBLISHED SIMULTANEOUSLY IN CANADA BY
THE MACMILLAN COMPANY OF CANADA, LIMITED

MANUFACTURED IN THE UNITED STATES OF AMERICA
AMERICAN BOOK—STRATFORD PRESS, INC., NEW YORK, N. Y.

PROLOGUE

I always figured that if you wanted to write a book, first off you'd have to have lots of peace and quiet. You'd have to be some place where there was nothing to worry you, no room rent, no board bills, no phones to answer, nothing. In other words, what the poetry writers call (*quote*) an ivory tower (*unquote*). See what I mean?

And that's just the sort of place I'm in right now. This is a jail.

How I got here, you probably know, because, after all, you can read, can't you? Therefore, what with all the publicity they've been giving me lately, you couldn't hardly help but know. I and the crowd I've been indicted with have been front-page copy for weeks. Moreover, just in case you can't read, we've already been in the newsreels at least twice that I know. That's one thing even I will say for the FBI: they sure can get you plenty of publicity.

But all that is neither here nor there. The point is, it makes no difference how much you may or may not have read about me and the others, what you know is practically nothing to what you're going to hear now.

Because this book is going to reveal all—and when I say all, I mean *a* double *l*, ALL.

First it's going to reveal all about me and how I came to get mixed up with the Crusade. Then it's going to reveal all about the others in the movement, and the exact extent of their innocence or guilt. (Incidentally, it's going to prove beyond the peradventure of a doubt that in my own case the innocence amounts to just about one hundred percent.) And I want you to believe every word in this book, because I don't intend, as the lawyers say, to mitigate, prevaricate, or equivocate in any manner, shape, or form whatsoever. In other words, and I state this on my oath and positively sincerely, I am going to tell the truth, the whole truth, and nothing but the truth, so help me God—and the Federal Court.

(*Signed*)
Clem Smullet

SEE WHAT I MEAN?

1

I was born in the city of Waterbury, Conn., on January 16, 1906. My father, Thomas J. Smullet, was a brakeman on the N.Y., N.H. & H. Railway, and he got killed in a train wreck the day the Armistice was signed, which was November 11, 1918. My mother, who had always been kind of delicate, died in the flu epidemic a year later, with the result that I was sent to live with an aunt in New Haven. Said aunt was married to a plasterer, and I didn't like her or her husband either. Moreover, now that I know they have come out and said things against me, I don't mind publicizing just why I didn't like them. They were stingy and kept crabbing because I had a healthy appetite, especially for a kid my size. (I've always been kind of small, taking after my mother, about whom people used to say she was no bigger than a minute.) Also they were religious fanatics, being Pentecostals, and they believed it was a mortal sin to smoke or dance or shoot pool or even go to the movies.

The night I graduated from high school, one of the boys in my class threw a party, and I got drunk on bath-tub gin and practically ruined my brand-new blue-serge suit. Knowing what would happen when my folks found out about that, I waited till they were asleep, got the cash-box they kept under a floor-board in the kitchen, and beat it to New York.

I figured I had a right to the money, seeing as how I had never got one cent of my old man's insurance.

My ambition at that time was to be a newspaperman, and my dough lasted just long enough for me to land a job as copyboy on the *New York American*. The following year I became a cub reporter, and right away I began to have visions of taking Mr. Brisbane's place, or maybe even Mr. Hearst's. But one day I got sore at the managing editor because he falsely accused me of charging for phone calls which he claimed I had never made. Moreover, when he threatened to fire me if I tried to do that again, I just blew up and quit. I was only a kid at the time, but I knew even then that I could never be happy working for someone who didn't trust me.

I decided it was time I saw something of the country, so I went to Chicago, where I worked for a while on the *Tribune*. After that I moved on to Kansas City, Denver, Portland and Seattle. Finally I came to the conclusion that a fellow with my brains was wasting his time in the newspaper game, so I bummed my way back to New York and took up another profession.

I became a press agent.

My first job was with a vaudeville booking office, and I liked everything about it—except the pay, of course. The work was interesting, the hours were easy, and the dames it put me in contact with were real sophisticated, if you know what I mean. But then I ran into one who turned old-fashioned on me and said we ought to get married. She was a cute little number, just the type I liked, being blonde and not too tall for me; but still and all I couldn't see myself hooking up with her for life. If I was going to take on a ball-and-chain, I wanted to pick one that was at least gold-filled —which this one definitely was not. So I talked my boss into giving me a week's wages in advance, and skipped town.

That happened in 1927, and it started me off on another spell of scuffling. For a while I had a pretty tough time of it, but I never starved. Only suckers starve, and, I don't mind telling you, I'm not the sucker type. All I needed was a break, and before long I got one. It happened in Tulsa. I got in there with a couple of promoters who were selling oil-stocks by mail, and I did such a bang-up job on the publicity that the syndicate cleaned up nearly twenty grand inside six months.

But then there was some sort of legal mix-up. It would take too long to go into the details, and anyway I don't recollect most of them, it being so long ago. The gist of it was that I got double-crossed by my partners. Moreover, by the time the lawyer I hired, one of the smartest in Tulsa, managed to clear me of the false charge, I was broke to the world and furthermore penniless.

Well, after that I did some more drifting until finally, in Chicago, I got another break. I connected there with an outfit that talked little towns into building big hotels, and the work gave me a chance to show what I really had in me, which I don't mind saying was plenty. In almost no time at all I was made director of publicity at a salary of $100 a week, plus expenses, and if the Crash hadn't come along the following year, there's no telling how far I might have gone.

However, and this is a matter of record, the Crash did come in October of 1929, and by November I woke up to find myself not alone unemployed but also broke once more. Like everybody else from J. P. Morgan up and down, I had been playing the market on margin, and notwithstanding that I had made some mighty shrewd investments, the brokers sold me out.

Thereupon, having no other recourse as the saying goes, I started scuffling again; and believe me, this time it was really tough, no kidding. President Hoover got hoarse talking about how prosperity was around the corner, and I developed bunions trying to locate where that corner was.

Still and all, I never gave up looking. Many a time I was tempted to swallow my pride and go on relief, but I always managed somehow to hold out. That's one thing I can say for myself honestly and sincerely: never once in all those years did I stoop to taking public charity. It was a matter of principle with me. I'd have starved rather than swallow my pride.

The fact remains, however, that I did not starve, though I will admit I lost weight for a while. There was a time out in St. Louis in 1936 when I got so thin I could have doubled for Gandhi. But it didn't last. Finding myself reduced to what was nothing less than desperation, I took a job peddling Fuller brushes.

That, of course, was an awful comedown for me, and I wouldn't even mention it now if it hadn't led to something better. What happened, briefly, was this: the second day, or maybe it was the third, that I went out with my satchel, I came to a door which was opened by a real friendly party, and the result was a kind of funny little bedventure. She was a schoolma'am in her early thirties, blonde, plump and not really bad-looking except for the way her gums showed when she smiled. She was sort of passionate, too. In almost no time at all, she was offering to stake me to a law course—I'd told her that was my ambition—so right then and there I quit my job and we became sort of engaged.

After a couple of months, though, I got fed up with trying to keep my mind on torts—yeah, it's spelled with an "o"—and when the second term came around I didn't sign up again. Instead, I cashed the check which my fiancée had made out to the registrar, and used the money to buy a ticket to Los Angeles.

In a technical sense, I guess maybe that wasn't the ethical thing to do, but on the other hand just consider what I *could* have done. I had enough on that schoolma'am to make her come through with every penny she owned. Besides, look at all the pleasure I had given her.

Be that as it may, the fact remains that I did cash that check, and three days later I was right where a guy like me belonged.

I knew that the minute I got off the train. Everything about Los Angeles, the sunshine, the palm trees, the sappy look on peoples' faces, everything seemed to shout, "Clem Smullet, this is just where you belong!" All I had in the world was eleven dollars, my pocket-comb, and a change of socks, but I swear John D. Rockefeller couldn't have felt happier than I did that morning.

And luck was with me right from the start. I'd heard that a fellow by the name of Ivan Kohn, whom I'd known back in Chicago, was doing publicity out at Paramour,* so I got in touch with him, and right away he took me to lunch. Moreover, that same day he got me a job. It didn't pay much, fifty a week, but I was satisfied. I had my foot inside the door, and that was all I needed—for a start.

Nine months later I had my name on that door and my fanny in one of the cushiest swivel chairs in Hollywood. I had become the ace idea-man in the Paramour publicity department, and was making a hundred a week—besides extras.

It didn't last, though. The dope at the head of the department got jealous because of the way I was making good, and the first thing I knew he was knifing me in the back. So I finally up and quit.

The next day I went over to another major studio where I had

This is of course not the real name of the studio, but an alias adopted on advice of counsel.

already started something cooking, and inside an hour I had them eating out of my hand. They had just had a reorganization on that lot—the umpteenth, I guess—and the new publicity chief was a right guy, with plenty of guts and imagination. He was an old carnival plugger, the finger-snapping kind, and all he wanted was results, no questions asked. We got along swell.

But after about six months there was another reorganization, and the new guy they put over me was a jerk of the worst order. He kept objecting to my ideas, and do you know on what grounds? Because they were too sensational! I'm not kidding! That squirt actually wanted me to tone my stuff down! You see, he was one of those elegant Hebes that had gone to collitch, and learnt to call himself a Counsellor on Public Relations instead of just a press agent. I couldn't stand the bastard.

So I eventually quit and moved over to Warner Bros.* I had to take a cut to do that, but I didn't mind. I knew I'd more than make it up once they gave me a chance to show how good I was. And I was right. In almost no time at all I was drawing my $100 a week again, and a little later $125. I was on my way to becoming a real somebody around Hollywood, in fact a sort of Lubitsch of pub-licity. People began recognizing what they called my "touch," and when they wanted to describe my type of promotion they'd say "if you can smell it, it is Smullet's." That'll give you some idea of what a dent I was making.

But then something happened that I still can't think about with-out getting boiling mad. One of the stars that I had done any num-ber of favors for, a nympho that I'd been protecting from all sorts of scandals, suddenly turned on me and claimed that I had been shaking her down. It was a bare-faced lie, of course. All I had done was borrow some money from her occasionally, and she couldn't prove even that, because it just happened that all the transactions had been in cash. Nevertheless the front office believed her, and as a result, it was curtains for me.

I was out.

---

* There's no need for me to camouflage this name, due to the fact that it has already been publicized in connection with my case. Here, however, you will read the only true version of what really occurred on said Warner lot.

And I mean *out*. From then on I couldn't get a job in any studio in town. There had naturally been no noise about what had happened at Warners, yet the story got around anyway, and the first thing I knew I was being ostracized, practically. I swear, I couldn't have been snubbed more if I'd been an Oakie.

I tried not to worry at first. I had a bankroll stashed away, plenty of clothes, and of course my car. It was one of those sporty Cords with the guts hanging out, and it had set me back two grand. I figured everything would blow over after a bit, so I took a trip to Palm Springs with a little canary I was acquainted with, and then drove her to New York, where she had a job waiting for her in a night-club. I put up at the Astor, and stayed almost a month.

But when I got back, damned if the heat wasn't still on. No matter where I turned, I was given the brush-off. Whoever I phoned was out of town, or in conference, or something. "Yes, Mr. Smullet," each and every secretary would say, "I'll tell him you called. . . . No, you don't need to leave your number, I'm sure he has it. . . ."

I guess that was the trouble. All Hollywood had my number, but wrong.

I had to give up my apartment and move into a hotel. First I lived at the Plaza, then the Coolidge, then a dump called the Majestique. Finally I had to move into a rooming-house off Vine Street, and that was where I hit bottom. I got so broke that I actually had to give up my car!

2

The lady who owned the rooming-house was a widow by the name of Mrs. Gunderson, and if it hadn't been for her, I guess I wouldn't be here now. In jail, I mean. But I don't hold that against her. If there is one person in the whole world that I don't hold anything against, it's Mrs. Gunderson. Because even though it was through her that I got mixed up with the Crusade in the first place,

I know she meant well, and wasn't in the least to blame for the result. I made that clear to the FBI the day they picked her up with the rest of us, and the fact that they didn't hold the old lady for more than a couple of hours goes to prove that I was correct. It also kind of eases my conscience. She treated me real decent, in fact like a mother, and it makes me feel right to know that I did her a good turn when I got the chance.

I didn't pay much attention to her when I first moved into her house. She was just someone who asked for the rent, and tidied the rooms, and called you downstairs if the phone was for you. All I noticed was that she was small and gray and gabby, with little gray eyes as bright as a kitten's, and a tiny, puckered-up mouth. She tried to get me into a conversation once or twice, asking how I was getting along, and whether I had found a job yet; but I always managed to brush her off. I was afraid she was leading up to the question of when I would be able to pay the month's rent, which was due in advance. Most of the time I tried to keep out of her sight. I would leave the house the minute I got dressed before noon, and not come back until way after midnight.

Of course, I still had my Cord then, so it was easy for me to do that. I'd cruise around all afternoon, tracking down job-prospects or just rubbernecking, and at night I'd sit it out at Slapsie Maxie's or some other joint.

But finally that day came when I lost the car, and then everything changed. I'll never forget that day. It started out kind of foggy and cold, so I stayed in bed reading the morning paper that somebody had left in the bathroom. It was the *Examiner,* and practically the entire front page was taken up with stuff about a sex-maniac who had been terrorizing Beverly Hills for months, but had finally been caught. Otherwise there didn't seem to be much news. The Yankees had beat Detroit 22 to 2, the World's Fair was off to a bad start, that guy Franco was all set to enter Madrid, and Porter's Mite wasn't going to run in the Derby.* Nevertheless, what with that

---

* *In case you're wondering how I remember all those details, I might as well admit that I got a pal to look them up in the* Examiner *files. The exact date, if you should care to check on me, was Tuesday, May 16, 1939. This, incidentally, will prove to what lengths I have gone in order to give this whole record absolutely straight!*

fiend story and the comics and the movie gossip, I managed to stay interested till almost one o'clock.

But then I just had to get up because I needed breakfast, and I was supposed to be down at KHJ at two. A guy I knew at that station had promised to give me a knockdown to the head of the publicity department, and though I was sure nothing would come of it, I felt I ought to show up anyway. So I dressed quickly, slicked my hair back, put on my camel-hair sport jacket, and ankled down the stairs.

When I got to the front door, though, who should be standing there, all primed to pounce on me, but a couple of ghouls from the finance company? I tried to stall them, of course, like I had done more than once before, but this time they wouldn't even give a listen. "It's the dough or else," they said.

So I had to let 'em else.

I can't tell you what that did to me: seeing those ghouls drive off with my car. It made something inside me go snap, like a spring had broken, and I thought I'd collapse. I actually had to hang onto the garage door, I felt so weak.

"Jesus," I groaned, "what'll I do now?"

I couldn't think any more of keeping that appointment down at the radio station. It would have meant taking a street car, and that was too much. The idea was so humiliating, it made me shake like I had malaria or something.

I wasn't really sick, you understand. It was just a case of mind over matter, or, in other words, psychology. But the fact remains that even if I wasn't sick, I *felt* sick. Believe me, I felt so sick that it was about all I could do to crawl back into the house and get to my room.

I caught a squint at my mug in the mirror over the washstand, and I swear it gave me a fright. Said mug had never been what you could call handsome, owing to the nose being kind of sharp, and the teeth irregular; but still and all it had always seemed at least passable. Now, though, it looked positively repulsive. The skin was the color of dirty blotting paper, and there were lines around the mouth a mile deep. "Grrr!" I went, shutting my eyes.

I had an old 3-Star Hennessy bottle that I kept up on a shelf for show, and I reached for it and started to drink. The stuff in the bottle was actually nothing but cheap grape brandy, but I kept gulping and gulping until finally I thought my guts had caught fire. Nevertheless, I still continued to shiver. I piled into bed, yet even that didn't help. I had all my clothes on, but still I shivered. So then I started to cry. I'm not exaggerating. I started crying just like a baby, the tears rolling down my cheeks and soaking the pillow.

How long that went on I have no idea, but finally I must have fallen asleep. Anyway, the next thing I knew, the light was on in the room, and there was Mrs. Gunderson leaning over me, her face full of fright. It must have been late, because she was wearing a flannel robe and her hair was in curlers.

"You sick, Mr. Smullet?" she said, in a scared voice. "You been groaning something awful. I could hear you clear over in my room."

I didn't answer. My head felt as big as a cement mixer, and the brains seemed to be churning gravel.

"You ain't been drinking, have you?" she asked.

"No, I'm sick all right," I managed to get out.

"Think I ought to call a doctor?"

I rolled my head. "It's not that kind of sickness," I said. "My nerves are shot, that's all."

She stared a minute, like she didn't believe me. But then she seemed to melt, and suddenly asked, "How long since you had something to eat, Clem?"

It was the first time she had ever called me by my Christian name, and that on top of the way she asked the question made me go all weak inside. I started to cry again. I just couldn't help it.

The next thing I knew, she was unlacing my shoes. I didn't try to stop her. I was too weak to try. I just lay there and let her fumble around till she got my shoes off and put them under the bed. Then I felt her give me a pat and heard her say, "Now you get out of them clothes, son, while I go downstairs and heat up a bowl of soup."

The next day I wanted to get up, but she wouldn't let me. The minute she heard me stirring she came bustling into my room without even knocking.

"Now you go right back to bed, Clem," she ordered. "You're all run down, and need a rest."

I didn't try to argue with her. I really did need a rest, what with all I had gone through in the last months. I had been worrying myself to a frazzle, and also drinking too much, and not eating the way I should. So I was darn glad to crawl back into bed.

Fifteen minutes later she was back again, this time with my breakfast all laid out pretty on a tray. There was even a tiny bunch of flowers on it. And it was a real tip-top breakfast: orange juice, bacon and eggs, buttered toast, and a whole pot of Java. Moreover, when I finished it, she brought me the morning newspaper and said, "Now you jest lay there, Clem, and take it easy."

I did. I stayed in bed all day, and she nursed me like I might have been her own son. I mean that. I was nothing but a stranger to her, just a roomer who hadn't even paid his rent, yet she couldn't have treated me nicer if I had been her own flesh and blood.

I guess it was because she just wanted to mother somebody. I found that out when she came up to keep me company during the afternoon, and started telling me her whole life history. Her own children were married and living back in North Dakota, and she was all alone out here. She had come west with her husband eight or nine years earlier, on account that she had rheumatism and couldn't stand the climate back home. He'd been a rancher, and must have been pretty well fixed. They bought property when they landed in Los Angeles, and figured to live off the income. But then came the Depression, and they had lost everything excepting this house she was in now. On top of that, her husband got a stroke, and all his insurance money went to pay off the doctor bills. She had to start taking in roomers after he passed away, and that was how she was getting by now.

She told me all that and a lot more during the time she sat in my room, doing her mending, that afternoon. Then she asked me to tell her my story, and I made it so good she nearly cried.

"It ain't right!" she said when I got through. "People like us shouldn't have to suffer the way we do. Here we are, millions of us, jest trying to live decent. That's all we ask, jest to be allowed to live decent, and look what happens to us. I tell you, Clem, it jest ain't proper!"

"Yeah," I sighed, reaching for the comb on the bedside table and starting to slick my hair. "But that's the way it is in this world.

Honest people don't stand a chance." I wasn't ribbing her. I meant that.

"Well, we ought to do something about it," she said, real fierce. "We ought to get together and change things."

"Aw, what's the use?" I answered, wiping the comb on the bed-clothes. "That's the way the world is, and there's nothing we can do about it. The trouble is God didn't create it right in the first place." I settled back on the pillows and grinned at the old lady. "Yeah," I went on, "He didn't give enough time to the production. Just six days, that's all. *Boom, boom, boom,* and there you are! Heck, He went at it like it was nothing but a quickie."

She didn't seem to appreciate my humor. "You mustn't talk like that, Clem," she said, frowning at me over the top of her glasses. "That's blasphemy."

I pushed the grin off my face and snuck down in the bed. "I was only kidding, Mrs. Gunderson," I apologized.

"Well, you shouldn't, Clem. I'm old enough to be your mother, so I've got a right to tell you. You oughtn't ever kid about things like that."

"Yes, ma'am," I said, real contrite. "But you know I didn't mean what I said."

"Of course you didn't," she declared, putting away the pillow slip she had been mending. "You're a good boy at heart, Clem. It's jest on the outside that you're so hard—and . . ."

"Cynical," I helped her out.

"That's it. But you're not *really* that way, not underneath. You just put it on." She paused to rethread her needle, and started to work on a torn towel. "I guess it's because of the sort of people you been with all your life, city people that ain't got any principles, and jest try to cheat you all the time."

I reached for a cigarette and struck a match. "Yeah, that's the truth, Mrs. Gunderson," I told her, taking a deep drag. "But there you are! Those are the people who are on top in this world, so what's the good of having principles? You've just got to be like them, if you want to get anywhere. If you're stubborn and try to hold out, you get it in the neck every time." She made as if she wanted to argue the point, but I wouldn't let her. "No, ma'am," I insisted, blowing smoke at the ceiling, "you'll never convince me it pays to have principles. Look at Jonah. Why do you think he had to stay in the belly of that whale for so long? Because he had his principles, that's why. He just wouldn't give in to the whale and leave by the regular exit!"

She had to laugh at that one even though it did kind of shock her a little. "There you go blaspheming again," she complained, but kind of smiling. "Jonah stayed in the belly of the whale because he knew that was what the Lord wanted him to do."

"Maybe so," I said, flicking the ash into the tray she had put at my side. "But take me, now. How am I to know what the Lord wants me to do? I'm just a common ordinary human, not a prophet."

"That's true enough. But you can at least listen to a prophet."

"Yeah? Who, for instance? There isn't any prophet around."

"That's where you're wrong, Clem," she cried, her little eyes flashing behind her spectacles. "There's a real prophet right here in Los Angeles. I listen to him every week."

I stared at her, wondering what I was getting into. "You don't mean Aimee McPherson?" I queried.

"Of course not! *That* woman! Why, she's nothing but—well, never mind." She frowned for a minute, her mouth very firm. Then, giving her head a shake, she drew in a deep breath and said, "No, I mean J. C. Power."

"Who?"

"John Christian Power. Ain't you ever heard of him?"

I shook my head. "What is he?" I asked. "A preacher?"

"No. He's—well, it's hard to explain. I guess you'd call him a leader, that's all."

"Yeah? Who does he lead?"

A look of positive awe came into the old lady's eyes. "Some of the biggest people in this town, that's all," she declared. "And I mean really the biggest. You'd be surprised if I mentioned the names of some of them."

"Is that a fact? Say, what does he tell them? I mean, what does he want them to do?"

Now she narrowed her eyes and looked mysterious. "I can't reveal that," she said, almost whispering. "It's a secret."

"No kidding."

"Yes, it's a deep secret. We're sworn not to let it out even at the point of the sword. . . . All right, you can laugh at me if you want to. I don't mind. But it's the truth jest the same."

"I'm not laughing, Mrs. Gunderson. Honest I'm not."

"Yes you are. I can see it in your eyes. But I don't mind. I'm used to it." She paused to heave a sigh. "But believe me, if you knew the secret you wouldn't laugh. No, Clem, if you knew even the least little part of it you'd—you'd jest tremble. That's how big it is."

"Is that so?"

"I mean it. You'll find out one of these days."

"Yeah? When?"

"Oh, you'll know in time. Right now that's also part of the secret."

"But you can give me a little hint, can't you? You've got me all curious. What does this man Power do? I mean, does he hold meetings or something?"

"Naturally. He meets with us once a week. He calls 'em conferences, though. I'm going to one tonight."

"Gosh, I wish I could come along," I said, still keeping a straight pan.

"Oh, they wouldn't let you in," she cried, shaking her head. "Only people who've taken the Blood Oath can attend our conferences. But if you're interested, I'll talk to Mr. Gribble tonight. He's sort of the manager of the movement. Maybe he'll let you apply for membership."

"Aw, that'd be putting you to too much trouble, Mrs. Gunderson," I said real quick. "Besides, I'm not sure . . ."

"Stuff an' nonsense!" she cut in. "I'll be glad to do it. It's our duty to try to bring in new members. Of course, I'm not saying you'll be accepted, Clem. But I'll vouch for you." She reached over and looked at my wristwatch lying on the table. "My, it's after five already!" she cried, folding up her mending and jumping to her feet. "I've got to get supper on the stove."

3

Well, that's how it all began. I guess it was Fate or something, because if I hadn't happened to move into Mrs. Gunderson's house and if she hadn't taken pity on me when I collapsed there, I might never have even heard of John Christian Power, let alone got mixed up with him. The point is, however, that all those things did happen, and what they led to eventually landed me where I am right now. So it does look like it must have been Fate.

Because the next thing I knew, there she was dragging me down to what she called the Citadel. It happened the very next day after our conversation, and I still don't know why I let her do it. I guess it was owing to the fact that I was still kind of unstrung.

I had stayed in bed that second day, too, but only till around 6 o'clock. By then, however, I'd had enough of being cooped up, and felt I just had to get some fresh air. And a drink, too. So I washed and dressed, but quietly, in order not to let the old lady catch on, and then tried to slip out of the house. She must have heard me, though, because I no sooner got to the hallway than she came rushing out of the kitchen.

"You're not going out now?" she cried, drying her hands on her apron. "I was just fixing supper."

I tried to tell her I wasn't hungry, and that anyway she'd been feeding me long enough, but she wouldn't listen. "Stuff an' non-sense!" she cried. "You've got to eat even if you ain't hungry. It's the only way you can get back your strength, Clem. Besides—" she narrowed her eyes and gave me that mysterious look— "I've got it all arranged to take you some place tonight."

I felt like telling her she had her nerve, making dates for me like that, but somehow I didn't have the heart. So all I did was sort of scowl and ask, "What kind of place?"

[16]

"Oh, you'll find out," she answered, smiling to herself. "First come and have your supper. I've made you a meat-loaf."

It was a good meat-loaf, I guess, but I couldn't hardly get it down. There was something about the way the old girl kept smiling to herself that made me choke.

"Come on, Mrs. Gunderson," I finally snapped, "let me in on it. Where are you figuring on taking me?"

"Now jest you be patient, Clem," she said. "You'll know when we get there. Jest finish your supper like a good boy."

When I was through, she stacked the dishes in the sink and went off to get her hat and coat.

"Look, Mrs. Gunderson," I made one final try. "I can't go with you tonight. I've got some business I ought to attend to. There's a fellow . . ."

But she wouldn't let me finish. "This is more important," she said, squinting her little blue eyes in that funny way of hers. "You take my word for it, Clem. This is the most important thing you could ever do. *Ever!*"

"But wait a minute. . . ."

"No, we're late already. We've got to go pretty near all the way downtown."

"You mean in a street car?"

"You don't suppose we're going to walk, do you?"

"But I don't think I'm up to it. I feel all woozy right now. Maybe I really ought to go back to bed."

She looked me in the eyes and then shook her head. "No," she said, putting on her coat, "you're strong enough. Come along."

We had to take two street cars and then walk a couple of blocks before we finally came to the place she was headed for. It was a big house down in that old-fashioned district below Westlake Park, a sort of broken-down mansion with a wrought-iron railing in front, and lots of weeds and bushes and palm trees all around. There was a big sign on the railing that said "For Sale," and another on the empty lot next door. If it hadn't been that a light was burning on the porch, I'd have sworn the place was deserted.

"Who lives here?" I asked Mrs. Gunderson.

[17]

"Now don't be so impatient," she said, tugging at my sleeve. "You'll find out soon enough now."

She had been saying that ever since we started out, and I knew there was no use arguing. I followed her up the gravel driveway, and climbed the wooden steps to the porch. They sounded like termites had been at them.

The door opened a crack even before we could find the bell, and Mrs. Gunderson leaned forward and whispered something. Then the crack widened enough to let us in. A hefty square-headed lug in a khaki shirt and denim pants was standing in the hallway. He had a gun on his hip and a belt full of cartridges. For a minute I thought he was going to frisk me, his eyes were so suspicious. Finally, though, he just jerked his thumb, and growled: "Come along with me."

I looked at Mrs. Gunderson, and she gave me a nudge. She didn't seem in the least scared. On the contrary, the way her eyes danced I could see she was all happy.

"I'll wait down here," she said.

I followed the gunman up a flight of broad stairs that must have had a carpet on them once. You could see where the varnish left off.

"In here," he said, opening a door.

I walked into an enormous room full of old furniture. There were plush arm chairs and sofas everywhere, most of them not quite large enough to hold elephants, and cracked marble-top tables, tattered footstools, and lots of other junk. At least a dozen faded oil paintings hung in heavy gilt frames on the walls, and there were hunks of tasseled velour in double layers over the windows and doors. A dummy dressed in a complete suit of rusty armor leaned half-crocked in one corner, and potted palms and rubber plants crowded all the others. It was like going into an auction room, even to the mothball smell.

Two men were sitting in easy chairs, and one of them got up as I entered. He was blond and fat, with ploppy cheeks full of dimples, and at least four chins. I guessed him to be around fifty, and probably in the dough, from the way he was dressed. I couldn't be sure though, because the light in the room wasn't any too bright. It came from a couple of floor lamps that had pink-silk shades on them, and fringe a foot long.

[18]

"Mr. Smullet?" this guy said, holding out a pudgy hand with a big Masonic ring. "My name's Gribble. And this is Captain Cleaver."

The other man got up and gave my hand a shake that all but crushed the knuckles. He was a big bruiser with a lantern jaw and shifty eyes set very close together. A few long, sandy hairs were plastered across the top of his dome to hide the bald part, and tufts of hairs stuck out of his red ears. He held himself as though someone had stuck a poker up his rear, and he seemed unable to smile. I decided he must be a captain in the National Guard, or some other tin-soldier outfit. He looked too full of himself to be a cop.

"Sit down," the fat fellow said, pointing to a chair next to one of the floor lamps. "We understand you're interested in joining our organization."

I had to clear my throat before I could get out an answer. What with that gunman downstairs, and everything else, I felt kind of jittery.

"No," I finally managed to say, "I'm afraid there's been some kind of mistake here. I never said I wanted to join anything."

At that the Captain glared and opened his mouth. It was a big mouth full of ugly black teeth, and put me in mind of the jagged end of a broken beer bottle. "Does that mean you're hostile?" he barked at me.

"Who said I was hostile?" I came back. "The fact is, I don't know what the organization's all about. Mrs. Gunderson said it was something secret."

"And that's right," the fat guy said, his voice all buttery. "But you've got some idea of its aims, haven't you? In general, I mean."

"Not the faintest," I said.

"Well, it's this way . . ."

"Just a minute, there," the Captain cut in. "Ain't you gonna find out somethin' about him first?"

"Yes, of course," the other fellow agreed. "That's what I was just about to do." He turned to me and smiled. "Where were you born?"

"What's it to you?" I snapped. I was beginning to get sore now.

"Aw, don't take that attitude," he said, leaning forward and putting a hand on my knee. It was about the pudgiest hand I'd ever seen. "We only want to make sure we can trust you. You're a real American, aren't you? I mean native-born."

"Don't I look it?"

"And a Protestant, eh?"

"Naturally. But what the . . ."

"Fine," he cut me off, flashing his dimples, "that's fine! Now one more question. Have you ever been in any trouble with the police?"

"Say," I bust out, "what the devil is this? The third degree? I'm getting out of here."

I did actually jump up and start for the door.

"Aw, don't run away like that," Gribble smiled, catching hold of my sleeve. "This isn't personal. It's just part of the routine."

I stared at him. I could have sworn he had given me a wink. "Well, I don't like it," I said, still on my feet. "What the hell are you grilling me for, anyway?"

"He told you," the Captain butted in. "We wanna find out if we can trust you."

"For what?"

"Well, it's like this," Gribble said, drawing me back to my chair. "We think we've got a proposition that might interest you."

I thought I saw his eyelid kind of flutter again, but couldn't be sure, so I side-mouthed, "Oh, yeah?"

"Yeah. That is, if you're the sort of man we've been told you are."

"And what sort is that?"

"First of all, an expert on publicity. You are that, aren't you?"

"That's the rumor," I answered, taking out my pocket-comb and starting to run it through my hair.

"Good. And second of all, you've been given a dirty deal. Correct?"

"Yeah, that's correct."

"You're sore, eh?"

"You bet I'm sore. Wouldn't you be, if you'd been framed and put on the blacklist?"

"Sure, sure. I know exactly how you feel. So does Cleaver here. That's why we're in this movement."

[20]

"But for crisake," I yelled, "what *is* the movement? Quit beating around the bush."

Gribble looked at the other fellow as if to ask how about it, but all he got in reply was a shrug. The Captain evidently wasn't taking any responsibility.

"Well, to put it simply," Gribble began to explain, "our aim . . ."

Suddenly there was a noise somewhere behind me. It sounded like a cross between a cough and a snort. I jerked around and saw a man step out from behind a pair of heavy plush portieres. He was very tall and very thin, with a long, thin, hawkish head that was completely shaved. His skin was practically leather, it was so heavily tanned, and his eyes looked like bits of blue bottle-glass. He had on a cheap flannel suit that he must have worn out in a rain, and a polo shirt that made his skinny neck look a mile long. Also he was wearing canvas shoes, and apparently no socks. On a studio lot I'd have sworn he was an extra made up for some horror picture.

"Just a minute there, Gribble," he announced in a voice that sounded like a truck on a wooden bridge. "I'll take charge now."

The fat man turned pink. "Sure, J.C.," he mumbled. "Go ahead. I only thought . . ."

The other waved him quiet, and came straight toward me. "My name's Power," he said. "John Christian Power."

I jumped up and let him give my hand a slow crush. "Glad t'meet you," I stammered.

That wasn't like me, to jump up and stammer, but the fact is, this bird had me all nervous. It wasn't just his looks that did it, but his whole manner.

He brought up a straight chair and sat down square in front of me. Then he leveled his eyes like they were two blowtorches, and started melting me down.

I felt around in my pocket for a cigarette the way a drowning man would reach for a life-preserver. "Have one?" I asked, holding out the pack.

He reacted like I was offering him a tarantula. "Put that away!" he ordered.

"Eh?"

"I said put that away. I don't allow smoking in this house."

[21]

I almost dropped the pack, I got rid of it so fast.

"Now then," he said, sitting back and folding his arms. "How long have you been employed out here? In the movies, I mean."

"About two years. No, two and a half."

"Got many friends?"

"Yeah. Quite a few, I guess."

"Any of them Communists?"

I stared. "Communists? Hell, no! I've never even met a Communist, so far as I know."

He didn't seem to believe me. "Don't you know James Cagney?"

"Oh, sure. That is, I've met him. But Jimmy's no Communist. He's Irish, that's all. Just likes to scrap all the time."

"How about Melvyn Douglas? Do you know him too?"

"No," I admitted. "He was never on any lot where I worked. Why? Is *he* a Communist?"

"He's a Jew, isn't he?"

"Yeah. At least, so I've been told. He doesn't look like a Jew, though."

"But he *is* one," the man barked. "Real name is Hesselberg."

"Is that so?"

He sniffed and curled his lip. It was a long thin lip, and seemed custom-tailored for curling. "For a man who's been around here as long as you have," he said, "you don't seem to know very much."

"Oh, I wouldn't say that," I started to argue.

"*I* would, though," he slapped me down. "You're like all the rest. Totally blind to what's really going on all around you. For example"—he raised his head and began riding me with a stare—"who d'you think is running this country right now?"

"Who? Why, F.D.R., I guess."

"Yes, but who's running F.D.R.?"

I suppose I should have said Eleanor, but my mind wasn't clicking that way. As a matter of fact, it just wasn't clicking—*period!* So all I did was look at him.

"You don't know, eh?" he sneered. "Well, it's about time you found out." All at once he leaned forward and started poking a hairy finger in my chest. "Smullet," he said, speaking slow and tapping out each word, "the people who are keeping Roosevelt in the

White House are the *same* people who are keeping *you* out of Hollywood."

He sat back as if waiting for that to sink in.

"I don't get you," I blinked.

"Of course you don't. That's the trouble with this country." He turned and sort of appealed to the two other guys in the room. "Men like that," he barked, indicating me, "men with brains, the sort that do all the constructive work, *real Americans*—they don't know a thing. Not a God-damned thing."

He jumped up and suddenly began to pace the floor. I just stared. The guy was nuts, of course; yet there was something about him, don't ask me what, that somehow made me feel he really knew what he was talking about.

Finally he sat down again. "Where was the last place you worked, Smullet?" he shot at me.

"Warner Brothers."

"And *who* are the Warner Brothers? I mean what race do they belong to?"

"Oh, that. Why, they're Jews, of course."

"Exactly! *Now* do you get it?"

I tried to look wise, but didn't get away with it.

"Don't you realize the Jews are behind everything?" he bellowed.

All I could do was blink.

"You don't, eh?" he went on. "Well, answer me this: Aren't they in control of Hollywood?"

"Why, yes. That is, in a way."

"What d'you mean, '*in a way*'? Don't they run every studio in town?"

That wasn't exactly true, and I knew it. Darryl Zanuck over at Twentieth Century wasn't a Jew, nor Sidney Kent, who was the boss over at Fox, nor half a dozen other top men I could have mentioned. As a matter of fact, I'd always resented the claim that the Hebes were running Hollywood. It sort of implied they were smarter than we were, and even if that had been the case, which I knew damn well it wasn't, I wouldn't have admitted it. But the way this crazy lug was worked up, I didn't see much sense in trying to argue. So I said, "I guess you're right at that."

[23]

"You bet I'm right. And it's the same way in Washington. Just think of it!

"Who runs most of the government bureaus and departments? Jews, all Jews, and everybody knows it."

"It's all a part of the great international conspiracy," he continued, answering his own barrage of questions, his eyes burning into me like blue blazes. He was trembling a little with anger and sweat was breaking out on his dome and upper lip.

I merely said, "Oh." With those eyes on me, there didn't seem to be anything else for me to say.

He started to go through every department of the government, rattling off name after name like he had them at his fingertips. And I must say, he sounded mighty convincing. It was the way he talked, the passion he put behind every word, that got me. I swear, if he'd told me the entire Catholic Church was run by Jews, or by Ku Kluxers for that matter, I'd have believed him.

"You sure do make out a strong case," I said when he let up for a second.

He scowled like he didn't want to be interrupted. "And that's just Washington," he snarled. "What about London and Paris and Prague"—he drew his long lips back—"and Moscow? They're all controlled by the Jews, every one of them. In fact, right at this minute there are only three capitals in the entire world that aren't in their hands—Berlin, Rome, Tokyo." He stopped short and twisted his mouth in a grim smile. "No," he corrected himself, ticking another finger, "there's a fourth now—Madrid." He turned to the other guys and let out a cackle. "We mustn't forget Madrid, must we?" They nodded and echoed his laugh. "But that's all!" he went on, suddenly glaring at me again as if I were to blame. "Just four nations in the entire world that aren't caught in the coils of the Hebrew octopus! Do you realize what that means, Smullet?"

I didn't, and he evidently realized it, because he started off on another harangue. Now he mentioned more names, maybe twenty more, but this time they were all new to me. Nevertheless I took his word for it that they were the names of Jews who were secretly conspiring to run and ruin everything. He called them the Elders of Zion and seemed to have all the dope on them; just how they had caused the revolution in Russia, the inflation in Germany, the corruption in France, the depression in America, and so on and so forth. According to him, pretty near every calamity that had occurred anywhere on earth in the last hundred years was traceable to those Elders of Zion. And when, having hammered that point home at least four or five times, he finally paused for me to make some comment, all I could do was say again, "Yes, sir, you sure do make out a strong case!"

He gave a side-glance at his two stooges as if to see if they had heard that, and then turned back to me. "You bet I do!" he said. "And you know why, Smullet? Because I've got the facts. I've been studying this situation for years, and there's nothing I don't know about it. Yes, sir. I'm *informed!*"

"You sure are," I said.

"So what are you going to do about it?"

"Do?"

"Yes, *do!* We can't just sit back and let 'em get away with it. This is *our* country, isn't it? Yours and mine and every other real American's. Are we going to let a bunch of God-damned Jews take it away from us?"

I ran my tongue over my lips. "You really think they're trying to do that?" I asked.

"Think? I *know* it! You ought to know it too, now. Haven't I just proved it to you?"

"Yeah, that's right," I said.

"So I repeat, Smullet: what are you going to do?"

I looked down at the floor a minute, and then at the walls. Finally I confessed, "I swear I don't know. Not off-hand, I don't. What's your idea?"

"Organize!" he barked. "That's the first step. Organize a conspiracy of our own! And we're doing that right here. What do you think of that?"

I felt myself wetting my lips again. "Mighty good idea," I managed to say.

"Well," he snapped me up, but with his eyes on the ceiling, like he wasn't really anxious, "how about joining us then? We could use a man with your background. What we need . . ." Suddenly he broke off and scowled nastily. "Would you *please* stop combing

[25]

your hair?" he barked. "You've been doing nothing else all the time I've been talking."

For a split second I wasn't sure whom he meant. I must have been fooling with my comb unconsciously, because I had no recollection of even taking it out of my pocket. I felt myself go red when I saw the damned thing actually in my hand, and got rid of it fast. Then, mumbling something about being sorry, I made like I hoped he'd go on. Inside, though, I was boiling. I knew of course that the habit I had of constantly slicking my hair was kind of annoying to some people. I'd been criticized for it more than once by friends. But this lug was a total stranger, and for him to make a scene about it really got my goat. I couldn't even hear what he went on to say, I was so mad.

All at once he broke off again, and sat back like he was waiting for my answer. I looked at him, and then at the other two guys, sort of hoping for a clue as to what I'd been asked. Finally I faltered, "Why, I guess maybe . . ."

"No, you can't guess!" the crank shot at me. "You've got to be *sure* you want to join us! Our work is *dangerous!*"

"Well, if you put it that way, maybe I ought to do a little thinking first."

He scowled a minute, his eyes narrowed down to pinpoints, and then suddenly jumped up. "Maybe you should," he said in a voice I didn't like at all. "Yes, maybe you should."

And with that I'll be damned if he doesn't turn right around and stamp out of the room!

I looked at the other two men. Now that that nut was gone, I didn't feel nearly so scared. "Say, who the hell does he think he is anyway?" I exploded.

The Captain made a sound like a cough, and got up. Then, mumbling something I didn't catch, he too left the room.

Gribble heaved himself out of his chair, his face kind of severe. "I'll show you downstairs," he said in a formal tone of voice.

Once we were on the other side of the door, though, he gave my arm a squeeze, and whispered, "What d'you say we go some place and have a drink?"

I looked up at him, and he gave me a wink.

"How about the old lady?" I asked.

"Aw, I'll send her on home. She'll be all right."

4

Gribble's car was parked in the empty lot back of the house. It was a Chevvy and looked pretty old.

"Hop in," he said.

I did, and we started off.

"I know a quiet joint over on Alvarado," he said when we turned out of the rutty driveway. "That okay with you?"

"Any place you say, just so we get there," I groaned. "I need a drink bad."

He chuckled and gave me a little dig with his elbow. "What's the matter?" he asked. "He didn't scare you, did he?"

"That nut? Christ, he just handed me a laugh!"

"Yeah?"

"Yeah."

"You didn't act it," he sort of needled me.

"Didn't I? Well, let me tell you . . ."

"Aw, don't get sore, Smullet. I was only kidding."

"Okay. But get this straight: I wasn't scared."

"Sure, you weren't. I could see that right away. But he sure does scare most people."

"Yeah, I can understand that," I said after a pause. "Say, why the hell did he walk out on me that way? Did I hurt his feelings?"

"And how!"

"But what did I do?" I asked, almost yelling.

"That's just it—you didn't. He expected you to say yes right away when he asked you to join, but you wouldn't."

"Oh, so that's what it was?" I chuckled, kind of proud of myself. But then I started to frown. "Say," I said, "who the hell is he anyway? I mean, what's his racket?"

"Can't you guess?"

"No."

"Well, if you're real interested, maybe I'll tell you."

He looked around at me and grinned.

"Go ahead," I said. "Spill it."

"No, it'll keep. Tell me something about yourself first. What really happened that you got blacklisted in the studios? On the level, now."

"Aw, what's the difference? It was just one of those things."

"Come on," he chuckled. "You don't have to hide anything from me."

"I've got nothing to hide."

"No?"

"No. They were just prejudiced against me because I'm a Gentile."

He let out a roar of laughter. "Boy, you sure do learn quick!" he said.

"That's my nature," I grinned. "I'm just naturally bright."

"I can see that."

"You don't look so dumb yourself, Gribble."

"How did you guess it?"

"I told you. I'm bright."

We both began to laugh, and then waited. It was like one of those pauses in a ring when the pugs start circling around while they look for an opening.

Finally I wore out. "How about a cigarette?" I asked, fishing the pack out of my pocket.

"Okay," he said, reaching for one without looking.

"Say, what the hell's he got against smoking, anyway?" I suddenly remembered. "Does he think it'll stunt his growth?"

"That's right."

"Quit kidding. He must be six-feet-four right now."

"Yeah, but did you notice his chest?"

I admitted I hadn't and Gribble went on, "It's all sunken in. Personally I think he must have had T.B. at one time or another. He's never admitted it though. He claims he's against smoking on general principles. Says it saps your vitality. Liquor too."

"Crazy nut!" I said, blowing smoke against the windshield. "Why the hell do you stand for that? I mean, what do you want to hang around him for?"

"I'll tell you after a while. Let's get to that joint first. It's only a couple of blocks away now."

We turned into Alvarado, and he pointed to a neon sign that read PEARL DIVE.

"That's it," he said.

We pulled up and entered the joint. It looked like it had been rigged up out of the salvage from a South Seas set on one of the quickie lots. There were fake palms all over the place, and fishing nets, sea shells, oars, anchors and old hula skirts. The light was bad and the air was worse.

The only customers were a couple of Sadie Thompsons sitting at the bar, and they gave us the eye as we came in. Gribble, though, walked right past them and took the farthest booth in the rear. He carried himself kind of impressively, like he might be a big-shot executive; but I suddenly noticed that the seat of his pants was shiny, and his rubber heels were worn way down.

The bartender came over and started wiping the table. He looked and moved like a strictly career bartender, the kind that had learnt his trade in the Free Lunch Age. He was not as large as a beer truck, had sad eyes and hurty feet, and seemed to know my friend.

"What'll it be?" he sighed as he set down a plate of popcorn.

"Bourbon and ginger ale for me," I said.

"Make mine straight, Chuck."

"I guess I'll take mine that way too," I corrected real quick. I wasn't going to let him think me a softie.

"And let's have a little music," Gribble added. "We've got business to talk over."

Chuck left us, and pretty soon a jukebox began to give out just loud enough to cover our voices.

I brought out my pack of Luckies and tossed it on the table. "Well, spill it, friend," I said, starting to light up. "What's the story?"

Gribble fished himself a cigarette, tamped it a couple of times, struck a match with his thumbnail, and drew in deep. "Got you kind of mystified, eh?" he grinned.

"Yeah," I admitted. "I just can't figure out what that guy's up to."

Gribble emptied his lungs slowly. "Oh, it's simple enough," he said, eyeing the tip of his cigarette. "He's merely grooming himself to become the Dictator of the United States."

"The hell you say!"

The guy leered at the look on my face. "That's a fact though," he said. "He expects to do for America what Hitler's done for Germany, only faster and better."

"Well, I'll be damned! He must be completely bugs."

"Sure he is." The fat face was still wreathed in a leer. "That's why I picked him."

"*You* picked *him?*"

"That's right. I gave him his start, practically."

"But what for? I figured you for a guy with brains."

Gribble took the cigarette from his lips, made his mouth small to blow out a long column of smoke, and then leaned forward. "Well, sir, it's this way. That nut . . ."

But he had to break off because the barkeep was back with the order.

We clinked glasses and drank up.

"Go ahead," I said, when I got through coughing.

Gribble took a minute to sip his chaser, and then leaned forward again. "Well, sir," he began again, "maybe I shouldn't spill this, but I'm going to anyway. I've got a hunch you're my kind of guy. Right?"

"Right."

"Well, here it is. I took up with Power because I could see there was jack in it." He nodded his head emphatically. "Yes, sir, a mine of jack."

"You mean he's rich?"

"Naw, he's as broke as you are."

I resented that crack. "Who told you I'm broke?" I flared.

The guy grinned. "Okay," he said. "So you're a millionaire. That's why you're living off your landlady."

I could see he had my number, and gave up. "You win," I said. "I'm broke, all right. But about His Nibs—what's he doing in such a swell house if he's broke?"

"He's living off *his* landlady."

I had to laugh at that.

"Yeah," he went on, "she's a crazy old bag by the name of Sally Garth Krutch. Ever heard of her?"

I shook my head no.

"Well, she's the widow of Adolph Krutch, whose beer you probably drink when no one's around to blow you to bourbon. Right?"

"Wrong," I back-cracked. "I like Budweiser."

"My error. But anyway, that's how J.C. happens to live in that mansion. I introduced him to old Sally, and she fell for his line one-two-three. She turned the whole place over to him."

"Oh, so that's it! You're working the dame, eh?"

Gribble tapped the ash off his cigarette. "No, now it's your error. Sally's tight, and besides, she hasn't got much any more. All we can gouge out of her is petty cash."

"Then where's the pay-dirt?"

He let out a light chuckle. "In Mrs. Gunderson," he answered.

"*Who?*"

"You heard me. Mrs. Gunderson. She and all the rest like her. They're the ones I'm figuring on tapping—at least to start with. And that's why I have to have J.C. around. I use him to hold 'em while I do the tapping."

"What do you mean, you use him? The way he acted up in that room, it looked more like he was using you."

Gribble crinkled his eyes in a cagey grin. They were regulation-size eyes, but in that fat face they looked almost piggish. "Don't you believe it," he snorted. "That's nothing but an act on my part. Actually I'm the one who's boss." He leaned back and pointed his cigarette at me. "Take tonight, for instance. He walked out on you, didn't he? Well, tomorrow I'll have him welcoming you back like a long lost brother."

"You will, eh? Well, who says I'll be willing to come back?"

"I do," he answered calmly. "That's why I'm talking to you now. The minute I saw you, Clem—that *is* your name, isn't it?—yeah, well, right then and there, Clem, I knew I wanted you in with me." He paused and smiled. "You're smart," he said.

"Thanks. And I don't mind telling you, Gribble . . ."

"Ben's the name," he broke in. "My friends, though, call me Doc."

"Okay, Doc. As I was about to say, I have an idea you're pretty smart yourself."

"Good. That makes us even. Now how about coming in with me?"

I paused to down the rest of my drink. I didn't want to seem too anxious. "What's the proposition?" I finally asked.

"Well, it's like this. We're organizing . . . Say, how about another drink first?"

"Okay, but this one is on me," I said, making as if I really meant it.

"Forget it," he said. "I'm buying tonight—all the way through." He yelled to Chuck to serve a second round, and then got up to go to the men's room. His feet, I noticed, were kind of small, and the way he moved, I had the feeling he'd be the sort of guy who'd be swell on a dance floor in spite of his weight.

When he returned, the fresh drinks were already on the table, and I watched him finish his in one gulp again. "Well, how about it?" I tried to prompt him. "What's this proposition you want me to come in on?"

He reached for a cigarette and started lighting it slowly. "Maybe I ought to do a little explaining first," he said, blowing out the match. "What I mean is, give you kind of a little background." He dropped the match in the ashtray, and leaned back from the table. "The way I size it up," he went on, squinting at me through the smoke, "this country's full of people who are scared. What I mean is, the average man is just naturally in a panic pretty near all the time. And that's what gives guys like us our opportunity. For instance, it used to be that the average man was scared of going to hell, so what did we smart boys do? We became preachers. Do you follow me? We had brains enough to realize that the fear of hell could be made to pay." His fat face suddenly broke into that dimpled leer again. "Believe me, I ought to know. I was a preacher once myself."

I stared at him, like I thought he was kidding. He wasn't, though. He went on to tell me how he'd been a lay evangelist back in Kansas years ago. He'd been good at it, too, he said, and I was ready to believe that. He had just the right voice for a gospeleer. But he'd got into some sort of domestic jam, and finally quit. "It wasn't just on account of that," he explained. "The real reason was that I couldn't see much future in religion. The whole thing had become sort of a dying industry. People had quit worrying about hell. They'd begun to think it was just nothing more than a cussword." He chuckled and flicked his cigarette against the rim of the ashtray. "But did that stop 'em from feeling scared?" he went on. "Not so's you could notice it. No, sir, now they began worrying about their bodies instead of their souls. They started worrying about cancer and colitis and high blood pressure and God-knows-what-all. So then what did guys like us do?" He chuckled again and spread his hands. "We became doctors!"

I echoed his laugh and slapped my thigh. I was getting to like this guy more and more.

"Well," he continued, flashing another grin, "that was my next move. I started a health clinic."

"You mean you became a regular M.D.?" I snickered.

He shook his head, still grinning. "Not exactly," he said. "I did study to be a chiropractor, though. I can show you my diploma. But I never practiced at it. I discovered there was more money in electrical diagnoses and all that sort of bunk. I made quite a bit of money out of it, too. Especially after the radio came in. I used to broadcast three times a week, explaining how you could cure pretty near anything with the help of orange juice and vibrations. I had people coming from as far away as Oregon and Texas to get treated." He paused to chew a piece of popcorn. "That's how I came across this guy Power."

"Don't tell me he was one of your patients!" I snorted.

"No, he was on my staff. He gave treatments in the clinic I was running here in town."

"You mean he was in on the racket?"

Now it was Gribble's turn to snort. "*That* nut?" he said. "Christ, he wouldn't know a racket if it reared up and kicked him in the teeth! No, he thought the clinic was strictly on the level. As a matter of fact, the treatments he specialized in *were* on the level."

"What sort were they?" I asked.

"What sort?" Gribble repeated, like he was thinking of something else. "Oh, he had charge of the colonic irrigations."

I let out a howl that made the girls at the bar turn around and stare.

"What's so funny about that?" Gribble demanded, suddenly frowning. "Colonic irrigations are mighty good for certain things. I take them myself when I've got a cold."

"Aw, don't get me wrong, Doc!" I tried to explain, but still laughing. "I was just thinking of the future Dictator of the United States starting out as a jerk that gives enemas for a living. Isn't that something to howl at?"

He had to smile. "Yeah," he admitted, "come to think of it, I guess it is."

"Still and all," I hurried to point out, "there's one thing you must say in his favor. He sure has started up from the bottom."

That made Gribble let out a laugh that set all his chins shimmying. "Not bad," he said, "not bad at all. In fact, it's good enough to call for another drink. Right?"

"You're the doctor," I grinned, draining my glass.

He waited for Chuck to bring the third round, but this time he let his glass stand a while.

"Christ, what a sweet racket that was!" he started to reminisce. "There was a period when I was cleaning up as high as a grand a week, net. And talk about fun! Most of my patients were women, of course, and you can imagine what they really wanted." He started to tell me, and I listened in spite of the fact that I wasn't really interested in such matters at the moment. Finally I butted in with some remark about how I couldn't understand why he'd ever given up a racket that was that good.

"Hell!" he came right back. "I had no choice in the matter."

"Why? Did the cops get after you?"

"Nah, that wasn't it. I was operating strictly within the law. I always have. The way I look at it, a man's a chump to do anything he can't defend in a court—with the help of the right kind of lawyer, of course."

"You said it!" I agreed.

"No, what got me was the Depression. People simply quit worrying about their health, because that was about all they had left after '29. So the result was curtains for my clinic. Not right away, of course. I managed to keep going till '35. No, '36. But then I just had to shut up shop."

He broke off to take a swallow. What he had just told me seemed to leave him kind of sad.

"But I bet you didn't stay busted," I tried to cheer him.

"Oh, sure," he bounced back with a smile. "The way I see it, if you have brains, you can always get on your feet again. Am I right?"

"One hundred percent."

"You betcha sweet life! . . . Well, so I put my brains to work. I said to myself: Look, when the boobs worried about their souls, what did you do? You became a preacher. And when they worried about their guts, what did you do? You made yourself a doctor. Okay then. Now they're worried about their pocketbooks. They're broke, or going broke, or scared that they might go broke. In other words, they're all stirred up now because they think the country's going to rack and ruin. So there's your opening. All you've got to do is turn politician."

He broke off and beamed at me.

"And did you?" I asked.

"I'll tell the world!" he laughed. Then, turning his head, he yelled, "Hey, Chuck, fill 'em up again."

5

Three drinks in a row were my limit normally, but I didn't want to be a quitter, especially when the drinks were free. Such being the case, I went at the fourth without batting an eyelash, trying to make out I was as good a toper as this guy Gribble was. I wasn't, though. I could tell that by the way he was able to go on talking real clear, as if he hadn't been drinking anything but grape juice.

He went into a long account of his experiences as a promoter of various pension schemes, but there's no call for me to repeat the details here. The gist of it was that he got nowhere. For a while he hooked up with Robert Noble, who was trying to put over one of those schemes locally. Then he joined the "Ham and Eggs" movement, because it looked at the time as if that was going to sweep the whole state. Finally he switched to Doctor Townsend, who was operating on a national scale. Gribble became a regional organizer, and traveled all over the Middle West setting up Townsend Clubs. As I have said, though, in the end he came out with nothing.

In February, 1939, he returned to Los Angeles as broke as ever. He had to come back by bus, he told me, which shows how hard up he must have been. It happened to be a sunny day when he landed, so naturally the first thing he wanted to do was go to the beach. Well, that's what he did do. He went out to Santa Monica, picked himself a quiet spot on the sand and prepared to make up for some of the sleep he had lost on the bus. But then, just as he was about to close his eyes, who should he see coming out of the water but—yeah, you guessed it—John Christian Power!

"You're kidding!" I broke in when Gribble got to that point. "You mean that guy had actually gone into the ocean in February?"

"Oh, sure," Gribble said, not even smiling. "That's the kind of guy he is. Just a bug on keeping fit. He makes a religion of taking a certain amount of exercise every day."

So then I understood. On top of everything else, the nut was evidently a Bernarr McFaddist.

"Well," Doc went on, "as I was saying, there he was, coming out of the water right in front of me. He was wearing practically nothing but a jockstrap, and he'd shaved his head since I'd last seen him. That had been more than two years before, and I was so surprised to run into him so unexpectedly that I clean forgot I still owed him a couple of months' pay.

" 'Hiya there, Long John?' I yelled to him. That's the nickname we always used for him around the clinic.

"He stared a minute before he recognized who it was, but then came right over and sat down next to me. He was breathing hard, like he'd been swimming a long distance."

" 'I didn't hardly know you with your head shaved,' I says. 'What's the idea?'

" 'It's more hygienic,' he answers, real solemn.

"I let out a laugh, because I suspected that wasn't the only rea-son. He really was hypped on the subject of hygiene, but I was ready to bet he'd shaved his head because he didn't want people to know he was turning gray. However, I felt I'd better not go into that, so I changed the subject. 'How's tricks?' I asked. 'Still poking 'em up people's behinds?'

"He kind of frowned at that. He never did like anyone to kid about his specialty. Matter of fact, he never liked anyone to kid about anything. No sense of humor. So he just sat there and started rubbing himself all over with sand.

" 'Haven't you got a towel?' I asked him.

" 'Don't need one,' he answers. 'Sun and friction, that's the natu-ral way to get dry.'

"I made like I agreed with him, and then asked again what he was doing for a living. But he still wouldn't tell me, so I figured he must be out of work. 'I haven't forgot I owe you that money, John,' I told him. 'But I'm still kind of strapped.'

" 'That's all right,' he says. 'I'm in no hurry for it.'

" 'Gee, that's swell!' I says. 'I was afraid you were hard up.'

" 'No, I'm getting by,' he says.

" 'Doing what?'

"He gave me one of those long stares of his. You know the kind. Like he was looking right through me. Then he says, 'I've started mobilizing my Crusade.'

"That made me want to laugh; but I didn't. I knew how sore he'd get if I laughed. All the time he worked for me he'd talked about starting that Crusade of his. Against the Jews, I mean. At first I'd treated it as a joke. Every time a fat old Jewish mamma would come around, I'd prescribe colonic irrigations, just to see his face when he had to work on her. But after a while I had to cut that out, because he got wise to what I was doing, and started mak-ing remarks so the patients could hear. The result was, naturally, that they quit coming. It got to be almost a boycott, and believe me I didn't like that at all. Jews are about the best customers you can have if you're running a health clinic. So I had to tell him to pipe down. 'John,' I said, 'I don't like Jews any more than you do, and if you want to talk against them, go ahead. But do it on your own time. This is a health clinic, not a beer hall.' "

[37]

Gribble broke off to take another swallow of his drink. Then he dug into my pack of cigarettes again. "What did he do?" I prompted, offering a light. "Did he get sore?"

Gribble let out a snort. "*Get* sore? How could he? He was born sore. All he could do was get sorer. But he did cut out talking in front of the patients. That is, unless he knew they were Gentiles. And of course he kept on bringing around anti-Semitic pamphlets for me and the staff to read. Hating Jews was an obsession with him. Know what I mean?"

"Yeah," I said. "I've come across quite a few guys like that lately."

"Sure. But I bet they weren't as hypped as John."

"That's true," I admitted. "I wonder what's back of it. I mean, what got him started? I can understand a guy not liking Jews. But to hate them like that, there's got to be a reason."

Gribble squirmed a second, struggling to cross his fat legs. "Yeah," he said, when he finally accomplished the feat, "that's what I thought."

"Did you ever ask him about it?"

"Lots of times. But he'd evade the question. The most I ever got out of him was that a Jew did something once to his sister. Knocked her up, I guess. He never would tell me the details, though."

"Did you ever try to find out from her?"

"You mean his sister?"

"Yeah."

"I've never seen her," Gribble said. "She must be living back East, unless she's dead, of course. . . . But anyway, to get back to what I was telling you, there he sits on the sand and announces that he's got his Crusade started. 'What d'you mean?' I says. 'Can you make enough out of that to live?'

" 'I don't need much,' he answers.

" 'Yeah, I can see that,' I says, looking him up and down. He was practically nothing but skin and bones. 'Still and all, though,' I argued, 'you've got to get *some* money. Who's keeping you?' "

" 'My followers,' he says.

"Well, at that point I got really interested. I began to ask him how many followers he had, and what dues they paid, and so on and so forth. His organization didn't amount to much, but I could

[38]

see it had possibilities. I'd been running into others like it all over the country on my tour. Pelley's Silver Shirts, for example. I'd come across them in lots of places. Then there was Winrod's Defenders of the Christian Faith, and Edmundson's Knights of the White Camelia, and maybe a dozen more. I guess you've heard about them, haven't you?"

I nodded. I really had heard about the Pelley outfit, vaguely.

"Of course," Gribble continued, "none of them amounted to a damn, but there they were. The way I figured it, there must be a market for the bunk those outfits were handing out, or otherwise they wouldn't be able to exist. So I listened to what John had to report, and did some quick thinking. Here maybe was just the opening I was looking for. It was a chance to get in on the ground floor of something that might build up to God knows how big a proposition if it was handled right."

Gribble must have read the look that crossed my face, because he stopped and frowned. "You don't think so, eh?" he asked.

"What's the difference?" I sidestepped. "Go on with the story."

He hesitated a minute, but finally did go on. "Well, as I was saying," he said, "I let John tell me all he had done, and then I pulled a fast one. I sat up, looked him square in the eye, and said: 'J.C., I take it all back.'

" 'What do you mean?' he asks, kind of surprised. It was the first time I had ever called him by his initials.

" 'J.C.,' I says very solemn, 'I used to be skeptical about that belief of yours. Yes, sir. I regret to say I used to think it was the bunk. But not any more. I've learnt a lot in the last couple of years, a hell of a lot. I've been pretty near all over the country, and I know now that what you've been saying all along is nothing but gospel truth. We Americans have really got to wake up! J.C., we've got to wake up *right now!* Or we won't have any country left to wake up in. Yes, sir. I'm absolutely convinced of that now!'

"He was so pleased, I swear he almost smiled. 'I'm glad to hear you say that, Gribble,' he says. 'Mighty glad.'

" 'What's more,' I went on, 'I'm ready to join you. I can't help you out financially. You know that. But I can offer you my organizing ability, and that's worth—well, I don't need to tell you how much. So what do you say?'

"He just looked at me, and for a second I was afraid I wasn't going to get away with it. But then all at once his whole face sort of lit up and he started giving me his hand. 'I'm going to accept your offer!' he says. 'Welcome into the fellowship of the Crusade!' "

Gribble paused and leered at me. "And that," he said, spreading his paws, "is how I got into this racket."

6

The guy heaved himself up, threw his head back, and tossed off what was left in his glass. He was beginning to show his drink at last. His fat face was getting flushed, like there were rashes under the skin, and one eyelid was starting to droop. His speech, though, was as clear as ever.

"Well, sir," he said, reaching for some popcorn, "that was less than three months ago, and now look where I am."

I didn't say anything, but he could tell what I was thinking.

"What the hell!" he growled, furling his bushy eyebrows. "I'm practically running the whole show now."

"Yeah, but what does the whole show amount to?" I couldn't keep from asking.

He leaned away and scowled for a minute, but then pushed the smile back on his face. "No kidding, Clem," he started arguing, "there's a mint in this proposition. Just figure it out for yourself. Here you've got millions of people who are riled, or in a daze, or just plain scared, and every one of them is just aching to blame somebody for the way they feel. Right? Every one of them is running around looking for a goat. . . . Well, we give 'em a goat. We tell 'em it's the Jews who are at the bottom of everything, and we've got to organize against them. Christ, it's a cinch! Can't you see it?"

I shook my head. "Frankly, no," I said. "Anybody with an ounce of sense would know better than to fall for that line."

"Sure, but what about those who haven't got an ounce? I'll

admit they're nothing but the lunatic fringe, but at the rate economic conditions are unravelling things, it looks as though this country's going to be nothing *but* fringe before long. And that's why I'm so sold on this Crusade. I'm telling you, it's going to sweep the nation."

"With that nut at the head of it?" I snorted. "Don't make me laugh!"

"Okay, go ahead and laugh. That's what they did when Hitler started out. They laughed and laughed at him. They laughed because he'd been a paperhanger, and wore a funny mustache, and wouldn't eat meat, and couldn't talk sense. And look what happened. First thing they knew, there he was, the boss of all of Germany."

"Yeah, but that's Germany. It never could happen here."

"Like hell it couldn't! Americans are human, aren't they? Well, being human, they can be scared, and if they're scared enough they'll go batty, and once they're batty enough they'll think a real bat like Long John is sane. Is that logic, or is that logic?"

"Wait a minute," I said, leaning forward and poking my cigarette at him. "Are you really figuring on that? What I mean is, are you actually banking on this Long John to become the Dictator over here? Because if you are . . ."

The smile that crept across Doc's face made me realize I didn't need to finish.

"What do you take me for?" he hooted. "All I'm figuring on is tapping the boobs who *are* going to bank on him. And believe me, this country's lousy with them."

"But why, for crisake, should they pick him of all people? What's he got to sell except just Jew-poison?"

"But that's all he needs to sell. He's like the people who put out mouthwashes. First they scare everybody about halitosis, and then they peddle their Listerine. Get the point?"

I didn't answer.

"Just figure it out for yourself," he pressured. "Is there anybody who really likes Jews? Of course not. Do you, for instance?"

"No, why should I?"

"Exactly. You feel about them the way everybody else does. They're too damn smart."

[41]

"Not for me, they aren't," I said flatly. "I haven't met a Jew yet who could put anything over on me."

"Naturally," Gribble admitted. "But you take the average Gentile —he thinks he's no match for them a-tall. Am I right?"

"Yeah . . . I guess so."

He paused to put out the cigarette he'd been smoking. "And don't forget the others," he said, wiping a smudge off his fingers, "the superior ones, I mean. We'll be able to get plenty of them too, and they'll come through with more than just nickels and dimes. Take a guy like Henry Ford. He's a Jew-baiter from way back, and he'll be tickled to death to support us once we've got a real movement going. So will any number of other tycoons, whether they're Jew-baiters or not. Because we'll be able to show them that in attacking the Jews we're really attacking the New Deal, and Communism, and the labor unions, and all the other things that they're scared of. Christ, there's no limit to what we can do with this racket! Can't you see that?"

I was still skeptical, and said so.

"Aw, don't be ornery!" he snapped at me.

"I'm not being ornery, Doc," I insisted. "I'm just using my head. If what you say is true, why haven't you made more headway already? Here you've been plugging away for the past three months, and where the hell are you?"

I had him there, and he knew it. His piggish little eyes dropped, and he suddenly began rutching around to recross his legs. In a minute, though, he seemed to regain his poise. He gave his face a quick wipe with the palm of his hand, and leaned forward on the table. "Clem," he said, looking at me real frank and open, "I knew you'd ask that question. I knew it because it's exactly the question that I'd ask if I were in your place. And here's the answer—I've been handicapped."

I could see he was leveling with me now, and I was glad. "Just how have you been handicapped?" I asked.

"Well, it's this way. To begin with, I'm all alone. There just isn't anyone in the whole organization that I can work with. You know what I mean—the way I could work with you, for instance."

"What's the matter? They all crackpots?"

"No, not exactly. Of course, most of them are that, but not all. Take Cleaver, for instance. He's no crackpot. He may act like one, especially when he's sucking up to J.C. But don't let that fool you. He's one of the shrewdest sons of bitches I've ever run into. But what he's shrewd about isn't what I'm shrewd about, so we just can't co-operate. All he's interested in, so far as I can make out, is glory *plus*. The whole Crusade means nothing to him except a chance to build up a private army that he can be the general of. He wants to ride the wave of the future on a white horse. See what I mean?"

I nodded.

"So that's one problem I've had to contend with, and it explains why I'm trying to get you in with me. I need you, Clem."

"Yeah?"

"Yeah. It wasn't so bad up to now, but from here on I simply got to have someone like you to work with. Because we're ready to start rolling now. I mean that. We're just about ready to go to town. You see, it's like this." He reached for his glass and then suddenly realized it was empty. Instead of doing anything about it, though, he merely ran his tongue over his lips, and went on talking. "J.C. started the Crusade as a secret organization, and in one way that wasn't a bad idea. It drew a lot of followers that he mightn't have been able to get with any other bait. Of course, he didn't think of it as a bait. He really believed that secrecy was necessary. He's like a kid that way: crazy about initiations and passwords and so forth. . . . Well, as I said, that has its merits. After all, there's nothing that has more sucker-appeal than secrecy."

"Yeah, I know," I said, grinning down my nose. "I fell for it once myself."

"No fooling!"

"It's a fact. One time I joined the Odd Fellows."

"The hell you did!" he laughed. And then, suddenly putting his hand on his lapel, he whispered, *"Are you looking for me?"*

I recognized the high sign. *"For you!"* I came right back, giving him the clasp.

We both started to roar.

"Say, that calls for another drink," he said, waving to Chuck.

"No, I've had enough," I said.

[43]

"Aw, come on. Just one more. Hell, we're fraternity brothers!"

"Okay. But this has got to be my last. My old landlady will get all grieved if I come home stewed."

Chuck limped over with the bottle and refilled our glasses. He had evidently gotten tired of serving us from the bar.

"Well, here's to Brotherhood!" Gribble said, raising his glass.

We clinked and drank.

"Isn't that a sketch though!" he began to laugh. "Here we are, both of us Odd Fellows. It just goes to show . . ." He leaned over to get a light from the match I had just struck. His hand, I noticed, was only the least little bit unsteady, which was a hell of a lot more than I could say for my own. "Yes sir," he went on, "it just goes to show you how much appeal there is in a secret order."

"Yeah," I said. "I guess it's because a guy just naturally wants to know something that other people can't find out about. It makes him feel important."

"Yeah, I guess that's it," Doc agreed. "But on the other hand, there's one drawback to secrecy. From the promotional angle, I mean. You can't expand fast enough. And that's why we're going to loosen up a bit now. My idea is that we should copy the system that I understand the Communists have set up. We'll go out for what they call fellow-travelers. Know what I mean?"

"Sure," I snickered. "In other words, saps that you can take for a ride."

"That's it exactly."

I nodded my head appreciatively. "Sounds like a good idea," I said.

"Good, hell! It's perfect." He broke off to reach for the salt shaker at the next table, and sprinkled a little into his drink. Then, taking a sip, he made a face, wiped his fat lips, and started talking again. "All we need is a proper start," he said, "and I'm planning to get that right away now. Next week, in fact. I've hired the Philharmonic Auditorium for a mass meeting next Thursday night. What d'you think of that?"

I couldn't answer at once because my thinking machine wasn't functioning so good any more. Finally, though, I did manage to say, "Aren't you being kind of ambitious? That's a hell of a big house to pack."

He switched on his dimples full strength, and sat back in the seat. "That's where *you* come in, Clem," he said.

"Me?"

"Yes, you. You're going to put on a publicity campaign that'll fill that hall right to the doors."

"Nh-nh!" I said, shaking my head. "You've picked the wrong guy."

"What's the matter? Aren't you that good?"

"Sure I'm that good. And even better."

"That's what I thought, Clem. With all your experience, a little job like this ought to be a pipe."

"I know that."

"So what are you scared of?"

"I'm not scared. It's just that I like to get paid for my work."

"Naturally, Clem. I figured on that."

Suddenly my brain seemed to clear. "You did?" I bleated. "Well, that's a horse from another stable! What are you offering?"

He sort of shied at that. "It depends," he started to say. "You see, here's the proposition. . . ."

I listened to him for a while, but finally started shaking my head again. With all his fumigating, the proposition was still lousy. He was offering me practically nothing but a share of the take—if any.

"Forget it," I sniffed. "I'm strictly a professional. You can't get me to take a job on nothing but spec."

He started to argue some more, but I stood pat. "I want real dough," I said, "and in advance. I've got to eat, remember."

"What's the matter with your landlady?" he said. "She'll be tickled to death to stake you if you're working for the Cause. And incidentally, have you thought how she'll feel if you refuse to work for it?"

There at last he had me, and we both knew it. If he could turn Mrs. Gunderson against me, I'd be in a hell of a spot.

I sat back and thought the situation over. Then I said, "Just a minute," and went off to the men's room.

He was at the bar when I came out again, talking to the two floozies who'd been sitting there all this while. The minute he saw me, though, he came right back to the booth. "Well?" he asked, resting a knee on the end of the seat. "What's the decision?"

"Hell!" I said, sitting down and starting to run my pocket-comb through my hair, "I'll take the lousy job."

He smiled and patted my shoulder. "I knew you would," he said.

He seemed anxious to return to the girls, but I caught his sleeve. "Just the same, Doc," I pleaded, "you really ought to give me *something* in advance. Not much. Say fifty bucks. Just to make me feel like really putting my heart into the work."

He shot a glance at the bar and then turned to me impatiently. "I'd like to, Clem," he said, "but the fact is we're kind of limited in our finances."

"Then make it twenty-five," I begged.

He still held out, but I pressured him some more, and finally he gave in. "Okay, Clem!" he said, sticking out his paw. "It's a deal! Now let's see if we can't promote those dames. They look like they might be fun."

7

And that was how I got hooked into the Crusade. I didn't believe in it, and wanted no part of it, but there I was, broke and black-listed, so what could I do? The way I figured, there was at least twenty-five bucks in the job for me, no matter how it flopped, and in the condition I was in right then, believe me, twenty-five bucks was only a little less than a fortune.

As to the right or wrong of the Crusade, that naturally was none of my business. I was functioning as a press agent, not a boy scout. I was being paid to do a job, and the only thing that was up to me to decide was how to do it—not why it should or should not be done. If you think that wasn't the proper attitude for me to take, that's your privilege. All I know is, I didn't invent the attitude. A press agent is like any other professional man. Take for instance a chemist. If you offer to hire him to fix up a mess of poison gas, he doesn't ask whether you're going to use it on rats or your mother-in-law. All he asks is how you want the stuff packaged. Am I right?

However, let's not go into that question, because as the lawyers say, it's incompetent, irrelevant and immaterial. The fact remains that I had given in to Gribble and agreed to do the publicity for that meeting. What is more, the job was tricky enough to appeal to my fancy, so I went to work on it right away.

By right away I mean as soon as my head cleared the morning after the night before, and that naturally wasn't in the morning at all, but around 2 P.M. As a matter of fact, it hadn't really cleared even by that time, but at least it wasn't churning any more. So I dug out my portable, set it on a bridge table, rolled up my sleeves, and started pecking. First I outlined the general plan for the campaign, listing the essential items such as news releases, feature stuff, colyumny, posters, throwaways, sound trucks, and so forth. That was easy, of course, and even though my brain was still pretty muzzy, the job didn't take very long. By the time Gribble showed up an hour later, I had enough wordage down on paper to make it look like I had worked all night.

Mrs. Gunderson answered the doorbell, and from the sound of her voice you would have thought he was royalty or something. "Come right in, Brother Gribble!" I heard her chirp, all excited. "Clem told me he was expecting you. My, I can't tell you how proud I feel . . . !"

But Doc evidently wasn't interested in how she felt, because the next thing I knew he was climbing the stairs.

"Well, well, my little man!" he chortled as he bounced into my room. "Right on the job, eh?"

I gave him a nasty look. It didn't seem right for him to appear so fresh and pink after the way he'd been lapping it up the night before. Besides, I didn't see why, just because I'm kind of short, he had to go and call me his *little* man. So I scowled and said, "You bet I'm on the job. How about you? Did you get me that dough you promised?"

He tried to register surprise, but saw he wasn't getting away with it. So then he says, "Oh, you mean the advance? Say, you don't have to worry about that. It's practically in the bag."

"What do you mean, 'practically'? I thought from the way you talked last night that it was all set."

"Sure, it's all set. Long John's waiting down at the Citadel right now to close the deal."

"You mean I've got to face him again?" I yelled. "Jeez, if I'd known that I'd have held out for fifty."

"Aw, it isn't that bad," he said, waving his pudgy hand. "Besides, you'll get more'n fifty bucks out of this before you're through. You see if you don't."

"I'll see all right," I said, gathering up my papers.

He tried his damnedest to jolly me out of my dumps as we drove downtown, but I wouldn't co-operate.

"Aw, can it, Doc!" I finally snapped. "You can't con me. I know the score."

He could tell by the look on my face that I meant what I said, so he didn't waste any more breath. Instead he suddenly slowed down and pulled into a parking lot.

"What's the idea?" I asked.

"Let's have a drink," he said. "You sound like you need one."

He was right, of course, but I wouldn't give him the satisfaction of admitting it. "Forget it," I said. "Let's drive on."

"Aw, don't be stubborn, Clem!" he said, starting to heave himself out of the car. "I need one even if you don't."

We went into the bar next door, and had a couple of snorts. He insisted on paying for both rounds, and between that and the effect of the drinks, I began to feel a little better toward him. In fact, I was almost friendly when we returned to the car and got going again.

"How d'you think he'll act toward me?" I asked. "His Nibs, I mean. He seemed kind of sore last night."

"Aw, he's all over that now. I told him you've seen the light since then."

"And he believed you?"

"Sure. He always believes me. . . . But I want to warn you—he can be smart about some things. Not about money. He's not interested in that. And not about people either. Half the time he doesn't seem to know they even exist. But it's different when it comes to theories. He can be plenty smart about them. The best thing to do is not to try to argue with him when he starts theorizing. Just let him rave on."

"I get it," I said.

"And another thing: don't get personal with him. He gets sore as a boil if you try to pry into his private life."

"Yeah? What's he trying to hide?"

"Search *me*. All I know is he just won't talk about himself. Would you believe it, after all these years I still don't know even how old he is! No one seems to know."

"Say, that puts me in a hell of a spot," I said. "How am I going to write my press stories if I can't find out anything about him? I certainly can't play up his ideas. All I'd have to do is just hint at the way he feels about the Hebes, and I wouldn't be able to get a line in any paper in town."

"I realize that. You'll just have to find some other angle."

"For instance?"

"Don't ask me. That's your problem, Clem. After all, why do you think I've taken you in on this proposition?"

"Taken me in is right," I growled. "Believe me, if I didn't need that dough so bad . . ."

"Aw, that isn't the way to talk. You're smart, Clem. You'll think of a way to crash the papers."

He seemed so sure of it that I didn't like to disagree. I just stared through the windshield and thought.

Finally I said, "How about my giving a sex slant to the story? That's always good for a spread, especially in the Hearst sheets. Think I could get him to come out in favor of free love or something like that?"

"Not a chance," Gribble said, starting to grin. "He'd bite your head off if you even suggested it. He doesn't believe in sex."

"No fooling! Say, what's the matter with him? Is he queer?"

"No, not really. At least, so far as I know, he isn't. He just hasn't any use for women, that's all."

That started me snickering. "Now I get it!" I cracked.

"Get what?"

"Why he took up that enema business. Those swishes just naturally go in for interior decorating."

[49]

Gribble let out a guffaw and slapped my thigh. "That's a good one!" he laughed. "Yes, sir, that's a damned good one. It beats me, Clem, how you think them up like that, right on the spur of the moment. You're better than Fred Allen."

"Go on!" I said, trying to look modest. "I bet you say that to all the boys who are better than Fred Allen."

That made him start laughing all over again. "You're all right, Clem!" he said. "Yes, sir, you're all right." He had to break off owing to the traffic, but the minute he was in the clear again, he resumed his speech. "And that's why I've got such confidence in you," he said. "All you've got to do is put the old noodle to work, Clem, and I bet you'll think of something. For the papers, I mean."

I lit a cigarette and started thinking once more, and meanwhile he drove on. I continued to think all the rest of the way, but in the end I had to admit I was still stuck.

"Well, don't worry," Gribble said as he parked the car behind the old mansion. "You'll think of something."

8

The same guard in the khaki shirt opened the door, and he went through the same routine of taking a peek before he would let us in. This time, though, it was daylight, and he didn't look nearly so tough to me. In fact, I got the feeling he was nothing but a dumb Swede janitor who carried a gun for the same reason that a sappy high-school girl will put on black lace underwear.

Gribble waddled past him, and led me into what must once have been the dining room. It was a sort of office now, with a big roll-top desk in the middle of the floor, and a mimeographing machine on a long table against one wall. The corners were piled high with bundles of literature, and the built-in sideboard was leaking with pamphlets and stationery. The place looked like it hadn't been dusted in months.

"Sit down," Gribble said, putting his hat away. "I'll go call J.C."

I took the big easy chair near the window and reached for one of the magazines on the side table. It was something called *World Service,* and stated right on the front page that it was published in Germany. The articles in it seemed to be about nothing but the Jews. The first one was entitled "Czechoslovakia's Role in the International Jewish Game," but I skipped it to read the next, which was headed "Jews Control the British Cinema." It turned out to be pretty dull though, so I put the magazine back, and started looking at the others on the table. There must have been at least a dozen of them, all with more or less crackpotty names like *Social Justice, The Octopus, Liberation, The White Knight, X-Ray,* and so forth. But then I noticed a copy of the local *Examiner* in the wastebasket, and that being more my kind of reading matter, I fished it out and turned to the front page. The lead story was about that sex-maniac again, the one that had been attacking little girls in Beverly Hills. He had just been arraigned, and the paper was full of pictures and interviews.

I didn't get a chance to read much beyond the headlines before Gribble returned. He looked upset about something.

"Where's His Nibs?" I asked out of the side of my mouth.

"He wants you to come upstairs."

"Anything go wrong?"

"No, of course not. It's just that it's more comfortable upstairs."

I could see he was weaseling, and for a minute I felt like I had lead in my pants. Nevertheless, I got to my feet and followed Doc upstairs.

Power was waiting for us on the other side of those portieres I had seen him come through the night before. The place was a sort of sleeping porch, part glass, part screen, and the rest knotty wood that needed a fresh coat of paint. The floor was bare, and the only furniture was an army cot, a kitchen table, and a couple of plain wooden chairs. A pair of heavy iron dumbbells lay in a corner, and a set of pulley-weights was screwed to the back wall. A dish of raisins stood on the table, and next to it a torn carton of crackers and a bottle of what looked like buttermilk.

Power was sitting behind the table in a sweat shirt and pants. His feet were bare, and he seemed to be trying to braid his long bony toes.

"Come in, Smullet," he boomed. "I want to talk to you." He put down the glass from which he had been drinking, and pointed to a chair near the table.

I parked myself and tried to act at my ease. Doc, I noticed, did the same, though he hadn't even been asked to come in.

"So you've changed your mind, eh?" Power said, fixing me with his blue eyes. They looked even fiercer than I remembered, almost as if they were burning calcium.

"Yeah, that's right," I answered, clearing my throat.

"You sure about that?"

"Why—yeah, naturally."

"Because if you're not sure, Smullet, we don't want you. You don't belong with us. Understand?"

I cleared my throat again and said, "Yeah, I understand."

He eyed me like he still wasn't satisfied. "I hope you realize what it means," he said, "joining a movement like ours. We're not fooling, you understand."

"Yeah. I know."

He paused and looked me up and down as if he was trying to guess my weight. "Can you handle a gun?" he suddenly asked.

"Me? Why, no!"

"Well, you'll have to learn if you expect to be one of us."

"I will? Say, wait a minute. . . ."

Gribble put out a hand to keep me in my chair. "That's all right, Clem," he said. "All J.C. means . . ."

"I don't need you to tell him what I mean!" the other barked.

Gribble glared around at him, and for a minute I thought he was going to blow up. He didn't, though. He just gave a shrug and started looking at the floor. "Okay," he said. "Have it your way."

Power let out a little snort, and began pouring himself some more buttermilk. He was slow and deliberate about it, as if he was showing off. Then he threw his weird head far back and took a long swallow that made his Adam's apple bob up and down like it was on a string. He took another swallow, smacked his lips, examined the glass carefully to see there was no drip on the outside, and finally set it down. Then he turned and began searing me again with those blue eyes of his.

"You're not scared to use a gun, are you?" he demanded.

I figured I'd had about enough of this third degree. "I don't know," I came back at him.

"What do you mean, 'you don't know'? You're an American, aren't you?"

"Sure I am, but what's that got to do with it? I've never believed in fooling around with munitions. I'm not the type."

"You're not, eh? Well, the time's coming when you may have to be."

"Yeah? Who says so?"

"I do."

It was all I could do to keep from yelling, "And who the hell are you?" He must have realized it, too, because of a sudden his glare seemed to flicker. That was all it did, just flicker, but it was enough. I'd been scared of him until that minute. In spite of the back talk I had given him, I'd been scared as hell. But not any more. That flicker had given him away. I suddenly realized that fundamentally he was nothing but a bulldozer.

I can't tell you how that made me feel, but you can guess when I describe what I did next. I just looked him square in the eye and snapped, "So what?" And then, without giving him a chance to answer, I sprang up and barked, "Listen, Mister Power, let's get this straight. I'm a press agent, that's all. If you're willing to use me in that capacity, okay. Otherwise, to hell with it! I'll just tear up the plans I've made for your publicity campaign, and forget all about it."

That got him. I guess he wasn't used to having anyone slug back to him like that, because he seemed floored for a second. But only for a second, for then he saw me take out the papers I had typed and make as if I was going to tear them up, and that seemed to shock him to life again. "Hold on a minute," he said, making a grab for the sheets. "You don't want to do that, Smullet. What are these plans?"

I let him take them and stood back while he started to read. He held the pages way off, like he needed glasses, and yanked at his long nose as he read. I turned to wink at Gribble, who was also on his feet now, looking kind of worried.

Finally Power put the papers down and raised his eyes to me. "This sounds mighty impressive, Smullet," he said in a new kind of tone. "Do you mean to say you intended to do all that just for our meeting next Thursday?"

"That's right," I answered. "The way I figured it, that meeting's a sort of premeer for you. If it's a success, you're made, and if it's a flop, well . . ." I said the rest with my shoulders.

He started rubbing his hand over his dome, making it sound like sandpaper. Then he said, "Sit down. I'd like to know more about this. Do you really think you can do all these things? Get write-ups in the papers, for instance?"

"Sure. Why not? With my contacts, it'll be a cinch. Of course, I'll need your co-operation."

"In what way?"

"Well, for example, you'll have to come out to the airport so I can shoot some pictures of you stepping out of a plane. That's always good for an advance spread. Then again I might be able to get some movie star to pose with you. . . ."

"What kind of movie star?" he cut in sharply.

Doc rushed to the rescue. "He means one of the men," he explained. "Somebody like McLaglen."

"Oh, that'll be all right," Power agreed.

I looked at them kind of impressed. "Do you know Victor Mc-Laglen?" I asked.

"No," Doc started to explain, "the one we're talking about is Leopold, his brother."

J.C. nodded. "Leopold used to be a great worker for the Cause around here," he said. "He'd be that now, if those God-damned Jew Dealers in Washington hadn't deported him."

"Is that a fact? Say, are there any other movie people like that? Sympathetic, I mean?"

He started rubbing the bristles on his dome again, trying to think. "No," he finally came out, "none that are prominent. Of course, we've got quite a few electricians and people like that. But I guess they wouldn't be much help, would they?"

"No," I said. "But don't worry. I may be able to fish up some big names for you in the next day or two. What I'm more concerned with right now, Mr. Power—yeah, and that reminds me. If I'm to handle you, I'm in favor of dropping the Mister in connection with your name. It's too common. I'd refer to you as The Power. See what I mean? John Christian *the* Power! How does that sound?"

His face lit up as if a battery of Klieg lamps had been turned on inside his skull. "That's a very sensible idea," he said.

"And how!" Gribble broke in. "Say, that's a real inspiration!"

I smiled at their looks. "Shucks," I said, "that's nothing compared to some of the ideas I'm going to come up with yet. Just give me time, gentlemen, that's all." I drew my chair closer, and fished out paper and pencil. "Now then, J.C.," I said very businesslike, "the first thing I need is some biographical dope. Just the bare facts, that's all. Where you were born, what you've done, and so forth."

I could feel him get taut.

"I don't see why that's necessary," he said, frowning. "Just say I'm a 100% American. That ought to be enough."

I started to argue the matter, but he was hard to budge. The most he would tell me was that he was raised on a farm near Elizabethtown, Kentucky—"just like Abraham Lincoln"—and that he had spent all his life studying medical science and philosophy.

Finally I said, "I guess I'll just have to bill you as a sort of Mystery Man."

He didn't seem to get the sarcasm in my voice. "Yes, that's the idea," he said right away. "I'd like nothing better than for the world to think of me as something kind of shadowy."

"But why?" I tried to corner him.

"Why? Because—well, that way people will maybe realize that I'm more than just a man. I'm an Idea."

"Huh?"

"Yes, that's the important thing about me, Smullet. Not what I am, but what I stand for. Get the point?"

I didn't, and said so; whereupon he went into a long spiel that left me even more balled up. Most of what he said sounded like double-talk. As best I could make it out, what he believed was that there were two different kinds of what he called philosophies of life. The way he put it was this: "One philosophy is rooted in blood and soil, so it's natural and true; but the other is tied in with money and cement, so it's artificial and false." And his big beef was that people were ditching the natural philosophy in favor of the artificial one. In the good old days, he said, they'd all lived on farms, and grown up tough and honest. But now they were flocking to the cities and becoming soft and slick. They were coddling themselves all the time, eating canned food, living in heated houses, riding around in automobiles, and going to the movies. And such things, he said, were unnatural. That's why so many people were losing their teeth ahead of time, and suffering from diabetes, high blood pressure, and constipation. It also explained why there was so much divorce and birth-control and general jazzing around. City-life, he insisted, was making the entire human race nothing but a pack of sloppy, slobbering, diseased and degenerate mongrels.

And it was the Jews, he went on to say, who were chiefly responsible for this. They couldn't exist except in cities, so they wanted everybody else to exist in them, because in that way they made themselves less conspicuous, and in addition created more scope for their dirty work. As you know, he'd given me quite an earful on the Jews the day before, but now he really cut loose. I shan't even try to repeat all the things he said about them, because it would take too long, and sound too silly, and anyway there's a limit to what you're allowed to print. The gist of his complaint was—and I quote his exact words—"The Jew is the Pied Piper who's leading the entire Aryan race to destruction."

It struck me he wasn't being very complimentary to us Aryans, comparing us to kids who could be led astray that way. But I let it pass. I remembered what Gribble had said about never arguing with him, and just sat mum and let him rave on.

When he got through with the Jews, he took up the colored people. Apparently he didn't like them either. Nor the bankers, even the Gentile ones, nor the New Dealers, and so on and so forth. Fundamentally, and notwithstanding Father Coughlin, he was down on the Catholics, too. They were too international, he said.

He must have raved on in that vein for at least an hour before he finally let up, and then, as I have said, I was more in a fog than ever. The reason was that I knew he was nuts and yet at the same time I was kind of impressed. I guess it was because he seemed so convinced of what he was saying, and because he was so wrought up about it, like it was a matter of life and death. I had never come up against anybody who talked as he did—with such passion, I mean. Listening to him, I felt like a guy who'd never slept with anything except chippies, and then for once gets a loving from a real decent girl. It left me kind of thrilled and breathless, and at the same time a little ashamed of my past.

"Lord!" I said when he ran down. "I had no idea there was all that philosophy in back of your movement."

"There is, though," he said, shooting out his lip. "And that's what I want the world to understand. I want people to realize that the real issue here is one of Principle, not personality. I'm not just another individual. I'm a Force!" He leaned back and got a funny faraway look in his eyes. "That's what I am," he went on, like he was talking to someone behind me. "I'm an incarnated Force!" Then, after a pause, he suddenly brought his eyes back to me and mumbled, "See what I mean?"

"Ye-ah," I managed to say. "Yeah, I get the point."

"Then will you do it?"

"Do what?"

"Leave me kind of shadowy, and throw all the light on what I represent."

I scratched my head. "I'll try," I said. "I don't know if I can get away with it, but I'll try my best."

He let out a sigh and stood up. His feet were bare, as I have said, and I was wearing my built-up shoes, but nevertheless he seemed maybe ten times my height. "That's all any man can do," he said, holding out his bony hand. "God bless you, Smullet."

"Thank you," I said, feeling almost as if he was consecrating me.

"Don't thank me. Thank the God who gave you the vision to see the light."

"Yes, sir."

"Remember, it's the light of Destiny!"

I blinked.

"Good-bye, Brother Smullet."

"Good-bye."

9

So now I was in. It took me a little while to realize it, because I had had an idea that first I would have to take that "blood oath" Mrs. Gunderson had talked about. It turned out, though, that J.C.'s handshake had been all that was necessary to make me a Crusader. From then on I was right in—up to my neck.

I still can't figure out how it all came about. My original idea, as I have explained, had simply been to earn that twenty-five bucks. But somehow, once I got started, I found myself getting more and more involved. One thing led to another, and before I knew what was happening, *boom*—I had been made an officer of the organization! I'm not kidding. I'd been put on what was called the Supreme Council.

I wasn't elected to that position. The Power, I discovered, didn't hold with the idea of elections. He believed all officers should be appointed—by himself. He called that the "Leader Principle," and claimed it was the only proper way to run an organization. Some day, he said, the entire government would be run that way.

I naturally thought it was a compliment when he first suggested putting me on his Supreme Council, but once I lamped the sort of people he'd already given that honor to, I wasn't so sure. Excluding Gribble, there wasn't a one of them that I'd have cared to be caught dead with.

For example, there was that Captain Cleaver, whom I have already described. He was exactly what I had guessed him to be: to wit, an amateur soldier on a professional basis. He'd stopped a few bits of shrapnel at Belleau Wood, and on the strength of that he considered himself a career-warrior. He belonged to five different veterans' associations, and walked, talked, and carried on like every day was the Fourth of July. And he was the least queer of the lot, so you can imagine what the rest were like.

Take old Mrs. Krutch. When I first set eyes on her I'd have sworn she was made up to play a part in *Arsenic and Old Lace.* She was wearing a rusty black dress with a high net collar around her wrinkled neck, and an antique black straw hat pinned to what couldn't have been anything but a wig. A big gold watch studded with corals hung from a big coral barpin on her bosom, and both her hands were loaded with cracked and yellow rocks. She was slightly deaf, had hair on her upper lip, and false teeth which she kept pushing around with her tongue, like they didn't fit right.

There was another female on the Council, a Miss Mabel Haight, and she in her own way was even queerer. She was in her thirties, built like a wrestler, wore mannish clothes, and had a goiter with pop-eyes to match. Her stiff black hair was cut very short, and her teeth looked as though they had been worked on by a saw-sharpener. She had big hands red as beef, square nails bitten down to the quick, and not a speck of powder or rouge on her face. She believed in theosophy, astrology, numerology, and Moral Re-Armament, and ran a health food store for a living. Listening to her talk, I knew exactly why she said she was what she called the "Amazon" type. Like the river by that name, she was practically all mouth.

Then there was a party named Max Kronkhite, a perfect Heinie type, built like a barrel, with a blown-up sort of face, and a fat neck that ran straight down from the back of his close-cropped head. He had a thick accent, of course, and could have stepped right out of a Warner Brothers spy picture. As you undoubtedly know if you've followed our case, he actually was a spy; but I had no suspicion of that until much, much later. Neither did any of the rest of us, I'm quite sure. All we knew about him then was that he was a big shot in the local Bund, which naturally made him mighty useful to the Crusade.

Finally there was a guy named Cyrus Peavey, and he might have come out of a comic strip. He was a skinny little mildewed man with long sideburns, a twitch in one cheek, and practically no chin. Properly he should have been a bookkeeper or maybe a watchmaker who'd been out of work for months. Instead he was a pretty successful merchant, owning three drugstores out in the Fairfax district. That, apparently, was why he rated the Supreme Council, being good for a touch once in a while. He was very insistent, however, on keeping his contributions a secret, and in general tried to stay in the background.

One look at that crew, and I understood why Gribble had been so anxious to have me come in with him. Furthermore I realized I'd been a sap to let him buy me with a measly twenty-five bucks. I discovered he'd raised a special fund for the meeting, and right away I hit him up for a little extra. I did that twice with a certain amount of success, but the third time he got positively sore. "For crying out loud!" he squawked, "who d'you think I am? Jesse Jones? All I've got to work with is two hundred bucks, and I'll need more than that to pay for the hall and the decorations."

Well, when I heard that I really blew up. I'd taken it for granted that he'd set aside at least a hundred for the publicity. "What about the printing?" I yelled. "And the sound-truck, and the newspaper ads?"

He shook his head. Apparently there wasn't going to be more than maybe fifteen dollars for those essentials.

So I took matters into my own hands and went direct to J.C. He was in the backyard of the Citadel at the time, taking his daily exercise in nothing but a pair of shorts. He wouldn't stop when I came up to him. He just kept on swinging his iron dumbbells and panting all the while I talked. I felt like a fool, because I couldn't tell whether he was even listening.

Finally, though, he dropped his skinny arms, waited to catch his breath, and said, "I can't concern myself with such problems. It's up to Gribble to raise any money we need."

"But he says he's already raised all he can," I explained. "I just been talking to him, and he says . . ."

I broke off because the nut had started exercising again. He was on the ground now, arms folded under his head, and legs circling like he was riding a bicycle upside-down. "Has he been to Peavey?" he panted.

"Yeah, twice," I yelled. "He says he can't get another cent out of him."

The hairy legs continued circling through the air. "Why don't *you* go to Peavey then?" he panted.

"Me?"

"Yes, you. Tell him I sent you."

So I did do that. I located Mr. Peavey at one of his drugstores, and he turned out to be just about as soft as reinforced concrete. I had to drill away at him for fully an hour before I finally managed to make him come through. Even then, all I was able to get was fifty bucks.

That, however, was better than nothing. It enabled me to sugar a press photographer into taking those shots at the airport, and also to leave a small deposit with the printer who was to run off the handbills. That left barely $40, so I decided to forget about the posters, sound-trucks, and so forth. I even gave up all thought of putting ads in the papers, which was more serious, because it meant I had no way to blackjack the city editors into giving me the free space I needed. I figured, though, that if I made my copy bright enough, they might print it anyway.

I pecked out a dozen different advance releases on the meeting, and they were damn good ones, even if I say so myself. They described Power as "one of the profoundest philosophers and spiritual statesmen of modern times . . . a most unique and original thinker whose doctrines combine the native soil-born wisdom of pioneer America with the latest findings of medical science and sex psychology." (When I have to sling high language, believe me I can sling it!) I made him out to be practically related to Abraham Lincoln, and also linked somehow to Plato, Aristotle, and Teddy Roosevelt. I hinted that he had discovered all sorts of startling facts about our "social degeneracy," and that he was going to reveal sensational truths about "the growing menace of racial mongrelism." To top everything, I promised that the meeting was going to be attended by "nationally prominent figures in political and patriotic life," and also "numerous Hollywood celebrities."

Even Captain Cleaver—and he, incidentally, had taken a strong dislike to me for some reason—even he had to admit my stories were lulus.

Nevertheless they failed to make the grade. Day after day I kept hammering away at the city editors, sending them Special Delivery letters, calling them on the phone, even dropping in to see them personally. But I got practically nowhere. All I could scrounge was a couple of sticks in one of the minor sheets, and I figured it would draw maybe twenty people—if they had no other place to spend Thursday night.

But in spite of that, I was still hopeful. For one thing I knew Kronkhite was planning to bring a mob from the German House, and Cleaver was going to rout out a crowd of Legionnaires. In addition, Gribble was contacting various shirty outfits like the Silver Legion, the Actioneers, the National Defenders, and Rev. Joe Jeffers' crowd. All of these were really in competition with the Crusade, but Doc hoped to be able to get them to attend our meeting anyway. Finally, I still had an ace of my own to count on, and that was the handbill.

I had ordered 10,000 to be delivered at the Citadel on Monday, and the following morning I got down bright and early to start the distribution. Kronkhite had promised to line up plenty of volunteers for the work, and about a dozen were already on hand when I arrived. Most of them looked like cleaning women on their day off, and they all had Dutchy accents. Their leader was a big krauthead with a broken nose who could have doubled for Schmeling if he had trained down a bit. He told me his name was Pfortz, or something like that, and I saw at once that he was an old hand at this game. He followed me into the office and brought out a map of the downtown area with the corners marked where he planned to station his distributors.

"That's fine, Pfortz," I said. "How about dispatching them right away?"

"Goot!" he snapped like a regular Heinie corporal.

I went out to the hallway and called the dope with the gun who guarded the door. "Where are the bundles, Hank?" I asked him. He didn't seem to know what I was talking about. "The ones from the printer," I explained. "They're here, aren't they?"

He started shaking his head. "There ain't been nothing come from no printer," he answered.

I flew to the phone, and almost wrecked the dial getting the printer's number. I heard the bell ring four times before there was any answer. "That you, Rodeheaver?" I hollered. "This is Smullet. . . . Yeah, Clem Smullet. Say, where the hell are those throwaways?"

"I'm sorry," the voice started to apologize. "I was just going to call you. They aren't ready."

"But dammitall, didn't you promise . . . ?"

"Yeah, I know what I promised. But I've been having trouble here. My men have gone on strike. Some sonova-bitch of a Red . . ."

I didn't wait to hear any more. I just slammed the receiver, and started tearing my hair.

I was still sitting there, tearing away, when Gribble showed up half an hour later. He must have had an extra heavy night. His skin was the color of herring filet, and there were tea-bags under his eyes.

"What's the matter?" he asked. "Didn't Kronkhite's gang show up?"

I explained what had happened.

"Wow!" he yammered. "Now we're up the creek for fair! Have you told Long John?"

"No. I've heard him stirring around upstairs, but I figured I'd better let you break the news."

"That's real nice of you."

His sarcasm made me want to paste him one. "For crisake!" I blatted. "Didn't you tell me only yesterday not to keep running to him?"

That made him change his tune. "Okay, okay," he said. "I'll tell him. Let's duck out and get a drink first."

We drove around to the Pearl Dive and sat at the bar.

"You're kind of early today, gentlemen," Chuck greeted us, hurrying to climb into his white coat. "What'll it be?"

Gribble started to order a double-rye, but changed his mind. "Gimme a Bromo-Seltzer!" he said, making a face.

I took a beer.

Chuck set them up and then went back to mopping the floor. "Wish I could get off today," he started to gab as he lunged back and forth. "I'd sure like to listen in on that trial."

"What trial?" I asked, though I didn't really give a damn.

He stared like he thought I was spoofing. "Don't you read the papers?" he said. "I mean that sex-maniac case. The jury's pritnear all picked, and they're likely to start dishin' the dirt today."

"That's right," I said, just to shut him up. "I'd forgotten."

But it didn't shut him up. "They ought to lynch the bastard," he began growling. "Yessir, they ought to take him right out and lynch him!" He almost knocked over a chair with his mop, he was so wrought up. "Why the hell should they worry about being fair to a degenerate like that? Gud-damit, was he fair to those pore little innocent kids?" I didn't answer, but that didn't seem to discourage Chuck. "A *trial* for that degenerate?" he went on, spitting in the bucket. "Kurryst, they ought to just string him up! Yes, sir. The law's all right in its place, but the way I look at it, there's sump'n higher than the law, and that's justice. The trouble with this country is . . ."

I didn't bother to listen to what the trouble was. I had other things to worry about. So had Gribble, judging from the way he was struggling to belch.

Finally Chuck finished mopping the floor and came back behind the bar. "Just look at that face!" he growled, opening the *Examiner* and spreading it out in front of us. "Degenerates like that ought never be allowed to get into this country."

I glanced at the picture, and started to read the caption underneath. The case, as you know, had been in the papers for weeks, but I hadn't followed it except casually. There was nothing really sensational in it for me. It was just the same old story of a quiet little bank clerk that everybody had taken to be a saint, yet who all the time had gone around picking up little girls and raping them in the bushes. I'd worked on hotter stories a dozen times when I was a reporter.

"Goddam furrin degenerate!" Chuck went on. "Lynching's too good for him!"

"What makes you think he's a foreigner?" I asked. "He doesn't look it."

"I bet, though, he is one," the barkeep said. "Look at his name. Conrad Wulff! Kurryst, if that ain't foreign, I'll eat it."

Gribble had got up the gas at last, and was belching fine. "Probably a Hebe," he said, grinning sourly.

I started to grin back at him, but then suddenly stopped. "Say, wait a minute," I muttered, rubbing my forehead.

"What's the matter?"

I waved him to shut up so that I could concentrate. Then I gave my fingers a snap. "I think I've got it," I said "Yeah, I'm sure of it. . . Doc, we're saved!"

[64]

"You gone nuts?" he said, letting out another belch.

"Come on!" I said, grabbing his fat arm. "We've got to get hold of J.C. right away."

10

Mrs. Gunderson was set on coming along the next morning, so I was kind of late getting to the Court House. However, the second I stepped out of the elevator, I knew everything was going to be jake. Power was right there at the head of the crowd, ready to rush in as soon as the court-room doors were opened. He was dressed entirely in white, and held himself like he knew, but didn't mind, that everybody was staring at him. Captain Cleaver was at his side, flanked by five or six bozos in veterans' overseas caps. I spotted Doc Gribble and at least a dozen other people whom I had seen around the Citadel. Kronkhite and Pfortz were there with what looked like a whole battalion of hausfraus.

Mrs. Gunderson was tagging at my heels, and I tried to barge a path for her through the mob. I couldn't, though, so I left her standing there, and slipped around to locate another entrance. I found one all right, and flashed my old press card so fast that the cop thought it was kosher and let me go through.

I recognized one of the guys at the press table, an old souse I'd known years back when I was on the *Chicago Tribune*. He was a bald-headed little geezer who could have doubled for Donald Meek, except that his eyes were glassier and he had varicose veins in his nose. His name was Duranty—Tom, not Walter—and I had almost forgotten he was still alive. I rushed over and started slapping him on the back. "Well, if it isn't my old pal, Tom Duranty!" I yelled.

He stared for a second, and finally remembered who I was. "Hiya, half pint!" he mumbled.

I'd always hated that particular nickname, but I let it slide. "Say, this *is* funny!" I guffawed. "Only last night I was saying to J. P.

McEvoy—you remember old Mac, don't you—well, only last night I was saying to him, 'What's happened to Tom Duranty?' Yes, sir, that's what I was saying only last night, and here I go and bunk right into you! Well, if that ain't psychoanalysis!"

The gag made the whole bunch snicker.

"What're you doing here?" Tom asked me. "I thought you were working for the movies."

"Not any more," I said. And then, edging closer, I started talking in his ear.

"You don't say!" the old guy spoke up when I got through. "What's he look like?"

"I'll point him out to you," I whispered, but loud enough for the other newshawks to hear.

"What's up?" one of them asked.

I didn't answer because just then the doors opened and the mob started pouring in. Cleaver was in the lead, and I motioned for him and his bonus boys to hog a couple of benches up front. It worked like a charm. In a minute we had The Power sitting right by the railing, with at least twenty of our people packed solid around him. I even managed to find a place for Mrs. Gunderson, though she was nearly the last one to get through the door. I could almost hear her heart hammering, she was so excited. It was probably the first time she'd ever been inside a courtroom.

I went back and started whispering to Duranty again. The effect was just what I had planned on. In a minute I had every newshawk at the table looking at me and asking questions.

"Shall I let 'em in on it?" I asked Tom.

He said, "Sure," so I leaned forward and gave them an earful. Then they all craned to look at The Power, and I had to smile at the way their eyes bugged. Even sitting, he was a head taller than anybody near him. And what a head! It could have been carved out of mahogany, the flesh was so brown and shiny over the skull. And the eyes looked like chunks of blue glass.

A sob-sister at the table let out a gurgle. "My, he gives me goose pimples!" she thrilled. "Who is he?"

I spilled a few more details, safe ones, and then clammed up. The judge had come in, and the bailiff was announcing the court in session.

I slipped back to the second row and squeezed in so I could be right behind J. C. He was as tense as a hopped-up racehorse. I could tell it by the way the cords in the back of his neck were quivering. I've got to admit I was kind of tense myself. I'd pulled promotion stunts in all sorts of places in my time—in colleges, hospitals, wedding chapels, even cemeteries. But this was my first offense in a courtroom. I'd always felt that a courtroom was one place it was good policy to steer clear of. So you can hardly blame me if I was tense.

Everything depended now on the judge. If he was planning to run for re-election, the way I'd been told, then we'd probably get away with it. In that case he'd want to play along with us for the sake of the publicity. He was a bald-headed shrimp with a long nose, a pointed chin, and large horn-rimmed glasses tied to a wide black ribbon. I could tell by the way he struck a pose every time a hocus-focus boy stuck a camera in his face that he was strictly ham.

Nevertheless I was plenty scared. I leaned across Mrs. Gunderson to give Gribble a nudge. "How do you size him up?" I whispered.

"Who?" he asked out of the side of his mouth.

"Hizzoner."

He shrugged and motioned me to sit back. He seemed to want to concentrate on the prosecutor, who had already started addressing the jury.

I mopped my face and tried to pay attention.

It was a good opening statement, full of fire and hokum. That prosecutor really knew his stuff. He was a tall, hawk-nosed fellow with buck teeth and shaggy hair, and he seemed hep to every trick of courtroom roaratory. He would yell and then suddenly start whispering. He would stamp and pound, and then all at once go limp, like he was about to break down and weep.

And the crowd lapped it up. Only the prisoner didn't appear to pay any attention. He was a skinny little punk, and the way he sat hunched over in his chair, he might have been asleep or dead. Everybody else, though, sat bolt upright. I saw some of the women begin to dab their eyes, and heard a sob or two. Somewhere behind me a man started cussing under his breath. I felt myself get tenser and tenser.

Suddenly I turned and whispered something to Pfortz, who was sitting right behind me. Then I watched him duck down and whisper to one of the hausfraus in his row. She was a screwy-looking frump with bulging eyes and an awful complexion. There were so many blackheads in her greasy skin that it put you in mind of flypaper in July. At first she didn't seem to understand what Pfortz was trying to tell her. Finally, though, she must have got it, because all at once she drew herself up, closed her eyes, and let out a screech that made even the prisoner jump in his seat. Again and again she screeched, her arms tight at her sides and her head bobbing up and down like it was on a pogo stick. The judge started banging his gavel, and cops came running from everywhere. They had to plough in and lift her up bodily before they could get her out and haul her away. One of them put his fist over her mouth to shut her up, but she bit it and screeched all the louder. All the way down the aisle she kept throwing herself around and screeching her head off. Finally they got her into the corridor, and only then did the crowd seem to notice that the little judge was still banging his gavel.

I felt like hugging myself. The stunt had got the whole courtroom so jittery that anything could happen now. The prosecutor must have felt the atmosphere, because right away he started winding up his speech. Flinging his arms wide, and flopping his mane, he blasted away till I thought he'd have a hemorrhage. Then, dramatically, he let his voice crack, broke into sobs, and staggered back to his seat.

I craned forward, my eyes on the attorney for defense. He was John W. MacNamara, the big-shot criminal lawyer from Chicago, and the minute I saw him start slouching across to the jury box, I gave J. C.'s shoulder a poke.

"This is it!" I whispered.

He jumped up like I had jabbed him with an ice-pick.

"Your Honor!" he boomed out. "I protest! My name is John Christian Power, and I protest! We're wasting time! That vicious fiend there in the dock. . . ."

The judge was so startled that the glasses fell off his nose. He fumbled for them, got them on again, and reached for his gavel. But then he saw the flashlights start popping, and paused. Every photographer in the room was shooting at J. C., and at the cops trying to get at him. Cleaver and his Legionnaires were barricading the way, yelling, "Let him alone! . . . He's right! . . . Let him talk!" The hausfraus too were yelling. Everybody was yelling.

For a minute it looked like there was going to be a riot. The cops broke through, collared J. C., and started hustling him out. One of them tried to clout him, but he grabbed the arm and pretty near tore it off.

"Don't you dare use violence on me!" he roared, straightening his ice-cream coat and stalking down the aisle. "I'm an American. You can't . . ."

I didn't hear the rest. Our crowd was yammering too loud, especially the hausfraus, who acted like they had been coached for the job. I ploughed through to get to Cleaver, who was covering J. C.'s rear.

"Get him out quick!" I said. "I'll meet you on the sidewalk!" Then I turned around and waved to Duranty and the other newshawks.

They didn't need any diagrams. Grabbing their hats, they came flying after me.

When I got downstairs, there was J. C. still holding forth at the top of his lungs. He was standing on the marble pedestal that held the flagpole in front of the courthouse, and the mob around him was yelling like crazy. I spotted Gribble and Cleaver, and started talking to them fast. Then I rushed back and collected the news-hawks.

"Follow me," I told them. "He'll be waiting for us around the corner. And get out your pencils, boys. This is going to be terrific!"

It was.

11

The minute I saw how the papers played up the ruckus in the courthouse, I knew our meeting was made. There were pix on the front page of practically every sheet in town, feature stories under two-column heads, and even editorials. Only the *Times* tried to crack down, barely mentioning the demonstration, and not saying a word about the interview that J. C. gave out afterwards. But it ran an editorial deploring the "shameless antics of publicity-seeking demagogues," and that was even better than a news story.

I called a war council late that evening to consider a switch in our tactics. "Gentlemen," I said, leaning back in my chair, "this changes the entire picture. The whole town's been given to understand that The Power's going to tell all about the sex-maniac tomorrow night, and that means we're going to draw a crowd big enough to fill a hall twice the size of the Philharmonic. So here's my idea. Let's charge admission!"

Gribble was immediately for it, but Cleaver and Kronkhite started arguing that we ought to consult J. C. first. They were kind of stubborn about it, too, and if it hadn't been that His Nibs had left strict orders not to be disturbed under any circumstances—he was upstairs working on his speech—they might have carried their point. Finally, though, I talked them into leaving it to me to get his okay in the morning. Then I sent them on home.

"Get a good night's sleep, boys," I told them bossily. "We've got a hard day ahead of us."

It was a hard day, all right, and by the time evening came around I was pretty near a wreck. I had had to do so much running around and arguing that my arches ached, my voice was hoarse, and my nerves were all in a frazzle. Gribble was about in the same condition, so we stopped twice on our way down to the auditorium to get refreshed.

As it turned out, however, we could have skipped the refreshments. Just the sight of the crowd in the lobby would have been enough to soup us up. It was barely seven o'clock when we arrived, yet at least a hundred people were already standing there, and more were arriving every minute. By seven-thirty they were actually jamming the sidewalk, and though most of the ushers hadn't shown up yet, we decided to open the doors anyway.

That didn't seem to help, though. We had evidently drawn nothing but pikers, for hardly any of them would buy tickets and go inside. All they did was just stand around and gawk. So I finally called a cop, and that got them moving. Once they saw they were going to be chased away unless they went into the hall, they started bellying up to the ticket window in droves. I swear they couldn't have pushed harder if we'd advertised that Sally Rand was going to be on our program—without fans.

I had posted a dame in the booth, one I had hired especially for the job, and she proved to be a real hustler. I had got her through a friend of mine who worked the county fairs, and he hadn't lied when he'd said she knew all the angles. Nevertheless, what with the arguments she kept getting into over short change and so forth, I eventually had to open up a second front to help her out. But even after that we still had a hard time keeping the queues moving fast enough.

Finally we ran out of tickets. I thought I'd brought along an ample supply, including one roll that I hadn't told even Gribble about. Apparently, though, I had miscalculated, and we had to start using slips of paper marked with my initials. But that didn't last long, because the deputy from the Fire Department came rushing out to order the doors closed. I tried to talk him into letting me crowd just a few more people into the side aisles, and I might have succeeded if he hadn't been scared because there were so many photographers around.

I slipped him a fin anyway, paid off the dame, and started counting up. I figured out the amount that the organization could check me up on, cached it in the office strong box, and pocketed the rest. Then, slicking my hair back and buttoning my coat, I ankled out to join the crowd in the hall.

I still can't understand what made me do that. Stick around, I mean. If I'd been really smart I'd have taken the entire receipts and made for the depot. That wouldn't have been so unethical, would it? After all, what receipts would there have been if it hadn't been for me?

But there's no use going into that now. The fact remains that the idea of skipping never even occurred to me at the time, which just goes to show how even the brightest of us can slip up once in a while. I guess it must have been because of the sort of company I'd been keeping all week.

Be that as it may, instead of walking out, I walked in, and there I was, one more goof crowded into that hall. Cleaver was holding forth at the moment, and I must say he looked real impressive up there on the platform. Probably it was because he was dressed in his American Legion uniform. He was just finishing his speech, and from the hand he got as he bowed himself off, he must have been pretty good. I couldn't be sure, though, for I knew shills had been planted all over the hall, and there was no telling to what extent they were needling the applause.

Then Gribble got up to introduce the next speaker, and the way he did it, I had to admit to myself that *he* was definitely good, no question about it. Of course, his looks were in his favor, his big dimpled face and bushy blond hair and two hundred and forty pounds of beef neatly packed into a smart double-breasted suit. What counted even more, though, was his manner. He had the poise of a bishop combined with the zip of a night-club m.c. And the language! That smoothie used five-dollar words like he'd bought 'em two for a nickel.

I listened a while and then started snaking down the side aisle to see if there might be a seat up front. There wasn't, so I made for the narrow door that led to the wings. It was quite dark back there, and at first I thought the place was empty. But then I made out J. C. hiding off in a corner. I spotted him because of his ice-cream suit. He was sitting on a little folding chair, hunched over with his elbows on his knees and his head in his hands. I walked across and touched him on the shoulder. "Some mob out there, eh, J. C.?" I chirped.

He swung his arm like he meant to knock me down. "Go away!" he snapped, not even looking around.

I didn't say another word. I just backed away on tiptoe, and parked on a trunk near the open wings. I felt hurt, of course, but not badly. I figured there was nothing personal behind the way the guy had acted. Just temperament.

I decided to concentrate on what was going on out front. A woman was talking now, a socialite by the name of Mrs. Louise Ford Fry, whom Kronkhite had contacted for us in Pasadena. She was a short fat woman trussed up in a pink silk evening gown that seemed about to pop where her girdle left off. Her bosom stuck out straight as a shelf, and the gardenia on it kept shimmying like it had St. Vitus Dance. Kronkhite had cracked her up to us as a big-shot clublady, a leader in the D.A.R. and so forth. She had tried to get into Congress the year before, and might have made it if she could have got the nomination, and the Republicans had won. Neither of those things having happened, she was plenty sore, and even if Kronkhite hadn't told us that, I would have known it by the way she was spouting now. She had a voice like a she-elephant in a tantrum, and every time she mentioned Communism, or the C.I.O., or the New Deal, or That Man in the White House, she pretty near made the walls quiver.

She wasn't holding the crowd, though. She tried hard enough, God knows, but the setup was against her. She roared and stamped and sprayed sweat all over the front rows, but she was just another preliminary, and the crowd was itchy for the main event.

Gribble must have sensed what was happening, for he began to cough and shuffle his feet where he sat, right behind her. Finally I saw him reach forward and tug her skirt. She gave a start like she'd been goosed, threw Doc a mean glare, and went on talking. But she was rattled now, and began to run out of wind. She let out one last blast at Roosevelt, added a couple of hoots for Eleanor and Madame Perkins, and then flounced around and took her seat. She all but broke it, she came down on the chair so hard.

The applause was only so-so, but Gribble made her bob up for a bow anyway. He went further, started shaking her hand, and made the crowd clap for her to take a second bow. She did, her sweaty face all smiles now, and then Doc seemed satisfied. Returning to the stand, he threw out his chest, switched on his smile full strength, and began: "And now, my good friends, I want to bring you the man you have been waiting for, the man you have been reading about in the papers, the man . . ."

Cleaver came soft-shoeing out to the wings. "Where is he?" he asked, peering around in the dark.

Before I could answer, there was The Power right at our side. He didn't seem to see us, though. We might have been air, the way he passed us.

Doc was still giving him the build-up. ". . . I don't mind telling you, my friends," he was saying, "it has been my proud privilege to know some mighty dynamic personalities in my time, real leaders in public life, great statesmen and thinkers, like for instance Senator

[73]

Bob Reynolds and Congressman Clare Hoffman and a dozen more that I could name if I cared to take up the time. But I want to testify right here and now that of all of them, and mind you I say of *all* of them, I have never met a one to come up to the man I am about to present. He towers above the rest as the noble redwood tree towers above the petty scrubpines, as the snow-capped mountain towers above the rolling foothills at its base. . . ."

I wondered how J.C. was taking it, but he had his back to me, so I couldn't tell. The way he stood there, his arms folded and his eyes on the roof, I had a feeling he wasn't even listening.

Finally Doc began to wind up. ". . . and so, my friends," he big-mouthed, "I bring you now the man who I sincerely believe will go down in history as the Abraham Lincoln of our generation, the man destined to be recognized as the greatest spiritual force and dynamic personality of our day and age, none other than"—he paused and pointed to the wings—"John Christian *the* Power!"

The crowd went wild. Everybody got up and started yelling and stamping as J. C. stalked forward and took his stand at the rostrum. He didn't bow, or even smile. He just stood there, head up, and waited. Finally the crowd stopped yelling and sat down. Still he waited. For ten seconds, maybe fifteen, he stared out, not saying a word. You could have heard a pin drop, it got so quiet in the hall. A pin? Hell, you could have heard a hair drop!

And then at last he opened his mouth.

"My fellow Americans," he began in his deep hollow voice, "my countrymen, the time has come to speak the truth!" He waved his long arm to keep the crowd from starting to yell again. "The time has come, I say, when real Americans, honest, red-blooded, God-fearing Americans, have got to rise up and shout the truth from the housetops. Our world is in danger! All that we hold dear, the sanctity of our homes, the security of our little ones, the virility of our sons, the purity of our daughters, all that we have lived for, all that our forefathers shed their blood on a thousand battlefields to preserve—our honor, our might, our way of life—they are being undermined! They are being debauched and debased and corrupted before our very eyes. They are being *raped!* . . ."

He was terrific! I want to tell you, that guy was just terrific! He was as good as one of those prophets you read about in the Bible, all fire and scorch and fury. *As* good? He was even better! He talked plain United States, and you could understand him.

I turned to grin at Cleaver, who was still in the wings. He had brought up a folding chair, and was sitting on the edge, listening like he was magnetized. "Boy, is he terrific!" I chortled.

The man of war looked around, scowling, and flagged me to shut up, so I turned back and started listening again.

Now J. C. was talking about the sex-maniac, and his voice was all gravelly with disgust. He was going into details, telling just what the crazy punk had done, and how, and where; and his language was enough to make your insides squirm. He wasn't smutty, understand. He didn't use one real smutty word from beginning to end. Yet it was somehow the rawest talk I'd ever heard.

And the crowd loved it. I could tell that even from where I was sitting. I had a view of the front rows over on the other side of the hall, and most of the people there were crouched forward, their mouths practically drooling. Were they getting their money's worth!

But then all at once he switched. Drawing himself up and shooting out that long finger of his, he suddenly roared:

". . . And who is this fiend? I ask, who is this monster who polluted those babies, mauling them, raping them, tearing their flesh with his bloody claws? Just another helpless maniac? Just another crazy imbecile who didn't know what he was doing? NO! That's a lie! I know, and I tell you that's a damned lie! . . . Don't believe what you read in the papers. They lie! They have to lie because they've been paid to lie. *I* am the only man who dares to tell the truth, I, John Christian Power! . . . And here it is. *Conrad Wulff is sane!* He did what he did because he was put up to it! Every one of his crimes was deliberate! Every one of them was planned in advance, and carried out in cold blood! And do you want to know why? I'll tell you why. It's because *they were all part of a plot!* Each and every one of these crimes was part of a world-wide plot! Do you hear me? *A world-wide plot!* And do you want to know who's back of that plot? I'll tell you. The papers won't tell you. They don't dare. The lawyers and judges and doctors and college professors, they won't tell. They're scared. But *I'll* tell you. . . . IT'S THE JEWS!"

For a split-second there was a gasp all through the hall. You could almost feel the sucking sound. And then came the explosion. I thought the roof would come off. The entire audience seemed to be roaring and hooting and stamping. From where I sat in the wings it sounded like the start of a free-for-all.

Cleaver jumped up and rushed to the front of the platform. Even before he could get there, four or five of his troopers collected from nowhere and ringed themselves around J. C. I too rushed out, but only because I wanted to duck down into the orchestra pit to see the fun. Several reporters were there, Tom Duranty among them, and they were scribbling their fists off. A couple of camera boys were making lightning with their bulbs. Half the audience was on its feet, and I saw maybe a dozen of Cleaver's men shoulder their way out into the aisles. I couldn't tell whether they were trying to prevent trouble or stir it up. Apparently they were out to do both—and succeeding.

But then, almost as suddenly as it started, the ruckus gave out. It was Gribble's doing. He gave our shills the signal to pipe down, and that did the trick. Good old Doc! He had evidently organized the whole business so well that he could turn the hullabaloo on or off like with a faucet. In a minute the whole place was practically quiet again. The cordon on the platform melted away, leaving J. C. alone once more by the rostrum. He stood there absolutely rigid, his arms folded, and his eyes shooting sparks. His weird hairless head might have been varnished, it was so dark and shiny, and the vein down the side of his neck throbbed something awful. I swear, he looked like he was in some sort of trance.

Finally he began to speak again, and I edged over to the press table to sit down. The reporters were trying to take every word, and I couldn't blame them. What The Power was saying now was a revelation even to me. I had known all along that he would claim this Conrad Wulff was a Jew. I had put that flea in his ear myself. But according to his statements he could prove much more than that. This ripper, he swore, was not only a Jew but an agent of Jews. Hadn't he been employed in a bank, and weren't all banks controlled by Jews? Furthermore, wasn't he being defended by a lawyer who had been brought in specially from Chicago, and wasn't this the same lawyer who'd worked with Clarence Darrow on the Loeb-Leopold case? Nor was that all. Who were the doctors who had come out in the papers to plead mercy for Wulff on the grounds of insanity? Israel Rosenberg, a Jew; David Fink, a Jew; Gordon Myers, a Jew.

". . . Do you see?" he put it to the crowd in a voice that roared like a French 75. "It's as plain as two and two makes four! They're all in on this. This whole thing is part of a Jew conspiracy. I know! I've made a study of the subject, a scientific investigation, and I *know!* Conrad Wulff isn't just an accident. He's a symptom. He's a cog in an infernal machine. He's a tentacle of the hellish octopus that's spreading its slimy arms all over the earth. I know! The whole of Jewdom is in back of Conrad Wulff. They want to pollute our Christian blood! They want to defile our Christian homes! They want to mock our Christian morality! And that's just what this pimply-faced Jew runt did do right here in Los Angeles! *Can't you see that?*"

Apparently they could. I could tell by the way they clapped and yelled. It wasn't just our own gang that was doing that now. J. C. had got the bulk of the audience hopped up by this time, and they were applauding like mad. Even I was applauding. I couldn't help it. There was something about him, something in his voice and appearance and awful sincerity, that just carried me away. I knew even at the time that what he was saying was pure hooey. Even his two and two were wrong, and on top of that he didn't make them add up to four at all. The way he talked, two and two came to twenty-two! I could see that clearly. His whole speech was nothing but a pile of apcray, and I knew it. Yet there I sat and just ate it up.

It was manure, and I knew it was manure, yet I ate it up, and even smacked my lips. That's how good he was.

And he stayed that good right to the end. He talked on for upwards of an hour, yet to the very end he had me tingling. He went on to tell the crowd the things he had tried to explain to me that day on his sleeping porch: how the Jews were naturally parasites because they were born city folk, and why they therefore wanted to corrupt our life so that they could ruin us and make us their slaves. He offered evidence to prove the point, all sorts of evidence from ancient history down to modern times. He quoted chapter and verse from something called the Talmud, and also from the Protocols of Zion, and the secret minutes of the Russian Revolution. He revealed how the Jews started the last World War, and were plotting now to start the next one. He referred to Trotsky, and Barney Baruch, and Morgenthau, and Blum, and somebody named Laski, claiming they were all working underground to set off a universal revolution. And I sat there and took it all in goggle-eyed.

Don't get me wrong. I didn't really believe all those things he said. I merely took them in. However, I must admit they didn't sound near as screwy as they had the first time I heard him say them. I guess it was because he was on a platform now, and I was down below, at his feet. That gave him an advantage over me, for I couldn't talk back to him. I couldn't even think back. All I could do was just listen.

And the longer I listened the more I became hypnotized. I stamped and cheered like I'd gone plain nuts. In fact, by the time J. C. finally got through speaking, I swear I *was* nuts. Here's the proof: he wound up with a plea for money to help him fight the Jews, and I'll be damned if I didn't immediately jump to my feet and start waving a ten-dollar bill in the air! If an usher had reached me fast enough, he'd probably have got it too. Luckily, by the time one did come around, I was myself again, and instead of giving him the bill, I grabbed the hat he'd been passing around. The usher recognized me and didn't stop to argue. He let me empty the hat into a big pasteboard carton that Gribble had set down on the edge of the platform, and then rushed off to collect some more money. Other ushers came running up, and I relieved them in the same way. It was a good thing I did that, for otherwise there's no telling how much of the take might have gone astray.

It must have been twenty minutes before our scavengers got through with their work, and then Gribble, who had been directing the operation, started a spiel about enrolling new members. Application blanks had already been distributed, and he called on the people to sign and hand them to the ushers on their way out. Then, drawing himself up, he yelled:

". . . And one last thing, folks! We're going to close this meeting with the pledge of allegiance to the Flag. (*Cheers*) But get this! We don't want anyone to take the pledge who isn't heart and soul *for* the Flag! (*Cries of 'Attaboy!'*) So stand up, all you who are with us in this great Cause! Every one of you who is already a member of the Crusade, or who's going to join tonight, stand up! (*Shuffle of feet.*) The rest of you stay in your seats. No, crawl under them! (*Cheers and Laughter.*) That's what you'd better do: crawl right under your seats. (*Cries of 'That's tellin' 'em!'*) Because we don't want you in on this! Only real Americans. . . ."

But the crowd wouldn't let him go on. Everybody was up now— at least, that's the way it looked from where I was in the orchestra pit. They were all on their feet, whooping and whistling. Gribble grinned and stepped back to let The Power take the center of the stage again. There was a pause while Cleaver and his guard of veterans took their stand around the flag at the right of the platform. Then everybody turned and started to recite the words: "*I pledge allegiance* . . ."

It sounded just like thunder, all those hundreds of voices reciting in unison. The sound came rolling down from the balconies and echoing back from the stage exactly like thunder. I didn't know the words, but I moved my lips anyway, and when the rest stuck out their right arms, I did the same. Most of the people kept their arms horizontal, but The Power held his high like in a Nazi salute. So did Kronkhite and most of the others on the platform. It gave me a turn to see that, but then I remembered I had something more important to think about. I could see the carton of money under Doc's chair, and I had a feeling he'd want me to get it out of the way when the meeting broke up. So, while everybody else was still saluting, I backed over to the platform steps and got ready to pounce.

I was on the carton the minute the pledge was finished. No one tried to stop me. There must have been at least twenty people on the platform, but they all started crowding around The Power. I grabbed the box and darted out the dressing-room backstage. Gribble had told me he would have a suitcase in readiness there, and I spotted it right away. Closing the door, I jammed a chair under the knob to keep things private, and started transferring the loot. There was quite a little folding money, and I must admit I was strongly tempted to do what wasn't more than natural in such a situation. Before I could yield, though, there was Doc yanking at the doorknob.

I couldn't help grinning at the relief in his fat puss when I let him in. "Thought I'd skipped, eh?" I haw-hawed.

He closed the door fast and started to smile. "Who, me?" he cried. "Why, the idea never entered my mind!"

"The hell it didn't!" I needled.

He took a friendly jab at my jaw, and then sat down. "We'd better stall here till the coast is clear," he said, mopping the sweat trickling down his chins.

"Okay," I said, starting to fish out a cigarette.

Ten minutes later we groped our way through the darkened hall to the front office. There we picked up the dough I had parked in the strong box, added that to the load in the suitcase, and quietly went on our way.

I didn't roll into bed that night until almost 3 A.M. And I mean roll.

12

There were no two ways about it: that meeting had been a wow! I forget now the full extent of the take, because Doc and I were kind of complicated bookkeepers; but the final accounting showed the organization richer by well over $600. In addition we had enrolled nearly 300 new members, and put the Crusade right on the map. Not a single paper even mentioned the meeting the following day, but word got around just the same, and soon the whole town seemed to know about our movement. Well, maybe not exactly the *whole* town, but certainly a big part of it. Because we had really put ourselves on the map now, no fooling.

So the first thing we did was reorganize. By "we" I mean Doc and myself, since the whole plan was ours, and between us we carried more than enough weight now to put it over. As a matter of fact, I could probably have put it over single-handed, for after what I had done to promote the meeting, I was definitely the white-haired boy in the organization. However, I knew better than to try to ditch my sidekick. Gribble was undoubtedly a slob in many ways, a booze hound and a blowhard and a faker from way back. But he had a great front, and was a real ace as an organizer. Besides, I figured there was no sense in trying to be a hog. The way it looked, there was going to be ample in this racket for the both of us.

So, as I have said, Doc and I combined our talents to establish a new setup which we diagrammed thus:

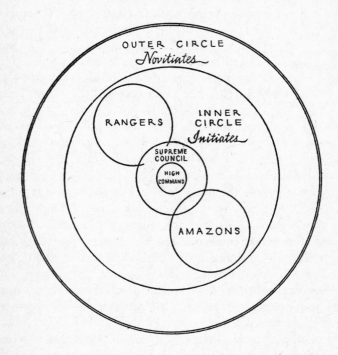

All new members belonged automatically in the Outer Circle and were called Novitiates. They were expected to pay $5 a year (in advance) or 50¢ a month, in return for which they were entitled to reserved seats at our general meetings. Any Novitiate, however, could qualify for the Inner Circle, and become an Initiate, by doing the following three things: (*a*) recruit one new member for the Outer Circle; (*b*) agree to shell out $10 a year (in advance) or $1 a month; (*c*) take the "Great Oath." The reward was the privilege of attending J. C.'s "secret" conferences and receiving certain "confidential" reports.

Within the Inner Circle there were to be two inner-inner groups: the Rangers for men and the Amazons for women. To belong to these an Initiate had to pass special tests, take the "Blood Oath," and agree to perform any and all duties that might be assigned to him or her. Captain Cleaver was named the Chief Ranger, and Mabel Haight the Chief Amazon, and they together with certain other officers were to form the Supreme Council. The ultimate authority, though, was to be vested in a High Command, consisting of just three people: The Power, Gribble, and yours truly.

Cleaver naturally raised holy hell when we proposed this arrangement, because he felt he ought to be included in the High Command. He argued that he not alone deserved the honor, but also needed the $50 a week which went with it. Most of the others were inclined to agree with him, and if the thing could have been put to a vote, he'd undoubtedly have carried his point. But, as I have already said, voting was taboo in the Crusade. The Power alone was supposed to decide all questions, and he didn't care for Cleaver. He objected to the way the ape drank and cussed and kept bragging about his battle scars. So the reorganization went through in spite of all the yammering. To make the thing stick, Doc hired a shyster to draw up papers of incorporation right away.

The papers were signed by the entire Supreme Council with the exception of Peavey, who said it was against his principles to sign anything not related to his own business.* The exact date when that was done was May 30, 1939—in other words, Memorial Day—as I recall, because Cleaver showed up late, and in his uniform, and drunk. Gribble, the old fox, had figured on that, and it worked out just as he had hoped it would. Cleaver arrived all primed for a knock-down-and-drag-out battle, but he was barely able to start slugging before The Power jumped on him for being soused. So that ended the argument. Cleaver signed without as they say further ado.

---

* *Smart guy! That must have been one of the reasons why he wasn't picked up with the rest of us after Pearl Harbor.*

The next day Doc and I got right down to business. First off we arranged to rent the Senate Auditorium on South Grand Street for an open meeting every Sunday evening. We would have preferred the Philharmonic, of course, but that hall belonged to some Baptist outfit that was kind of persnickety about the sort of organizations it would accept as regular tenants. The Senate, on the other hand, was owned by a regular business corporation, so there was no non-sense about ethics and so forth. The place was more a barn than an auditorium, with rickety folding seats, torn scenery, and awful acoustics. However, the location was swell, being right downtown, and the rent was dirt cheap. Moreover, there was a hotel next door belonging to the same corporation, and the agent agreed to throw in the use of a room free gratis if we'd sign a six-month contract. I was the one who mooched that extra concession, so Doc was a good sport and didn't object when I said the room ought to be mine. To clinch the matter, I moved in that same afternoon.

It was a hayseedy hotel, with leather rockers in the lobby window, and battered brass spittoons all over the place. My room was on the second floor, and had a swell view of the fire escape. You can picture what the hole was like when I tell you the phone was screwed to the wall and the bathroom had linoleum on the floor. Nevertheless I was glad to move in, and not alone because of the free rent. With all the dames that were certain to be attracted to our meetings, I figured it might come in handy to have my living quarters right next door.

Mrs. Gunderson was naturally disappointed to see me leave, but I convinced her it was for the good of the Cause. The result was that she not alone refused to accept the back rent I still owed her, but actually insisted on my taking along some ornaments to decorate my new domicile. That, I must admit, made me feel a little cheap, but she wouldn't have it otherwise, so what could I do? They were corny-looking ornaments made of imitation marble and so forth; but I took them anyway. To ease my conscience, however, I made her a present of a brand-new Philco radio which cost me $27 wholesale. Also I took her for a long ride the following Sunday in my new car. It was a rebuilt Auburn, full of rattles and squeaks, but with bright fresh yellow paint, and real sporty-looking. I explained that it had been turned over to me by a Hollywood friend in payment of an old debt. She believed me, of course.

By this time practically everybody connected with the Crusade was believing me no matter what I said. The only exceptions, so far as I could make out, were Doc, whom I could trust, and Cleaver, whom I tried to steer clear of. For a while I had my suspicions of Peavey, because I figured that a businessman ought to have at least some brains. But if he did see through me, he gave no sign of it.

All in all, therefore, I was sitting pretty, so I decided I might as well try to sit tight. The job wasn't exactly the sort that a press agent of my caliber would want to write home about, but seeing as how I had no home anyway, I figured what the hell. Wasn't it going to pay me $50 a week—besides the extras?

Accordingly, I started to dig in. I organized what I called the "Department of Public Relations," fixed up an office next to Gribble's on the ground floor of the Citadel, ordered a flock of stationery, and began looking around for a secretary. I would have wanted one even if there hadn't been any work for her to do, because my morale demanded it, if not my morals. My experience had taught me that there's nothing so inspirational as having a cute young thing around to look at during office hours.

As it happens, though, I could see I was really going to have plenty of work for a secretary to do. In the first place, we were beginning to draw fan mail that needed to be answered. In the second place, I had to plan on getting out mimeographed programs for our meetings, and also those "confidential" reports, and so on and so forth. In the third place, I was figuring on starting a house-organ for the Crusade. All that naturally called for a highly efficient Girl Friday.

Thus far most of the office chores had been done by one of the members, a Miss Alice Twitchell, whose only recommendation, so far as I could see, was that she was willing to work for free. She was in her late thirties, built like a stepladder, and wore cotton stockings and orthopedic shoes. Her eyes were the color of raw oysters, and she was constantly licking what appeared to be a permanent cold sore in the corner of her mouth. I realized she wouldn't do at all for what I had in mind. Accordingly, I told The Power he ought to appoint her his personal secretary, and there being prac-

[84]

tically nothing but saltpeter in her chemistry, he agreed. Then I went on a hunt for something more my speed.

And that's how I acquired Miriam Cabot. I spotted her . . . But hold the phone a minute. Maybe I'd better start a fresh chapter before going into that story.

13

I spotted the girl at our first or second meeting in the Senate Auditorium. There must have been at least 500 people present, yet I couldn't help spotting her. The rest were the sort you'd expect to see in such a place: elderly couples with pinched lips and gleaming eyes, middle-aged spinsters with too much powder on, and hairy-eared lugs who looked like they were sore about something. She stood out in that crowd like a poppy in a field of mud and stubble. There was nothing flashy about her, understand. Her curly bobbed hair was that light brown color that no Hollywood doll would have left natural, and her mouth was practically without any lipstick. She was wearing a plain tweed suit under a polo coat, and she had no hat on. Nevertheless, it didn't take a talent scout to size her up as something definitely special.

I was up on the platform, helping Doc with the collection, when I first noticed her. She had her head down, and was apparently taking notes, so I decided she must be a reporter. That naturally made me all the more curious, because I couldn't figure out what paper would want to cover any meeting of ours now. I understood the slug had been put on us by every sheet in town. So the minute the meeting was over, I made a beeline to catch her before she could get away.

"Pardon me, miss," I said, grabbing her elbow just as she was going through the door. It felt like a nice elbow. "You with one of the papers?"

She gave such a jump that she dropped her notebook. I ducked to pick it up, sticking out an arm to keep the crowd from stepping all over me. Then, handing the pad back to her, I put on a real sweet smile and said: "You *are* a reporter, aren't you?"

Apparently she was still scared, for she just looked at me, kind of trembling. I noticed she had nice eyes, large and brown, with nice long lashes.

"Let's get out of this crush," I said, taking her arm and leading her back into the hall. "I'd like to talk to you a minute."

She allowed me to back her into a quiet corner, where I faced her, still holding on to her arm. I knew she wasn't going to run away, but I liked the feel.

"My name's Smullet," I said, real friendly. "I'm in charge of publicity here, so it's my business to contact any reporter."

"But I'm not a reporter," the girl stammered. "I'm a student at U.C.L.A."

"No kidding! The way you were writing everything down, I thought you must be on some newspaper."

"No. I was just taking notes for a paper I'm writing for one of my classes."

"Is that a fact!" I cried. "Say, you really ought to let me talk to you then. In private, I mean. I could give you all sorts of dope on the movement."

Her face lit up something wonderful. It was exactly as if a 300-watt bulb had suddenly been turned on. "Oh, I'd love that!" she sang out. "When would you be able to do it?"

"Why not tonight?" I suggested, giving her arm just the least little pinch. "It isn't ten o'clock yet, and my office is right next door."

The light in her face went out. "Next door?" she faltered. "But isn't that a hotel?"

"Yeah, in a way it is," I said. "But it's quite all right, believe me."

She shook her head. "No," she said, "can't we go somewhere else? I don't feel . . ."

"Oh, sure, sure," I cut in. "I understand. How about going around to Mike Lyman's? We could have a drink while we're talking. Coffee, I mean."

"Oh, that would be fine!" she cried, her face all bright again.

"Okay then. Just wait here a minute while I attend to one or two details. Don't run away now!"

"I won't," she smiled.

I gave her arm another pinch, and rushed off to tell Doc. He was sitting at a little table on the platform, counting the collection with Miss Twitchell's help. There were several other people up there, but they were gathered around The Power. I leaned over to whisper in Doc's ear, and he looked up kind of annoyed.

"Won't it keep?" he asked out of the corner of his mouth.

I shook my head and beat it before he could start an argument. I moved so fast that I almost fell over Cleaver, who was at the head of the platform steps, furling the flag. He started cussing me out, but I didn't stop to argue with him either. I just mumbled something and raced on up the aisle.

She was still there, standing just the way I had left her. Now, though, she seemed poised again. When I took her arm I could feel it wasn't trembling any more.

I led her through the crowd standing around in the lobby, and started toward the parking lot across the street.

"I've got my car here," I explained, catching the look she gave me.

"Oh, let's walk," she said. "Lyman's is just around the corner, isn't it?"

"Sure, but we'd better take the car anyway. I'll be able to drive you home then."

"That's awfully kind of you," she said, flashing me that bright smile again. "But I have my own car here."

"Yeah?" I challenged, sure she was lying. "Which one is it?"

She nodded toward a shiny big station-wagon standing against the wall. It was a Chrysler, and looked like it was slumming among the jalopies parked all around. For a second I didn't know what to say. I wasn't used to picking up dames who drove around in station-wagons. Finally I managed to mumble, "Gee, that's too bad!"

She gave a little laugh. "How was I to know I'd meet anyone who'd be nice enough to offer to take me home?"

"You've got a point there, sister," I said, taking her arm and starting to walk.

She was pretty tall for me—she must have been at least five-feet-seven in her high heels—and that together with everything else somehow robbed me of my normal nerve. By the time we'd walked half a block, though, I was myself again. "Say," I piped up, "this is practically against the Mann Act! Here we are, going out together, and I don't even know your name yet!"

I watched to see how she'd take that smut crack, but it seemed to go over her head. She merely smiled and answered, "My name's Miriam Cabot."

It was all I could do to keep from dropping her arm. "N-not one of the Boston Cabots?" I stammered.

"Yes, my father was born in Boston. Why? Do you know my family?"

"Naturally—that is, by reputation. I'm a New Englander myself. I was practically raised in New Haven."

"How wonderful!" she cried. "Then we're almost related, aren't we? Did you go to Yale?"

I swallowed and said, "Aw, sure!"

"Isn't that funny?" she laughed. "The minute you spoke to me I had a feeling you were a Yale man."

"You did? Why?"

"It's hard to say, Mr. Smullet. I suppose it's just that—well, you had the air of a Yale man."

I struggled to grin. "Is that supposed to be a dirty dig?" I queried.

"Why, of course not, Mr. Smullet!"

I gave her a quick look and saw she really wasn't ribbing. Jeez, I thought to myself, she's just a dumb kid! And then I felt better. Taking a firmer grip on her arm, I said, "How old are you—Miriam?"

She gave a slight start and turned red. "I know why you asked that!" she pouted. "You think I'm nothing but a silly little girl, don't you?"

I tried to deny it, and we volleyed the point back and forth for a while. Finally she broke down and confessed she wasn't quite twenty yet. "But I'm getting my B.A. next year!" she boasted.

"Is that a fact?"

"Yes," she said. "Just because I'm so impulsive, that doesn't mean I'm stupid. I'm pretty smart, really."

"Sure," I said, giving her arm a squeeze. "I could see that right away."

We had reached the restaurant by this time, and the headwaiter came rushing up to greet us like we were a couple of movie stars.

He was a big roly-poly Jew in a tux that fitted him as if he'd been poured into it. "How's this?" he asked, showing us to a booth near the entrance.

I thought I saw the doll hesitate, so I said, "No, further back."

He beamed and paraded us to a booth way in the rear. I couldn't help sticking out my chest at the way every guy in the place turned around to stare.

We sat down and I helped her slip out of her coat. The label, I noticed, said "Saks Fifth Avenue."

"Something to eat?" asked the h.w., handing us a couple of menus the size of bill-posters.

"Just coffee," the doll spoke up.

"Aw, gwan and take a sandwich," I urged. "It won't break me."

She laughed, but shook her head. "No, I'm not hungry," she said. "But don't let that keep you from eating."

I ordered a kosher corned-beef sandwich and a glass of beer, and the h.w. waddled off.

"Cigarette?" I asked, holding out my pack.

She took one and tamped the end on the table like a veteran. Her brow, I noticed, was wrinkled, as if she was troubled about something. "I hope you won't mind my asking this, Mr. Smullet," she suddenly blurted out, "but do you think it's right for you to order that kind of food?"

It took me a couple of seconds to figure out what she meant, and then I naturally had to grin. "Why not?" I shrugged. "It's the influence of the Jews that we're against, not their cooking. Personally I'm nuts about kosher corned-beef. Kosher pickles too. Have you ever tasted 'em?"

She shook her head, still frowning. "But what about your Leader?" she asked.

I looked at her and decided she was even dumber than I had thought. She evidently considered J.C. somebody to be taken seriously. So I wiped the grin off my face and said, "Oh, him? Yeah, I guess he really wouldn't think it just right. But then, he's a vegetarian."

"He is?" she cried, all excited. "My, that makes him even more like Hitler, doesn't it?"

[89]

"Nh-nh! It's the other way around, sister. That makes Hitler more like *him!*"

She blushed as if I'd caught her in a crime. "Yes, I suppose that *is* the way I should have put it," she apologized. Then, pausing to get her cigarette lighted, she went on, "I thought he was wonderful, the way he spoke tonight! I could hardly take any notes, I was so thrilled."

"Is that so?" I remarked solemnly. "Well, let me go over them for you. Maybe I can fill in the parts you missed."

"Oh, that would be wonderful," she said, starting to hand me her notepad. "But they're in shorthand."

I opened the cover, and riffled through the pages. "So they are," I grunted. "Too bad." I gave the pad back to her. "Say, what's all this for, anyway?"

"Oh, I'm writing a paper on Fascism in America for my sociology prof." She caught the look that came into my eyes and smiled defiantly. "He'll probably flunk me for what I'm going to say, but I don't care. I *believe* in Fascism!"

"Good for you!"

"Yes," she said, wrinkling her lovely puss, and sounding very earnest, "I think Fascism is the only way out for America. We've tried democracy, and all it's done is bring the worst elements to the top. Look what's happened in New England. Our kind of people don't stand a chance there any more, do they? It's those Irish and Portuguese and Italians who run everything."

"Don't forget the Jews," I pitched in.

"Yes, and the Jews, too, of course," she agreed. Then, after a worried pause: "By the way, do you believe Christ really was a Jew? Because I don't. I think His father must have been a Nordic soldier in the Roman army. Otherwise how can you account for His blond hair?"

That was an entirely new one to me. I'd always understood that Christ's father was God. I was afraid, though, that it would sound kind of corny to say anything like that, so I merely frowned and nodded.

"Of course," she rushed on, "there's always the possibility that the whole story's a myth. Christ may really have been nothing but another oriental sun-god like. . . ." She mentioned three or four names that I'd never heard before, and then started to tell me about a book called the *Golden Bow,* or something like that.

I decided we were getting off the subject. "About this Fascism," I broke in. "Are there many people in your set who feel the way you do about it?"

"No," she answered, clenching her fist. "That's what makes me so mad. They won't even bother to try to find out what the movement represents. All they're interested in is clothes and gossip and having a good time. Except the intelligent ones, of course, and they're mostly Reds. Well, anyway, Pinks. I mean that! You'd be shocked if you knew how much radicalism there is on our campus."

"Aw, you're talking about the kids," I said. "I wasn't referring to them. What about the older generation? Your parents and their friends? I bet they're no radicals."

She hesitated and bit her lip. "My mother is," she finally admitted. "So is my father, in a way. Of course, they insist they're merely liberals. They're like the professor for whom I'm doing this paper—always quoting the *Nation* and the *New Republic.* You know the type I mean."

I didn't, so I got her to describe her parents. Apparently they weren't at all what I'd imagined. They had dough, all right—her father, she told me, was a retired banker—but nevertheless they actually believed in the New Deal. "The trouble with them is," the girl said, "they're not realists. They're still living in the eighteenth century."

"Why don't you bring them up to date then?" I started to argue. "Get them to come to one of our meetings. They're just the sort we need in the Crusade—people with prestige and—and . . ." I was about to say "dough," but caught myself in time.

"Oh, they wouldn't dream of coming!" she cried before I could go on. "They think Fascism is something dreadful. They're so prejudiced . . ." She saw the waiter come up with our food, and fell silent till he set it out on the table. When he finally left, she'd apparently lost the thread of the discussion. Stirring her coffee, she suddenly asked, "How long has the Crusade been in existence, Mr. Smullet?"

"Just since last fall," I answered. "Actually, though, you might say it didn't get going until about a month ago. That's when *I* joined!"

"You mean you're the one who's made it such a success?" she cried.

"Well, not exactly. But I'll have to take credit for most of what's been accomplished."

The starry-eyed look she turned on me made me stop chewing. "Gee, you must be a real genius, Mr. Smullet!" she gushed. "How in the world were you ever able to do it?"

I swallowed what was in my mouth and tried to act modest. "Aw, it was easy enough!" I answered. "I just applied what I call the scientific principles of advertising psychology. Get it?" She obviously didn't, so I began to elucidate. I went into a long routine about "mass suggestion" and "shock propaganda," illustrating my points by telling her how I had put over that first meeting. I naturally omitted some of the details, and colored most of the rest. In fact, the way I fancified the yarn it sounded good enough for a fan magazine. And she just lapped it up. She acted exactly like a kid listening to a bedtime story, begging me to tell more and more. And I wasn't what you would call loath to oblige, because by this time, I don't mind telling you, I was all in a stew to make a hit with her. She had everything I most admired in a dame: namely, looks, class and dough. Of course, she seemed awfully dumb, especially for a girl with her education; but that too was an attraction, from my point of view. When it comes to tossing for a dame, men of my type, you'll notice, practically always favor tail over head. I suppose it's just Nature's way of keeping things balanced.

So I talked on and on, cracking myself up to be not alone a super press agent but also a colossal Fascist. And when I finally ran out of wind I had her practically swooning.

"Gee, Mr. Smullet!" she panted, "that's wonderful! It must give you tremendous satisfaction to know you're accomplishing so much. Why, you're making history!"

"Yeah," I said, starting to go at my sandwich again, "it really is kind of thrilling."

"You can't imagine how I envy you!" she went on.

"Aw, you don't have to do that," I said. "You can have the same thrill easy enough if you want to. All you've got to do is join us."

"You mean I *could?*"

"Shucks!" I answered, spattering crumbs all over the place. "We'd just about break our necks to get a member of your type!"

"Oh, but I wouldn't care to be just a member," she pouted. "If I joined, I'd want to be right in the thick of things. I'd want to work."

"So much the better. We'd give you more work than you can handle. What would you like to do?"

She hesitated a moment. "Well, I suppose I'd be most helpful around the office. Of course, I'm not very experienced, but . . ."

I snapped my fingers. "That'd be perfect!" I cut in. "I've been looking everywhere for a secretary. How would you like that job?"

"You mean you'd really give it to me?" she cried.

I almost choked on the beer I had just swallowed. "Just say the word!" I said, as soon as I could breathe. "Just say it, that's all. Of course, we wouldn't be able to pay you much."

"Oh, I wouldn't dream of asking any pay at all!" she exclaimed.

I'd expected that, but nevertheless put on an act of happy surprise. "No?" I piped. "Well, that settles everything."

"But I may not be good enough . . ."

I wouldn't let her finish. "Let me be the judge of that," I said, reaching for her hand. "What d'you say, Miriam? Are you game to take the job?"

"Why, I'd consider it an honor!" she cried, looking at me round-eyed. But then a frown crossed her face, and she drew her hand away hesitantly. "Of course, I'd have to keep it a secret. My parents would be terribly upset if they found out. So would all my friends. They'd think I'd gone crazy."

"Don't let that worry you," I snorted. "They needn't know a thing. We'll enroll you under an alias."

"You will? Oh, that would be wonderful! I'd feel like a real conspirator!" She could barely breathe, she seemed so thrilled over the whole idea.

I grinned and took her hand again. "Exactly," I said. "So when do you want to start in? Tomorrow?"

"But don't I have to be initiated first?" she asked.

"Leave that to me, kid," I said, holding on to her hand. "From now on you're one of us."

And she was, too.

14

She was a real prize, that kid. Everybody took to her right off the bat, including even The Power. He was naturally suspicious when I told him about her the next morning. "How do you know she isn't a spy?" he growled. I didn't bother to explain. Instead I waited for her to come around that afternoon, and in no time at all he got the answer for himself. There was absolutely no doubting her sincerity, nor any resisting her daffy charm. Two minutes after he met her, damned if he wasn't acting almost human. He even began to twist his features into what he evidently thought was a smile. And before a week was out, damned if he wasn't calling her by her first name! That's how wonderful she was.

I have to admit, of course, that part of the reason why she made such a hit was on account of her family. We had enrolled her as Miriam Cable, but all the insiders knew she was a Cabot, and they were naturally proud to be associated with someone by that name. And the added fact that she wouldn't take any pay for her work didn't hurt either. It proved that she was not alone Society, but also had dough, which was a mighty rare combination around our movement. In fact, with the exception of old Mrs. Krutch, it was practically unique.

But even if this kid had been just Sally Glutz, and a hired hand, she'd still have been the darling of our organization. Her personality alone would have made her that, her way of smiling at everybody, and agreeing with everything, and never trying to put on airs. In a word, she was what a tony writer would call beguiling, and so much so that it kind of hampered me in a way. I had figured that once I got her initiated, I'd have her more or less to myself, because after all it was "finders keepers" according to my code of ethics. In other words, I had counted on making her my secretary —and etcetera. But no sooner did I get her all installed than she became practically surrounded by chaperons.

Doc was one of them, and to my great surprise as well as displeasure he turned out to be in many ways the worst. The minute he clapped eyes on the kid he seemed to feel he had to shield her from me. It was partially my own fault. I had no sooner put her into her car after her first visit to the Citadel than I came busting into his office with a grin on my face like I was the cat that had just swallowed a whole aviary.

"Boy, oh boy, oh boy!" I gloated. "Can you imagine the fun I'm gonna have with that cutie?"

"What d'ye mean, 'fun'?" he growled, looking at me blackly. "That girl's decent. She wouldn't let a runty little chaser like you even touch her."

"Is that so!" I flared. It always made me fighting mad when anybody called me runty. "What d'you think she and I were doing up in my room last night after the meeting? Cutting out paper dolls?"

He let out a nasty laugh. "Like hell you were up there!" he came back at me. "I phoned around eleven, and the clerk said you hadn't been in all evening." I turned red and started fumbling for an out. He wouldn't give me time, though. "Listen, Clem," he snarled, wagging a fat finger at me. "You let that kid alone. She's decent."

"So what?" I shrugged. "Somebody's got to slip it to her sooner or later, so why not me?"

"Because I won't let you!"

"*Tsk, tsk, tsk!*" I went, forcing a smile. "And supposing I tell you it's none of your damned business?"

"I'll make it my business!" he barked.

"Yeah? You and who else?"

"Well, Cleaver, for instance," he said. "He's just aching for an excuse to lay his hands on you, and so help me God . . ."

He broke off abruptly, for Miss Twitchell was at the door. She evidently had something to ask him, and while she was getting it out, I scrammed. I could see there was nothing to be gained by going on with that foolish argument.

[95]

We never returned to it. What's more, from then on Doc and I both acted as if the whole subject hadn't ever come up between us. I knew, though, that it was in his mind every time he saw me with the girl. That, of course, was fairly often, because Miriam started coming three or four afternoons a week to do my typing, and the result was a slight rift between Gribble and me.

It was very slight, though, because he was as anxious as I was to keep it that way. We continued to act as pally as ever, hobnobbing, and lunching together, and going off on sprees. We'd probably have done that even if we'd hated one another's guts, for we both realized we couldn't afford to split up. As it happened, however, deep down we really liked each other.

Anyway, I know I liked him. To tell the truth, down deep I even admired the way he tried to protect Miriam. The reason is that I thought I knew what was in back of his concern. He had a couple of daughters of his own, and he was obviously bracketing them in his mind with this Cabot kid. The girls were living in Attica, Kansas, with his first wife, and they were real beauties, judging from the photo he had of them. I guess that was what made it so easy for him to make the association.

I saw that photo the first time Doc invited me out to his apartment. He lived in a bungalow court on Echo Park Avenue, and the picture was hanging on the wall in his bedroom. It was nothing but an enlarged snapshot, but I couldn't help staring, it was such an eyeful.

"Jeez!" I cried, after he told me they were his daughters. "Why don't you bring them out here and try to get them in the movies? They'd make even Lana Turner look sick. I'm telling you . . ."

But then I shut up, for he was glowering as if he meant to bite my head off.

"I'd rather see them dead!" he said. "They're clean, and I want them to stay that way. Clean and pure!"

I stared at him like I thought he was nuts. "What's that got to do with their going in the movies!" I yelled. "You'll find any number of girls around the studios that are purer than Ivory Soap."

"Like hell you will!" he growled. "I know too much about what goes on in those studios. I'd rather see my daughters in their grave!"

He was slightly liquored at the time, and I figured maybe that was what made him talk as he did. I was wrong, though. He took exactly the same attitude, I discovered, when he was cold sober. Not that Doc was a prude, understand. On the contrary, the way he would blab about the leching he'd done in his day, he made Casanova sound like a Y.M.C.A. secretary. He'd already been divorced by three wives, and was currently separated from the fourth, all because he was such a chaser. He told me so himself. But he confined his chasing, so he said, entirely to used merchandise.

And that explains why I didn't really hold it against him for being so set on protecting our Virgin Miriam. Of course, I might have felt differently if his protection had been the only thing that stood in my way. The truth is, though, that it wasn't. The real obstacle was her own sweet self.

She had me completely buffaloed, that kid did. Even after I'd known her for weeks, in fact months, I still couldn't figure her out. In some ways she seemed real sophisticated. For example, she smoked—and inhaled, too—and was willing to take a drink once in a while. In addition, she read all those books with smutty words in them, like for instance *Grapes of Wrath*. But when it came to Adam-and-Eveing, it was no soap. She wouldn't even hold hands!

I tell you, I couldn't figure her out at all. The way I'd been given to understand, those college girls were all pretty negotiable, if you know what I mean. Especially the Society kind. Nothing but debutarts, so to speak. But not Miriam. I tried all the techniques, the Don Juan, the cave man, the brotherly, even the love-sick, yet none of them got me anywhere. And I was no amateur, understand. It isn't part of my nature to boast about myself, but I don't mind admitting I'd always been pretty successful with the fair sex. I'd even made the grade in my time with one or two dolls who were pretty close to being stars. Ask any of my old Hollywood buddies if you don't believe me.

But here was one case where I couldn't get as much as started. That first evening, for example, after she and I left the restaurant, I must have worked on her for fully half an hour, just trying to wangle one little kiss. And did I succeed? In a pig's eye!

And it was the same the next day, when she came down to meet

The Power, and the third, when she started in on her job, and the fourth, and the fifth—and the fifteenth.

It wasn't that she didn't think me good enough for her. On the contrary, she kept saying she considered me wonderful, in fact, a genius. Therefore I could see only one way to account for her attitude. I decided she must be frigid.

Nevertheless I didn't give up hope, because she was still awfully young, and I figured maybe she'd thaw out eventually. Meanwhile I was glad to keep her as my secretary minus any etcetera. Not that she was so hot in that role either. On the contrary, as just a secretary she was distinctly on the underdone side. She could make the damnedest mistakes, especially when she was cutting stencils for the mimeographing machine, always skipping lines and misspelling names and overworking the shift-key. Worse still, every once in a while she'd leave out a word like "not" or "unless," and thereby make a sentence say exactly the opposite of what I meant. That naturally proved mighty embarrassing at times, because I didn't always catch the slips until too late.

I never had the heart to bawl her out, of course. Could she help it if she was just naturally a lame-brain? Besides, she was working for nothing, and trying to do her very best. Miss Twitchell wasn't able to show up more than one afternoon a week—she kept house for her father who was an invalid—so Miriam had to do most of the typing for Doc as well as for me. Occasionally she got so snowed under that she'd have to finish part of the work at home on her own typewriter. As a matter of fact, she actually preferred doing that, especially if the stuff was important correspondence which had to be typed neatly. She said she didn't like the old L. C. Smith we had at the Citadel, and I couldn't blame her, because it really was a wreck. It was as noisy as a threshing machine, and just about as easy to work.

Once or twice I suggested coming out to her house to pick up the finished copy, but she wouldn't hear of that. In the first place, she said, it would be too much trouble for me—she lived way off in Brentwood—and in the second, it would be too risky for her. She was still keeping her parents in the dark about her connection with the Crusade. She let them think she was doing research at the library on the afternoons she spent at the Citadel, and always locked her room when she worked on our stuff at home.

So I never got to see her except during office hours, or when there were meetings, especially the "secret" conferences for the Initiates which were held every other Wednesday evening at the Citadel. Personally I found those conferences a pain in the so-and-so, and not alone because there was nothing to sit on except wooden folding chairs. The Power wasn't at his best in such confined quarters. He couldn't let out his voice, or work up a sweat, and the result was that you were able to realize the complete screwiness of everything he had to say. It was exactly like having a greasy goulash served up cold.

But Miriam seemed to find those bull sessions fascinating. She would take down every word, and then rush straight home to get her notes transcribed while they were still fresh in her mind. That, of course, seemed the height of foolishness to me, and also annoying. It prevented her from going out with me after the meeting for a cup of coffee or anything. But I just couldn't win her over to my point of view. She insisted that she owed it to posterity to keep a complete record of our doings. "We're making history!" she would say with a starry look.

So I was stuck. All I could do was wait and keep my fingers crossed. And that, believe me, was no end annoying.

15

However, the way things were going, I didn't have much time to fret about that Cabot kid. My mind was too occupied with other and more pressing matters. Doc Gribble had been right, I decided. The country was full of goofy people, so a movement as goofy as the Crusade could hardly help but succeed. The best proof of it was our growth, which was positively staggering during those first months. In spite of the fact that it was already summer, we were pulling in new members all the time. Unfortunately, most of the records of that period somehow got mislaid, so I can't give you the exact figures of the growth. But it really was staggering, believe me.

Of course, the thing didn't happen all by itself. There was a hell of a lot of effort behind our success, and since I've sworn to tell the truth, I might as well admit that the best of that effort was put out by me. It practically had to be that way, seeing what our setup was. The Power was great at hooking the suckers, and Gribble couldn't be beat when it came to cleaning them. But I was the one who had to lure them in the first place.

How did I do it? Well, how did Barnum do it? I simply went in for ballyhoo, that's all. But not just ordinary ballyhoo. That wouldn't have worked, and anyway it was out of my reach. Every paper in town was dead set against us. Most of them wouldn't even take paid ads from us, let alone hand out any free space. My old friend Tom Duranty, who was willing to do practically anything for a bottle of booze, tried in every which way to get us a break in his sheet. So did two or three other newsmen who had heavy thirsts. But all of them failed. So far as the city desks were concerned, the Crusade just didn't exist.

But did that feaze me? It did not. On the contrary, it merely needled me into putting my brains to work.

First I let Cleaver pull a fast one on those papers just for the hell of it. The idea was really Kronkhite's, but Cleaver was the lug who actually carried it out. He fixed it so that a couple of his Rangers could climb on board an *Examiner* truck around 5 o'clock one morning, and insert handbills into a few hundred copies of an edition that the newsboys were going to distribute on their regular rounds.

The result, of course, was a sensation. Those handbills didn't mention the Crusade by name, and they were mimeographed so that no one could trace them to a printer; but they were loaded full of our dynamite, and right away every Hebe in town started yelling for J.C.'s blood. With all the stir he had already made in town, it was only natural for them to suspect him of being at the bottom of the thing. Just to make sure, Cleaver got on the phone and called a lot of prominent Jews, saying his name was Sam Cohen, or Abe Ginsburg, and swearing that he knew for a fact that The Power was *it*. Kronkhite did likewise, figuring that with his German accent they'd be sure to take him for a fellow-Hebe. At the same time, they started a rumor that the *Examiner* had secretly connived at the crime, because Hearst himself was supporting the Crusade.

They would have liked to pull the same nifty on the other papers, but the risk had become too great, and besides they couldn't find any truckdrivers willing to co-operate. For my part, I was just as pleased. As I saw it, our real need was to pack the hall every Sunday evening, and to accomplish that we had to be free to give the name and address. So, after allowing those apes to indulge in a couple or three more pranks, I finally called them to heel, and insisted that they leave me to do all the plugging. They squawked, of course, but since I was in the High Command and they weren't, they squawked in vain.

There was no local ordinance at the time against distributing handbills in the streets, so that became my main method of getting publicity. Kronkhite wanted me to use the old Bund stunt of showering leaflets from the roofs of buildings downtown; but I turned thumbs down on that. Those "snowstorms" were too wasteful, and besides there was the danger of getting in bad with the cops. I favored a technique that was less hit-or-miss, and also strictly legal. Every Saturday a crew of our Amazons would pass out throwaways on busy corners, and on Sunday mornings another bunch would cover certain churches, especially the Holy Roller joints. A third group worked the factory districts each week, sticking leaflets into mailboxes, parked cars, etc. Finally, a squad of Rangers made regular rounds of the public comfort stations downtown, leaving our literature in all the toilets. I called that squad the "Privy Council," and rated it tops in drawing a type which Cleaver considered particularly valuable to the movement. Doc and I were naturally of a different opinion, but we decided what the hell. Bums might be poor contributors, but they did help fill the hall. Also they were great when it came to yelling.

Anyway, we were catching plenty of people who weren't exactly bums. What's more, we were putting lines out with a view to hooking some real income-poops. Doc took charge of that project, because he alone had the proper finesse for it. He worked mostly through old Mrs. Krutch, who was the only one around who could give him any entree to high society. Mrs. Louise Ford Fry would have been a better bet, but she refused to co-operate. Someone must have got to her after our Philharmonic shindig—probably Joe Shott or some other Republican big-wig—because she never came around again. Peavey was no bet at all, for though he had dough, he was strictly codfish. His idea of high society was the Jonathan Club, and he didn't belong even to that. Of course, Miriam Cabot would have been the perfect bet, but there was no way to use her on account she was keeping her affiliation with us a secret.

So Doc had to make do with old Sally. Her social connections were not the best, because even in her prime she'd never belonged to anything but the beerocracy. However, she did have a big estate out in Pasadena, and though it was no longer the showplace it had been in pre-Volstead days, it was still good enough to give her a certain amount of standing.

Doc would get her to invite select groups of Society dames to come out and see her sunken gardens, and then introduce himself around and maybe make a little speech. He took me along with him once so I could see how he operated, and I must say it was quite an education. There were about twenty ladies present, and though every one of them was as homely as La Krutch, and almost as old, he played up to them as if they were all Earl Carroll girls. Big as he was, he managed to flit from one to another like he had wings. In fact, all I could think of as I watched him was a butterfly in heat.

He seemed to get them in heat, too.

But that, I must admit, was about all he did manage to accomplish. The proof is that though he got Mrs. Krutch to throw at least half a dozen such parties during that summer, he failed to make a single convert.

Nevertheless he refused to give up trying. "Give me time, Clem," he kept telling me. "All I've got to do is land one of those barracudas, and then we'll have some real roe to eat."

So I let him go ahead. If he got a kick out of angling for those big fish, why should I object? The only thing I cared about was that he shouldn't neglect my small fry—and that, I must say, he didn't do. He fried 'em good, and over and over again. Hardly a day passed but what he thought up some new way to raise money. First he designed a secret token which all members had to carry for identification. It was in the form of a metal coin which cost us 7¢ and sold for a quarter. Then he devised a super-secret token for the initiates which cost us 11¢ and sold for a dollar. One month he promoted a special levy to buy flags for the platform, the next a general levy to equip our Rangers, the third another general levy to doll up our Amazons. And all the time he kept selling subscriptions to the magazine we said we were going to bring out.

By mid-August the Crusade was raking in enough dough each week for me to be able to double the payments on my Auburn, and for Doc to open negotiations for his divorce. I'm not letting out any secrets when I confess those things now, because the FBI has already published how much we got away with altogether. The only thing they haven't published is how they found it out, and that I can't reveal for the simple reason that I just don't know. The way Doc and I kept mislaying the books, we were never able to figure out the amount ourselves.*

And that of course explains why no one in the organization was able to catch on to what we were doing. The High Command had sole authority over the finances, and that meant just Doc and me, because The Power couldn't be bothered. He had no interest in money.

All he was interested in was power.

16

At this point I think maybe I ought to talk some more about The Power. I'd naturally prefer to go on talking about myself, be-

---

* I will state, however, and under oath, if necessary, that the amount mentioned by the FBI is a gross exaggeration.

cause it isn't often that a man in my profession gets the chance. However, it wouldn't be right nor proper to neglect him any longer, since basically this story should be about him, not me. I realize that the way I've slanted the script thus far, I may have given the impression that I was tops in the Crusade, with Doc right below me. But that wasn't the situation at all. The truth is, we two played merely supporting roles. The real star all the way through was no one but John Christian Power.

It's hard to explain why that was the case, but only because the explanation is so simple. The gist of it is this—he was cracked, and we weren't. Of course, if the Crusade had been what you might call a normal racket, that difference would naturally have given us the lead over him. But it was the very reverse of normal, so *he* had the lead. Here's the proof: whereas we could get away with murder, he could murder without even needing to get away. See what I mean?

His particular form of murder consisted of stepping on everybody around him. You never saw a guy with such a passion for making a bar-rail out of people's necks. He seemed to crave power the way hopheads crave dope. And that, as I have already said, accounts for the way he allowed Doc and me to do as we pleased with the finances. Money meant nothing to him. All he wanted was worship.

The way he lived, I must admit he didn't really need money. Not much, anyway. He ate practically nothing but crackers and raw vegetables, drank absolutely nothing but buttermilk and fruit juices, didn't own a car, never went to the movies, and wore his clothes till they all but fell apart. He was supposed to draw $50 a week as salary, but would he take it? Not on your life! Whenever he needed cash for groceries and so forth, he would tell Hank, the janitor, to go ask Doc for it. He himself seemed to hate the very feel of cash.

I remember asking him about that on one occasion. I was driving him down to the auditorium at the time, and he told me to stop and buy a paper from a newsboy who was yelling, "Wuxtra, Wuxtra!" It was all about Hitler taking over Slovakia, and J.C. wanted to learn the details so he could play them up in his harangue that evening. He always liked to hook his speeches to whatever was in the headlines.

I did stop, but when I dug into my pocket I found I had nothing smaller than a five-dollar bill.

"Got a nickel, J.C.?" I asked.

"No," he answered, kind of loftily. "I never carry any money."

So I started to hold up the traffic while the newsie hunted for the change, and the honking that resulted was something awful.

"I'd better let 'em pass," I said, preparing to turn the corner.

"What for?" J.C. barked. "Stay where you are. They can wait."

I didn't argue. I just sat there and let the cars behind me keep on honking till I got my change and could drive on. Inside, though, I was sizzling.

I had to go half-a-dozen blocks before I could trust myself to speak again, and then I asked him what the devil he had against carrying money.

"I just don't believe in it," he answered.

"But why?" I yelled. "There's got to be a reason."

"Sure there's a reason," he growled, looking straight ahead. "It's my way of showing how different I am from a Jew."

I drove on without another word. I knew he'd get sore if I tried to argue the point, and I preferred to keep him soothed. Not that I was scared of him, understand. Not in the least. As I have already related, the very first time I'd had a real talk with him I'd caught on to the fact that he was fundamentally nothing but a bull-dozer. From then on I'd always known that all I needed to do was stand up to him, and nine times out of ten he'd go to pieces. But I'd also discovered that he'd never stay in pieces. No matter how hard I jolted him, he'd always manage to pull himself together again, and then I'd be right back where I started.

That's why I'd finally given up arguing with him. I'd learnt to follow Doc's practice, which was to avoid even trying to converse with him except when absolutely imperative. For the guy simply didn't know how to converse. He could talk all right, but never with you or even to you. It was always *at* you. If you did try to discuss something with him, he either slapped you down or went off into a speech.

Just a born monologist, that's what he was.

But a good one. Yes, sir, one of the best. No matter how much he fell short in all other respects, when it came to making with the words, John Christian Power was unquestionably Grade-A plus. I have already described how he panicked me the first time I caught his act. Well, it was almost the same every time thereafter. Not that he ever changed his plot. Week in and week out it was the identical old meller about a vile villain (Jewdom) who was bent on ruining a fair maiden (Aryan civilization), only to be foiled by a brave posse (The Crusade) led by its stalwart sheriff (John Christian Power). But he always managed to work in new business, and that was what kept me fascinated. There seemed to be no limit to the variety of ways in which he could dish out the corn.

Most of his inventiveness was devoted to the villain, of course. In fact, he paid so much attention to that character that the others became little more than walk-ons. That, however, seemed to me to be good showmanship on his part. In the first place, there was more scope to the villain, more room for what scenario writers call "characterization." Jewdom was something vague and mysterious, so J.C. could say practically anything about it and still sound plausible. In the second place, this villain was full of hate-appeal, and the customers we catered to were the sort who couldn't respond to practically anything else. They were mostly bellyachers and soreheads, total losers in the battle of life, and the chief reason they flocked to our meetings was because they wanted to let off steam. Even those who were naturally gentle inside, like for instance my old Mrs. Gunderson, even they had an urge to gripe a bit. And J.C. gave them the chance. It made no difference what they were sore about—unemployment, usury, flaming youth, vivisection—no matter what it was, he'd always tell them the Jew was to blame. And that seemed to make them feel swell.

But don't imagine he was deliberately trying to kid the boobs. In other words, there was nothing phony about his act. I'll go further and say that so far as he was concerned it wasn't an act at all. Of course, our meetings were bang full of hokum, especially after we got going good. We learned to stage them almost like a Reinhardt production. We'd have the Rangers troop to the platform, and drill the Amazons up and down the aisles, and bring on The

Power with a spotlight and a blare of bugles. We'd even rehearse the demonstrations and half-cocked riots. But it was Doc who arranged all that, usually with a good deal of help from Kronkhite. The Power himself had absolutely no part in contriving the razzle-dazzle.

Because that guy was *sincere!*

Yes, sir, John Christian Power was sincere. He was able to fool the public only because he had already fooled himself. He really believed everything he said, believed it with all his heart and soul. He even believed the things I made up for him to say!

That's the truth, so help me. For instance, there was that time when I told him Conrad Wulff, the sex-maniac, was a Jew. Did he stop to ask me how I knew? He did not. The minute I spilled the yarn, right away he took it for gospel, and though it came out later that Wulff had an unbobbed dingus to prove that he couldn't possibly be a Jew, nevertheless J.C. kept on saying that he must be one anyway.

And the same thing happened over and over again, because once I discovered what an appetite he had for baloney—so long as it was strictly anti-kosher—I just naturally couldn't resist dishing it out to him in slices thick as truck wheels. It was all in fun, of course. I did it for the same reason that kids will feed soda-mints to a monkey in the zoo—just to get a laugh out of seeing him burp. I used to let Doc in on the game, and we'd almost die laughing at the way J.C. would swallow my whoppers.

One time, for example, I got him to believe, and publicly state, that Harry Bridges' real name was Brodsky, and that he was plotting with President Cardenas, whose real name was Caplan, to bring a Mexican army into California! Another time I sold the screwball on the idea that the new Pope was secretly a Jew, and that he'd been elected only because Rabbi Stephen S. Wise had raised a million dollars in Hollywood to grease the cardinals! My prize lulu, though, was the one I made up about Fritz Kuhn, the Bund leader, after he was sent up for grand larceny. I convinced J.C. that the Heinie had been working all the time for his Hebe relatives, who were none other than *Kuhn, Loeb and Company!*

In the beginning I used to go easy on that stuff for fear he'd catch on. After a while, though, I saw my caution was wasted, because other sources were feeding him wilder yarns than any I could make up even if I strained. Those sources were the papers he read all the time, the sheets put out by the Nazis, and by Pelley, and the other Fascist crackpots in the East. And could those guys build 'em tall! With them the sky seemed to be barely the ground floor.

They invariably described their whoppers as "exposés" or "revelations," but most of them sounded more like hophead nightmares. Let me give you an example. According to one source, the Elders of Zion, in collaboration with renegade Gentiles like Joe Stalin, J. P. Morgan and Anthony Eden, had already perfected plans not alone for the second World War, but also for the peace that was to follow. According to these plans, 33% of the entire human race was to be wiped out during the fighting, and then 99% of the remainder was to be permanently enslaved. The poor survivors were to be herded into tremendous super-skyscrapers, each a small city in itself, and surrounded by barbed wire and mine fields. This arrangement, it was claimed, was already in operation in Russia, and the infernal plotters expected to extend it throughout the globe. The buildings were to have fifty floors of nothing but sweatshops, then another fifty where the slaves slept in dormitories and ate in messhalls, and finally a luxurious penthouse with hanging gardens for the ruler and his family. Ninety-five per cent of all the male slaves would be castrated, and the other 5% allowed out only for stud purposes. The cutest females would of course go to the ruler, as would everything else worth taking. And there'd be no chance of rebellion, because said ruler would have a flock of push-buttons in his penthouse by means of which he could flood poison gas into any part of his domain at the first sign of trouble. . . .

And J.C. believed that! I know because I heard him repeat the yarn over and over again!

And yet—here's the topper—he wasn't what you could call a dumb cluck. On the contrary, he was bright in certain ways, in fact brilliant. I guess that was part of the reason why so many people took him seriously. It's true that most of those people were saps, but even the rest—and they had at least a little sense—even they felt respect for him. As for me, I was convinced that he had plenty of milk in his cocoanut, and the only thing wrong was that the milk was curdled.

In other words, he wasn't dumb. He was crazy.

Don't get me wrong now. I'm not saying he was crazy in the sense that he seemed to need to be put in a padded cell. At this period he impressed most people as merely high-strung and eccentric. Even Doc was convinced he was nothing more than that. I, though, knew better. Right from the start I suspected that deep down he was genuinely nuts. What's more, even though I'm no long-haired professor of psychology, I managed to figure out just what he was nuts about. Fundamentally, I mean. It wasn't the Jews. The more I studied him, the surer I became that his Jew-complex wasn't basic at all. He knocked them only because he wanted to boost something else. And do you know what that something else was? I'll tell you. It was *himself!*

I'm not kidding. Fundamentally John Christian Power was in the strict literal sense just crazy about himself. I don't mean that he simply thought he was good. A lot of people think that of themselves. Take me, for example. I think I'm damn good. But that guy? Hell, he thought he was perfect!

Do you recall the time when I came out with the idea that we ought to bill him as *The* Power? Well, right then and there was when I caught on to the basic flaw in his cranium. If he'd been in the least sane about himself, he'd have grinned at that moment, or at least looked kind of embarrassed. But instead, as I told you, he just nodded solemnly and said, "That's a very sensible idea." So how could I fail to catch on?

And as a result I was able to understand why he could repeat the wildest whopper as though it was the soberest truth. It was simply because he was so stuck on himself. He was convinced that if he chose to repeat a thing, that in itself was enough to make it true.

Believe me, I know. I tried to correct him once when I heard him call Louis B. Mayer a Communist. "J.C.," I said, real friendly, "you're all wrong about that Hebe. He may be everything else you say, but he's no Communist. As a matter of fact . . ."

But that's as far as I got. "Are you calling me a liar?" he roared, grabbing me by the lapels. "When John Christian Power says a thing is so, it's so! Get that?"

I got it all right. I had to. It was a case of bow down or bow out. So I naturally bowed down. It was humiliating, of course; but on the other hand, as Doc liked to point out, that position worked to our advantage. The more we stooped, the less we had to reach for what we were after.

17

So Doc and I didn't rebel. We saw no reason to rebel. We let the Power grab all the glory, and meanwhile went after the cash. We got it, too. As I have already reported, the Crusade kept growing all through those first months, and between the dues, collections, assessments, and so forth, we were able to rake in quite a fair amount of cash. It wasn't enough to get rich on, understand. I don't care what the FBI may say, the God's honest truth is that Doc and I didn't take a penny more than we needed just to get by. I'm not saying we wouldn't have, if the penny had been there to take. But it wasn't, so we had to make do with barely enough to keep ourselves going. And we certainly did deserve that much, didn't we?

Because we were putting in all our time on the movement, and the work wasn't exactly pleasant. In fact, to me personally it stank. To begin with, look at the sort of company it forced me to keep. I'm not referring now to The Power, though he was bad enough. I'm thinking, for example, of Captain Cleaver, who was even worse. The Power was at least crazy, so you could excuse what he did, but Cleaver was as sane as you or me. That's why I insist he was by far the worse of the two. Fundamentally Cleaver was a gangster who lacked the guts to admit he was one, and therefore wore a flag instead of a bullet-proof vest. In other words, in addition to being an ignorant, loud-mouthed, unprincipled hoodlum, a tinhorn braggart and all-round bum, he was also a hypocrite.

Maybe you think I'm prejudiced when I describe him in such language, but I'm not. To be prejudiced I'd have to be unfair, and that's one thing no man could possibly be to Captain Douglas C.

Cleaver. You'll discover that for yourself before I get through with this story, but let me give you one or two indications right here and now.

From the very outset that ape's sole interest in the Crusade was to use it as a means of raising hell. I don't mean just ordinary playful hell like getting a crowd of saps excited, and giving a few Hebes a scare. I mean *revolution*. He was set on organizing an army of his own, and talked openly of marching on Washington, to take over the government. And he wasn't kidding, either. The minute we put him in charge of the Rangers he began drilling them with no other thought in mind. He ordered every one of them to join the National Rifle Association so that they'd have the right to carry guns, and made them take target-practice in the country every Sunday morning. In addition he got Kronkhite to arrange for them to be allowed to use the pistol range in the German House one evening a week. Moreover, he kept yammering for money to buy more rifles and ammunition, and even wanted us to let him build a range right in the basement of the Citadel. If he could have had his way, he would have turned the entire joint into an armory.

And that was why Doc and I had such trouble with him. Hardly a day passed but what he came around to cuss us out because we wouldn't support his schemes. He even threatened to beat us up, and if it hadn't been that he was so scared of The Power, he probably would have. And believe me, merely standing for that was worth ten times the amount of money that Doc and I got out of the Crusade.

Nor was that all we had to stand for. In addition to holding Cleaver down, we had to keep other scoundrels out. There seemed to be no limit to the variety of foolmongers who tried to hop on our train once we got rolling. Some were just petty grifters who'd organized for the Ku Klux Klan, the Silver Shirts, the Christian Mobilizers, and so forth. They were fairly easy to handle, because we could see through them at a glance. But others were real slickers who almost fooled even me. If we'd ever allowed them to get to His Nibs, there's no telling what might have resulted.

Let me cite a case for illustration. One day Hank came to my office and announced there was an honest-to-God, real, live bishop at the front door asking to see The Power. Ordinarily Doc or I quizzed all strangers before allowing them to proceed upstairs, but he wasn't in at the moment, and I was busy, and besides this was a bishop, so I thought maybe I ought to make an exception. It didn't seem right to make a bishop run our gantlet. Nevertheless, just to play safe, I went out into the hall to take a look at the gent.

He was a bishop, all right. At least, he was dressed like one. His collar was the wrong way round, and there was a silver cross the size of an altar-piece dangling down his purple front. Except for that, though, you'd never have taken him for any kind of Holy Joe. He was small and blond, with pink cheeks, soft lips, eyes the color of dishwater, and delicate hands and feet. He might have been anywhere from fifteen to fifty, and smelled of scented talcum.

"I em Bishop Pehcival Eton Meckel," he sang out in a high soprano. "I em most eagah to hev a chet with your Mahster, if I may."

Right away I gave him the glassy eye. His accent was about as phony as any I'd ever heard even in Hollywood, and everything else about him was wrong. "Sorry," I lied, "The Power isn't in now. Is it something important?"

He sort of pouted for a second, but then suddenly switched on a dazzling smile. I'd never seen such a smile outside of a toothpaste ad. "Yes, it's most frightf'ly important," he trilled. "When do you expect him to return?"

I said I wasn't sure.

"Then let me chet with you," he piped, starting to prance into my office. "I know you'll be frightf'ly int'rested."

I saw I had no choice, so I told him to sit down. Miriam was at the typewriter, and she gave me a look that asked if I wanted her to leave. "It's all right," I told her.

"Yes, of course, my deah," the twerp nodded, drenching her with his smile. "Do stay. You are very dec'rative." Then, leaning back in his chair, he turned to me, pressed his fingertips together, and said, "Now, let's chet, shall we? I hev plenty of time."

His gall took my breath away. I sort of collapsed in my chair and goggled. Miriam, too, seemed staggered. She quit pecking at the keys and just sat and stared at him. But he either didn't notice how we reacted, or didn't care. He simply smiled with all his beautiful little teeth, and launched into a monologue.

I won't try to give it to you word for word. You'd swear I was making it up. I'm not sure I can give you even the gist of it without straining your powers of belief. To begin with, he claimed to be a Catholic bishop, but not of the Roman branch. He belonged, he said, to something called the True Catholic Ecclesia, which considered the Pope nothing more nor less than an impostor. His diocese included the entire Pacific Coast, but for the present he was concentrating on Los Angeles, owing to the fact that his Ecclesia hadn't drummed up a following anywhere else as yet. Even here, though, his following evidently didn't amount to much, because it was meeting in his own apartment in Hollywood.

And that was what he had come to "chet" about. He wanted to know whether he couldn't join forces with us, and maybe use our headquarters as his "cathedral." Because fundamentally our beliefs were right in line with his own, he said. In fact, the only real difference was that ours lacked what he called the "mystical touch," and were therefore less "illumined." In other words, we were doing the right things, but for the wrong reasons.

"Is zat so?" I dead-panned when he got to that point. "And what might be the right reasons?"

I thought he'd hop on my lap and kiss me, he looked so pleased. "I just knew you'd be intrigued!" he cried, clapping his little hands. Then he started to explain. It seems our mistake was that we were attacking the Jews on any number of grounds except the one that was the most important of all. We were accusing them of being usurers, panders, wreckers, warmongers, but failing to expose their very worst crime, which was that they were—*pretenders!*

I had to hold on to myself when he lobbed that one at me. I swallowed hard, coughed, and finally managed to ask what they were pretending.

"But don't you knyow?" he cried, positively shocked. I shook my head. He turned to Miriam, and she shook hers. "Why, they're pretending they are Israelites!" he shrilled.

Well, that was too much. I just had to let out a laugh, and so did Miriam, though in a sort of polite and puzzled way. Whereupon the little man put on a look of anguish and moaned, "You don't understand, do you?"

[113]

"Sorry, bishop," I said, struggling to straighten my face. "I guess I don't."

So then he went off into another monologue. The Jews, he insisted, weren't Israelites at all. They were a tribe of fakers who had stolen that trade-name in order to pass themselves off as the Chosen People. Actually, the English were the true Israelites. He claimed he could prove it, too. The English, he pointed out, were originally called Saxons, and didn't that really mean "Isaac's sons"? They were also called the British race, and wasn't that name derived from the two Hebrew words *brit*, meaning "Covenant," and *ish*, meaning "man"? *

He rattled off a dozen other proofs of the same order, and then plunged into a spiel that made me sit there, bug-eyed. Because, according to his claim, what he was telling me wasn't something he had thought up all by himself. It was a belief shared by lots of people—millions, he said—who called themselves "Anglo-Israelites" and carried on propaganda all over the world. He ticked off the names of some of those people, Lord Whozis, Lady Dizzidame, and a dozen more with titles, and also W. J. Cameron, the Ford Sunday Evening Hourator!

So I listened, kind of fascinated, unable to decide to what extent this daisy was a crook, and to what extent a crank. For all of an hour I must have listened before I finally decided he was worse than either, because he was both combined—in short, a croonk †
So then I started looking at my watch, and scraping my feet, and fussing with the papers on the desk. He wouldn't take the hint, though. I had to practically heave him out before I could get rid of him. Then I called Hank and told him never to let that character inside the door again. "He's poison," I said.

That sort of shocked Miriam. Apparently, she hadn't seen through this bishop at all. "I thought he was sweet," she said, sounding kind of sad and bewildered.

I smiled at her indulgently. After all, was it her fault that she

---

* *Miriam Cabot took these words down at the time, and left me a memo of them, which is how they happened to have stuck in my mind. I can't guarantee the spelling, however.*

† *This word is not in the dictionary, but to my way of thinking, it should be.*

wasn't quite bright? "Ant-paste, too, is sweet," I answered, giving her cheek a pinch. "Nevertheless it's still poison."

And my judgment was right—as usual. About a week later the papers reported our sweet little bishop had been picked up on a morals charge. It seems he'd been using his apartment not alone as a church but a fag-joint!

Well, that will give you some idea of what Doc and I had to contend with. If it hadn't been for us, the Crusade would have gone hog-wild right from the start, and then the effect on the community might really have been bad. (If you doubt that, just read on. You'll discover what actually did happen once Doc and I lost control of the movement.) All in all, therefore, I insist we had a just right to every penny we paid ourselves. And plenty more.

Because God knows we got no other reward. It would have been different, of course if there had been any prestige connected with the work, but it goes without saying that there wasn't. If anything, there was a definite taint to it. Practically all the best people in town seemed to look down on the Crusade, and by the best people I naturally don't mean the Jews. I mean the top-flight Gentiles—the sort who got their names in the papers even without the help of press agents. Some of them actually took it on themselves to attack us publicly, sponsoring meetings against us, and signing petitions to have us investigated by the Dies Committee. About the only people that appeared to be for us were the riffraff. And to me, I must state, that was real humiliating.

Doc, of course, was less touchy on that particular score. In fact, he thought my reaction totally uncalled for. In the first place, he argued, the best people weren't nearly as much opposed to the Crusade as they tried to make out; and in the second, even if they were, what the hell! They had never cared about my feelings, so why should I care about theirs?

Nevertheless I did care. I guess it was because, as old Mrs. Gunderson once said, at heart I'm really kind of a sensitive guy. You may not believe it, but for a while I was even upset at the thought that I was getting the Jews down on me. Understand, I'd never been what you could call a Jew-lover. At the same time, however, I'd never been a Jew-hater either. I'd just taken them for granted.

the way I had the Irish and the Wops and the Swedes and all the other elements that were sort of foreign in the U.S.A. As a matter of fact, and I can say this sincerely, in the past some of my best friends had been Jews.

Take Ivan Kohn, for example. He was the guy, you may recall, who got me my first job in Hollywood, and he'd remained a close pal of mine from then on. I still don't know what drew us together, because except for the fact that we were both press agents, we had almost nothing in common. He was nearly twice my size, and I had more than ten times his brains. He'd been a prize-fighter in his younger days, and always looked and acted as if he was still punch-drunk. When we walked together, I'd feel like a little tug dragging a rusty old freighter. When we talked together, he'd do practically all the listening. Nevertheless, he and I were very close, especially after I got into that trouble over at Warner's. He not alone stuck up for me then, insisting to all and sundry that I'd been framed, but also loaned me money, and even offered to let me bunk in his apartment when I got too broke to stay in a hotel. If it hadn't been for his wife—and she, incidentally, was a Mick—I'd probably have accepted his offer. But she had never liked me, so I went to live in Mrs. Gunderson's rooming house instead.

Nevertheless, as I have said, Ivan and I remained good buddies. I mean even after I hooked up with the Crusade. Of course, I didn't tell him about that. He wasn't much of a Jew, in fact except for his name you wouldn't hardly have taken him for one at all, but just the same I felt it was better policy not to tell him. I let him think I was doing publicity for the hotel I'd moved into downtown.

Eventually, though, someone must have tipped him off, because the next time we met there was a brutal scene. It happened in the Melrose Grotto, where I'd dropped in to have lunch, the way I usually did at least once a week. The place was crowded, but I had no trouble spotting Ivan. He was sitting alone in a corner, hunched over a plate of food, with a copy of *Variety* propped against the sugar-bowl in front of him. I saw several other guys whom I knew, mostly press agents and writers from the studios in that neighborhood, but I passed them by with just a nod. I wanted to eat with my pal.

"Hiya, Champ!" I yelled, giving the back of his thick neck a pinch. "Don't you know it's bad manners to eat when you read?"

He looked up kind of startled, and I noticed him scowl. I paid no attention, however, because I knew that reading was quite a task for him, and always caused him to scowl. I slid into the chair next to his, and started mopping my face. It was June, and I'd worked myself into a sweat edging into a parking space near the restaurant. I looked at his plate, saw he was eating pigs' knuckles and sauerkraut, and asked how it was. Instead of answering, though, he continued to scowl, and it suddenly dawned on me that something was wrong. "Anything the matter, Ivan?" I asked.

He still didn't answer. His big pop-eyes just glared at me, and his jaws sort of twitched. Finally he wet his lips and blurted out in a husky voice, "Is that true what I heard about what you're doin'?"

I felt myself turn pale. "What d'you mean?" I asked.

"You know what I mean!" he came back at me, still speaking in a low growl. "Are you working for that crazy bastard they call The Power?"

"Aw, who told you that?" I tried to stall.

"Never mind who told me!" he snapped. "Is it true or not?"

I struggled to fake a cagey smile. "Well, if you must know . . ."

Suddenly he was on his feet. "So it *is* true!" he roared, kicking his chair out of the way.

"But let me explain!" I yammered. "All I'm doing . . ."

That, however, was as far as I got. I felt a clout that rattled every tooth in my head, and the next thing I knew he was lifting me out of my chair. Then, taking hold of my coat-collar with one fist, and the seat of my pants with the other, he began carrying me bodily through the restaurant. I struggled, of course, but it did no good. All the way to the door he carried me, scattering waiters and upsetting trays. Finally, reaching the sidewalk, he heaved me up like I was a dummy, and threw me into the gutter.

I raised my head, half-dazed, but then quickly covered it with my arms. I thought he was going to hit me again. He didn't, though. Instead he spat somewhere—I guess it must have been on my suit—and I heard him say in a thick voice, "If you ever come near me again, you little rat, by God, I'll break your neck!" Whereupon he turned on his heel and walked back into the restaurant.

I stayed in the gutter, too scared to think of moving. After a minute, though, I saw that a crowd was collecting, so I crawled to my feet and staggered away. Somebody offered to take my arm, but I shook myself free. "I'm all right," I growled. Luckily my car was only a little way down the block, and I climbed in and slammed the door. Then, starting the engine, I pulled out with a jerk, denting the fender of the car ahead of me. I heard a yell, but paid no attention. Ramming the gears into second, I stepped on the gas and raced off.

I didn't dare go back to the Citadel that day. One whole side of my face was swollen, and my spine was so sore I could barely move. I phoned Doc from my hotel room to say I'd had an accident, and then went to bed and stayed there.

I don't need to tell you how I felt. I was so mad that if I'd had it in my power, I'd have massacred every Hebe in creation. It wasn't just on account of the physical pain I was in. What hurt even more was the humiliation. That restaurant had been one of my favorite hangouts ever since I'd worked on the Paramour lot, and I knew I'd never be able to show my face there again. Nor practically anywhere else in Hollywood. I was through now for good in the movie world. Finally and completely washed up.

So I lay there in bed and cussed the Jews. For maybe an hour I did that, calling them every foul name in the language. But then, thinking the matter over, I started cussing the Crusade as well. I realized that if it hadn't been for that movement, I might never have gotten into the jam I was in now. Ivan would have remained my pal, and through him or someone else I might still have been able to get back into the studios. Because after all the blacklist wasn't written in indelible ink.

Now, however, that chance was gone. Apparently I was stuck for good and all with the Crusade. And, once I realized that, I became almost frantic. As you know, I'd never had anything but contempt for the Crusade. I'd despised everything about it from the very start. Not for any moral reasons, I will admit. As I've said before, I figured I was strictly a press agent, not a boy scout. What made me loathe the Crusade was that it was so mangy and cheap. For me to have to work for it was like for Paderewski to have to play the piano in a honky-tonk. Yet now it looked as though I'd never be able to do anything else. I'd crawled so deep into that mucky outfit that I'd smeared myself up for life. At least, that's the way it looked to me at the moment. I guess I was kind of hysterical.

Finally, though, Doc blew in, and then I gradually quieted down. He had a pint of rye with him, and between that and his calm counsel I was brought around to thinking that I was a sap to take on so.

"What the hell!" he said, turning on his dimples. "You don't have to be scared of those Hollywood Hebes. They're scared of *you* now. Mark my words, it won't be long before they come on their knees and beg you to work for them. Just to get you away from the Crusade. Don't you realize that?"

At first I didn't, but after he said it a couple more times, I began to think maybe he was right.

"You bet I'm right," he declared when I finally admitted the fact. "So why worry? All you've got to do is just sit tight. You're able to eat, aren't you? And you're getting this room for nothing. You're paying off on your car, and buying new clothes, and in general getting by nicely. So what the hell!"

That's the way he argued, and the longer I listened, the surer I became that he was as right as rain. I actually *was* getting by. And at the rate the Crusade was progressing, it looked as though I was going to do better than that soon. Our movement was booming beyond any doubt. Every week we were attracting more attention, and gaining new members, and raking in more dough. So what the hell!

18

But it didn't last. That boom, I mean. For about three months the Crusade kept going like a house on fire, and then suddenly—*psss!* It was exactly as if a hose had been turned on, because all at once the blaze started to die down. I recall the exact day when the turn occurred, because it was marked by a piece of news that was kind of memorable. The date was August 24, 1939. Doc and I were at the Pearl Dive, putting away a couple of beers around lunchtime, when the story broke. It came over the radio as a flash bulletin, and we could hardly believe it at first. *Hitler had made a deal with Stalin!*

"Can you beat that!" I gasped, wiping the beer that had spilled down my chin. "The crooked bastard has finally sold out his own movement!" I was more amused than anything else. I'd never had much use for Adolf.

But Doc wasn't amused at all. "To hell with *his* movement!" he growled. "What worries me is what he's done to ours!"

I set down my glass and looked at him. "Say, I hadn't thought of that!" I muttered. "Do you really think it'll hurt us?"

"Hurt us? Christ, it's liable to wreck us! Here J.C.'s been saying all along that Russia's run by the Elders of Zion, and now this makes him out a cockeyed liar. We'd better get hold of him right away."

He called to the bartender for the check and a packet of Sen-sens —we were always careful to stink up our breaths when we knew we'd have to talk to His Nibs—and then started for the car. Doc was in such a panic, he wouldn't even wait for me to finish my beer.

We found him in the backyard as usual. He had on nothing but a pair of shorts and a green eyeshade, and was reading a book of articles by Westbrook Pegler. His bony carcass was smeared all over with cocoanut butter, and he smelled rancid.

"Have you heard the news?" Doc panted.

The Power stopped stroking himself and looked up from his book. "What news?" he asked, giving us a slow scowl.

We spilled it, sure that it would bowl him over. It didn't though.

"Propaganda!" he snapped, squinting at us to keep the sun out of his eyes. "Nothing but Jewish propaganda! Hitler wouldn't any more shake the hand of that Red fiend than—than I would."

"But Berlin has just admitted it!" Doc yelled.

His Nibs still refused to believe the story. He even began to bawl us out for believing it. So I slipped into the house to get Hank's portable radio, and fiddled around with the knobs till I caught a newscast.

"Well, there it is," I said, planting the box down on the grass.

J.C. seemed to go cold as he listened. I could actually see the goose pimples stand up under the grease on his leathery skin.

"I wouldn't have believed it!" he finally came out, starting to stroke himself again, but fiercely now. "It just didn't seem possible that they'd be able to get to Hitler!" He caught the puzzled look that passed between Doc and me, and started to glare. "Don't you understand?" he hollered. "The Jews have bought him off!"

"Aw, now wait a minute!" I started to protest. "That doesn't sound reasonable. Hitler's too powerful a guy . . ."

"What do *you* know about it?" he cut me off. "The fact's plain now that nobody in Europe is powerful enough to buck the Elders of Zion. But nobody! It'll take an American to do that!" He narrowed his eyes and gave us a look that was cunning, mysterious, and goofy all at the same time. "Get it? Only an American!"

I started to say something, but he refused to listen. Closing his book with a slam, he jumped up and started to go indoors. Halfway there, though, he seemed to remember something, because he halted and screwed his head around. "What about the handbill for Sunday?" he called back, looking at the air over my head. "Is it out already?"

I struggled not to grin. He had written the copy for that handbill himself, and it was all about how he was going to expose the "vicious propaganda rumor" that Germany intended to make a pact with Russia. The headline on it read: THE JEWS ARE LYING AGAIN!

"Oh, that?" I answered, dead-pan. "No, Miriam's mimeographing it now. Why?"

"Well, scrap it," he said, still keeping his eyes down. "I'll get up a new one right away."

I went to my office and told Miriam to quit what she was doing. I hoped she would ask me why, and give me an excuse to sit down and chin with her for a bit. But she merely said, "Very well, Mr. Smullet," and beat it. Evidently she was still sore because I'd taken a chance a few nights earlier and tried a little cave-man stuff when I was seeing her to her car. I was tempted to call her back, but decided against it. I didn't want a scene, especially with Doc in the next room. So I said something under my breath, and walked out to my car to take a smoke.

An hour later His Nibs sent for me to come upstairs. He was still wearing nothing but his shorts, and his skin looked purple under the dry grease.

"Here it is," he said, handing me a sheet of pencilled scribble.

I read it over slowly. His handwriting was like a kid's, large and unsteady and all on a bias.

"Swell," I said, turning to go. It was what I always said when he handed me a piece of copy, and also what I never meant. He had practically no idea of how to put oomph into a handbill.

I beat it back to my crib, locked the door, lit a cigarette, and went at my typewriter. I whacked out three different versions of that handbill before I finally got one that satisfied me. Then I got rid of the cigarette butts, threw open the window to air the room, and went to show the copy to Doc.

He was sitting with his feet on his desk, dictating a letter to Miriam.

"Here's a honey for you!" I clucked, sticking the sheet under his nose. "If this doesn't draw 'em, I'll eat it, clip and all."

He put on his reading glasses and glanced through the copy. Here's what it said:

THE POWER
declares
NAZI GERMANY HAS SOLD OUT TO THE JEWS

Come & Hear Him Expose The Truth!

LEARN HOW THE ELDERS OF ZION HAVE MADE A JUDAS
OUT OF ADOLF HITLER!

Why is Leon Trotsky in Mexico?
Where is Maxim Litvinov?
Who is Stalin's new Concubine?
What is Frankfurter up to in Washington?

JOHN CHRISTIAN POWER
Founder and Leader
of

THE CRUSADE, INC.
Will Reveal All
SUNDAY, AUGUST 27, AT 8 P.M.
at the
SENATE AUDITORIUM
(Admission Free)
JOIN THE CRUSADE & SAVE AMERICA

Doc laid the sheet down with a grin. "Say, this is great!" he said. "Did J.C. get it up?"

I was about to let out a guffaw, but remembered Miriam was present. I knew how she felt about The Power. Straightening my face, I said, "Yeah, it's mostly his work. I just put the tease in it, that's all."

Doc gave me a knowing look, wiggled around to get more comfortable in his chair, and read over the copy a second time. "Know what I think?" he said, handing the sheet back to me.

"No, what do you think?"

"I think it's too good to be just mimeographed. Get it printed. Run off ten thousand copies and plaster the town with them."

I smiled at him. "That's just what I had in mind," I said.

As a matter of fact, I really had, and not solely because I stood to get a kick-back from the printer. I honestly did believe that that bit of copy deserved a special play.

The handbills didn't arrive from the printer until Saturday morning, and the first thing I did was rush right upstairs to show a copy to J. C. He was taking a shower at the moment—he took at least two a day, always with cold water—and I waited for him to finish. When he finally came out of the bathroom, water was streaming from his hairless dome, and practically cascading over his ribs. His teeth were chattering, and his skin looked blue where it was untanned, and almost liver-colored everywhere else.

He gave a jump at seeing me, and hastened to cover his front with a soppy piece of toweling. I too must have looked startled, for I had never caught him quite that nude before. He made me think of a mummy fished out of a sewer.

"What d'you want?" he growled.

I handed him the throwaway. "Isn't that a humdinger?" I sang out, trying not to look at his skin and bones.

He gave one glance at the sheet, and then crumpled it into a ball. "That's all wrong!" he snapped, giving me a cold stare. "I've changed my mind!"

"You've *what?*"

"Don't you understand plain English?" he shouted. "I've changed my mind. It was Stalin who sold out, not Hitler."

I stared at him, frog-eyed. "I don't get it," I said.

"But it's as plain as day!" he answered, curling his long upper lip. "Stalin has double-crossed the Elders of Zion. He's on *our* payroll now."

I could see he really believed that, and I felt like yelling, "You're nuts!" Instead, I looked at the waste-basket, where he'd tossed the handbill, and whined, "What are we going to do about that, then? We've got ten thousand of them downstairs!"

"Put 'em in the incinerator," he said, turning to go back to the bathroom. "Better do it right away, too."

"But wait a minute!" I yelled after him. "Only yesterday morning, when I showed you the copy, you said . . ."

"I know what I said," he cut me off. "It was an error. I can see now that Hitler's accomplished the greatest triumph of his career." He glared as if challenging me to deny it. "Yes, sir," he went on, giving his head a shake that sprinkled water all over the floor, "Within six months there won't be a Jew at large in the whole of Russia! Mark my words, this is the beginning of the end for the Jews everywhere!"

Then he stalked off and slammed the door.

19

Well, as things developed, it did look like the beginning of the end all right—but for us, not the Jews. Our meeting on Sunday drew little more than 300 people, and though J. C. bellowed as I had never heard him bellow before, the total collection came to exactly $28.84!

That was an awful jolt. For once I didn't try to get Miriam to come out and have a bite with me after the show. Instead I waited for Doc to finish his chores on the platform, and then trailed his car to the Pearl Dive.

Chuck started polishing the bar when we entered, that being his way of hinting for us to sit there and spare his sore feet. But we walked on and took our regular booth in the rear. "What'll it be?" he called after us in a kind of injured tone. "The usual?"

We nodded, and waited for him to bring the drinks.

Doc, I noticed, looked almost as worried as I felt. "Well, what d'you make of it?" I asked.

He reached for a cigarette, lit up, and inhaled deeply. "Aw, I guess it doesn't mean anything," he lied. "Just an off night, that's all."

"That isn't the way it looked to me," I said, frowning. "I'll lay a bet we're in for trouble from now on."

He must have felt the same way, because he suddenly began to act sore. "Christ Almighty!" he bawled, "you're the worst calamity-howler I ever came across! What if we did draw a small crowd tonight? After all, there wasn't any advertising."

I shook my head. "I wasn't thinking of the size of the crowd," I said. "It's the way they reacted. Notice how cold they were? Even the shills . . . And say, that reminds me. Where *were* most of our shills tonight?"

He shrugged his fat shoulders and looked away. "I guess maybe there was something going on over at the German House," he answered after a pause. "There were hardly any Heinies in the hall tonight."

I shook my head again. "No," I said, "that can't be it. Kronkhite would have told us in advance. I talked to him on the phone only yesterday."

"What did he say?"

I waited for Chuck to set down the drinks and leave before I answered. "Nothing about their throwing any shindig tonight," I said. "As a matter of fact, they're calling off the affair they'd announced for next Wednesday. You know—the big Anti-Communist rally J. C. was supposed to speak at. That's what Kronkhite called to tell me about."

Doc half-nodded, his eyes on the drink in front of him. He acted almost as if he was waiting to see if it would change color, or something. Finally he took up the glass and tossed it off in one gulp. Then, wiping his mouth with the back of his hand, he reached for some popcorn. "Hell," he said, leaning far back and tossing a kernel into his mouth, "what's the use of worrying? It's only natural that people should be kind of distracted right now. On account of that double-cross, I mean, and the war, and so forth. But they'll get over it." He scowled at the doubt that must have been plastered all over my face. "You wait and see," he said. "I bet next week we'll have as good a meeting as ever."

I should have taken Doc up on that bet, because the following week the meeting was even worse. Not alone was the crowd smaller and stingier, but for the first time we got an honest-to-God heckler. We'd had disturbances, of course, at practically all of our meetings, but they'd always been staged. Someone in the crowd would be primed to jump up at a given signal, point to a guy near him who was wearing dark glasses or some other disguise, and start yelling: "Throw him out! He's a Jew spy!" Other people would take up the yell, a bunch of our Rangers would rush in, there would be a phony tussle with lots of grunts and shrieks, and finally the plant would be thrown out on his ear. As a rule we'd pull some stunt of that sort just before The Power got up to speak, because it never failed to get the audience in a nice warm mood.

But this time the ruckus was genuine, and it didn't come until The Power was already on his feet. He was talking slowly at the time, and with his eyes closed, like he was fumbling to get a grip on the crowd, when suddenly a voice somewhere under the balcony growled, "You're crazy!"

It came so unexpectedly that for a second The Power seemed paralyzed. He just stood there, mouth open, and stared. Then, in a choking voice, he cried, "Who said that?"

"I did!" came a shout, and everybody turned to look at a man in the rear who was leaving his seat. He was tall and red-haired, and had no coat on. At a guess I'd have said he was a truck driver or maybe a cement-man. Reaching the aisle, he paused a moment, and pointed to J. C. defiantly. "And I ain't no Red either!" he yelled. "I've been one of your followers right from the start, but I'm satisfied now that you're plumb crazy. Anybody can see . . ."

But he wasn't given a chance to say what anybody could see. Half a dozen of our Rangers made a rush for him, and in no time he was out of the hall. The audience, however, reacted badly. Part of it seemed to side with the heckler, and several people started to walk out when he was bounced. Moreover, those who remained seemed unable to get back in a listening mood. They kept shuffling their feet, and looking around, and talking among themselves. The Power started running with sweat, but still he couldn't recapture their attention. For maybe ten minutes he struggled, and finally quit in disgust. Then Doc got up and called for the collection, whereupon more of the audience began walking out. When we counted the night's receipts, they came to exactly $14.83—including what had been taken in at the literature table.

And thenceforth things went from worse to worser. The next day we got fourteen written resignations, and at least thirty squawks over the phone. All the ensuing week we kept getting squawks, and the next month there was a brutal slump in the payment of dues. It began to look as though we were really in for it.

The fault, of course, was Schicklgruber's, fundamentally. First the rat pulled his switcheroo and teamed up with Stalin, and then he sent his pansy divisions into Poland and started World War II. That naturally hit us hard. Power had been saying all along that he meant to do over here what Schicky had done over there—and now a lot of our people were not so sure they wanted it done.

Even poor old Mrs. Gunderson, I discovered, began to have doubts on that score. She came down with a bad cold late in September as a result of going out into the rain to distribute our handbills, and I went to call on her one afternoon with flowers and a box of candy.

She began to cry when she saw what I had brought her. "Shame on you, Clem!" she scolded me. "Bringing candy and flowers to an old woman like me!"

"Who's an old woman?" I kidded her, sitting down on the edge of the bed. "You're my best girl!"

Well, we joshed back and forth like that for quite a while, and I guess I enjoyed it almost as much as she did. Deep down I'd always had kind of a soft streak in me, and it was a pleasure to give it an airing for a change. Finally, though, we seemed to run out of things to kid about, and suddenly became serious. Mrs. Gunderson began to ask me how the Crusade was getting along, and though I said swell, she could tell by my voice that I was lying.

"Clem," she said, starting to shake her little head, "I'm worried. I wouldn't say this to anyone else, and I don't want you to repeat it. But the truth is, I'm worried sick."

"What about?" I asked, as if I didn't know.

"Oh, everything." She hesitated a minute, like she hated to say more even to me. But then, sagging back on the pillow, she suddenly blurted out, "Clem, I—I'm afraid I'm losing my faith. Somehow I can't feel the way I used to about The Power. I keep wondering now if maybe he isn't a little wrong about some things. Tell me, Clem, honestly—haven't you begun to think that too?"

"Me?" I said, making a big play of looking for a match. "I should say not. My faith in him is as great as it has ever been."

"Honestly?"

"Cross my heart," I said, starting to light a cigarette.

"My, I'm glad to hear that!" She reached to the little table at her side and cleared a saucer for me to use as an ashtray. "But I must say," she went on, "things aren't the same somehow in the movement. There used to be so much enthusiasm, especially among the Amazons. But now you hear nothing but grumbling."

"Yeah? About what?"

"Well, for instance, about the way they beat up that fellow who yelled out at the meeting a couple of weeks ago. His sister's an Amazon, and she's been telling everybody he couldn't go to work for three days, he was beat up so bad."

I nodded understandingly. "But you can't hardly blame The Power for that," I tried to argue. "It was those Rangers who did it."

"I know. But he's our Leader, and he shouldn't allow things like that." She fell silent, her sad little eyes staring at the ceiling. Finally, turning back to me, she said, "And then there's the way he keeps on sticking up for Hitler. I don't think he ought to do that either. Not any more, he shouldn't. Even that sweet young Miss Cabot thinks that, and you know what a loyal one she's been."

"Did she herself tell you that?" I asked, scowling.

"Well, not in so many words, Clem. But she hinted at it plain enough. And not jest to me, either."

I looked away, unable to decide what to say.

Suddenly the old lady reached out and took my hand. "Oh, Clem," she cried, almost in tears, "I know this must sound terrible, but sometimes I think that if I could only find something else to believe in, I—I'd drop out of the Crusade right now."

"Aw, you mustn't say that, Ma!" I told her.

"It's true, though," she sighed.

I managed to talk her around before I finally left. At least, I thought I did. But I must say I myself felt lousy. I couldn't dream of going back to the Citadel, so I drove around to a house where I was kind of acquainted, and tried my damnedest to get cheered up. It didn't work, though. By 9 P.M. I was out on the street again, feeling even bluer than before, and sick to boot.

I didn't show up at the Citadel until around noon the next day, and then found Cleaver there, raising hell as usual. He was in Doc's office and I could hear him through the connecting door. It seems he'd just found out he could pick up a couple of dozen second-hand rifles cheap—$7.50 a piece, he said—and he simply wouldn't believe we weren't in a position to lay out the price. I listened a while, and then started looking over the pile of marked magazines The Power had left on my desk. He had been doing that regularly of late, thinking I'd need the stuff for the house organ we still talked of publishing. But I couldn't keep my mind on the drivel. In fact, the very sight of it made me want to throw up. Swiveling my chair, I leaned back, put my feet on the typewriter table, and let my mind wander. That wasn't pleasant either, but I kept it up until I finally heard Cleaver stamp out of the building. Then, ducking into Doc's office, I said, "I want to talk to you."

He gave me one look, and threw up his hands. "Christ Almighty!" he swore. "Haven't I been talked to enough for one day? I've just had Cleaver on my neck. . . ."

"Yeah, I know," I cut in, "but this is really serious."

"Then it'll have to wait until I've had lunch," he said, grabbing his hat. "I'm hungry."

I told him I'd go along. I'd just had breakfast, but I didn't want to let him out of my sight. We drove around to a hash house on Third Street, and I watched him put away a plate of spaghetti and meat balls, and some pie and coffee. Then we adjourned to a quiet bar a block away and ordered beer.

"Look, Doc," I opened up as soon as we got settled, "I'm beginning to think we ought to check out. . . . No, listen a minute. I know what you're going to say, but I really mean it this time." I told him of my conversation with Mrs. Gunderson. "So you see?" I concluded. "When even a person like that wants to quit, what chance is there? I'm telling you, Doc—this racket's played out."

He leaned back and looked at me like I ought to be ashamed of myself. "You're all wet!" he snorted.

"The hell I am!" I said. "I'm just trying to keep from getting wet. This ship's sinking."

"So you want to jump straight into the ocean, eh?" he sneered. "Does that make sense?" His sneer broadened at the way my face fell. "Use your brains, Clem. The only time to start diving is when there just isn't anything else to do. After all, is there anything sillier than a rat that deserts a ship that doesn't sink?"

I stared at him and then at my beer. I just couldn't think of a comeback. Finally I said, kind of weakly, "And you really don't think the Crusade's through?"

"Through?" he hollered. "Christ, it's barely started! Don't you see what an opportunity we've got right now? All our competitors are suffering worse than we are. Temple Luther—you know, the crank who runs that Christian Militants outfit—he was in only yesterday afternoon, offering to sell his mailing list for ten bucks. That's how broke he is. And it's the same with the others—the Silver Shirts, and the American Defenders, and the Great Phalanx, and the rest. They're practically all folding up locally. Even the Bund is having a tough time. . . ."

"But that just bears out what I've been saying," I broke in. "The public . . ."

"Nah, let me finish!" he barked. "Here's my point. If we hold out now, we'll be able to pick up what's left of all those other outfits. It's like what happens in the business world when there's a panic. The guy who weathers the storm is in a position to swallow those who go down, and, as a result, he's got everything practically to himself when the storm passes. See what I mean? All we've got to do now is keep going, and the first thing you know, we'll be enjoying what amounts to a monopoly. Every sap in this area will belong to the Crusade. Get it?"

I took a long slow swallow of my beer, and set the glass down gently. I could see he really did have a point. So finally I said, "Okay. . . . But if we're to keep going, we'll have to do something."

"Sure," he agreed. "We're got to start a new offensive, as Cleaver would say. In other words, take the bull by the horns . . ."

"And throw it," I cracked sourly.

"Exactly. Throw the bull as we've never thrown it before." He paused to drain his glass. "And here's my suggestion. Let's bring out that paper we've been talking about. . . . No, don't start objecting right away. I've been giving this a lot of thought, and here's my analysis. First off, a paper will help hold the members that we have right now. Second, it'll undoubtedly bring in new ones. And third, you and I'll be able to pick up a little extra change." He sat back and smiled. "Now what have you got to say?"

"But how'll we swing it?" I asked. "We've got to have enough capital to carry the thing through the first month, at least."

"I realize that," Doc admitted, fiddling with his empty glass.

"Well, where are you going to get it?"

"From Peavey," he answered serenely.

"You mean he's told you he'll stake us?"

"No, as a matter of fact I haven't asked him yet. I'm leaving that to you." He waved a hand to keep me quiet. "You've got a drag with Peavey," he said, flashing his dimples. "No, don't say you haven't. I know better. He's got respect for you. I heard him say once he considered you the smartest publicity man in town. That's straight, Clem. All you need to do is just talk to him. . . ."

"Nothing doing!" I yapped. "That's your job."

"But I can't even get him to let me come to his office. I've phoned a dozen times to try and get an appointment."

"Then I bet he'll turn me down too," I said.

"Okay," Doc snapped me up, laying a dollar bill on the table, "let's make it a bet. There's the phone right over there against the wall. . . . Come on, sport. It was your idea. You can't back out now."

He grinned, aware that he'd cornered me. Cussing myself, I got up and went to the phone.

20

It was the sort of drugstore that made you think a cyclone must have swept up a beanery and a liquor warehouse, dumped both into a bargain basement, and then added the salvage from a dozen sign-painters' shops. I picked my way between piles of glassware, haberdashery, toys, magazines, and auto accessories, and finally located the prescription department.

"I'm looking for Mr. Peavey," I told the clerk behind the counter.

He was short and pimply, and wore a doctor's smock that had probably been clean once. I was carrying a brief-case, so he must have taken me for a drummer. "What d'you wanna see him about?" he asked, running a finger over the little blond hairs that apparently represented a moustache.

"It's private," I snapped. "I've got an appointment."

The jerk eyed me a second, and then opened the swinging panel next to the counter. "You'll find him in the office back of the stock-room," he said, pointing with his thumb.

I edged through a narrow opening in the shelves, groped past a lot of packing cases, and came to a door on which someone had chalked the word PRIVATE. I knocked, heard a growl, and walked in.

Even a genius couldn't have rigged up a more perfect stage-set for Mr. Cyrus J. Peavey. The office was practically a crib with one little iron-barred window, and it was crowded with old filing cabinets and shelves of catalogues and junk. The cement floor was bare, and part of the plaster was gone from the ceiling. Peavey was seated at an old-fashioned roll-top desk, his little fanny sliding off a chair pad that had split its seams. He was wearing a black alpaca coat, and a soiled shirt and ready-made tie. One side of his horn-rimmed glasses was held together with a piece of dirty adhesive tape, and he needed a shave.

He looked at me over his shoulder and said, "Oh, it's you, Smullet?" Then, turning back to the papers on his desk, he muttered, "I'm kinda rushed this morning."

"So am I," I said, starting to look for a place to sit down. There was a wooden chair next to the desk, but it was piled high with catalogues.

He raised his head again, and peered at me with his mean little bookkeeper eyes. "Managing to keep busy, eh?" he sniffed.

"And how!" I chuckled, bending over to clear the chair. "I've hardly had time to eat since I phoned you day before yesterday." He gave me a look that practically yelled "liar," but I let it pass. I sat down, put the briefcase on my lap, and fished for my Luckies. "Cigarette?" I asked, tapping one out of the pack and poking it toward him.

He shook his head, but shoved a dirty glass ashtray in my direction. "I had an idea things were kinda dead down at the Citadel," he said.

"Dead?" I snorted. "Shucks, we're more alive than we've ever been! You evidently haven't heard what's happened. We're all set to start publishing our paper. I've just finished the dummy for the first issue." His cheek gave a nervous twitch, but otherwise there was no reaction. "I brought it along to show you," I said, opening the briefcase. "And believe me, it's a lulu. We're figuring the circulation ought to hit ten thousand right off the bat."

"That's pretty tall figuring," he said, leaning back and staring like he wasn't much interested either way.

I plunked the dummy in front of him. It was tabloid-size, and pretty thick on account of all the pasted parts inside. "For a sheet like that?" I cried, jumping up and pointing to the cover page. "Just look at that cartoon. There's enough dynamite in it to blow up Boulder Dam."

He gave it a glance, and then cocked his bifocals to get a good look. The drawing showed a fat Hebe in a silk hat sitting on a throne built of money bags, his clodhopper feet making a footstool out of the National Capitol. A half-naked girl with hair falling down her back was struggling to get off his lap. One of her hands was tugging against the hairy paw on her thigh, and the other was clawing the man's jowls. Below the drawing a heavy line of shocker type asked: HOW LONG WILL AMERICANS STAND FOR THIS?

Peavey picked up the dummy, held it at arms' length, brought it close again, and finally looked at me. His thin chapped lips were parted in a leer that showed yellow teeth, and his cheek twitched four to the beat.

"That's dynamite, all right," he sort of snickered. "Think you can get away with it?"

"Why not?" I snickered back, sitting down again. "We've still got freedom of the press in this country, haven't we?"

"Yeah. But what about the Post Office? You'll never be able to send anything as raw as this through the mails. Not second-class, anyway."

"So what?" I said, squinting against the smoke from my cigarette. "All I'm figuring on is local distribution to begin with, and we can handle that ourselves. We'll sell it on the streets, and from door to door. There's no law against that, is there?"

It was a foolish question, so he let it ride. He went on gawking at the cartoon, almost as if he expected the girl in it to break loose and maybe give him a front view. At length he muttered, "That's a mighty clever drawing. Who did it?"

"Search *me*," I chuckled. "I swiped it from a throw-away that the Bund put out back East some place. It isn't copyrighted, if that's what's worrying you."

It evidently wasn't, because he just sucked his teeth and continued to gawk. Finally he turned to look at the script inside. The lead article was by The Power, and was headed "Wake Up, America!" About every third word was in caps and half the rest were in bold type. There were practically no periods in it—only exclamation marks. Next came pieces by Gribble and Mabel Haight, and one that Kronkhite had ghosted for Captain Cleaver. The balance of the paper was filled with stuff from the magazines J. C. had marked up for me. It was real hot stuff, too, especially the bits from the Nazi organs.

Peavey leafed through the pages slowly, and then gave his teeth an extra hard suck. "I guess it'll do," he said, handing the dummy back to me.

"What d'you mean, 'do'?" I pressured him. "This is going to be sensational!"

"Think so?"

"I know it. I'm a trained newspaperman, Peavey, and I want to tell you, this is going to rock the town."

He turned away and swept his coat collar with a nervous gesture, as if he was trying to brush off the dandruff. "Well, don't let me discourage you then," he said. "Go ahead and print it."

"Shucks!" I growled, semi-circling an open hand through the air, "there isn't anybody who could discourage me about this! I've got too much confidence in it. So has everybody else down at the Citadel. You haven't been around lately, or you'd know that yourself."

"I been busy," he said, still looking away. "Running a chain of drug stores don't leave me much time for outside interests."

He began shuffling his papers, but I wouldn't take the hint. "I can understand that," I said, leaning forward to dump the butt of my cigarette in the ashtray. "But it's a pity you don't come around more. We need you. A man of your experience could give us all sorts of advice."

He let out a dry cackle, like a hen with the hiccups. "Don't try to fool me, Smullet," he said. "It's not my advice you want. You're after money."

I hesitated a second, wondering what tack to take. Finally I spread my hands and said, "Okay, Peavey. There's no sense my trying to beat around the bush with a man as smart as you are. The fact is, we do need a little cash. We can't go to press otherwise."

"I know it," he said, with his eyes screwed up. Then, suddenly making as if he were all sympathy, he went on, "And I'll tell you where you ought to be able to get plenty of cash for a thing like this."

"Yeah? Where?"

His yellow teeth showed in a ratty smile. "The German consul," he said, kind of low. "I understand he's got a special fund to finance papers of this sort. Kronkhite told me."

I shook my head. "We've already thought of that. In fact, Gribble had a long talk with the consul only yesterday. But we finally decided against taking that kind of money. The public wouldn't understand."

"But why tell the public?"

"That's the law now," I explained. "We'd have to register with the State Department that we're getting dough from a foreign government."

Peavey's smile vanished, and the tic in his cheek started working again. It seemed to be keeping time with his brains. Then suddenly he brightened once more. "Why not work it through a third party?" he winked. "Kronkhite, for instance. He could say the money's his personal contribution."

"Too risky," I sighed. "Besides, there's another obstacle. The consul's willing enough to give us a subsidy, but only after we've already got the paper started. In other words . . ."

"Yeah, I know," Peavey broke in nastily. "In other words, he turned you down."

"He did nothing of the sort!" I flared. "Ask Kronkhite, if you don't believe me. He was there at the time. In fact, he arranged the conference."

That seemed to stymie the cuss. His eyes shifted, and he started scratching the bristles on his chin. "Well," he finally said, "I guess you'll just have to give up the whole idea then. Because *I* can't give you the money." He looked at me kind of sore, as though I'd denied what he had just said. "No, I *can't*," he whined. "It ain't fair to ask me. Hell's bells, I bet I've contributed more than three hundred dollars to the Crusade already."

I looked him square in the smudged glasses. "And that," I said quietly, "is exactly why I expect you to give more."

"Yeah? How do you figure that?"

"Simple enough," I said, starting to light another cigarette. "You wouldn't have given a cent in the first place unless you had a good reason. A man of your caliber would know better. You must have figured it was an investment. Am I right?" He didn't answer. He just glared at me, his cheek twitching. "Well, give a little more now, and that investment may start paying off."

He seemed about to blow up, but then thought better of it. Fixing his red little peepers on my face, he finally said, "What's in your mind, Smullet?"

"That's neither here nor there," I smiled. "The important thing is what's in yours? Come on, Peavey. You can level with me. What are you after?"

He paused again, chewing at a fingernail. "Well," he spoke up at last, "there *is* something I'd like to see done. Something real concrete and practical. I've never broached it to Power because—well, I

[136]

kinda thought he might misunderstand my motive. Not that he'd object to the idea. It's right in line with his program. But I'd prefer it to come from someone else."

I nodded understandingly. "What's the idea?" I asked.

"Well, what I'd like to see us do is start a 'Buy Christian' campaign. You know—the sort of thing Father Coughlin's followers are carrying on in New York."

I leaned over and slapped the desk top. "Perfect!" I sang out. "That's just what I had in mind." I could see he doubted my word, so I went in deeper. "As a matter of fact, Gribble and I got together only last night to work out a plan. I've got it with me right now." I opened my briefcase again and started rummaging through the compartments. Then I felt in my coat pockets. "Shucks!" I finally said, "I guess I must have left it at the office."

It was hard to tell whether I'd put it over. He just looked at me, his cheek twitching. "What sort of plan was it?" he quizzed.

"Well, in a general way our idea was . . ."

"To heck with the general way!" he snapped. "Tell me exactly how you were gonna start."

"Well, sir," I plunged, thinking fast, "we figured we might start with a boycott of the Jew drugstores. What do you think of that?"

He bared his teeth in a grin of satisfaction. "Now you're talking!" he said. "How did you plan to go about it?"

"Well, to tell you the truth, Peavey, that's one of the things I came to consult you about."

He sniffed to show me he knew I was lying but didn't mind. "Okay, Smullet," he said, sitting back and giving his coat collar another quick swipe. "Here's one suggestion. How about a blast in this paper exposing the way the Jews fill prescriptions with adulterated drugs? That happens to be the truth, and I can prove it. Take that kike Gessner, who's just opened up one of his stores right across the street from here. I know for a fact . . ."

"Aw, that's all right, Peavey," I said, waving my hand. "You don't have to prove it to me." I smiled knowingly, and flicked cigarette ash on the floor. "The point is, though, could you prove it to a judge? In case of a libel suit, I mean."

"But who's gonna sue? I'm not telling you to give names in the article. The whole thing can be sort of general."

I wrinkled my brow, making like I was thinking that over. Finally I said, "We-ell, I guess maybe we could get away with that."

"No question about it!" he snapped. "So what d'you say?"

I continued to play coy. "I don't know," I said. "It's kind of risky, but—well, if there's no other way to get the money we need to start this tabloid. . . ." I finished the sentence with a gesture.

He seemed to take fright of a sudden. "Hold on a minute!" he bleated. "How much money do you expect?"

"Aw, not much. A grand, maybe." He apparently didn't understand the term. "A thousand dollars, that's all."

I thought he was going to have a heart attack. "Did you say a *thousand?*" he squeaked.

"Yeah. Of course, that'll include a nice big ad for your stores. We could run it right in the middle of that article."

He eyed me a minute, his cheek twitching like it had gone plumb haywire. Then all at once he let out a snort and turned back to his desk. "Forget it!" he said, starting to fuss with the papers in front of him. "I'm not interested any more."

"But wait a minute!" I hollered. "You can't expect to start a weekly of this type . . ."

"I said forget it!" he repeated, not even looking up.

"But be reasonable. Figure what this'll mean to your business."

"I haven't the time. Good-bye, Smullet."

I glared at his ugly profile, thinking what a pleasure it would be to give it one good poke. But then I got hold of myself. "How about seven-fifty?" I said hoarsely.

He kept on reading.

I became desperate. "Well, then, five hundred! If it isn't worth that to you . . ."

"It isn't," he rapped, still pretending to read his papers. "I'll donate two hundred, and not a penny more. Take it or leave it."

I hesitated a minute. Actually I had come with the idea that I'd be lucky to get two hundred—but that was before I'd known what this foxy little chiseler would expect for his money. So I sat there and breathed hard. Then suddenly I whined, "But what about that article? You can't ask me to write it for nothing."

"Why not?" he asked, barely turning his head. "You're getting paid by the organization, aren't you?"

"Not for work like that, I'm not."

He gave me a quick look. "All right, I'll pay you twenty dollars for the job."

I said a word that I can't print, grabbed up my briefcase, and made like I was going to walk out.

I thought he would call me back, but he didn't. I got as far as the door, opened it, and still he didn't make a sound. So at last, completely disgusted, I let go of the doorknob.

"Oh, hell," I said, returning to the desk. "You win."

21

So at last we had our house organ. We called it *The Crusader*, and brought out the initial issue early in December, 1939. It was an eight-page tabloid all broken out with scare-heads and black-faced type, and I'm not exaggerating when I say it contained some of the wildest reading matter ever published this side of the Rhine. Two whole pages were given over to the "Buy Christian" campaign, and carried not alone the piece I had written for Peavey, but also a three-column directory of various local merchants who had proved to our satisfaction—*i.e.* with a $10 donation—that they were 100% Gentile. The Power was all for ordering an edition of 10,000 copies, and so was practically everybody else at the Citadel; but I played safe and cut that number in half. However, I told the printer to be sure to keep the plates ready for a second run. It certainly looked like we were going to need it, and maybe even a third.

Doc and I took charge of the circulation. We were the only people in the organization with enough brains for the job, and besides it looked like there was going to be a lot of cash involved. First we put in an application for second-class mailing privileges, and to our surprise the Post Office said okay right off the bat. Then we announced that for $25 anybody could become a life-subscriber, and though we carefully failed to state that we meant the life of the paper, we actually got all of eleven suckers to bite. (One of them, a daffy old dame, came to the Citadel with $14 in nickels and dimes, and promised to pay the balance out of her next week's relief check.) Annual subscriptions were priced at $2 each, or $1.50 in lots of four or more, and a cash prize plus an autographed photo of The Power was offered to whoever sold the largest number during the first month. Each member was of course ordered to take at least one subscription just to keep in good standing.

But all that was merely incidental. The real dough, we felt, was going to be in the sale of single copies, so our major thought was directed at getting street distribution. Cleaver wanted us to leave that to his Rangers, and started raising the roof when he found that Doc and I had another idea. However, we had taken good care to nail the roof down tight, so he wasn't able to get very far in spite of all his heaving. Our plan was to hire a crew of youngsters to handle the street sale, high-school kids who'd be willing to work for peanuts. We'd already lined up a dozen or fifteen, most of them sons of our members, and in the end they were the ones who did get the job.

We picked a Saturday for the opening of our campaign. Doc and I got down bright and early that morning, and by ten o'clock we had the whole crew saluting and trooping off to their assigned stations. Each kid wore our red-white-and-blue armband, and carried a bundle of fifty copies in a cloth sack specially provided for that purpose. We had promised them $1 for the day, plus a cent on each copy they sold, plus also a badge of honor to the one who was the first to return for fresh stock. To make sure they'd stay on the job, we warned them we were going to make the rounds of all the corners several times during the day.

Once they were gone, Doc and I locked the door of his office and opened a couple of cans of beers. Hank was mowing the grass in the backyard, and The Power was taking his regular morning hike around Silver Lake, so we felt safe from interruption.

We must have sat there that way, smoking and drinking, for maybe three-quarters of an hour, when finally we heard the front-door bell ring. Doc made a lunge to get the beer-cans out of sight. "That's probably Long John," he said.

"It can't be," I declared, keeping my feet on top of the desk. "He always uses the back way. I bet it's one of our sales-force returning for more papers."

Doc's fat face lit up, and he started heaving himself out of his chair. "You're right," he chortled. "We better see him outside. He might smell the smoke in here."

I made a dirty sound with my lips. It always riled me that we had to act like Sunday-school kids around the Citadel. Nevertheless I followed Doc out of the room.

Hank was already hurrying through the hall, struggling to buckle on his gun as he moved. When he reached the entrance he peered out first and then swung the door wide. I had guessed right—it really was one of our boys. But the minute I looked at him I also saw that something was wrong. There was dirt all over him, and his face was bruised. In addition, he wasn't wearing his armband.

"What happened to you, Jack?" I yelled. Jack was actually his name, Jack Todd. His mother was a friend of Mrs. Gunderson's, and one of our most faithful members. She did dressmaking by the day, and had been largely responsible for running up those sacks for our sales force.

The kid limped in and looked at us like he was about to start bawling. He was a sturdy youngster with tow hair and a pug nose, but he couldn't have been more than maybe fifteen. "They ganged up on me," he said in a choked voice. "There was two of 'em, an' they jumped me. They didn't gimme a chance. . . ."

"Who's they?" I cut in, taking him by the shoulder.

"The newsboys on the corner you sent me to. They were bigger'n me, an' one of 'em looked like a nigger. You gotta believe me, Mr. Smullet. They just didn't gimme a chance. The minute I showed up, *wham*, one of 'em socked me from behind, and the next thing I knew, I was down on the sidewalk. That's the honest truth, Mr. Smullet."

I looked at Doc, and then at the kid again. "What became of the papers?" I asked.

"They dumped 'em in the storm-drain. I tried to stop 'em, but there was the two of 'em against me, an' . . ."

"Why didn't you call a cop?" Doc broke in, scowling.

"There was a cop right there when it happened," the kid answered, struggling to keep back his tears. "Honest, Mr. Gribble! He was right there, directin' traffic, an' I know he musta heard me yellin'. But he wouldn't turn around."

Hank, who was standing behind me, let out a growl. "The sunvabitch!" he said. "He musta been in wit' 'em!"

"That's what *I* think," the kid cried, giving his nose a quick wipe with the heel of a palm. "It was all fixed." He could tell we were skeptical, and his voice became shrill. "You gotta believe me!" he shouted. "They musta found out I was comin', an' laid for me."

I turned to Doc, real puzzled. "What's your opinion?" I sidemouthed.

He ran a hand through his bushy blond hair, and looked away for a second. Then he said, "Damned if I can figure it out. Maybe we ought to drive around there and take a look for ourselves."

He turned to go for his hat, and I yelled for him to bring mine too. When he came back he motioned for the youngster to follow us, and we started for the door. We had no sooner got to the stoop, though, than we heard the phone ring, and I yelled to Hank to find who it was for. A minute later he was back in the hallway, his muddy eyes popping.

"It's another one o' them kids," he announced, hoarsely. "Dick Allen. He says he's in jail!"

I rushed to get on the phone. "This is Mr. Smullet," I yelled. "What the hell's happened?"

"I'm in jail!" the voice began to babble. "Listen, Mr. Smullet, I'm in jail. They're gonna lock me up. Can you hear me, Mr. Smullet? I'm in . . ."

"Yeah, I know. You're in jail. Now take it easy, son, and tell me what you're doing there."

But all he seemed able to do was inform me over again that he was in jail.

I turned to Doc, who was at my side now. "See if you can make him out," I said, handing over the phone.

Doc had no better luck, and finally hung up. "We better run over there right away," he said to me, mopping his chins.

I gave him a startled look and then led him to one side. "Why not send a lawyer?" I said out of the corner of my mouth. "I don't like walking in on cops."

"What the hell!" he blew up. "They've got nothing on us."

"How d'you know? Maybe . . ."

He shushed me with his fat hand. "Come on!" he growled.

It wasn't far to the Police Station, but I got tied up in a traffic jam, and by the time we got there we found that young Allen had company. Two more of our kids were lined up with him in front of the high desk, one of them nursing a bloody nose. All three looked like they'd been mussed up plenty.

The desk sergeant eyed us up and down, and then down and up. I could see he belonged to the new crop of police officers that had come up with Mayor Bowron and the reform crowd. In civilian clothes I'd have cast him for a young business executive, the kind they gave the title of vice-president to instead of a $10 raise. I didn't like his looks a-tall, and I must say, from the way he acted, he didn't like ours either.

"What's the meaning of this?" he demanded with the edge of his voice. It was a sharp edge.

Doc put on a look of puzzled innocence. "That's exactly what we came here to find out, sir," he answered in his butteriest voice.

The sergeant, though, seemed to see through him, and there was a sort of duel between them that lasted ten minutes at least. Then finally we got the story. Our boys, it appeared, had been arrested for disorderly conduct. Brawling with nice, gentle, law-abiding newsies. No, there couldn't be any doubt about their guilt. In all three cases it was they who had picked the fights, not the newsies. That's why they alone had been hauled in. The sergeant was an absolute mule on that point.

It was an awful session. Before this Johnny Law was through he had Doc sweating through his clothes. Me, I could have been poured down a drainpipe. It wouldn't have been so bad if the sergeant had blustered, but instead he kept his voice low and hard, and never stopped looking at us like we were dirt under his feet. Finally, though, he seemed to tire of expressing his opinions, and told the lot of us to get the hell out of there.

"But remember," he warned as we made for the door, "don't let it happen again. This isn't Berlin. Or Yorkville, either."

When we reached the sidewalk, Doc drew himself up and told the kids to go on home. "Don't worry, men!" he said, furling his blond brows. "We know who's back of this, and we're not going to let 'em get away with it!"

They stalled a second, like they were worrying about something quite different. It was probably the dollar we had promised each of them for the day's work, because one started to say as much. But Doc pretended not to understand. Raising his right arm in the Ranger salute, he mumbled something about getting in touch with them later on, and then turned on his heel so fast you could almost smell burning rubber.

I followed him straight to the nearest bar. It wasn't noon yet, but we ordered rye and took it neat. My drink hit me harder than a runaway truck.

"Well, Doc," I said, when my shakes finally quieted a little, "what do you make of it?"

He took the handkerchief out of his breast pocket and started wiping the cold sweat from his face. "It beats me," he admitted. "All I can see is that it's organized. Somebody must have found out about our plans and got to the cops.

"Yeah, but who?"

He shrugged his big shoulders, and looked off into space. Finally he turned and signalled the barkeep to hit us again.

I took my second drink slower and tried to think. "Wonder if it could be the man o' war?" I said after a pause. "You know how sore he was because we wouldn't let his Rangers do the peddling."

Doc shook his head. "Not a chance," he said. "That isn't the way Cleaver would operate."

"How do you know?" I started to argue. "Don't forget he's got lots of friends on the police force. I've heard him claim that Clynes is one of his best pals." I was referring to the cop who'd formerly headed the local Red Squad.

"Yeah, but that was in the good old days," Doc replied. "Red Clynes is out somewhere in the sticks now, driving a prowl car. So are most of the other johns of the old school. Cleaver wouldn't be able to get to first base with the type that's running the P. D. now."

I mulled that over and decided Doc was probably right. "But if it wasn't Cleaver," I said, "who the hell could it have been?"

My buddy shrugged his shoulders again, and stared into the mirror behind the bar. I could see, though, that he was thinking, not just looking at himself. Finally I came up with another suggestion. "How about the Hollywood Anti-Nazi League that used to go after us all the time?"

"No," he answered right away. "That outfit's practically folded up since Stalin got into bed with Hitler. It never was anything but a Communist front."

"Well then, what about that other organization, the Jew one that works on the quiet?"

"The Anti-Defamation Committee?" he asked. "Yeah, that's more like it. But I doubt whether those Hebes have enough drag down at the City Hall." He leaned both elbows on the bar to take some of the weight off his behind, which was way too big for the stool. Then he started looking in the mirror again, a heavy frown on his face. "I'll tell you the best bet," he piped up after a pause.

"Yeah? Who?"

"That reverend we keep hearing about. You know—Loring Keniston. I'll just lay a bet he's back of this whole thing."

I weighed the suggestion, and decided it really was the best yet. We had never been able to find out much about this Reverend Keniston. Even the Bund, which had spies in practically every anti-fascist setup, seemed unable to keep track of his activities. All we knew definitely was that he had quit the Unitarian Church, and was running something he called the Citizens' Research Service from an office downtown. Kronkhite had pointed him out to me once. The guy was sitting on the platform at one of those protest meetings against us, and I must say he didn't look anything like what I'd imagined. He was tall and dark, with bright eyes and a shock of curly black hair, and he had a way of laughing like he found life a hell of a lot of fun. Nevertheless we had ample reason for believing he was a plumb fanatic on the subject of Fascism. He seemed to be mixed up in every local effort to put a crimp in organizations like ours.

So I looked at Doc and said, "Come to think of it, he really could be the guy."

He nodded and got down from the stool. "Maybe I'd better phone to see if anything's happened to the other boys," he said.

I started to go with him to the wall phone in the rear of the saloon, but noticed the men's room on the way, and decided to duck in there first. When I came out, Doc was just hanging up, and I didn't need to ask what he'd heard. His face was the color of stale suet, and sweat was rolling down his jowls. "They're all back," he muttered in a hoarse voice. "Every damn one of them. We better beat it over to the Citadel right away."

I started to follow him out of the door when I heard a yell from the bartender.

"Ain't you forgot somethin', gents?" he asked.

I turned, stared, and suddenly got the point. "Sorry," I said, throwing a dollar bill on the bar.

"No harm done," he sighed, ringing the register. "Come again, gents."

22

That evening the Supreme Council met in a special session, and believe me, we got it good and proper. Cleaver tore into us like he meant to nail our hides to the wall, and for once he had the majority on his side. They all jumped on Doc and me, and I'm here to tell you we got one hell of a beating.

We didn't take it lying down, of course. Doc got so indignant he almost blew a gut, and I yelled plenty too. But in addition to outnumbering us, they had all the arguments, so we didn't stand a chance. No matter how we big-mouthed, we couldn't hide the fact that we'd made a mess of things. Eight of the kids we'd sent out got a mauling, three more were chased up alleys, and one just disappeared. Of the 700 copies of the *Crusader* with which they started out, they sold exactly eight. Anyway, they didn't bring back the money for more than eight.

So Cleaver had Doc and me over a barrel, and I want to tell you, he tried to make the most of it. His aim, of course, was to get us out of the High Command, or at least get himself in, and for a while it looked as though he might succeed. He probably would have, if it hadn't been for The Power.

I ought to explain, if I haven't already, that J. C. didn't like Cleaver. He claimed he objected to the latter's "lack of character," by which he meant that the bum was always getting liquored and using foul language. Right from the start, though, I sensed that the hostility was based on something deeper. I had an idea that fundamentally The Power was leery of Cleaver's intentions, suspecting that he was maybe trying to get control of the movement. I remember reading an article once in the *Reader's Digest,* or some such magazine, which told how all through history there's been a rivalry between the Man of the Word and the Man of the Sword—in other words, the priest and the prince. At the bottom I think that was exactly the situation here.

Be that as it may, the fact remains that The Power did definitely distrust the soldier-man, with the result that Doc and I were saved. At first His Nibs just sat there, arms folded and eyes on the chandelier, like it was beneath him even to notice what was going on. That was the way he usually sat at the Council meetings, aloof and mum, as if he meant for us to realize that he considered all our jawing a waste of time. On this particular occasion he may have had an extra reason for playing dead. I suspect he enjoyed seeing us get a good going-over. Finally, though, he came to life. Clearing his throat with a sound like a small landslide, he unfolded his arms and got up from his chair.

"Anything else on your mind?" he asked, staring at Cleaver. "Because if there isn't, we'll adjourn."

Just like that!

The suddenness of it left the ape positively gasping. His big, ugly mouth fell open, and his eyes bugged. After a second, though, he seemed to recall that he had a tongue in his head. "Heh, wait a minute!" he made it say. "What about taking some action?"

"I don't see any need!" J. C. barked. Then, shifting his eyes to Doc and me, he said, "But from now on you'd better let the Rangers handle the street sales."

So that was that. Two days later our tabloid was back on the streets, and this time it stayed on them. Cleaver picked half a dozen of his toughest babies for the sales crew, and they proved handsomely able to take care of themselves. They were real plug-uglies, and wore Sam Browne belts and Ranger caps, thus giving the impression that they were all Legionnaires. In addition, they worked in pairs, with the result that no one seemed to want to try and get rough with them.

But though there were no brawls or arrests, there was plenty of yammering. Practically every Hebe in town started wringing his hands and yelling "Oy-oy!" You'd have thought we were massacring them, the way they carried on. The Power, I might add incidentally, had an idea they'd go further and try violence. He got Cleaver to rig up a machine gun ready for action in a closet off the hallway, and stocked enough munitions in his own room to stand off a small army. In addition he made Hank buy the groceries in a different store every day, for fear of poison, and kept telling him to examine all incoming packages to see if they had bombs in them. Doc and I thought these precautions were plumb silly, but the rest of the gang took them very seriously. They seemed unable to realize that the Hebes were too smart to play into our hands by going Chicago on us.

But, as I have said, there really was a terrific amount of yammering. Moreover—and this certainly surprised me—it didn't come solely from the Hebes. Any number of Gentile groups attacked us, and even the American Legion gave us a blast. In fact, the only civic organization that seemed willing to stand up for us—this will give you a laugh!—was some radical outfit called the American Civil Liberties Union.

The climax came when the Reverend Loring Keniston and his mysterious Citizens' Research Service hired the Shrine Auditorium for a monster mass meeting against us. I attended that meeting personally, and I must say I got a tremendous kick out of it. There were enough big shots on the platform to make you think it was a benefit for the Community Chest or the Disabled War Veterans. The list of speakers included not alone the Mayor and a couple of judges, but also Eddie Cantor, Miriam Hopkins, Fredric March, Dorothy Parker and Melvyn Douglas. I came away from that show feeling so chesty I could barely breathe. I calculated there must have been at least a million dollars' worth of talent denouncing my little sheet, and I couldn't help saying to myself, "Clem Smullet, you really are somebody!"

Quite a crowd of our people attended that night, and most of them had the same reaction. Some of them, in fact, got so hopped up that they accepted Kronkhite's invitation and adjourned to the German House for a beer-bust that lasted way into the morning. There were, of course, some exceptions. Mrs. Gunderson, for instance, seemed quite upset about us and our paper. She phoned me the next day to say she hadn't been able to sleep all night, she'd been so upset. But the following Sunday she heard The Power explain how all those stars had had their speeches written for them by their Jew employers, and then she naturally didn't feel so bad.

On the whole, though, and in the long run, the yammering didn't do us any good. Not any *real* good, I mean. True enough, it did swell our Sunday night crowds temporarily; but the swelling was like what you get with dropsy. The newcomers seemed to be nothing but bums. Doc and I could tell that by the increase in the number of buttons and phone slugs in the collection plates. And the sale of our tabloid, after one short spurt, started slumping something awful. By the end of January we were failing to sell a thousand copies a week on the streets, and this in spite of the fact that we had hawkers all over town.

I couldn't figure that out at all. Our rag was getting more publicity in and around Los Angeles than *Life, Liberty,* and the *Satevepost* combined. Hardly a day passed but what there was some public blast against it. To be sure, that was all we got, just blasts; but I didn't see why that should make any difference. Wasn't it one of the first principles of the science of advertising that every knock's a boost? As old C. C. Pyle used to say: "I don't give a damn what they print about me, so long as they spell my name right!" But here was a case where the effect wasn't in any way according to Pyle.

So, as I have said, I couldn't figure it out at all. God knows the sheet was sensational enough. I had jazzed it up till it was practically nothing but cartoons and scareheads, and I allowed J. C. to say things in it that astonished even the Heinies. The krauthead who ran the Aryan Book Shop over at the German House told me himself that the *Crusader* was about the hottest publication on his racks. Nevertheless the damned thing wouldn't sell.

So there was trouble. It came to a head at the meeting of the Supreme Council late in February, 1940. As usual, Peavey was absent, and also old Mrs. Krutch, who was sick or something. Kronkhite too was absent.* But Cleaver was present, and all tanked up, so there just had to be a fight.

"Lookit here!" he started bellowing the minute The Power called the meeting to order. "We gotta do something about them boys of mine. Goddamit, they're not making enough to pay for the shoe leather they're wearing out!"

Doc wiggled himself upright in his armchair and put on a sympathetic look. "We all know that, Doug," he remarked sadly. "But it's the way I've said before. You've already made us give them fifty percent of what they take in, and we just can't go any further than that."

"Like hell we can't!" Cleaver snarled. "I say we gotta put 'em on the payroll. Christ knows, they deserve it!"

"Sure they do," Doc agreed, still keeping his voice on a vaseline base. "And if we could afford it, I'd be the first to favor the move. But the fact is, we're losing money on the paper even now."

I was about to back up that statement, but noticed the gleam in Cleaver's eyes and decided to stay mum. He looked like he was really on the warpath. "Goddamit!" he roared, "that's no argument! We can't leave those men to starve!"

"Aw, come on now!" Doc sort of laughed. "They're not starving, and you know it, Doug. Every one of them is getting relief money. And that's another reason why we can't pay them regular wages. They'd be dropped from the W.P.A. rolls."

"Not unless we told on them, they wouldn't!" the patriot came back, still roaring. "Anyway, that's beside the point. I can't go on asking 'em to work the way they're doing for nothing. Goddamit, they're my boys, and they expect me . . ."

"But wait a minute . . ."

"Wait nothing!" Cleaver hollered, lowering his head like he meant to butt Doc in the stomach. "I notice you took goddam good

* *We understood at the time that Kronkhite had gone East to attend a convention of the insurance company he worked for. Actually, as came out later, he was in Mexico on some mysterious mission.*

[150]

care to put yourself on the payroll. Fifty bucks a week! And the same for Smarty-pants over here. Yes, sir, I don't see you guys working on any percentage basis." He switched his bloodshot eyes to me. "Do I, Smarty-pants?"

I didn't answer. If he was that blind, why should I set him straight? I just sat back in my big plush chair and looked up at the ceiling.

Doc leaned forward to draw Cleaver's fire back to himself. "Let's stick to the subject, Doug," he said. "We haven't got the funds to pay those Rangers, and that's all there is to it. Do you know what we've got altogether in the treasury right now?"

"No, I don't. But I bet it's not as much as there ought to be."

Doc's eyebrows furled. "Just what do you mean by that crack?" he asked in a new kind of tone.

"You know well enough what I mean!" Cleaver sneered. "So does Mabel here. Don't you, sister?" The dame turned red, and shifted her bulging eyes. "Scared, eh?" Cleaver jeered at her. "Behind their backs you're a regular hell-cat, but now . . ."

Suddenly J. C. stirred. It was the first move he'd made thus far. He'd just sat there in his straight chair, arms akimbo as usual, and eyes on the lion in the oil-painting over the mantelpiece. But now he jerked his head around to glare at Cleaver. "Shut up!" he barked.

The Captain reacted like he'd been hit with a horseshoe. His head reeled and he sort of puffed. After a second, though, he seemed to recover himself and began to return J. C.'s glare. "What did you say?" he snarled.

"You heard me!" the other shot back. "I said shut up! You've been drinking!"

Cleaver stuck out his jaw. It needed a shave, and the bristles twitched like mice were running around under the skin. "Supposin' I have?" he yelled. "Goddamit, you'd be a hell of a lot more human if you took a drink yourself once in a while!" He suddenly began to leer at The Power. "Yeah, an' if you got a good loving, too! The trouble with you is . . ."

All at once The Power was on his feet. "Get out!" he thundered, pointing to the door. "Get out before I kick you out, you *bum!*"

I wanted to whoop. So did Doc, judging by the look on his face.

We'd been hoping for months that something like this would happen.

Cleaver's mug had turned green. He hadn't moved, but only because he was plumb paralyzed. The Power didn't move either. He just stood there, a regular pillar of wrath, his long finger still pointing at the door. Mabel Haight chewed at her nails like she'd forgotten all about being a vegetarian, and even Doc seemed nervous. There was silence for maybe ten seconds, and then the drunk seemed to sag. He opened his mouth, ran the tongue over his lips, wiped the five sandy hairs spanning his dome, and then made an effort to grin.

"Aw, hold on a minute, J. C.," he started to crawl. "There's no need . . ."

"*Get out!*"

The roar was so loud, I could have sworn it made the chandelier shake. Cleaver gave a jump, and the sick smile on his mug literally fell apart. He turned green again, and his eyes started darting this way and that. He was almost twice J. C.'s weight, and could have picked him up and broken him like a broomstick. Nevertheless he just sat there and cringed. For a minute he struggled to raise his eyes; but it was no go. He tried a second time, but again he failed. So finally, letting out a sort of grunt, he heaved himself to his feet, and started to slink out.

He didn't walk. He slunk. He was almost at the door before he was able to straighten his shoulders. Then he turned and looked at The Power as if he still hoped there might be a chance to come back. But the glare he got seemed to melt him to water.

"Aw, f——!" he said, and lurched out.

23

The next day not a single Ranger showed up on the streets. There were at least twenty who had stocks of that week's *Crusader* on hand, but only two had the decency even to turn them in. However, Doc and I didn't mind. On the contrary, we were delighted. Right away we rushed to The Power with the news, and he took it just the way we had hoped. He was shaving at the time, and had lather all over his face and head. One of his hands held the strop taut while the other moved the old-fashioned razor up and down in a way that gave me the creeps.

"I expected that," he said between his teeth. "I always knew Cleaver was a traitor at heart." He let go of the strop, and waved the razor at us. "I wouldn't be surprised if he's been in the pay of the Jews from the start!"

Later that day we got him to call Mabel Haight to a conference, and before the week was out we had a totally new kind of crew to peddle our tabloid. It was the largest crew yet—there were thirty in it, including the reserves—and each and every one of them willing to work for nothing! That was Doc's inspiration. He talked Mabel into ordering the Amazons to undertake the job of hawking the *Crusader*, and they obeyed as though we were doing them a favor. Most of those bags were on relief anyway, so they didn't really need to be paid.

The Citadel sounded like we were having a rummage sale the day we mustered that crew for its first assault on the town. Most of the recruits were middle-aged housewives, frowzy dames in butt-sprung coats, and worn shoes that showed the shape of their bunions. They were so excited and jabbered so loud that they had Mabel Haight running around like a chicken with her alimony cut off. Even Doc couldn't make them pipe down. Finally, though, The Power appeared on the scene, and that put an end to the ruckus. He had evidently been showering himself, again, for he was wearing his long Turkish-towel robe, and was dripping wet.

"What's the meaning of this?" he roared from the landing at the head of the stairs. "This is my Citadel, not a fish market!"

Instantly there was quiet in the hallway. The women took one look at his eyes, and backed away like they'd been scorched. I watched the effect, and couldn't help marveling. It was no wonder, I thought, that everybody was willing to call him The Power. There he stood in that sopping wet robe, his long hairy legs making a puddle, yet I swear he couldn't have inspired more awe if he'd been a swami dressed in full regalia. He was *the* Power all right.

Well, after that things went more smoothly. In fact, it wasn't more than three-quarters of an hour before the last of those dames was assigned her corner and given her carfare and bundle of papers. And thereupon, leaving Mabel to hold the fort, Doc and I went off to make the rounds of the stations.

First, though, we stopped in at the Pearl Dive. It was a little out of our way, but both of us were kind of broke, and we thought Chuck still had some space left for us on his cuff. From the way he acted when we showed up, the space couldn't have been as big as Texas. Still and all, he didn't turn us away. We sat at the bar and ordered bourbon straight.

It was a typical February day in Los Angeles, which means the mist was chilly enough to make you think you were in San Francisco. Between that and our nervous exhaustion we had to down three apiece before we felt equal to going on about our business. Then we climbed back into the car and started downtown. Doc was at the wheel, so he gave me the list of corners where our hens had been told to set. Miriam had typed it out the day before, and there were pencilled notations in Mabel Haight's handwriting giving the names of the women at the different stations.

"Let's cut over to Seventh Street," I suggested. "We've got 'em strung out there all the way from Figueroa down."

He nodded and stepped on the gas. He was a creepy driver ordinarily, but with a few drinks in him he thought he was Barney Oldfield. That, I will admit, was the only way he did show his liquor, but I often wished he'd been able to hit on a safer one. By the time we neared Seventh and Figueroa my feet were halfway through the floorboards, I'd pressed so hard on the brakes that weren't there.

"Take it easy, Doc," I yelled, "This is where we're supposed to start looking. Pull over to the outside lane."

He couldn't, on account of the traffic, and furthermore the light was green. He had to drive right past the corner. According to the list, a Mrs. Tillie Gall should have been there, and I tried to spot her as we swept by. I knew what she looked like. She was a tall, rawboned mare who'd formerly worked in the County Hospital, but had been fired because, according to her story, some Jew on the medical staff had caught her slipping our leaflets to patients. She was big enough to be lamped in any crowd, especially if she was displaying the tabloid according to instructions. But I couldn't see her anywhere.

"Let's turn back," I said to Doc.

We had to go around the block to do it, and when we reached the corner this time the light was red. That gave both of us a chance to look, and we craned around till we pretty near dislocated our collar bones. Nevertheless we failed to see hide nor hair of the woman.

"Think we ought to stop and try to find out what's happened to her?" Doc asked.

"No, let's go on," I advised. "According to this list my old land-lady's supposed to be at the corner of Olive, and we can ask her. . . . That is," I added, "if she's still there."

He could tell by my voice what I was thinking, and tried to make light of it. "Hell, there's nothing to worry about!" he snorted. "Nobody would try any rough stuff with women."

I didn't say anything. I reached for a fresh cigarette, lit it on the butt of the last one, and puffed hard. Then, nearing the corner of Olive, I leaned forward to look ahead. I thought I made out a small crowd there on the sidewalk, not right on the corner, but about fifty feet this side of it. Then, getting closer, I was sure I could see Mrs. Gunderson in the middle of the crowd. Two young fellows were standing on either side of her and shouting something. The rest of the people seemed to be grinning.

"Pull up," I yelled to Doc, starting to open the door. Before I could get out, though, she came rushing toward me.

"Oh, thank God, it's you, Clem!" she cried, struggling with the handle of the rear door. "Don't stop! Just take me away from here!"

I caught her before she could collapse, and bundled her into the rear compartment. Half her papers slid into the gutter, and the rest fell on the floor of the car.

"What's the matter, Ma?" I yelled as I got in at her side. "If those apes have been bothering you, I'll kick the teeth down their throats!" I meant it, too, though they looked twice my size.

"No, no, don't stop!" she cried, hammering Doc's shoulder. "Drive on, *please*, Mr. Gribble!"

She sounded so frantic that he didn't try to argue. We saw a woman shake a fist at us and yell, "Go back to Germany, you dirty

Nazis!" She was wearing a fur coat, but didn't look a bit Jewish. Doc shot the gears into low and started off with a lurch that almost threw us from the seat.

I put my arm around the old lady and held her tight. She was trembling something awful. "What happened, Ma?" I asked her. "What did they do to you?"

She couldn't answer at first. She just lay there with her head on my shoulder, and shook like she was going to fall apart. Finally she got hold of herself and sat up. She started hunting for her pocket-book, found it on the floor, and took out a piece of Kleenex.

"Oh, Clem, it was just wicked!" she said, wiping her eyes. "I thought I'd never live through it!"

"But what did they do?" I repeated. "Those bastards didn't try to hurt you, did they?"

I was too wrought up to notice my language, and so was she. Anyway, she didn't bawl me out for using the bad word. She started straightening her old hat, which had fallen to one side, and pulled down her skirts. Then at last, still trembling, she came out with her story.

It seems that almost the minute she got to her station and opened up her bundle of papers, the newsie on the corner came up and told her to beat it. He looked like a Mexican, she said, and she tried not to pay any attention to him at first. That was what we had told all our women to do: just stand their ground and refuse to get into any arguments. But then this newsie started talking rough, so she moved away from the corner to the entrance of the department store halfway up the block. He followed her, though and a crowd began to collect. There were jeers, and someone yelled "She ought to be arrested!"

Then all at once those two young fellows appeared out of no where, pushed through to her side, and said, "Don't worry, ma'am We'll protect you." She started to thank them, because she though they were going to chase the newsie away, but instead she dis covered they meant for her to go. They actually took her by th arms and started leading her off. "But I don't want to go," she tol them. "I have a right to stand here." So then they said, "All right ma'am, if that's the way you feel about it," and suddenly turne on the newsie. "Why don't you leave her alone?" they yelled. "I she wants to spread Hitler's propaganda, let her go ahead. This is a free country, isn't it?" That, of course, made the newsie laugh. The whole crowd started to laugh, and the poor woman thought she would die of shame.

Nevertheless she stuck it out. She was a game one, that old girl! In spite of everything, she just wouldn't go away. But neither would those two wise guys. A cop came by and ordered them and the rest of the people to move on. A minute later, though, they were back again, and giving her the same horse laugh. Every time anyone came up to look at the tabloid, they would make cracks about its being printed in Germany and so forth. She wasn't able to sell a single copy.

Finally the cop showed up again, but this time he walked right by. She ran after him and cried, "Please, Officer, drive these boys away!" At first he pretended not to hear, but when she caught his sleeve, he wheeled around and asked, "Whatsa matter, lady?" She told him, still hanging onto his sleeve. "They won't let me sell my papers! They keep shouting that I'm working for Hitler!" So then he bent his head down to look at the tabloid, examined the cartoon on the front page, and growled, "Well, ain't you?" And with that he turned and walked away.

How she managed to stick it out after that I can't imagine, but the fact remains that she did. She stuck it out until finally her poor old legs seemed about to give way under her. And then, just in time, Doc and I arrived.

"I swear, Clem," she wound up, "if you'd been a minute later, I'd have fainted."

My own car was parked behind the Citadel, so we drove back there, and then I took Mrs. Gunderson straight home. I could see she was in pretty bad shape. She didn't seem able to stop trembling, and the tears kept flowing down her cheeks. When we finally reached her house, I had to practically carry her up the stairs.

I wanted to call a doctor, but she wouldn't hear of it. "I'll be all right, Clem," she said, when I got her to her room. I could see, though, that she wouldn't be all right unless she had someone to help her undress, so I went next door and asked the woman there if she'd kindly come and give a hand. She was a Mrs. Newmark, and might have been Jewish, because she was dark and plump and had a New York accent; but nevertheless she didn't hesitate a second. She got Mrs. Gunderson into a flannel nightie, tucked her in bed with a hot-water bag, made her a cup of strong tea, and promised to stick around till the masseuse who lived in the first-floor front came home from work. Seeing there was nothing more I could do, I left.

I knew I ought to return to the Citadel, and actually got into my car with that in mind. When I reached the corner of Vine and Hollywood, however, I decided I needed a drink, and drove into the parking lot next to the Plaza Hotel. I ordered an old-fashioned, and slipped out to the phone booth while the bartender was getting it ready.

Doc answered when I got my number. "Where in hell are you?" he yapped.

I told him, and then asked how things were going.

"Awful!" he groaned. "Just awful! Half the women are back already, and the rest seem to be on the way."

"But why?" I began to ask, though I didn't really need to. "Is it the same business . . . ?"

"Exactly," he cut in. "They're all being razzed the way your Mrs. Gunderson was. The whole goddam thing seems to be organized. . . ." I listened to him fume for a while, and then asked what he thought we ought to do about it. "Damned if I know!" he said in a voice that sounded like he was ready to cut his throat. "I guess maybe we'll just have to quit trying to sell the paper on the streets. . . ."

I finally hung up and hurried back to the cocktail lounge. I really needed that drink now—but bad. My stool was occupied, but I saw the old-fashioned standing on the bar untouched. I reached in to grab it, hitting the elbow of the man who had taken my place. He turned to glower at me, but then gave a second look and suddenly started to grin.

"Well, if it ain't Clem Smullet!" he cried in a barker's voice. "What the hell are you doing in these parts?"

I looked at him, kind of puzzled. He was a short fat man with a heavy Irish face all filigreed with fine blue veins. He was wearing a loud plaid suit and a broad-brimmed Stetson hat, and had a

Shriner's pin in his lapel, a huge elk's tooth dangling from his watch-chain, and a diamond ring on his hand. Suddenly I remembered who he was. "I'll be a dirty name!" I yelled. "Sam Mulligan!"

We started pumping each other's arms, and then he turned to take up his beer. "Let's find some place to sit down," he said, climbing off his perch. "Christ, I bet it's all of ten years since the last time I seen you!"

I started counting on my fingers as we pushed our way to an empty table across the lounge. "No, six," I corrected him. "Remember? It was back in '34."

"That's right," he said, as he shoe-horned himself into the tiny booth. "Cincinnati, wasn't it?" He got himself set, and began to chuckle reminiscently. "Say, that sure was a raw deal you pulled on old Kipling! Christ, if you hadn't scrammed in time, I bet he'd have had you thrown in the can!"

I took a swallow of my old-fashioned and grinned. "Aw, it wasn't that bad!" I said. "And anyway, that old crook had it coming to him."

We fell to talking over the incident, which hadn't amounted to much, really. I'd been the advance man for Colonel Kipling's International Super Carnival Show, and finally got a little too careless with the palm-grease. Mulligan, though, seemed to think I'd got away with a fortune. I didn't bother to set him right. Instead I switched the conversation by asking what he'd been up to since then, and learnt he was still in the carnival game, only now he had a show of his own. That's how he happened to be passing through L.A. at the moment. He had just brought his outfit across from Texas, and was working his way up the Coast. From the way he talked he was apparently doing right well.

Then he asked me what I was doing, and I told him. I tried to make it sound big, of course, and I'd probably have gotten away with it if the talk I'd just had with Doc hadn't left me so blue. Feeling the way I did, though, Mulligan caught on right away. "Whatsa matter, Clem?" he said, giving me the old gimlet-eye. "Don't this racket pay off?"

"Aw, it isn't that," I said.

"Then what is it?"

I fished the slice of orange out of my glass and nibbled at it a minute. "Well, it's this way," I finally said, dumping the peel in the ashtray. "I just can't get any fun out of what I'm doing. You see, Sam—it's one thing to skin people who know you're out to skin 'em. Like in the shell game, for instance, or the greengoods racket. It's a real battle of wits then, and there's a kick in it. But these crackpots I have to deal with—hell, they take it for granted I'm on the level! Skinning 'em is just like stealing candy from a kid that's crippled and—and blind to boot. See what I mean?"

Mulligan seemed skeptical. "That don't sound like you, Clem," he laughed. "You talk like you've worked up a conscience, an' I know better'n that." He turned to call the waiter, and ordered a second round. Then, leering at me again, he said, "Come on now, Clem. On the level. What's the real drawback to this racket?"

"I've told you," I insisted. "What I can't stand, goddam it, is the fact that it's not supposed to be a racket at all! It's a Cause!"

He must have seen I was really sincere, because he dropped his leer at last. "Well, if that's the situation," he said, "why don't you quit?"

"And do what?" I growled. "Join the navy, maybe?"

"Hell, there's any number of things you could do!" he answered. "What about coming back into the carnival game?"

I made a sour face. "No future in it," I snapped. "Besides, I don't know of an opening."

"I do," he said, kind of off-hand.

"Yeah? Who with?"

"Me," he answered. He smiled at my look of surprise. "That's straight. As a matter of fact, one of the reasons I'm laying over in this town is to pick up a new press agent. I understand Hollywood's lousy with 'em."

"Not with good ones," I came back real quick.

"No? Well, I wouldn't know about that." He paused to let the waiter set down the drinks, and reached for the check. "Forget it," he said, seeing me make a show of fumbling for my wallet. "You'd probably put it on the expense account anyway." He grinned and handed the waiter a dollar bill. "Well," he went on after we'd sipped at our drinks, "what do you say? Want to take the job?"

I didn't really, but I saw no harm in finding out what it would pay. When he said fifty a week, I was surer than ever that I didn't want it. Even after he offered to include the upkeep on my car, I still turned thumbs down. I knew what press-agenting for a carnival involved—eating in greasy truck-driver joints, sleeping in lousy tourist camps, arguing day after day with hick mayors and printers and cops. Besides, there was the question of prestige. After the sort of jobs I'd held, how would it sound for me to go back to plugging for a crummy little gilly show?

"Nah, it's out of the question!" I finally told him.

"Suit yourself," he shrugged, starting to crawl out of the booth. "But if you change your mind, Clem, gimme a buzz. I'll be stopping here till Monday—unless I pick up somebody before then."

"Thanks all the same," I said, shaking his hand.

"Well, glad I bunked into you anyway, Clem."

"Same here, Sam."

I watched him walk out of the lounge, and then moved to the bar. "Gimme a shot of bourbon," I told the bartender.

Somehow my running into Mulligan had left me feeling worse than ever. I decided to get drunk.

24

I didn't unglue my eyes the next morning until almost eleven o'clock, and then I shut them again right away. My head ached something awful, and my mouth tasted like I'd been sucking a motorman's mitt all night long. It was Saturday, and I remembered I was due at the Citadel to parcel out the handbills. Nevertheless I just lay there.

Even when the phone started to ring I still wouldn't stir. I figured it must be Doc, or Hank, and simply pulled the covers over my ears. After a while, though, I thought the sound would drive me nuts, so I started to get up. By the time I crawled out of bed, however, it was too late. The girl at the hotel switchboard said the party had just hung up. So I rammed the receiver with a wallop that pretty near tore the phone from the wall, and began making breakfast. This consisted of coffee brewed on the electric ring in the bathroom, and two stale crullers. I had to drink the coffee black because I'd forgotten to get a fresh can of condensed milk, and the crullers tasted like they'd been dug up in the La Brea pits. The general effect, though, was beneficial. By the time I finished downing the bilge I was sufficiently braced to consider going out.

It was a lovely day, real springlike, and I decided to take a ride to the beach. I had a lot of thinking to do, and I figured a snootful of ozone might help clear my head. So I walked to the garage around the corner, climbed into my car, waved away the attendant who wanted to start jawing again about the bill I owed, and drove off.

As I have said, it was a lovely day, and when I got to Santa Monica I was sorry I hadn't brought my trunks along. Not that I'd have gone into the water. Only a nut like The Power would have been equal to that so early in the year. But I'd certainly have enjoyed taking a sunbath. It was almost hot on the sand.

After a little while, though, the fog started rolling in, and the next thing I knew, I was all goose pimples. So I got up, brushed the sand from my pants, and went to sit in my car. I fiddled with the radio till I caught a sweet dance band, tuned it low, and then tried to concentrate once more on the problem in my mind.

I hardly need to tell you what that problem was. I was trying to decide whether I should grab Sam Mulligan's offer, or take a chance and stay with the Crusade. I slumped down behind the wheel, tipped my hat over my eyes, and thought and thought and thought. But I made no more progress than a worm in a bait-can. I tuned the music lower, tried another program, then switched the radio off altogether. Nothing seemed to help, though.

Finally I came to the conclusion maybe I'd have better luck if I began driving again. There was very little traffic on the coast road, especially toward Malibu way, so I started off in that direction. I drove slowly, barely ambling along, because I wanted to have nothing on my mind except that problem. Even the trucks were able to pass me up, I drove so slowly. And the nice easy motion did appear to help somewhat. I got the feeling that if I'd keep going just a little longer, say another five minutes, ten at the utmost, I'd have the problem completely solved. So I kept going.

But then all of a sudden I swerved off the paving and rammed the foot brake. Something about a station-wagon parked on the other side of the road had hooked into my mind like a thorn, and made me stop. I turned to squint out of the rear window, and then backed up to get a better view. That was her car all right! It was a Chrysler station-wagon, and her old man's initials, J.Q.C., were right there on the door-panel.

I scratched my head, deeply puzzled. Miriam had phoned only yesterday to say she was sick in bed with a cold, and here . . . I scratched my head some more, wondering whether I ought to get out and investigate. I wasn't worried. Just intrigued, that's all. Somehow I had the feeling that our sweet little virgin had driven out here for reasons that were maybe more sufficient than good. "You know what?" I said out loud. "I'll lay a bet she's alley-catting!"

The station-wagon stood in front of a cottage that looked like an ideal hide-out. It was a shacky wooden affair, painted dark red, and built on two levels from the road to the beach below. The upper floor seemed to consist solely of a garage, and was connected with the lower one by a flight of outside stairs. I looked at it a minute, suddenly getting sore. "The dirty little tramp!" I thought to myself. "She won't let me even get near her, and here all the while . . ." I shut off the engine with a snap that almost broke the key, and got out of the car. Then, waiting for a couple of trucks to pass, I tore across the highway.

First I stuck my head into the station-wagon to take a peek at the registration slip. It said exactly what I had expected. So then I went over to the mailbox in front of the cottage, and looked for a name. Finding none, I put my hand inside to see if there were any letters. Stumped again, I turned to the garage, which was open and had a car in it. Walking on tiptoe to keep from being heard below, I stuck my head into the tonneau to see what that registration slip had to say. There wasn't enough light, however, and I had to strike a match. Then I gave a jump that made my skull go crack against the steering wheel.

The name on the slip was Loring C. Keniston!

I sagged to the running-board, the lighted match still in my hand. I didn't realize it was there till it scorched my fingers, and then I dropped it with a yelp and began to stamp it out. I stamped so hard I made the whole building shake. Whereupon, realizing I had given myself away, I beat it out of the garage—but fast.

I was barely able to get across the road in time. In fact, I was still closing the door of my car when I saw a man come running up the steps alongside the cottage. I ducked and then raised my head just high enough to take a gander at him through the side window. It was Keniston, all right. He was wearing a white turtle-neck sweater and corduroy pants, and looked more like a playboy than a clergyman. Nevertheless I recognized him instantly. I ducked again and waited till I heard his sandals go slip-slopping back down the steps. Then, letting the car roll a few yards, I pressed the starter and made a U-turn so that I could park behind a jacked-up trailer alongside a neighboring cottage. I wasn't more than maybe fifty yards from the station-wagon now, and yet pretty well hidden, so I shut off the motor and prepared to wait.

I didn't have to wait long. In about two minutes, there he was coming up the steps again. He had a pipe in his mouth, and stopped to knock out the ashes when he got to the top of the bank. For a second I thought he noticed that my car had moved, but I decided it must be my imagination, because he turned right away and waved to someone below. "Okay!" I heard him shout.

And then I saw her. Up to that minute I had still hoped it might be someone else, perhaps her old man, or some other member of her family. But now I knew. She was wearing dark glasses, but I recognized her figure, and also the briefcase under her arm. It was the one in which she always carried the work she did for us at home.

I hunched down behind the wheel and watched. Something passed between them, and she turned and seemed to look in my direction. Then I saw Keniston open the door of the station-wagon, help her in, and wave as she drove off.

I inched up, released the hand-brake, and waited for the man to go indoors. I figured it would be too suspicious if I started out after her while he was still watching. But instead of turning away, he began walking toward me! There was no mistaking what was in his mind. He was looking straight in my direction. For a minute I sat absolutely paralyzed, and then I kicked at the starter. My only thought now was to get going. I was ready to run him down if he tried to stand in my way. But the damned engine wouldn't turn over. I kicked the starter again and again, but still got no result. "Kurryst!" I swore, staring at the dashboard in a panic. And then I suddenly realized what was wrong. I had forgotten to switch on the ignition!

It was too late to do anything about it. Keniston was already at my side, and turning the door handle.

"What's the hurry, Mr. Smullet?" he drawled, smiling at me in a way I didn't like at all.

I hesitated a second, and then struggled to register surprise. "I don't get you!" I said. "You must have me mixed up with someone else. My name's Sm—Smith."

"Oh, no, it isn't!" he came right back, opening the door. "I know who you are. Miss Cabot recognized your car."

I looked at him and then suddenly kicked again at the starter. But he was too fast for me. Reaching in, he pulled the hand-brake and grabbed my arm. "Come along, old man," he said, still smiling. "Now that you're here, we might as well have a little talk. Let's go into the house."

I could see there was no sense trying to argue. He was big enough to pick me up and carry me in. Locking the ignition, I climbed out of the car and started walking. My legs felt like rubber.

He made me go ahead of him down the steps, and then bowed me through a door into what must have been the living-room. I noticed an enormous window facing the sea, a log fire, and a lot of books.

"Sit down," he said, pointing to one of the chairs in front of the hearth.

I hesitated a second, but then obeyed. He sounded almost friendly, and I figured even if it was an act there was nothing to be gained by being stubborn. Besides, my pins were so wobbly, I was glad to sit down.

He turned to throw a fresh log on the fire, fooled for a while with the poker, and finally sank to the couch opposite me. "Ciga-rette?" he asked, opening a box that stood on the low table between us. It was a silver box, I noticed, and had a large crest on the lid. Everything else in the room, though, looked kind of junky, especially the books. There must have been at least a thousand of them lining the walls, but no two seemed to match.

He held out a lighter, waited for me to get a good draw, and then started filling his pipe. "Well, Smullet," he said, flicking the lighter again, "what made you think of trailing Miss Cabot out here?" He paused to draw on his pipe, his eyes narrowed. "Or did you just happen to drive by and notice her station-wagon outside?"

I didn't answer, but my face must have given me away.

"So that was it!" he began to laugh. "Sheer coincidence, eh? Well, I suppose you would have had to find out sooner or later." He picked up a little gadget on the coffee table and began tamping the tobacco in his pipe. "I'm sorry, though," he went on. "Now I'll have to plant someone else in your organization."

"You mean," I couldn't help croaking, "you mean she's been working for you all along?"

"Certainly," he smiled. "And very effectively, I don't mind telling you. But don't worry. I'll be able to replace her soon enough." He leaned back and puffed smoke at the ceiling as if trying to think whom to pick, but then suddenly brought his eyes back to me. They were large dark eyes and had a glint in them now. "That is," he added casually, "unless the FBI decides it's got enough on you people already."

I caught the cigarette before it could fall from my lips. "The FBI?" I echoed.

"Yes, of course," he answered, raising his brows. "You don't mean to tell me that's a surprise to you? After all, you know how the FBI cracked down on the Christian Mobilizers in New York last month. Arrested seventeen of them. Well, I presume your crowd comes next."

"But why?" I tried to yell. Actually, what I let out must have sounded more like a squeak. "We've done nothing against the law!"

He reached for the lighter and set fresh fire to his pipe. His movements were very slow and deliberate, as if he was enjoying my panic. At last he sat back and said, "Haven't you? What about

[166]

those guns you've been buying, and all those plans for an insurrection?"

Suddenly I was able to breathe again. I even managed to twist my lips into a sort of smile. "Shucks!" I snorted. "You know who was responsible for all those things! It was Captain Cleaver! And he's out of our organization now!"

"Not for long," Keniston answered. "Oh, I know all about that quarrel he had with Power, but that's going to be patched up any day now. As a matter of fact, Cleaver's trying to do that right this minute." He turned his head to look at the clock on the mantelpiece. "No, in five minutes," he corrected himself. "They have an appointment to meet at the German House at three-thirty. Kronkhite arranged it."

"Kronkhite?"

"That's right."

I thought for a second, and then started to grin. "Nh-nh!" I said. "That's where you slipped up, Reverend! I happen to know that Kronkhite's out of town." I waited for him to go to pieces, but he didn't. "That's a fact!" I hollered. "He left for the East ten days ago."

Keniston's lips parted in a gentle smile. "No, he didn't," he said. "Actually Kronkhite went to Mexico City. He was sent to . . . But never mind that. The point is, he returned the night before last. Cleaver got in touch with him yesterday afternoon. I can tell you the exact hour, if you're interested."

I stared, all numb inside.

"So you see?" he continued, still smiling. "I know a good deal more than you do about what's going on. As a matter of fact, Smullet, you know practically nothing. You think you're smart, but the truth is, you've been just a sucker. That's why I wanted to talk to you." He leaned forward and pointed the stem of his pipe at me. "Smullet," he said, frowning hard, "you're being *used!*"

I felt myself lick my lips. "I—I don't get it," I stammered. "Who the heck's using me?"

"The Nazis, of course! They're using you to confuse and demoralize this country. You couldn't be serving them better if you were actually on their payroll."

[167]

I pushed a sneer to my lips. "Aw, that's the bunk," I said, though kind of shakily.

He didn't appear to like that. His black brows came together in a heavy scowl, and I drew back, expecting a blast. It didn't come, though. Instead, he let his breath out in a long sigh and said, "Listen, Smullet. Let me try to explain."

I swung my hand through the air to flick the cigarette ash into the fireplace, and nodded. I was less scared now. I could feel I wasn't even trembling. Somehow the tables had been turned, and here he was doing the explaining, not me. So I settled back in my chair and said, "Sure. Go ahead."

He did. He started talking my ear off about how the Nazis were conspiring to spread their ideas all over the world, and how organizations like the Crusade were playing into their hands. He referred to Goebbels and Viereck, and somebody named Colonel Fleischauer, and talked of Trojan Horses and Fifth Columns and so forth. I sat and listened. I didn't try to argue with him. I figured it was wiser not to, and besides I wasn't really interested. I didn't know then what I know now, so I imagined he was talking pure bushwah.

Finally he must have caught on to my attitude, and gave up. "I'm not making any impression on you, am I?" he asked.

"I wouldn't say that, Reverend," I lied. "I just think you've got this whole thing out of focus. What the heck d'you think our Crusade amounts to anyway? Why, it's nothing but"—I paused and flashed a grin—"just a tempest in a crackpot."

That was an old flip-quip of mine, but I pulled it as though I'd just made it up. All it got out of him, though, was a scowl. "This is no matter for wise-cracking," he said. "I know well enough that your little racket doesn't amount to much. But neither does one plague-rat."

"Aw, be reasonable," I pleaded. "What's so wicked about the Crusade? Come right down to it, the worst it's doing is raise a little hell with the Jews. That's no skin off your nose, Reverend, is it?"

I thought he'd jump down my throat. "You fool!" he snapped.

"Jeez!" I gasped, suddenly afraid I'd pulled a real boner. "Are you a . . . ?"

"No, of course I'm not a Jew!" he cut me off. "That's not why

[168]

I called you a fool. It's because you don't seem to realize that raising a little hell with the Jews is the surest way of raising a lot of hell with everything that keeps a country decent. It's a smokescreen to cover an attack on the basic principles of civilization. No, don't shake your head. I'm not talking theory. This whole thing has been proved in practice. Look at Germany. The Nazis started by attacking the Jews there, and ended by enslaving the entire population. And they're trying to work the same trick over here. Isn't that so?" He waited for me to answer, but I merely stared. "They may get away with it, too. All they need is enough cranks like Power, and agents like Kronkhite, and ruffians like Cleaver, and—and petty crooks like you to help them."

I gave a jump, and struggled to put on a glare. "That's an insult!" I burst out. "You've got no right to call me a crook!"

Suddenly he began to laugh. It was a gay laugh, almost like a boy's. "Relax, old man," he cried. "You're evidently not as bad as I thought. I was afraid you weren't even capable of being insulted."

I looked at him, not quite sure how to take that. The remark should have made me all the sorer, but it didn't somehow. I suppose it was because of the grin on his handsome puss. There was something almost affectionate about it. I paused a minute, trying to think of a squelcher, but failed. So finally I said, "Is zat so?"

He put out his hand and opened the silver box. "Here," he said, still grinning, "take another cigarette and let's try again."

I pretended not to want to smoke. "What's there to try?" I asked sulkily.

He knocked out his pipe, refilled it carefully, and got it going once more. "Well," he said between puffs, "I'd like to come to some understanding with you."

"About what?"

"About this work you're doing," he answered. "It isn't worthy of you, Smullet."

I could see he really meant that, and it made me feel almost warm inside. I was glad he seemed to recognize that I really was above what I was doing. Nevertheless I didn't say anything.

"You've got ability, man," he went on. "You shouldn't be wasting it on a filthy little racket of this sort. Because, honestly now, that's all it is to you, isn't it? Just a racket."

"Aw, I wouldn't say that," I stalled.

He smiled knowingly. "Of course you wouldn't *say* it. But you think it. Don't you?"

"All right," I granted, "supposing I do?"

"Then why don't you quit?"

"Because I like to eat," I came right back. "Don't you, Reverend?"

He winced, but managed to keep his voice calm. "Yes," he said, recrossing his legs, "I'm human. But it seems to me I'd find it easier to starve than earn my bread the way you're doing now."

"Maybe so," I shrugged. "But don't forget, you're supposed to have ideals. After all, you're a preacher. Me? I'm just a press agent."

"That's an evasion," he answered sharply. "You're an American, aren't you?"

"Sure. But what's that got to do with it?"

He started to shake his head. "Haven't I made that clear?" he sighed.

"Not yet you haven't."

"Very well," he said, running a hand across his eyes. "Let me make another attempt."

"Aw, save your breath," I snorted. "I know that what I'm doing is pretty lousy—stealing nickels and dimes from those poor boobs who flock around Power. But the fact remains that I've got to live. If you want me to quit this job, you've got to offer me a better one. See what I mean? Maybe you think that's a mercenary attitude to take, but what the heck! This is a mercenary world, Reverend." I could see he wanted to object, but I wouldn't let him. "There's no use arguing," I said. "Just get me a better job, that's all."

"In other words," he said, eyeing me gravely, "you want me to buy you off."

"Sure. That's kind of a coarse way to put it, but I don't mind. Here's the proposition. You get some Jewish producer to fix it so that my name's taken off the studio blacklist, and I'll quit the Crusade tomorrow." I fished a cigarette out of the silver box and worked the lighter. "That ought to be easy enough," I went on, puffing nervously. "The way you've been sticking up for those people, they ought to be tickled to death to do you a favor. Come right down to it, it'd really be a favor to themselves. Because I'm not exactly a help to them, working for the Crusade. No, sir. The fact is, I'm doing them plenty of dirt—and I can do lots more, if I want to. You bet your sweet life I can. There's some things I can do . . ."

All at once I felt my throat go dry, and I stopped talking. It was because of the look on Keniston's face. His upper lip was drawn back tight against his white teeth, and there was a sort of curdled sneer in his half-closed eyes. "Go on," he said quietly.

"What for?" I faltered, wetting my lips. "You got the point."

"Yes, I got it all right," he answered, spacing his words. "What you want me to do, Smullet—correct me if I'm wrong—what you want me to do is blackmail Hollywood into forgetting that you were fired for blackmail."

I jumped to the edge of my chair and let out a bleat. "That's a lie!" I bleated. "If you're referring to what happened over at Warner's, I'm telling you it's a lowdown lie. So help me God, Reverend, all I did . . ."

But he wouldn't listen. Suddenly he was on his feet and looking at me like I might be a worm or something. "Listen, Smullet," he said, struggling so hard to keep his voice low that he pretty near choked. "The only reason I asked you in here was because Miss Cabot felt sorry for you. She insisted you weren't really vicious. Just pathetic, that's all. So she wanted me to try to straighten you out. She thought I could save you before the FBI closed in. Well, she was wrong. I wouldn't want to save you now even if I could." He strode to the door and held it wide open. "That's all," he said, standing there with his long arms limp. "You'd better go now."

I stared at him, completely dazed. "But wait a minute," I started to yammer. "Gimme a chance to explain. All I meant . . ."

"I know exactly what you meant!" he cut me off. "That's why I'm telling you to leave." He jerked his head toward the door. "Go on. Get out!"

I did get out. Don't ask me how. I must have walked, but what gave me the strength I can't imagine. All I know is that all of a sudden I found myself in my car again, and driving like the rear end was on fire. Scared? Christ, I was so scared I shook worse than the old wreck I was driving! There were seams of tar across the paving, and the way they sounded under my tires, they seemed to keep clicking, "F-B-I—F-B-I—F-B-I . . ."

I didn't take my foot off the throttle till I reached the mouth of Santa Monica Canyon, and then I pulled up in front of one of the big hot-dog stands there. "Got a phone?" I yelled to the fat dame behind the counter.

She pointed to a corner in the rear, next to a door marked, "Gents." The sign suddenly reminded me there was something else I needed to do, and bad—but I grabbed the phone anyway. "Get me the Plaza Hotel in Hollywood!" I barked into the mouthpiece.

It seemed to take hours before the operator finally made the connection, and then I dropped three nickels into the box. "Hello?" I yelled. "Plaza Hotel?—Gimme Mr. Mulligan's room. And make it snappy. I'm talking long-distance. . . . Yeah, Sam Mulligan. . . ."

25

We'll have to skip the next year and a half, because this book is supposed to tell about the Crusade, not me, and I was completely out of the movement during all that period. I was chasing around the country, desperately trying to get out from behind the eight-ball, and becoming more convinced every day that I really was what Keniston had called me—to wit, a sucker. Because, as I eventually discovered, that noble-talking Holy Joe had actually played me for one—but good. All his gab about the FBI had apparently been nothing but bluff. The Crusade continued to carry on without the least interference on the part of the law, and what's more, before long it was on the upgrade again. And moving fast, too.

You remember Doc Gribble's crack about a rat that deserts a ship that doesn't sink? Well, the way things turned out, that seemed to be exactly what I had allowed myself to become. Only I proved thereby that I wasn't even a rat. I was a mouse.

The net result was a year and a half of pure hell for me. What I mean is, I really suffered. Take for instance that job with Sam Mulligan—it proved to be something awful. He sweated me worse than a nigger, and at the same time kept griping that I wasn't earning my pay. How I stuck it out as long as I did—pretty near six months—I still don't know, nor why he suddenly turned around and fired me. All I do know is that one day I found myself ditched in a little burg in Northern Montana with hardly enough cash to buy gas to the next town.

Luckily there was a Silver Shirt organizer stopping at the same hotel, and with his help I managed to land another berth before long. It was with a local goat-gland quack who was running for Congress in the elections that fall, and my duties included everything from writing his radio scripts to chauffeuring his mother-in-law. Still and all I didn't kick, for the job not alone kept me in eats, but even enabled me to catch up on some of the delinquent payments on my Auburn. However, came the first Tuesday after the first Monday in November, and my baby-kisser was of course left holding the diapers—he was a Republican—so there I was, out in the cold once more.

Well, that's the way it went throughout the rest of those eighteen months. In all, I must have tried a dozen different jobs, but not a one of them panned out right. By May of 1941 I was forced to part with my car, and by August I had to hock my typewriter. I was in Chicago at the time, having hitchhiked all the way from Cheyenne, Wyoming, and I finally got so strapped there that I couldn't afford to stay even in the Y.M.C.A. So then I decided I might as well quit trying to buck Fate. Swallowing my pride, I sent Doc an airmail letter asking for the fare back to L.A.

He was at the depot when I got off the train five days later, looking fatter and more prosperous than ever. It was all I could do to keep from breaking down at the way he behaved. I had expected that he'd greet me with an I-told-you-so look, and act patronizing or maybe even get sore. Instead he fell on me like I was a long-lost brother. "Christ, it's good to have you back!" he hollered, pounding me all over. "I sure have missed you, Clem!"

I was too choked up to answer, so I pretended to rest my suitcase on the ground.

"Here!" he yelled, craning around. "Let's get a redcap to carry that!"

"No," I managed to mumble. "It isn't heavy. Anyway, I'm kind of out of the habit of using redcaps."

He flashed his dimples at the sheepish look on my face. "Had a tough time of it, eh?" he remarked. "Well, I guess we all make mistakes." Then, giving my arm a squeeze, he turned and started for the exit. "You wait here, and I'll go get my car," he said when we reached the sidewalk. "It'll save you toting the valise all the way to the parking lot."

He was back in a couple of minutes, but not in the dinky little old Chevy I remembered from former days. Now he was driving a shiny new Buick sedan with white sidewall tires and giant bumpers.

"How d'you like it?" he smirked as I got in at his side. "Pretty snazzy, eh?"

"I'll tell the world! What the hell you been doing, Doc? Robbing banks?"

He winked and nudged me with his fat elbow. "Nah!" he guffawed. "Just saving the country, that's all!" He threw in the clutch and pulled away from the curb. "Yeah, that was a great mistake on your part, Clem," he said, "leaving town when you did. You should have had more faith in this racket." He broke off to attend to the traffic, and then added, "but I guess you know that now."

"Yeah," I admitted, staring out of the window. "I was just a goddam fool."

He took a hand off the wheel and patted my knee. The big Masonic ring, I noticed, looked like it had a real diamond in it now. "Well," he said, kind of consolingly, "no use grieving, kid. As I said before, we all make mistakes." He smiled and suddenly changed the subject. "How about food? Or did you eat before you got off the train?"

"No, the diner was too crowded," I lied. "I guess I could do with a bite of supper. But I'd like to clean up first. A guy gets awful sticky, riding all that distance in a day coach."

He nodded and began to turn a corner. "Okay," he said, "we'll go straight to the hotel then."

"You mean the old Senate?"

"Sure. I've been living there ever since you left. But I've got a suite, so you can be my guest until you get yourself settled. Come to think of it, we might have our supper right there. I can order it up while you're taking a bath." He turned his head around and grinned. "That suit your Royal Highness?"

"And how!" I answered, struggling to keep my voice steady. Then, after a pause, I cleared my throat and added, "I don't mind telling you, Doc, I really—well, I do appreciate the way you're acting. You're a real pal, Doc. What I mean . . ."

"Aw, forget it!" he said, patting my knee again.

Doc's suite didn't amount to much, just two dinky rooms crowded with old slip-covered furniture, and a bath built into what must once have been part of the outside corridor. The lace curtains looked like they hadn't been laundered in years, and the faded wallpaper was practically all smears. However, after some of the mouse-holes I'd been forced to bunk in during the past year and a half, the place looked a regular palace to me.

The food came up while I was still in the tub, so I hopped to it wearing nothing but a bathrobe. I was so hungry I didn't even mind that the liver tasted like it had been vulcanized, and the mashed potatoes were soggy and cold. The pie too was pretty gruesome, but I ate Doc's portion as well as my own—he suddenly remembered he was on a diet—and then I finished off what was left of the butter and rolls. Finally, there being nothing more to eat, I flopped in an easy chair and loosened the rope around my middle. "Jeez," I sighed, "I sure feel good now!"

Doc got out some rye and a couple of glasses, and sank into the chair opposite me. "I bet this'll make you feel even better," he said, starting to pour me a drink.

It did. In fact, in a little while I was feeling so damned much better that I was all for getting dolled up and going out somewhere. "Tell you what!" I suggested. "Let's drive around to that house on Highland Avenue, and see if those two redheads are still there!"

"No, some other time," Doc said. "We've got business to attend to tonight."

"Can't it wait till tomorrow?" I whined.

"No, we've got to act fast. You'd like to get back into the Crusade, wouldn't you?"

[175]

"Naturally. That's the only reason I returned." I wasn't lying about that. I'd learnt enough during the past eighteen months to convince me that the organization really did have a future. I'd found others of a like nature cropping up everywhere, and apparently coining money.

"Well, then," Doc said, "you'll have to get busy right away. There have been a lot of changes around here since you left."

I looked at him, kind of worried by his tone. "What kind of changes?" I asked, lighting a cigarette.

He fidgeted around in his big chair. It evidently had a broken spring in the seat, like mine did. "Well," he came out after a couple of seconds, "for one thing, Cleaver's with us again. In fact, he's in the High Command now."

A gust of smoke got stuck in my windpipe, and I thought I'd choke. "Wow, that's not so good!" I finally managed to say. "Why in hell did you take him back?"

"Aw, it's a long story." He sat up to pour himself a fresh drink, and then, taking a gulp, wiped his mouth. "You see," he began, "it was like this . . ."

26

And then Doc started telling me what had transpired while I was away. At first, it seems, the Crusade had kept going from bad to worse. Doc made no bones about that. In fact, he went so far as to admit that a couple of months after I ducked out, it all but folded up. Partly that was due to my old friend, Reverend Keniston. The holy so-and-so started a regular blitzkrieg against the organization, going after every member he could contact, and trying to scare the b'jesus out of them the way he had out of me. Of course, he didn't always succeed. In fact, some of them reacted the other way round. The real fanatics got hopping mad, and became more loyal to the Cause than ever. They took their cue from The Power, who started to yell that he'd like nothing better than to be arrested. On one occasion he actually got a gang to march right down with him to the local FBI office and *demand* that he be arrested.

Nevertheless the movement suffered. Before long there was practically nothing left of the Outer Circle, and very little of the Inner one. The Sunday night crowds became so slim that the collections hardly covered the cost of the announcements, let alone the hall rent. It finally got so bad, Doc said, that even he began to consider pulling out.

But then, just when there appeared to be absolutely no hope left, the entire situation changed. Some of the old members started shuffling back, new ones joined up, and the revenues began to grow again. By the end of July—I'm still talking of 1940—there was enough money coming in for Doc to start drawing his regular pay once more. By mid-September he was even able to collect some of his back pay. "It was just like a miracle," he told me. "All at once we were rolling again. And I mean *rolling!*"

I looked at him, puzzled. "How do you account for it?" I asked. "Did you hit on a new approach, or something?"

"Nah, we didn't have to do a thing," he answered, grinning smugly. "It was Hitler who did it all. He'd started knocking over countries the way Al Capone used to knock over beer joints. Norway, Holland, Belgium, France—remember how he blitzed 'em one after the other? Well, that's what gave us our fresh start. We'd been for Adolf from the outset, and now that he was riding high, we naturally rode right along with him." Doc started to take up his glass, but saw it was empty, and reached for the bottle with the other hand. "Y'see," he went on, pouring himself a good three jiggers, "it was like what happened the previous fall, only in reverse. Remember how we lost out when Hitler made his deal with Stalin? Well, now he won on that deal, so we cashed in. In fact, we're still cashing in."

I watched him add a little water to his drink and take a couple of sips. "And d'you mean to tell me that's all there was to it?" I asked, still frowning.

"Absolutely," he said, resting the glass on the arm of his chair. "Of course, I'm not saying all the people who're coming to us are out-and-out pro-Hitler. Most of them, I guess, don't give a damn about him either way. What draws them is the fact that they know we're fighting the anti-Hitlerites who're trying to get us into the war. What's more, we're fighting 'em with our gloves off. We're sort of the vanguard of the America Firsters around here." He went on to tell me how the Crusade had managed to tie in with those big-shot isolationists. The Power was actually making speeches for them in the outlying districts, and he'd been put on the reception committee when Lindy was in town. "Long John's really going places now," Doc laughed. "Wait till you see how he's changed. He's gained ten pounds and allows his clothes to be pressed once in a while."

"Good Lord!" I said. "Don't tell me he's getting house-broke!"

Doc waved his hand. "Not a chance," he snorted. "Basically he's as wild as ever. Maybe even wilder. You should have heard him during the election campaign last fall. Boy, he really outdid himself then!" Doc paused to take another swallow, and then set the glass down on the floor at the side of his chair. There was a reminiscent smile in his eyes. "Yes, sir," he continued, "he sure was good then. I'll never forget the speech he made the Sunday after F.D.R. was nominated for a third term. The way he cut loose, it was a wonder to me the cops didn't stop the meeting. He kept calling him Mr. Rosenfelt, and swore he was part-Jew on both his mother and his father's side. And Eleanor, he said, was not alone part-Jew by blood but all-Jew by religion. He claimed there was actually a synagogue in the White House basement."

I let out a cackle. "That's one I never heard before," I admitted.

"Wait," said Doc, grinning from ear to ear, "you ain't heard nothing yet. He went on to tell the crowd there was documentary evidence that F.D.R. had taken an oath in that synagogue way back in 1936 to make war on Hitler. Yes, sir. The oath was signed in ritual blood prepared by the Elders of Zion!"

"'I'll be damned!" I cried. "And did the crowd swallow that too?"

"Aw, sure. They just lapped it up. And when I got to my feet after he was through, and announced we were raising a special fund to keep Roosevelt from being re-elected, how much d'you think we collected?" I shook my head. "Over two hundred bucks!" he gloated.

I suddenly felt sick inside. "That's just like my luck!" I groaned

"If I hadn't been such a sap . . ." I left the sentence unfinished, because all at once I thought of something else. "Say, where was Keniston all this while?" I asked.

"Aw, he was around."

"Didn't he try to gum the works?"

Doc nodded. "But it wasn't so easy for him any more," he explained. "He had too many other organizations to go after now, especially the America First Committee. And besides, he no longer had that Cabot girl to tip him off on what we were doing."

"But wasn't he able to plant someone else in her place?" I asked.

"Not so far as I know. I guess he tried hard enough. As a matter of fact, I think he's still trying. But he hasn't succeeded." A worried look darted across Doc's face. "At least," he said, half to himself, "I *hope* he hasn't."

I looked up sharply. I had the feeling he was holding something back. "What's the matter?" I asked. "You're not doing anything now that he could get you on, are you?"

"No, of course not!" Doc answered, but with more heat than seemed called for. "What the hell gave you that idea?"

"Aw, nothing," I said quickly. "I was just asking, that's all."

He continued to scowl for a second, but then seemed to decide to let the matter drop. "Where the devil are those matches?" he suddenly asked.

I threw him the pack—it had fallen under the table—and he lit a fresh cigarette. Then, taking a deep draw, he settled back again in his chair, and went on with his story. The Crusade, he said, continued to boom all through the election campaign. Several people with dough began to interest themselves in the movement, and though they wouldn't actually join, they did come through with small contributions. On the q.t., of course. One of them—I think it was Mrs. Louise Ford Fry—even offered to buy some radio time for The Power. But it was on condition that he'd come out for Willkie, and he absolutely refused to do that. He'd become convinced that Willkie was just another tool of the Jews.

"Too bad," I broke in. "You might have been able to pick up some heavy cush if he'd been more reasonable."

"You said it," Doc agreed. "But you know how stubborn that

crazy lug can get." He fell silent a minute, evidently brooding on the lost opportunity. Then, taking another gulp of his liquor, he returned to his tale.

There was naturally a let-down once the campaign was over. A lot of the new members decided there was nothing more to do once Roosevelt was re-elected, and they started dropping out. Even The Power seemed to lose heart temporarily. The morning after the election he stamped out of the Citadel and didn't show up again for four days.

"What happened to him?" I asked. "He didn't go off on a drunk, did he?"

Doc snickered and said no. Apparently the nut just wandered away somewhere. How he managed to live is a mystery, because so far as anyone knew, he left without a cent on him. He didn't take his overcoat, either. The result was that when he finally returned, he was not alone half-starved, but also running a fever. He'd evidently slept out in the open, and caught a terrible cold. He had to stay in bed for over a week, and wasn't able to do any speaking for almost a month.

"Who ran the meetings meanwhile?" I asked.

"I did," Doc answered. "With the help of Kronkhite, of course. He got us a string of guest speakers, and some of them were pretty good, too. That Heinie seems to have an awful lot of connections. And he's a hell of a hard worker." There was a second's pause and I noticed the little eyes get shifty. "That's why I finally agreed to let him into the High Command."

I gave a sudden start. "You mean Kronkhite's in it too now?" I yelped.

"Sure. Didn't I mention that?"

He knew darn well he hadn't, and I began to wonder how much more bad news he was going to come out with before he was through. All I said though was, "Jeez, that must make it kind of tough on you!"

"Yeah, in a way it does," he admitted, running a hand through his hair. "But Kronkhite's not so bad. He doesn't draw any pay, and he's a great help. It's really through him that we got our angel."

"Did you say an *angel*?" I cried.

Doc beamed. "That's right," he answered. "We've hooked a guy that seems made of dough. He came through with four hundred smackers just last month alone.

I let out a whistle. "Now I begin to understand," I said. "Criminy! With that on top of everything else, Doc, you must be cleaning up."

"Aw, I'm getting by," he smirked.

"I'll bet you are! Say, what sort of goof is this angel? Another Heinie?"

"Nah. His name's Flanahan. Francis X. Flanahan. He comes from New York originally."

"Oh, so he's that type," I said, curling my lip. "A left-hander, eh?"

"Yeah, but what's the difference? I've no objection to taking money from a Catholic. And this one's got plenty. I understand he's worth four or five million."

My sneer gave way to a look of awe. "How much did you say?"

"You heard me! Four or five million! What's more, he says he's ready to spend half of it to get rid of Roosevelt. He figures that's the only way he can be sure of keeping the other half."

"He must be nuts!" I said.

"I'm not so sure," Doc answered, knitting his brows. "If Roosevelt ever gets us into this war, the first thing he'll do is start conscripting all the wealth. Anyway, that's what Flanahan says. He claims he got the dope straight from someone on the Military Affairs Committee in Washington."

"I still think he's nuts. Neither Roosevelt nor anyone else can get us into the war. The public won't stand for it. You should hear how they talk in the Middle West. They'll start a revolution before they'll let our boys be sent overseas."

Doc nodded agreement. "That's what Flanahan's counting on," he said. "As a matter of fact, that's why he's backing us. He figures the Crusade is paving the way for the revolution right here on the Coast. Cleaver sold him the idea."

Suddenly I felt all the joy leak out of me. "Oh," I said, "has Cleaver got next to this guy too?"

"Yeah. As a matter of fact, he's closer to him than I am. He's known him longer. I have an idea Kronkhite brought them together last winter, just before he started his own organization."

Now I was completely balled up. "Wait a minute," I said. "Who started what organization?"

"Cleaver. I guess you didn't know he was in competition with us for a while. He started an outfit called the True Crusade."

"And you took him back even after that?" I cried. "You must have been crazy!"

"Yeah, like a fox," Doc snapped. "Don't worry. I knew what I was doing." He frowned and started rubbing his solar plexus. He'd already done that several times since supper. Suddenly he growled, "Guess I'd better take some bicarb," and got up to go to the bathroom.

I slumped in my chair, trying to think, but then reached for the bottle and poured myself another drink. I felt I needed it. I was absolutely convinced now that Doc wasn't leveling with me.

He was back in a couple of minutes, belching lavishly and looking relieved. "Let's see, where was I?" he asked as he sank into his chair again. "Oh, yeah, I was telling you about Cleaver. Well, to make a long story short . . ."

But somehow he didn't seem able to make it short. He kept wandering off and losing the thread of the story. The gist of what he had to say was as follows: Cleaver had launched his own movement about six months after he'd had that run-in with The Power. It was an entirely militant movement built around the Rangers who'd followed him out of the Crusade, and at first it had had its headquarters right in the German House. Cleaver's idea seems to have been to create an auxiliary for the Bund made up of 100% native Americans; but for one reason or another that didn't pan out. I guess it was too hard to get real Yanks to associate with those Heinies. Anyway, it wasn't long before Cleaver set up headquarters of his own, and though he continued to drill his men in Hindenburg Park, he claimed he no longer had any direct affiliation with the Bundists.

He must have got next to Flanahan by that time, because he seemed to have plenty of money to work with. He was able to equip his men with uniforms, and blow them to beer and pretzels after every meeting. He organized a fife-and-drum corps, paying the musicians full union rates, and arranged fancy drills with plenty of hoop-la all over the county.

Nevertheless he was still unable to make much progress. At the peak, it seems, he didn't have more than maybe a couple of hundred followers. So then one day Kronkhite came around to Doc with a proposition. He claimed he could get Flanahan to back the Crusade —if Cleaver was included in the bargain. It was kind of a package-deal.

"What would you have done?" Doc appealed to me when he got to that point in his story. "Could you have turned him down?"

I was forced to shake my head.

"So there you are," he said, spreading his hands. "I went to work on Long John, talked him into giving the bum another chance, and that's all there was to it."

I looked at him for a minute. I still had the feeling he was holding something back. Finally I asked, "How's it worked out?"

"Aw, swell," he answered, but just a shade too quickly. He must have read my face, because he scowled and added, "That's straight, Clem. Things have worked out fine. I mean that."

"Like hell you do," I came out bluntly. "Look, Doc, you're not fooling me. Why don't you break down and tell me what's bothering you?"

He paused like he was debating in his mind whether to stall any longer, but then suddenly found he had to bring up some more gas. That seemed to decide the issue, because once he got the belch out, he relaxed and began to smile. "Okay, Clem," he sighed, "I guess there's no use trying to kid a guy like you. The fact is, those lugs are getting to be kind of a problem now. I have an idea they're ganging up on me."

"So that's it?" I said, wagging my head.

"Yeah. I wouldn't be surprised if they're trying to crowd me out of the front seat." He drew himself tense to give another belch, and then sagged. "That's why I wired you that money right away. I need you around here, Clem. If I'd known where the hell you were, I'd have sent for you a month ago."

I sat up and smiled cheerily. "Well, I'm here now, pal," I sang out. "Once I'm back in the High Command . . ." I broke off, frightened by the look in Doc's little eyes. "Say, I *can* get back, can't I?"

"That's the question," he said, rubbing his forehead. "Cleaver's dead against it, of course. I've already sounded him out on the subject. And Kronkhite seems to feel the same way."

"So what?" I cried. "J. C.'s for me, isn't he? And after all, he's the one who has the say."

"Yeah, that's true enough. But as you know, he can be influenced. Those guys have sold him on the idea that you're not entirely reliable."

I can't quote what I said to that, but it was something very pithy about the real character of those two apes. Then, realizing that was beside the point, I went on, "But you can unsell him, can't you, Doc? After all, you've still got more influence with him than anyone else."

He pressed his lips together, and thought for a second. "I'm not so sure," he admitted at last. "Flanahan seems to have the inside track at the moment. That's why I wanted you to meet him right away. If you could make a good impression on him . . ."

I wouldn't let Doc go any further. "Where is he?" I interrupted. "Just let me get at him, and there'll be nothing more to worry about. I've always craved a chance to charm a multimillionaire. Especially a goofy one."

"Well, you're gonna get it right this evening," said Doc. He looked at his wristwatch and gave a jump. "Say, we better get a move on. I told him we'd be at his place by eight-thirty."

27

Doc pulled up in front of a small apartment-house on Eighth Street, not far from the Ambassador. It was one of those Spanishy stucco affairs, all broken out with fake stone-work, cast-iron grills, and faded awnings. A couple of sick-looking cement lions were stretched out on either side of the entrance, and there was a sign on the door reading VACANCY.

"This it?" I asked, like I thought there must be some mistake.

Doc nodded and started heaving himself out of the car. I followed him into the dinky hallway, and watched him press a button under a mail-slot that had no name on it. "Say," I side-mouthed, "this doesn't look to me like the sort of joint a multimillionaire would want to live in!"

"It's just his hide-out," Doc explained. "I understand he's got a regular palace down in Mexico. That's where he has all his silver mines."

I had no chance to ask anything more, because the electric door-latch was clicking. Doc led the way up a flight of steps, and knocked on the door of a rear apartment. "Who is it?" a man's voice called out. Doc answered, and I heard a bolt being drawn.

We were let in by a small, dark, youngish-looking guy, and when Doc introduced him as Mr. Flanahan, I thought I'd drop. I'd imagined I was going to meet someone built along the lines of a retired saloon-keeper, with a big beefy mug, and a 'Tent' Avenoo accent. Instead this bird looked more like he might be a snappy little college professor. He talked like one, too.

He showed us into the living room, and asked us to sit down. The furniture was typical apartment-house junk, all velour and fringe and big brass nails, but I hardly noticed that or anything else because of what was hanging on one of the rough-plastered walls. It was a big wooden crucifix, and the facial expression of the Christ on it was too awful for words. You could all but hear the figure screaming in agony. I turned to look at Flanahan, wondering what was wrong with him. It seemed to me a guy would have to be cracked to want to have a thing like that staring at him all the time.

Yet he didn't look cracked. He was evidently a little on the serious side, with a heavy furrow between his black brows, and a brooding look in his dark hollow eyes; but otherwise he seemed completely normal. He was about my size, and couldn't have been much over forty, I guessed. He had neat features, a high narrow dome, and very small ears set tight against his skull. His suit was gray, and looked like it had just been pressed. His tie, pocket-handkerchief, and socks were likewise gray, and must have come in a set. The only thing that didn't match was his shoes, which were brown suede and slightly faded. There was a knot, I noticed, in one of the laces.

He didn't offer us a drink or even a cigarette. The minute we were seated, he perched himself opposite me and started firing questions. He wanted to know exactly why I had walked out on the Crusade, and precisely where I had been and what I had done since then. My answers were pretty guarded, of course. Even if Doc hadn't warned me on the way over, I'd have known better than to try and pull too tall a line with this hombre. He'd have caught on in a second.

Even as it was he evidently saw through my tale, because when I got through he said, "I gather you've had a hard time of it, all in all."

"I wouldn't say that," I lied. "As a matter of fact, I was on the point of landing a real big job when I left Chicago. Balaban and Katz wanted me to take charge of their entire publicity department. I guess you know what that would have paid. They own the biggest chain of theaters in the Middle West."

"Then why did you leave?" he asked, eyeing the foot he was swinging up and down.

I faked a look of angry pride. "Because," I snapped, "I couldn't see myself working for Jews any more. That's why. I was right, wasn't I, Mr. Flanahan?"

He didn't answer, but Doc cleared his throat and nodded solemnly. "You bet you were right, Clem," he said.

There was silence for a few seconds. The Mick was still looking at his foot, which he was rotating now like he was exercising the ankle. Then, without any warning, he suddenly asked: "What's your connection with Keniston?"

I thought I'd keel over. "Connection?" I blatted. "Hell, I haven't even talked to him more than once in my life! And then it was only because he trapped me into it!"

"But wasn't it you who brought one of his spies into the movement?"

"Yeah, but how was I to know she was that? The girl fooled me the way she did all the rest of us. Didn't she, Doc?"

"Absolutely," Doc declared. "You can take my word for that, Mr. Flanahan."

"Besides," I rushed on, "wasn't I the one who caught her? That ought to prove to you I'm innocent."

If it didn't, it at least stumped him for a minute. I watched him loose one end of his watch-chain and start circling it in the air. It was one of those thin, snake-like silver chains, and there was some sort of charm on the end. He must have wound and unwound it around his finger at least three times before he finally spoke up again. Then, in a quiet voice, he said, "Not necessarily." He shook his head to keep me from interrupting. "You might have exposed her out of spite. Perhaps Keniston refused to keep you on his pay-roll any longer."

That was too much. "Wait a minute!" I exploded. "If you're going to accuse me . . ."

"I'm not accusing you," he said, still in that same quiet voice. "I'm merely saying that that *might* account for your conduct. What makes it even more plausible is the fact that you left town immediately afterwards."

I turned to Doc. "Can you beat it?" I appealed to him. "If there's one thing in my whole life that I'm completely innocent about, that's the thing he accuses me of! Lord, it's enough to make a guy give up trying!"

Doc was about to say something, but Flanahan got in ahead of him. "Give up trying what?" he pounced.

"Why—why, everything," I said lamely.

He fell silent again, staring at the charm which he was twirling now like a plumb-weight. I guess it was one of those St. Christopher medals that Catholics are always carrying around, but I couldn't be sure. At last, his eyes still on the charm, he said, "Supposing you tell me exactly what happened, Smullet."

"Yeah, go ahead," Doc urged.

I paused a minute, struggling to overcome my just indignation. It wasn't a light struggle either, I don't mind saying. Finally, though, I managed to get myself in hand, and sat back and related the entire story. Of course, I was careful to leave out the sex angle, but that as you know didn't amount to much, so I was able to sound like I wasn't leaving out anything at all. The result was that when I got through, Flanahan seemed to be completely satisfied. "Well," he said, catching the charm at the end of his chain, "I guess that settles that."

I waited for him to go on, but instead he started in to whirl the chain again. I looked at Doc out of the corner of my eye, and thought I saw him nod. Whereupon, drawing a deep breath, I asked, "So how about it, Mr. Flanahan?"

"How about what?"

"About my being reinstated in the High Command?" I explained.

He looked at me like he was surprised. "But I have no say in that matter," he said, tight-lipped. "I'm not even a member of the Crusade."

"Aw, don't gimme that!" I said, suddenly getting sore. "I know well enough . . ."

Doc went "*Hrmm!*" and gave me a hard look. Then, turning to the millionaire, he switched on his dimples and said, "What Smullet means is that—well, if you'd just put in a good word for him with The Power, it might—you know . . ." He shrugged and said the rest with his hands.

Flanahan lowered his head like he needed to mull that over. "Ye-es," he finally sighed, "I suppose I could do that." Then, addressing me, he went on, "I presume you'd like to take charge of the publicity again, is that it?"

"Yeah, naturally. That's what I'm best at."

He nodded as if to indicate he already knew that. "Of course," he went on, "I doubt whether there's much chance of your getting back into the High Command right away, but I suppose you could function just as well if you were in, say, the Supreme Council." He waved to keep me from interrupting. "Temporarily, I mean," he explained.

I looked at Doc, expecting him to come to my rescue. Before he could get out a word, though, Flanahan was talking again. "Even that, however, is contingent on one other factor," he said.

"I don't get you," I declared.

"Well," he said, talking very deliberately, "we'd have to feel assured that you're ready to follow our new line. Because you realize, don't you, Smullet, that things have changed lately? We're going in for direct action now. We're no longer sparring. The time has passed for that. We're *fighting!*" Suddenly his mild manner was gone. His eyes were flashing, and a thick blue vein stood out on his temple. His voice, though, was as low as before. "Yes, Smullet," he went on, "things are coming to a head now in this country. We're facing a crisis here like the one in Spain in '36. It's crush or be crushed! Either we destroy the Reds here, or they destroy us!" He repeated that thought maybe four or five times in different versions, and finally demanded, "You see that, don't you?"

I tried to say yes, but couldn't find my voice. My throat seemed all clogged up. It was because of the way he sat there glaring at me. I suddenly realized that this Mick was even worse than I'd figured. On top of being smart, he was a fanatic.

He continued to glare at me for a couple of seconds, and then his lip started to curl. "What's the matter, Smullet?" he queried. "You're not scared, are you?"

"N-no," I managed to stammer. "Why should I be scared?"

"If you're still worried about that renegade clergyman," he sneered. "Well, forget it! Keniston can't do a thing to us. He's nothing but an old woman, a miserable, spineless, meddling old woman. Just a liberal, that's all. The most he can do is snoop around and whine. When it comes to action, he's as impotent as—as all the rest on his side. They haven't got the *guts* for action." He looked at me, aware that I was trying to get up the nerve to say something. "You know that, don't you?" he cried.

"Ye-ah, sure," I answered. "But he *is* in with the FBI, isn't he?"

"And what if he is?" Flanahan snapped. "The FBI can't do a thing to us either. They don't dare! Remember what happened in the Christian Mobilizer case? Seventeen arrests, and not a single conviction. Well, that taught the FBI a lesson." He turned to Doc. "Isn't that so?" he demanded.

"I'll tell the world!" Doc replied, but kind of hoarsely. "Of course, we've got to be careful not to go too far . . ."

"No, that's where you're wrong!" Flanahan flared at him. "That's where you're completely wrong! Our only danger now is in not going far enough. I thought you and I had agreed on that, Gribble."

"Yeah, of course," Doc answered, licking his lips. "I only meant to say . . ."

"Yes, yes," the other cut him off. "I understand." He paused as if to get himself in hand. Then, taking a deep breath, he turned back to me and said, "So now you see the situation, Smullet. If you want to get into harness again, you've got to promise to pull with the team. Our publicity must match our action. It's got to be *militant*

[189]

from now on. Understand? It's got to go the limit—shock people, galvanize them, make them fighting mad! They're not that yet! They've been coddled so long with sweetness and light and the godless pap they call liberalism . . ." Suddenly he broke off and scowled irritably. "Are you listening, Smullet?" he snapped.

"Why, of course I'm listening!" I said.

"Well then, I wish you'd quit fooling with that pocket-comb!"

I turned red, suddenly realizing that I'd been at my old habit again. Slipping the comb into its case, I mumbled, "I'm sorry."

His eyes wandered, as if trying to recall what he'd been talking about. Finally, giving his head an impatient jerk, he said, "Well, what about it? Are you willing to work in that spirit?"

I hesitated, and looked at Doc.

"Aw, sure he's willing," my pal butted in. "I know that once he gets into the swing of things . . ."

But Flanahan wouldn't let him finish. "I want *you* to answer, Smullet!" he insisted, looking at me hard.

"Why, ye-ah," I managed to make myself say. "I guess it'll be okay with me."

All at once he started getting up. "We'll consider it settled then," he said, holding out his hand. "You'll be paid, of course. I'll see to that personally. You were getting fifty a week, weren't you?" I nodded. "Well, supposing we keep it at that—for the present, at least. Is that satisfactory, Smullet?"

"Ye-ah," I answered slowly. "I guess it'll have to be. But there's one thing I'd like to clear up . . ."

Apparently he wasn't interested. Right away he was saying good night, and the next thing I knew, Doc and I were out in the hall.

28

I turned on my pal even before we were down the stairs. "Say, I don't like this, Doc," I breathed. "I don't like it one little bit."

"For crisake!" he muttered, grabbing my arm. "Can't you wait till we get outside?"

I could and did, but not one second longer. We were barely in the car before I was at him again. "I don't like this a-tall, Doc," I repeated. "What the hell does he expect me to do? Start whooping it up for a revolution? Because if that's what he has in mind, I'm telling you right now . . ."

"Aw, keep your shirt on," Doc growled as he fumbled with the ignition key. "He just likes to hear himself talk, that's all."

"No, that isn't all," I insisted. "You can't fool me! What's this new spirit he was raving about? On the level now."

Maybe Doc was too busy starting the car to be able to answer, but I kept at him nevertheless. All the way down the block I kept at him, until finally he couldn't stand it any longer. "God Almighty!" he exploded. "Can't you let up for a minute? I'll tell you in due course . . ."

"To hell with the due course!" I came back at him. "Tell me now. What's going on in the Crusade? I mean, what's all this about 'direct action,' and so forth?"

Doc let out a laugh. "You worried about that?" he jeered. "Shucks, it's nothing but kid stuff. Cleaver gets his goons to go out and beat up some Hebes once in a while. Or they paint swastikas on synagogues, and scratch the word JEW on store windows. Just kid stuff."

I turned to look at him, but it was too dark in the car for me to read his face. I had to judge by his voice, and that I must say did sound like he was telling the truth. Nevertheless I wasn't satisfied. I grilled him some more, hurling one question after another; but no matter how I tried, I couldn't break him down. So then I went on to another matter. "Doc," I said, "exactly what do you make of this Flanahan guy?"

"How do you mean?" he stalled.

"Well, I think there's something fishy about him—and I don't mean just on Fridays. I don't trust him."

"Yeah? What makes you say that?"

"Quit stalling," I hollered. "You know well enough why I say that. You don't really think he's a millionaire, do you?"

"What makes you so sure he isn't? You haven't had a chance to count his money, have you?"

"I don't need to," I answered. "Everything about the guy gives him away. Look at the sort of dump he lives in."

"But I explained to you that's merely his hide-out."

"Then what about the way he dresses? Did you notice the crummy suit he had on? I'll lay odds it came with two pair of pants."

"So what?" Doc parried. "Maybe he's eccentric that way. Lots of rich guys don't like to spend money on clothes."

"Yeah, but then they don't keep them pressed like his were. He had creases even down the front of the sleeves."

"Christ, you notice everything, don't you? You and Sherlock Holmes!"

I ignored his sarcasm. I could afford to, because I knew I had him on the run now. "Sure I notice everything," I said. "That's why I'm convinced he's a phony. If that bird had the means, he'd dress like Adolphe Menjou." I waited to see if Doc would try to deny the statement, but he remained mum, so I started in to plead again. "Come on, pal," I said. "What do you really know about this Mister Francis X. Flanahan? On the level now."

Doc still refused to speak. He pretended to be worried about a street car just ahead of us, and when he passed it, he started racing with a truck. Finally, though, the red light on the corner of Vermont brought him to a halt, and then he just had to say something. Clearing his throat, he said, "To be honest, I don't know a thing more than what I've already told you." He turned to look me in the eyes. "That's straight. I don't even know what his middle initial stands for."

"So he's just Mister X to you?" I sneered.

"That's the truth, Clem. I realize it's hard to believe, but it's the truth, so help me God. I've tried my damnedest to find out more about him, but he just won't open up. Neither will Kronkhite, who brought him around in the first place."

"How about Cleaver?" I asked. "Won't he talk either?"

"Nah. He doesn't know any more than I do, apparently. He was telling me the other day that Flanahan helped finance Franco in Spain, but I think he was bulling. The fact is, we're all of us in the dark about that little Mick."

"Have you tried inquiring at his bank?"

Doc heaved a sigh. "First I'd have to know which bank. He never gives us any checks. Just cash. Twenty-dollar bills, usually. He seems to have wads of them in a briefcase that he always carries around with him."

I sat up and snapped my fingers. "That settles it!" I said, "now I've got the whole story. He's just a front. He's paying off for someone else." I watched Doc shift gears and start the car moving again. "And I bet I can guess who it is, too," I declared.

He waited to get into high before replying. Then, keeping his eyes on the traffic, he grunted, "I suppose you think it's the German consul, eh?"

"Sure. Don't you?" I didn't wait for his answer. "For crisake, you must be out of your mind, Doc! Don't you realize what you can get for a thing like that? It's a federal offense!"

"What is?" he said, trying to sound like he really didn't know.

"You know well enough!" I yelled. "You're supposed to register with the State Department if you take money from a foreign government!"

He turned and leered. "I didn't know there was a foreign government by the name of Flanahan," he said. Then, aware that he had me stumped, he started to laugh. "Don't you see, Clem?" he laughed. "They can't do a thing to us! We're in the clear even if this money does come from Germany."

I slumped in the seat and tried to think. For maybe three or four blocks I sat like that, staring at the dashboard, and then I started shaking my head. "Nh-nh," I said. "I wash my hands of this. Maybe you don't mind tangling with the cops, but I do. I'm allergic to the bastards. . . . No, there's no use arguing, Doc. From here on you can just include me out!"

I thought he'd blow up, he looked so exasperated. "You make me sick!" he yelled. "Where the hell do the cops come into this? You know what the trouble with you is, Clem? You're yellow!"

"Who's yellow?" I flared.

"You are!"

I glared at him, but then sort of sagged. "Well, you're wrong," I said. "I'm just smart. That's all."

"Oh, yeah?" Doc sneered. "I guess that explains why you're so well off right now, eh? Maybe it was because you're smart that you let Keniston scare you into running out on us and . . ." He didn't finish the sentence. He could see he didn't need to. He turned his head to eye me, kind of gloating, but then seemed to relent. "Don't be a sap, Clem," he went on in a different tone. "You ought to know by now that you can rely on my judgment. When I tell you we're in the clear on this, believe me, it's so." He sounded his klaxon to scare an old Ford out of his path. "After all, is there any law that says we've got to pry into where every contributor gets the money he hands us? If Flanahan's lying, that's his funeral, not ours. Am I right?"

I didn't answer.

"Besides," he went on after a pause, "how do we know he really is lying?"

"Quit kidding," I said hoarsely. "You know well enough it isn't his own money."

"Okay, and supposing it isn't? That doesn't necessarily mean he's getting it from the Nazis. Maybe he's fronting for some hundred-percent Americans who don't want their names known."

Suddenly I felt like I'd broken out of a locked icebox. "Say," I breathed, "come to think of it, that really could be the case!"

"Of course it could!" said Doc, grinning at my relief. "There must be any number of moneyed guys in this country who'd want to support us if they thought they could get away with it. Take some of those big tycoons who are backing the America First Committee. You know the sort I mean—the ones who think Roosevelt's worse than Hitler any day. Well, wouldn't they naturally want to help us? And I'll lay a bet that's exactly what some of them are doing right now." He put his hand on my knee and gave it a squeeze. "Like to take odds on that?"

I shook my head, no.

"So then what's all the squawking about?" he demanded. "If you're really smart you'll go ahead and do what Flanahan wants. All you'll be letting yourself in for is a chance to pick up some easy dough. That's the way *I* see it."

I took out my pocket-comb and started running it through my hair. "Yeah," I muttered slowly. "Maybe you're right at that."

29

The next day I got me a room of my own at the hotel. It was exactly like the one I'd occupied before, but on the fifth floor, right across the corridor from Doc's suite. The manager, being an old friend of mine, let me have the room at a special rate, and also promised to put in a studio bed and a desk so as to make it look more office-like. That's the way I'd had my original crib fixed up, and I must admit I'd found the camouflage kind of effective for certain purposes.

I made the move because Doc was confident that I was all set now. "That's one thing I do know about Mr. X.," he told me. "When he says he'll see to a thing, he sees to it." And within less than twenty-four hours I found that my pal hadn't been bulling me. I was right back at my old job again.

But though the job was the same, my position was different. And how! The minute I showed up at the Citadel I was made aware of the change. I'd had visions of a lot of handshaking and back-slapping and maybe even a small celebration. You know what I mean— the fatted calf, and so forth. But instead everybody gave me the cold shudders. When I came to the front door, Hank acted like he was doubtful whether he ought to let me in, and upstairs The Power greeted me with a sermon that left me feeling icy wet all over. He implied that I'd been a deserter, and plainly stated I was being taken back on strict probation. The entire Supreme Council was present, and if Doc hadn't sort of hovered over me, I swear I'd have told them all to go to hell right then and there.

And things were even worse the next morning when I reported for work. Right off I was informed by Cleaver that he himself was now using the office I'd once occupied, and that henceforth I'd have to make-do with a desk in Doc's room. Then I was given to understand that although there were now two Amazons serving full time on the office staff, both were already so overworked that I'd have to do most of my own typing. Finally I was told that I was not to order anything printed, or even mimeographed, without first getting the copy okayed by the High Command.

You can imagine how all that made me feel. In the old days I'd been able to run my department pretty much as I pleased, because my only superior had been The Power, and he'd been too superior to interfere much. But now I had Cleaver and Kronkhite over me, and I knew in advance that they'd be right on my neck. To make matters still worse, there was Flanahan to yank me by the nose. It looked like I'd have to become nothing but an acquiesce-man.

And that's exactly what happened. Knowing what I do now, I realize it was a lucky break for me. I was kept from becoming a conscious party to whatever it was that those bozos were up to.* I must admit, though, that at the time I felt hurt, as they say, to the quick. Just to be associated with such characters was bad enough; but to have to take orders from them—that was almost too much.

Nevertheless I stood for it. It was hell, believe me. But I mean really *hell*. Day in and day out those guys kept riding me to get more reckless and "militant." They weren't satisfied with the sort of bright little firecracker stunts I'd pulled off in the earlier days. They wanted me to blast with dynamite. And I had absolutely no way to resist them.

Except for Doc, no one in the entire organization would give me any support. And even he wouldn't give me much. When the two of us were alone, he'd be all on my side, but the minute they'd start barking, he'd crawl. If Peavey would have come around more often, I might have been able to get him to back me up; but that old fox was staying completely under wraps now. He'd even had his name taken off our mailing list, and though he still contributed, it was never in anything but currency. The only other person with any sort of influence whom I might have been able to scare was Mrs. Krutch, and she too kept herself way in the background. There were a couple of new people in the Supreme Command—an old

---

* *This is of course my main grounds for pleading "not guilty" to the charge that has landed me where I am right now—namely, in jail. Even if, as claimed, the Crusade really was a criminally subversive organization during those months, I for one am not to blame in any way, shape, or manner. If you still doubt that, please read on.*

crackpot named Henry D. Gallon, who claimed to be a mining engineer, and an old shyster named Lavery Andrews, who'd been disbarred for fixing a jury—but they were both as hypped on what Flanahan called "militancy" as he was himself. So I was helpless.

Of course, I could have quit. But I'd already done that once—and you know with what results. Before I could bring myself to quit again I wanted better proof of the need. And I must say, the more I studied the situation—at least during those first few weeks—the less I could see of such proof. Flanahan seemed to be right about one thing: the people we were attacking evidently lacked the guts to counter-attack.

I'm not referring now solely to the Jews. They were still getting most of our attention, but we were hitting plenty hard at all the other anti-Hitlerites. We were lambasting the British, the Dutch, the Poles, the Czechs, the Free French, the Red Wops, and every other foreign element that was trying to drag America into the war. We were tearing into Walter Winchell and Dorothy Thompson and above all F.D.R. The Power rarely made a public address without dragging in something about how the President ought to be impeached; and his favorite theme in private was what a blessing it would be if the entire Roosevelt family was wiped out. Yet, so far as I could see, nothing was being done to chop us down. Nothing serious, I mean.

Of course, there was any amount of yelping against us, especially on the part of Keniston and his crowd. He kept sending snoopers to our meetings, and then running to the Mayor with complaints. He also held meetings of his own, and wired resolutions to the Governor. He connived to have us investigated by a committee of baby-kissers from Sacramento, but the way the investigation was handled, it merely got us a lot of free advertising. He tried to get the Dies Committee after us, and we were sorry he failed, because that would undoubtedly have done us even more good. No matter what he did or tried to do, he seemed totally incapable of chopping us down.

The main reason, I suppose, was that we were doing most of our real dirty work under cover. Take, for instance, those paint jobs on synagogue doors, and glass scratchings on Hebe store windows. Or take the red-hot leaflets we were scattering from roof tops, and the dirty limericks we were smuggling into army camps. Or take the poison-pen letters we were pumping into the mails. All those activities were being conducted strictly on the sly.

Even so, I was scared of them, and never stopped saying so. Moreover, I want to state right here and now that I personally had no part in them. I know that I've been accused of writing the copy for those circulars and also of making up many of those limericks. But it's not true. Similarly with regard to the charge that I started that chain-letter about the nature of the President's affliction, and the one saying that Morgenthau makes a commission on every Defense Bond that gets sold. I understand the FBI has copies of those letters which were apparently typed on my own machine; but that's no proof that I personally did the typing. My guess is that Mabel Haight was the guilty party, because she was in charge of the entire chain-letter project.

If I had had any say at all in the organization, I would never have permitted any of those activities whatsoever. Neither would Doc. We both had sense enough to realize that, on top of the risk involved, there was no money in such activities. That's why we hadn't allowed them to be carried on in the old days. Cleaver and Kronkhite had agitated for them right from the start, but Doc and I had turned thumbs down. Now, however, we were powerless. Mr. X was really running the show, and he was all in favor of those crazy capers. He didn't give a damn that they were of no direct benefit to the organization. His first interest—he told me this himself more than once—was not to build up the Crusade but to tear down the government. And The Power, poor nut, thought that was as it should be. He'd been completely sold on the idea that as soon as this government was torn down, he personally would head the new one.

So we were helpless.

At first Doc pretended to be less jittery than I was about what was going on. "Keep your hair on, chump!" he'd snort. "The cops'll never bother about this kid stuff. They're too busy directing traffic and tagging parked cars." Inside, though, I could see he was plenty scared, and finally the time came when he was forced to break down and admit it.

I recall the exact date when that happened—October 16—because

it was Mrs. Gunderson's birthday, and I spent that evening showing her a good time. I more than owed her the treat, because she'd
been having me over for meals once or twice a week ever since my
return. I blew her to dinner at Al Levy's, then to a movie, and
finally to an ice-cream soda. By the time I got back to my hotel it
was way after midnight, and I was just getting ready to pile into
bed when Doc came knocking on the door.

I knew he and the rest of the High Command had been conferring up at Flanahan's place, and from the way he looked, it had evidently been a tough session. His fat face was all lumps, and as pale
as lard. "Christ," he groaned as he collapsed in a chair, "those screw-
balls are enough to drive a guy to liquor!"

"That what you're looking for?" I asked, kind of sympathetic.

He admitted he wouldn't object to a nip, so I dug out what I had
on hand. It was just about two nips, and he took both right out of
the bottle. Then, unbuttoning his overcoat and leaning back in the
chair, he started staring at the rug.

"What were they jawing about this time?" I asked, sinking to the
edge of my cot.

He didn't answer at first. Finally, pushing his hat far back on
his head, he sighed, "Aw, they just jawed."

I got up to get some cigarettes and offered him one. Then, taking
an ashtray with me, I returned to the cot. I could see he wanted to
talk, but couldn't get himself started.

"Something bothering you?" I tried to prompt him after a wait.

He took a deep drag and tried to blow rings. His heart couldn't
have been in it, though, because the smoke came out shapeless.
Heaving another sigh, he suddenly stirred and crossed his fat legs.
"God," he exploded, "you wouldn't believe what they're thinking
of now! I'm telling you, Clem, you just wouldn't believe it!" He
glared a second. "Listen—do you know what they want to do now?
They want to bomb the Citadel!"

I bug-eyed and asked what the hell was the idea, whereupon he
proceeded to explain in language too strong to quote. The sole purpose, it seems, was to attract attention. The plan was to have someone lob a bomb on the front porch, just a small bomb that couldn't
do more than maybe blast a couple of windows, and thus set the
entire country talking about us. Doc had of course tried to make

the lugs realize that everybody would know right away it was a put-up job; but they'd refused to listen. Millions of people, they'd insisted, would be ready to believe that the Jews, or the Reds, had committed the outrage. So then Doc had reminded them of the munitions stored in the Citadel. What would happen, he'd asked them, when the cops came snooping around and saw all those guns, etcetera? But they'd had an answer for that too. Flanahan had said he'd arrange to have the stuff carted away temporarily.

Doc mashed his cigarette on the sole of his shoe. Judging by the expression on his face, he must have been wishing the butt was Flanahan's head. "You know, Clem," he growled, "I'm beginning to think I wasn't so smart when I let that little Mick buy his way into the Crusade. He's turned out to be a regular Frankenstein." He stared at me like I hadn't been saying the same thing for weeks already. "Yes, sir," he insisted, pounding his knee, "that's just what he is—a Frankenstein with a Jesuit education!" He broke off to reach for a fresh cigarette, and then fumbled in his pockets for a match. "We'll have to shake him off somehow," he declared, filling his lungs with smoke. "To hell with his dough! We can get along without it." He let the smoke curl out of his nostrils slowly. "Yes, sir," he said, "we've got to edge Mr. X. right out of the organization."

"Don't forget Cleaver," I piped up, "and Kronkhite."

"Aw, sure," Doc agreed. "I'm not forgetting them. But they're nothing but the Y and Z that follow after X. Once we get rid of him, they'll go too." Suddenly he cheered up and flashed his dimples. "And then, pal," he cried, rubbing his hands, "then you and me get back where we belong. You betcher. We hop right back behind the wheel, and drive the way *we* please." He gave his face a quick wipe and smacked his lips. "And I know just what direction we'll take," he chortled. "Ever heard of this new racket called Mankind United?"

I had to stare. Mrs. Gunderson had been gabbing about that very movement all evening long. Somebody had just sold her a book about it, and she'd evidently swallowed it whole.

"I'm not surprised," said Doc when I got through telling him how she'd talked. "It's the sort of movement that her type would naturally fall for. There's something nice and spiritual about it, and at the same time mercenary." He started to tell me what Mankind United stood for, but I couldn't follow him except in a vague way. Apparently the program was a crazy jumble of Technocracy, Christian Science, and the Hidden World Rulers bunk. "Say," he glowed, "if we could only switch the Crusade over on a track like that, we'd really get somewhere!"

I hated to pour cold water on him, so I remained mum. "What's the matter?" he demanded. "Don't you think I'm right?"

"Aw, I guess you're right enough," I said. "All I'm wondering . . ."

"Yeah, I know," he cut me off. "You're wondering how we're going to dump those guys who're at the wheel now."

"Exactly."

He slumped in his chair and thought for a while. Finally he shook his head and let out a sigh. "That's what I've still got to figure out," he said, getting to his feet. "But don't worry, pal," he added at the door. "I'll find a way."

30

But Doc didn't seem able to find a way to dump those guys. Neither did I. We racked our brains day in and day out, but all to no purpose. What we had to do was get something on Flanahan & Co. that would antagonize The Power, and make him kick them out. But that's just what we weren't able to do.

First we thought of tattling our suspicions about the source of Flanahan's dough, but then we decided that that wouldn't do any good. To begin with, in spite of all our sleuthing—and we'd done a lot in the past weeks—we still hadn't found out what that source was.* In addition, we were pretty sure that even if we could prove our suspicions, The Power wouldn't be greatly shocked. He was no longer the pure and innocent crank that he'd been in earlier days.

---

* *Incidentally, we never did find that out until after we were all rounded up, and the FBI spilled the story to the press.*

There was just a touch of the croonk about him now. The slick little Mick had wised him up in many ways, and made him more of what he—the Mick—called a "realist."

Of course, The Power was still an absolute idealist about some things—for instance liquor—and that suggested our second strategy. We played with the idea of encouraging Cleaver to pull another one of those big drunk scenes. We realized, of course, that at best that couldn't accomplish much. At the same time, however, we thought maybe it would cause a rift that we could work on. But the bum had evidently had his lesson, because although Doc got him stinking on at least three occasions, nothing ensued. Each time Cleaver staggered straight home instead of to the Citadel, where he was expected. So that was that.

Our next idea was to ram in our crowbar via Kronkhite, but here again we were balked. There didn't seem to be a thing we could say against the Heinie that The Power didn't already know—and apparently think okay. Of course, if we'd been aware then of what has since come out, the situation might have been different. Even in his new "realistic" mood, I doubt whether J. C. would have stood for having an alien spy in his High Command. But at the time we believed Kronkhite was a full-fledged and legal American citizen.

So it looked like there was absolutely no chance of our getting anything on Flanahan & Co. The only thing left was for us to try the opposite angle—i.e., get something on The Power. It occurred to us that if we could do that, then we had maybe a club with which to force him to do what we wanted. But after due considera-tion we decided there was nothing to that idea either. Doc and I were sure, of course, that there was a scandal of some sort in Long John's life. Otherwise why was he so secretive about his past? But we'd never been able to discover what that scandal was, and any-way we figured it couldn't amount to much, or somebody like Kenis-ton would have exposed it long ago.

Apparently, therefore, we were stymied no matter which way we turned. Try as we might, we couldn't get at those lugs in the front seat. And that began to worry Doc as well as me. With each passing day it worried us more and more. In fact, by the first week in No-vember we were almost in a panic. The reason was that we could see they were up to something really bad now. What it was they wouldn't tell even Doc. They went further and swore there was nothing *to* tell. But the way they acted, we knew better than to believe them.

In the beginning we thought maybe all the hush-hush was connected with that crazy bombing plot. Doc had learnt of it in the first place only by accident—he'd overheard Cleaver blabbing about it in another room—and when the plotters refused to discuss it with him any further, he decided they were dummying up to keep him from interfering. But then we noticed they weren't doing anything to move the munitions, so we knew that couldn't be it.

Besides, there was more activity going on than seemed necessary for anything as minor as a fake bombing. The Flanahan trio kept going into huddles up in J. C.'s quarters, sometimes with strangers who'd been slipped in through the back door. Or the trio would go off somewhere in the middle of the day, taking J. C. along, and not return for hours. Long-distance calls began coming in for the Mick, and he'd make a point of our leaving the room before he'd answer them. Also a suspicious lot of mail began going out which neither Doc nor I were allowed to get even a peek at. Evidently whatever was being cooked up was no silly little kid affair. It was something real big—and serious.

For maybe two weeks those guys carried on like that. The Power no longer spent half the day doing his exercises and frying himself in the sun. Similarly Cleaver no longer spent hours thinking up ways to get me sore. Kronkhite, who'd formerly shown up at the Citadel at most a couple of times a week, began coming around daily now. So did Flanahan. Yet no matter what lengths Doc and I went to, we just couldn't find out what they were so busy about. We tried to pump the stenogs. We eavesdropped. We even trailed Flanahan's car a couple of times. But it was no use.

And then at last I got an inkling of what was up. I got it, of all people, from my old landlady, who incidentally had all but dropped out of the Crusade by that time. She phoned me one day to say she was sick again—lumbago this time—and I went to call on her that same evening with a bottle of her favorite tonic wrapped in fancy tinsel paper, like it was champagne. That pleased her no end, and she laughed like a regular kid. But then all at once the tears came to her eyes, and she said, "I suppose this is sort of a farewell present, eh, Clem? How long d'you figure you'll be away?"

I stared at her. "Who told you I was going away?" I cried.

"Oh, it's all right, Clem," she smiled. "You don't need to pretend to me. Sarah Ames let me in on the secret when she was visiting with me this afternoon. She got it from her son-in-law—you know, Jed Hinkley."

I did know. Jed was one of Cleaver's goons, a young Oakie with a harelip who was always getting in fights. "What did he tell her?" I asked.

"Oh, everything," Mrs. Gunderson replied. "He's promised to take her along, as well as his wife and the kids. I suppose you'll be riding with The Power, right in the lead, eh?"

"What *are* you talking about?" I almost yelled, "Who's riding where in the lead of what? . . . No, don't look at me like that, Ma. I'm not trying to stall."

I finally convinced her of that fact, and then she came out with the story. Apparently there was going to be a tremendous march on Washington in December. Millions of patriots from all over the country were going to drive to the capital and stage a mass demonstration against the warmongers there. Cleaver had already tipped off some of his boys, telling them they were going to police the caravan from Los Angeles. According to Jed, 10,000 people were expected to go from this area alone. It was going to be the most sensational event since the Civil War.

"But I guess it's all jest a rumor," Mrs. Gunderson ended up. "You'd know about it if it was true."

I said sure, and tried to look like I meant it. "There's nothing to it at all," I told her. Then I found an excuse to scram.

The minute I was out of the house I made for the nearest phone. I wanted to get hold of Doc right away. First I tried the hotel, but he wasn't there. Then, remembering he'd said something about a special meeting of the High Command, I called the Citadel. Hank answered, and said, "No, there ain't nobody here now." I knew that meant the meeting was at Flanahan's place, and realized I was stuck. I didn't have the phone number at that hide-out—almost no one did—and anyway I figured I'd get Doc in bad if I called him there.

So I went on home and waited for him to return. First I waited in the hotel lobby, playing the pinball machine till it went out of whack, and then I went up to my room and tried to read the book that Mrs. Gunderson had forced on me before she'd let me leave. It was the one put out by that Mankind United outfit, and she'd insisted I'd find it a "revelation." By the time I'd read the first ten pages I realized it was a revelation all right, but only of how much bunk some people were willing to swallow. I managed to read maybe ten more pages, and then I said some words that even Ernest Hemingway wouldn't put in print, and heaved the book across the room. Stretching out on the couch, I lit a cigarette and started counting the flowers on the wallpaper.

When Doc finally showed up it was way after midnight, and he was stewed to the gills. "I just had to stop for a coupla drinks on my way home," he tried to explain.

"Well, I been waiting for you for hours!" I said. "I've got news. I've just found out something."

I told him what I'd heard, but instead of reacting the way I'd anticipated, he merely shrugged his shoulders. "That's no news," he grunted. "I was told all about that at the session tonight. They're planning to spill it to you tomorrow, so's you can start getting out the publicity."

"Then you mean they're really in earnest?" I yelled.

Doc nodded and tried to focus his eyes. "Yup," he hiccuped. "They been working on the project for weeks, it seems." He broke off to let out a string of hiccups, and finally went to the bathroom for a drink of water.

When he returned he sank into the chair and told me all he knew. Apparently the tale I'd heard from Mrs. Gunderson was only slightly exaggerated. As yet not even a dozen organizations had promised to take part in the march, but Flanahan was satisfied that hundreds more would join up once the trek got under way. The whole scheme was to be officially announced by The Power at a monster open-air rally on Sunday, November 30th. Flanahan had already engaged Fillmore Stadium for that afternoon, and was hoping to get some radio station to carry the main address. The first caravans were to start moving the following Sunday, December 7th, with rallies in San Diego, San Francisco, Portland and Seattle, as well as Los Angeles. If everything went according to schedule, the climax would be pulled off in Washington on December 25th—in other words, Christmas Day.

"Well I'll be goddamned!" I exclaimed when Doc finished.

"You'll be worse than that," he growled, "if this thing comes off. So will all of us."

"Didn't you try to make them realize that?" I cried.

"Try?" he shouted. "Hell, I did everything except go down on my knees to 'em!" He went on to repeat some of the arguments he'd used. Winter was no time for driving across the country, especially in the jalopies that our sort of people owned. Besides, even if they were sure they could get through the snows, most of those people wouldn't want to, because they were good Americans and liked to celebrate Christmas in their own homes. A project of this sort couldn't be pulled off except maybe in the summer time, and even then only after months of preparation. "That's how I argued," Doc said, glaring at me with bloodshot eyes. "But d'you think they'd listen? They kept answering that it would be too late if they put the stunt off a single day. Flanahan says he knows for a fact that F.D.R.'s planning to have us in the war by spring." He licked his puffy lips and started looking around the room. "Got a drink handy?" he asked.

I rummaged in a bureau drawer and dug out a half-empty bottle of Schenley's. He wouldn't even wait for me to get a glass. Tipping his head back, he let a good four ounces trickle down his throat, and then started shouting again. The way he sounded, you would have thought I was on Flanahan's side instead of his. "God Almighty," he shouted, "this may wreck the entire movement! And land the whole lot of us in jail, too! Because it's not just a little street parade that'll get a couple of traffic cops down on us. It's liable to set the whole goddam U. S. Army on our necks. I mean that. Cleaver's organizing a regular militia to go along, goons with side-arms and rifles and even tommy-guns. Hell, it'll look like the start of a revolution!" He waved a hand to keep me from interrupting. "And you know what I think? I think that's exactly what it's intended to be.

Yes, sir! Mr. X wants nothing else but a revolution. He practically said so tonight. He's planning to route the autocade so it goes by all the big army camps, and he's got Long John all hopped up to tell the draftees to mutiny." He glared and nodded emphatically. "I'm not conning you, Clem. That's the God's honest truth, so help me!"

I tried to say something, but again he waved his hand. "Wait a minute," he said. "I'm not finished yet. Remember that bomb plot I told you about a couple weeks ago? Well, now I know why they haven't pulled it yet. They're saving it for the day after the big rally on November thirtieth. They figure that'll get the march in the headlines if nothing else does. And just to make sure, they're figuring on allowing somebody to get hurt a little in the explosion." He paused and let a leer flash across his boozy face. "Cleaver says he thinks it ought to be you."

I gave a jump that pretty near threw me off the cot. "He *does*, does he?"

"That's straight," Doc answered solemnly. "His idea is to trump up an excuse for getting everybody out of the Citadel except you, and then have some stranger come by and toss the bomb on the front porch."

"And what did the others say to that?" I cried.

"Aw, they said there's plenty of time to decide about details like that."

Now I really hit the ceiling. "So they think blowing me to bits is a detail, eh?" I yelled. "Well, I'll show 'em. You know what I'm gonna do, Doc? I'm gonna squeal. Yes, sir, I'm gonna spill the whole story to Keniston!"

A look of alarm shot across Doc's face. "Now don't be too hasty, Clem!" he said, laying a paw on my knee. "I think there's a better way to handle this. Let's play along with 'em temporarily . . ."

"Nothing doing!" I cut in. "Play along with guys like that? Not me! No, sir, I'm gonna squeal!"

"Yeah, but squeal what?" he asked, spreading his hands. "After all, you haven't got anything concrete to pin on them. Not now, you haven't. If you blab at this stage of the game, they'll be able to get off like"—he snapped his fingers—"that!"

I could see he had me there, so I let him go on. "Nah, the only smart thing to do," he said, "is to stall for the present. That way we at least get a chance to pick up some of the dough Flanahan plans to hand out in the next three or four weeks. Stall and keep throwing sand in the bearings. "See what I mean? Sabotage the whole affair!"

I slumped forward and thought for a couple of minutes. Then I asked, "How much dough does he say he's going to spend?"

"Twenty grand."

"*How* much?"

Doc repeated the figure and added, "He talks of shelling out a couple of grand just to put over the initial rally."

I slumped again and thought some more. Finally, cocking my head, I said, "Maybe you're right, Doc."

He put down the bottle from which he had just taken another powerful swig. "Sure," he said confidently. "You ought to know by now, I'm always right."

31

So I followed Doc's advice and played along with Flanahan & Co. All that month of November I played along with them, making out I was nuts about their project. Moreover I went through all the gestures of helping to put it over. First I thought up a snappy title for it: "The Continental Autocade." Then I went to work drumming up ballyhoo for the big sound-off at the Fillmore Stadium on November 30th. I edited a special issue of the *Crusader*, and wrote copy by the yard for throwaways, posters, and would-be press releases. I lined up printers, sign painters, sound-truckers, and so forth. I talked of how I was contacting every wire-service in town, and arranging for coverage by the newsreel boys and the radio commentators. When, just the week before the rally, one of the big national picture magazines led off a spread on the American Fascists with a full-page action shot of John Christian Power, I naturally claimed I'd arranged that too.

Of course it was all pure razzle-dazzle. My sole object was to make Flanahan hand out the dough, and I must admit—since the FBI has already advertised the fact—that I didn't fail entirely. All in all I must have cleaned up a couple of hundred bucks in kick-backs and hold-outs.* However, considering the amount of finagling and shadow-boxing I had to do, and also all the real worry, I guess that reward wasn't by any means out of line.

Naturally, I'd have acted different if I'd thought the Autocade had the least chance of success. In that case, believe me, I'd have gone straight to Keniston, or maybe even the cops, and blabbed the whole story. I really mean that. But the fact is, I was absolutely convinced the project was bound to be a flop. And not just on account of the way Doc and I were quietly foxing the works. Even without that I knew the thing was going to flop.

What's more, I had a notion Flanahan knew it too. With J. C. it was different. That poor crackpot was of course completely halluci-nated as to what was going to happen. He had visions of collecting such a mob by the time he reached Washington that he'd be able to move into the White House right away. Likewise Cleaver. The stew-bum could already see himself taking command of the Army, Navy, Marine Corps, and the FBI. Likewise most of the others who were in on the secret. The silly dopes seemed to imagine that all they needed to do was rush to the capital and yell "Boo!"—and right away the entire government would collapse.

But Francis X. Flanahan was too smart a guy to have any such ideas. It's true he kept big-mouthing about how the Autocade was going to start a "national upheaval," but he wasn't fooling me. I was confident he hoped to create at most a local disturbance. And I thought I understand what his aim was. I decided he was a local stooge working for some outfit interested in creating all sorts of disturbances all over the country in order to discredit what he called the "War Deal." Of course, had I been sure that that outfit was the German government, I'd have known better than to stick around. The same, I might add, goes for Doc. But we weren't sure at all. For all we knew, that outfit might have been some screwball clique

---

* The charge made by the FBI that I got away with "several thousands of dollars" during those weeks is of course just horse radish. I guess it was trumped up solely with the idea of getting me on an income-tax rap if, as, and when the present prosecution for sedition falls through.

in the America First Committee, or in the Republican Party, or even in the Catholic Church. See what I mean?

Anyway, the fact remains that I did stick around. Moreover, as I have already said, I pretended to work my fool head off. This was especially true on the last day before the rally, because thanks to my careful mismanagement, most of the throwaways didn't arrive from the printer until late that morning. The result was a small riot at the Citadel. Almost all our Amazons were on hand, plus a gang of hausfraus from the Bund, plus twenty or thirty Rangers, plus at least fifty kids, all yammering to be given their bundles and told where to distribute them.

Doc was supposed to be in charge, and he naturally did his utmost to gum everything. (His entire strategy now was to make the Autocade as huge a flop as possible, and then get Flanahan & Co. ousted for having sponsored it.) Around noon, however, he got a hurry call to meet the rest of the High Command at Flanahan's apartment, so he told me to take over. That naturally made Mabel Haight sore, both because she felt she ranked above me, and also because she could see I was suddenly acting kind of dim-witted. Several others who were present seemed to share her attitude, and they began picking on me till I finally blew up and told them to try to handle the job themselves. It was nearly two by then, and I wanted to duck out for lunch anyway.

I didn't return until well after three, and was surprised to find everyone gone except Hank. "Did they get through that quick?" I asked him, kind of upset that they'd managed so well. He wouldn't even bother to look up from the paper he was lip-reading. He just gave a long sniff and growled, "Didn't take 'em no time once *you* were out of the way!"

I decided to ignore the jibe. That dumb Swede hadn't been civil to me even once in all the weeks I'd been back in the Crusade. Turning on my heel, I stalked off to the office I shared with Doc, closed the door, and propped a chair under the knob. I thought I'd smoke a cigarette and relax for a bit. My desk was piled a mile high with things that still needed to be taken care of before the rally, but I was in no mood to go at them right away. What with the heavy food I'd just had, and one beer too many, I felt kind of logy.

Lighting a Lucky, I sprawled in a big chair, put my head back, and let my eyes close.

Then suddenly I gave a jump and let out a yell. I'd evidently dozed off with the lighted cigarette in my hand. I hopped around for a minute, blowing on my fingers, and then decided to go look for Hank. I thought maybe he could give me something to keep the burn from blistering.

He was no longer at his regular post by the front door, so I hollered up the staircase. "Hey, Hank!" I hollered. "Where are you?" There was no answer. I tried the basement door, but it was locked, so I knew he couldn't be down there. Then I looked on the back porch, where he sometimes ducked out for a smoke, but he wasn't there either. "That's funny," I muttered to myself.

Then all at once I felt my heart stop. "My God!" I let out a gasp. I'd just remembered the bomb plot. According to Doc, the final decision of the High Command had been not to risk getting anyone hurt. The stunt was still scheduled to be pulled on Monday, but at a time when there wouldn't be a soul in the Citadel. Now, though, the suspicion flashed through my mind that maybe they hadn't told him the truth. I recalled how the Rangers had been carting munitions out of the basement all week long, and with that the suspicion became a certainty. "Kurryst!" I yelled. "I bet they're gonna pull it right now!"

In two seconds flat I was through the front door, and out on the sidewalk. I was in such a panic, I wouldn't have stopped even there if I hadn't collided with somebody. It was with a woman I'd never seen before, a tall thin woman who was standing in the driveway and sort of eyeing the Citadel. Right away I decided she must be carrying the bomb. She had a small suitcase with her, and that seemed to prove it. I remained frozen for an instant, not knowing what to do. I wanted to snatch the suitcase out of her hand, but I was afraid it might blow up in my face. So instead I just backed away and yelled, "Don't, for God's sake!"

The woman looked completely staggered. "Don't what?" she asked, trying to set her hat straight.

In a flash I realized I'd made a mistake. This party wasn't the type that even lunatics would pick to deliver a bomb. She was white-

[211]

haired and nicely dressed, and looked like she might be an elderly high-school teacher, or a librarian. So then I sprang toward her, grabbed her arm, and started hustling her across the street.

"What *is* this?" she panted, struggling to break away. "Let me go! You have no right . . ."

"For God's sake, don't argue, lady!" I pleaded as I dragged her along. "There's liable to be an explosion any minute in that house!"

I guess I must have sounded convincing, because she began to move fast then. She almost ran. When we got to the opposite sidewalk, though, she suddenly halted and turned to glare at me. "Is this some sort of a trick, young man?" she demanded, laboring to catch her breath. "Because if it is, I want you to know it won't work! I'm going to go into that house, and neither you nor anyone else can stop me." She actually started to go back again.

"No, *don't*, lady!" I yelled after her. "Believe me, a bomb's liable to go off in there any minute now!"

I really meant that, and the expression on my face must have told her as much. She hesitated, looked at the house, then at me, then back at the house, and finally remained standing on the curb. "A bomb?" she echoed, all confused. "Who'd want to . . . ?" Suddenly she let the suitcase fall, and sort of staggered toward me. "Good Heavens!" she cried, tugging at my sleeve. "Is *he* in there?"

"No, don't worry," I told her. "Nobody's in there now." I watched her give a gasp of relief, and added, "Who're you talking about, anyway?"

"My brother," she blurted out.

"Well, don't worry," I repeated. "He isn't . . ." Then I shut up, because I could see her staring at the little dormer window on the third floor of the Citadel. Someone had just raised the shade.

"Who's that?" she cried, in a panic again.

I looked and knew it was Hank. That was his own room, up in the attic, and when I realized he'd probably been there all along, I felt myself go red in the face. "I guess I must have made a mistake," I stammered, starting to slouch back across the street. "There's not going to be an explosion, after all."

The woman stared at me, more puzzled now than ever. "I don't understand this at all!" she cried. "First you tell me . . ."

"Yeah, I'm sorry, lady," I cut in on her. "But don't ask me to explain. It's too complicated." I tried to grin and change the subject. "That's Hank Olsen up there," I said. "I guess he isn't your brother, though." I looked at the woman, took in her neat appearance and refined manner, and added, "He just couldn't be."

"No," she said, "my brother . . ." She bit her lip and looked annoyed. "Never mind that," she snapped, starting to hurry ahead of me.

"But hold on a minute, lady!" I called after her. "You can't go in there!" I was afraid she'd start asking Hank about my strange actions, and give me away. "That's straight, lady," I said, catching up with her at the foot of the driveway. "You've got to be a member and know the password." She shook off the hand I'd laid on her arm, and continued toward the house. "Now, see here!" I snapped, blocking her path. "We don't like strangers snooping around this building. If there's someone you're looking for . . ." All at once I noticed her eyes, and became dumb. They were a weird blue and blazed like only one other pair of eyes I'd ever seen. "Say, wait a minute!" I spluttered, grabbing her arm again. "Are you—say, is your brother The Power?"

She drew herself up and curled her long upper lip. "I believe that's the name he goes by at present. And now, young man, perhaps you'll allow me to go in and see him."

"Aw, but he isn't there!" I cried. "That's a fact, ma'am. He's at a conference uptown. I don't know when he'll be coming back. Maybe not until . . ." I broke off to look at a car that had just slowed up before turning into the driveway. It was Doc's Buick. "Say, hold on. Here's somebody who may be able to tell you exactly." I rushed over and flagged the car. "Heh, Doc," I said, poking my head through the open window. "Whadye know? Here's J.C.'s sister!"

He looked at me and then at the woman. For just a second I thought he was going to say something nasty and drive on. But then, giving the woman a second look, he pulled the hand-brake and started to get out. "Did you say his sister?" he side-mouthed, still with his eyes on her.

"Yeah," I answered. "I was just telling her maybe you know when he'll be coming back."

He swept right past me, and grabbed her hand. "Well, well,

well!" he sang out, flashing all his dimples. "I sure am glad to meet you, Mrs. . . ."

"*Miss* Bauer," she said in a prim tone.

"Ah, yes, Miss Power . . ."

"No, Bauer," she corrected him firmly. "B-a-u-e-r."

Doc looked at her kind of confused. "Oh, I see," he said lamely. Then, recovering his poise, he started pumping her hand again. "My name's Gribble," he informed her, turning on his dimples full strength. "Doctor Benjamin Gribble. Your brother's often spoken to me about you."

That seemed to surprise her. It did me too. So far as I knew, Long John had mentioned his sister only once in all the years he'd known Doc, and then only to let something slip about her having got a raw deal from a Hebe.

She gave Doc a queer look, and withdrew her hand. Apparently she wasn't falling for his line. "Can you tell me if he will be returning soon?" she asked, sort of frigid.

"No," Doc answered, shaking his head. "Probably not for hours. But I know where he is, and if you'll allow me, I'll be glad to drive you there right now."

"That's very kind of you," she said, still sounding icy. "I do want to see him before . . . I mean, it's rather important that I see him as soon as possible. But if you'll just tell me where he is, I'll find my way there. There's no need for you to go to the trouble of driving me."

Doc frowned like she'd hurt him to the quick. "Trouble, ma'am?" he cried. "Why, I'd consider it a privilege!" And with that he took the suitcase out of her hand and practically pushed her into the front seat of the car.

I caught his wink as he closed the door on her, and hopped into the rear seat. I thought I knew what was going through his mind. He was undoubtedly hoping to pump something out of this dame that he could hold over Long John. That was just the sort of break Doc had been praying for ever since he'd begun to worry about ousting Flanahan and Co. So I was anxious to stick around and see what luck he'd have.

"You must be very proud of your brother," he opened up after he'd backed out of the driveway. She didn't answer, and he evidently figured she hadn't heard him. "Yeah," he tried again, "you must be mighty proud of him."

I could see her draw herself up, and then heard her say in a clear cold voice, "On the contrary. I am thoroughly ashamed of him."

"You're what?" Doc cried, throwing her a startled glance.

"I said I am thoroughly ashamed of him."

"But why?" he cried, trying to stare at her and watch where he was going at the same time. "After all, think of the following he has! Thousands of people just worship him!"

She sniffed and said, "They must be fools."

"Aw, you've got no right to say that, ma'am," he protested. "You evidently don't know what a great personality your brother's become. How long is it since you last saw him?"

She plainly didn't want to go on with the conversation, but at the same time felt she had to be polite. So, after a pause, she said, "Thirty years."

"Oh, well, that explains everything," Doc came back. "He must have been a mere punk—I mean, just a youngster then." She didn't say either yes or no. "Well," Doc rushed on, "you wait till you see how he's developed. I don't mind telling you, John's probably the most dynamic speaker in the entire country today." She sniffed like she didn't believe it. "That's straight," Doc insisted. "You'll get a chance to see tomorrow. We expect ten thousand people to turn out to hear him, and when you see what he does to them, you'll know I'm not exaggerating. He's wonderful!"

"That's a fact," I chimed in from behind. "He's terrific!"

I expected her to make some response, and judging from the way Doc turned his head, so did he. But she didn't say a word. She just sat there, very erect, looking straight ahead. It was exactly the way her brother always sat when in a stubborn mood. So there was silence in the car, a prickly silence that lasted maybe three or four minutes. Then suddenly she stirred and said in a quiet voice, "I think he must be insane." She half-turned, as though daring us to deny the statement. "That's the only possible explanation," she went on. "He simply must be out of his mind." Again she seemed to wait for us to try and contradict her. We didn't open our mouths, though, so she breathed hard for a few seconds, and then suddenly snorted, *"Him* attacking the Jews!"

I saw Doc throw her another startled look. "Why, what's wrong with that?" he piped up. "After all, if he believes they're a menace to the country . . ."

"But how *can* he believe that?" she broke in, her voice almost shrill now. "He of all people?" She turned and caught our puzzled expressions. *"He's a half-Jew himself!"*

32

We made her tell us the whole story right there in the car. Doc drew up to the curb, shut off the engine, and went to work on her in a way that practically forced her to tell it to us. And when she finished, he said he didn't dare take her to the place where her brother was. He explained that J.C. was at the German House, conferring with the leaders of all the other organizations that Flanahan had lined up for the Autocade, and there was no telling what might happen if she made a scene there. "You've got to wait till you can get him alone," he insisted.

She wouldn't listen at first, but finally he managed to make her see he was right. Then he drove straight to the Y.W.C.A.—that's where she was stopping, she said—parked her there, and staggered off with me at his heels toward the nearest bar.

"Christ!" he swore as he collapsed in a booth. "I still can't believe it! *He* should turn out to be the son of a Hebe! It just can't be true!"

But it was, and Doc knew it as well as I did. Even if that dame hadn't had the documents right there to prove it—that's what she was carrying in her little suitcase—we would still have had to believe her. Because no one could have made up such a story. It was altogether too weird to be anything but true.

I shan't try to tell it the way she did, because that would take too long and be kind of confusing. At first we had to drag things out of her, and then, once we got her going at last, she seemed unable to stop. I guess she'd had that secret bottled up in her too long. She kept wandering off on tangents and wallowing around in details. Also she used a lot of high-brow words. So I'll give you the story straight and in my own plain language.

To begin at the beginning, J.C.'s real name wasn't Power at all. It was Bauer, like his sister's. And by rights it shouldn't have been even Bauer, but Rappaport! Bauer was his mother's maiden name. She'd given it to her two children because their father, a Hebe by the name of Israel Rappaport, had deserted her before the second one was even born. How she'd ever come to marry such a character is a story all by itself. Her old man, who was a pretty substantial farmer in southern Indiana, had wanted her to get a real good edu-cation, so he'd sent her off to college when she was seventeen. It was a hick Baptist institution half-way up the state, very religious and straitlaced, and he'd picked it because he'd figured the sort of education she'd get there would be nothing but good. He was fooled, though. Came Christmas vacation, and lo and behold the kid returned home pregnant! She seemed kind of proud of it, too. So Papa marched her straight back to the college, got her to point out the cause of it all, and then started fingering his shotgun till suddenly there was a wedding.

The groom was said Israel Rappaport, aged 30, a sort of special stu-dent on the campus, and hardly what a prosperous Indiana farmer would consider a catch. To the young bride, though, the guy seemed wonderful. Of course he was a Hebe with a Hungarian accent, and he had no home, and not a dime to his name. But on the other hand he was the most fascinating thing in pants that she'd ever met. Miss Bauer showed us a photograph taken shortly after the wedding—it was one of the mementos she was carrying in the suitcase—and we could tell from it that young Rappaport must have been quite a good-looker. In a foreign way, of course. He was tall and thin, with heavy black hair, smoldering eyes, and the sort of mouth there ought to be a law against. In addition, he was studying to be a preacher, having been brought to Christ right there on that campus only a few years earlier. That must have been his crowning attraction to the bride. She was apparently a high-strung kid who'd attended too many revivals, and she seems to have talked herself into believing she was marrying a second St. Paul.

She soon learnt better, though. He became a preacher all right, but more along the line of Elmer Gantry than St. Paul. She forgave him the first time she caught him off-base, and probably would have done it the second time if he'd given her a chance. But he didn't. Instead he just walked out on her one day and stayed out. I guess he'd had more than enough of her by then. At any rate, he never let her even hear from him again.

Well, knowing the type she was, you can imagine what that did to her. All her love turned to hate, and she spent the rest of her life trying to blot out the guy's memory. Her worst fright, it seems, was that the kids might learn about him, because she'd become convinced that all Jews were servants of the Devil. Her first child, who had originally been christened Judith Rappaport, she now renamed Jane Christina Bauer. When the second was born, and it turned out to be a boy, she called him John Christian Bauer. She'd had that second child while living in her father's house, but a year or two later she made her old man settle her on a place of her own over in Kentucky. It was a small farm surrounded by lots of woods, and she insisted on moving there because she was anxious to raise the youngsters where no one knew about her past. When they grew old enough to be curious, she told them their papa had been her own third cousin—that explained the name Bauer—and that he'd gone off to look for gold in Alaska and had died there.

Nevertheless the kids did catch on to the secret. The girl got wind of it at the age of six or so, when a gossipy grand-aunt came on a visit to the farm and made some remark about "your Hebrew father." That got little Jane all excited, and right away she ran to tell her baby brother. Then both of them, not really understanding what it was all about, went to their mother for an explanation, and an awful scene resulted. The woman went completely berserk, chased the old aunt with a carving-knife, wept, howled, beat her head against the wall, and finally collapsed in a dead faint. And that night, when the kids were ready to go to bed, she made them kneel and promise on the Bible that they would never repeat what they'd heard. "It's a wicked lie," she told them, "and God'll strike you dead if you so much as think of it again!"

That, of course, was the worst thing she could possibly have done, because it left those youngsters sort of haunted. They never brought up the matter again—they were too scared—but it was always there in the back of their heads. The effect was especially bad on the boy, he being the more high-strung of the two. He grew up to be a moody twerp who always wanted to be by himself. According to his sister, that may have been in part because he was too puny to be any good at games; but mostly, she thought, it was owing to that scar on his mind. He seemed to be jumpy all the time, like he had something to hide. When anyone tried to cross him, he'd get completely uncontrollable, cussing and screaming and throwing whatever he could lay his hands on. The only person he seemed to care about was his mother, who spoiled him no end, yet at times he'd act savage even to her. On one occasion, when she caught him doing a thing that I guess kids of his type just naturally do to themselves, he threatened to kill her, and then rushed off and attempted to kill himself. If a farmhand hadn't heard him strangling in the barn, and rushed in and cut him down in time, the attempt might actually have succeeded.

The boy seemed to improve slightly when he entered high school. His health was still poor, especially in the winter time when he was constantly coming down with colds; but he'd started reading books on physical culture, and exercising all day long. He set out to get on the track team, and though he failed in that, he made up for the disappointment by becoming captain of the debating team. He took to combing his hair once in a while, and shining his shoes, and even began writing poetry to a girl. But then, just when he seemed on the point of becoming almost normal, his mother suddenly started acting up. She'd always been kind of hysterical in her attitude toward the boy, but now she became practically nuts. She'd follow him around wherever he went, try to pry into his thoughts, and shoo off any friends he tried to make. If he complained, she'd throw a faint, and then cry for him to come and rub her arms and legs. She'd keep him at her bedside for hours on end, making him read to her, or hold her hand, or just sit.

That kept up until the boy was ready to go to college, and then she wanted to sell the farm and go with him. She said she was afraid he'd get sick and waste away unless she was there to cook his meals and look after him. He tried to balk, of course, saying he was old enough to take care of himself; and that made her go battier than ever. The two of them were living alone then—the sister was already away at college—and they began acting like a couple of cats in a sack. Day in and day out they argued and nagged and stormed. Finally one night they had a really terrible fight, and when the mother threw her usual faint, the boy just stamped out and left her lying there on the kitchen floor. There was no one else in the house, but he was so wrought up he didn't give a damn. He went off into the woods and walked and walked and walked till he was ready to drop. Then he crept back into the house. His mother was still lying there on the kitchen floor, but in a pool of blood now. She'd cut her throat almost from ear to ear.

The next day, when the sister came rushing back from college, she found the boy acting in a way she couldn't understand at all. She'd expected he'd be frantic, but instead he seemed like a stone. He didn't shed a single tear, even at the funeral. And two days later he disappeared. He'd borrowed fifty dollars from the lawyer who was handling the estate, and left a note saying he didn't care to claim any of the rest. Apparently he'd taken the night train to Chicago.

His sister tried to trail him, of course. She'd never gotten along with him—in fact they'd barely talked to each other for years—but he was still her brother and she felt an obligation to try and find him. Besides, there was the problem of settling the estate, which was fairly sizable on account that it included what the grandfather had left on his death. However, when seven years passed without revealing any clue to John's whereabouts, the courts declared him dead, and that was that. Most people who remembered him figured he'd probably done away with himself.

Meanwhile the girl had finished college and become a professional social worker. She didn't tell us what prompted her to do that. I guess she too must have been slightly screwy, because otherwise, what with the money she'd inherited, she could easily have copped herself a husband. Instead, she took up that weird career and remained an old maid. She settled on the East Side of New York, and that was one detail in her story that she did explain to us. It seems she'd found out at last the entire truth about her father, and it had given her an urge to go and live among his people. But after twenty-five years of that, she must have decided it might be a nice change to live among Gentiles for a spell. Whatever the reason, she finally upped and moved to California, where she became a social worker in one of the Oakie camps near Bakersfield.

And that's how she happened to get on the track of her brother. The very first time she'd heard the name John Christian Power it had sort of rung a bell inside her; but she'd shied away from trying to discover who he was. For almost a year, during which she'd spent several weekends in L.A., she'd never once dared attend a Crusade meeting to see what he looked like. But at last she came across his photo in that magazine article on the American Fascists—the one, you recall, that I'd claimed credit for planting—and right away she'd known all. Even after thirty years, and with his head shaved, she'd been able to recognize his odd likeness. So the next morning she'd caught the early bus to town, and kept going till I bumped into her in front of the Citadel. . . .

33

Doc swallowed his double-rye in one gulp and then gave a shudder. "I just can't believe it!" he repeated, scowling at the table.

I didn't speak for a minute. I just went at my own drink, and followed it with the chaser. Then, lighting a cigarette, I muttered, "It's the goddamnedest story I ever heard!"

There was another pause, during which he too lit up, but only to mash the cigarette after a single puff. "By God," he suddenly exploded, "I knew he was hiding something, but I never dreamed it would be anything like this!" He raised his eyes and looked at me like he was almost in physical pain. "Did you?" he asked.

I shook my head. "The question is," I said, "what're we gonna do now? I guess this just about finishes everything."

He didn't answer. Instead he looked at his empty glass and signaled the bartender to hit him again. The cluck must have misunderstood, because he brought two fresh drinks, but Doc said never mind, and downed both of them. Then he seemed to brighten suddenly. "You know what?" he cried. "If we play our cards right, I think maybe . . ." He didn't finish the sentence. Instead he caught his tongue between his lips and began drumming on the table. Evidently he wanted to think some more.

I said nothing. I was pretty sure I knew what was going through his mind, and it didn't interest me. Slumping in my seat, I started fooling with my pocket-comb; and then tiring of that, I lit another cigarette. Meanwhile he just sat and thought.

After about ten minutes, though, he seemed to give up. "Let's get the hell out of here!" he said. "This joint's too noisy!"

He was right about that. The place was jam-packed, mostly with middle-aged dames drinking cocktails and jabbering about the bargains they'd been stalking all afternoon. We tried another bar across the street, but found that just as crowded, so finally we decided to go to our hotel. It was only a few blocks away.

When we got there, we found three phone messages waiting for Doc, and one for me. They were all identical: Mr. Corcoran wanted us to call him at once at the Quaker Institute. We knew what that meant: Corcoran was our code name for Flanahan, and the Quaker Institute was the German House. "Lord!" Doc side-mouthed to me. "I forgot all about that."

"About what?" I asked.

"About bringing you to the German House," he said, still keeping his voice low. We were standing right by the desk in the hotel lobby. "That's why Flanahan sent me around to the Citadel," he explained. "He wanted you right away, so's you could tell the crowd what you'd done about lining up the reporters for tomorrow afternoon."

I gave a grim chuckle and asked what he thought we ought to do.

He shrugged his shoulders. "Forget it, I guess," he answered. "Just play dead." He turned to address the desk-clerk. "If you get any more calls for us, Sam," he said, "tell 'em we're still out. Don't forget now! We're out to everybody!"

When we got upstairs I asked Doc what was in his mind, but he wouldn't tell me. Instead he went into the bedroom of his suite and started getting a number on the phone. Apparently he was calling Miss Bauer to tell her that her brother was going to be tied up all evening. "You'll have to wait until morning," I heard him say to her. ". . . Yeah, he's sure to be alone then. . . . Now don't worry, Miss Bauer. You can trust us. We'll take you to him ourselves. . . . Yeah, we'll call for you around ten."

He hung up and came back into the parlor. "That settles that," he muttered, starting to grope in a closet. "Now let's have a drink."

I could see he wasn't just trying to keep me in suspense. He was stalling because he hadn't yet figured out his next move. I could tell by the scowl on his fat face. So I kept mum. If I could have suggested anything, I'd have done so, but my mind was on something else. I was still going over that story, fascinated by all the puzzles it solved. I'd always wondered what made J.C. behave the way he did, and now at last I was beginning to understand.

Doc poured the drinks and then sprawled in a chair. I was stretched out on the couch, staring at the ceiling. There was silence for a while, each of us sunk in his own thoughts. Finally I heard him stir and let out a sigh. "If I could just figure out some way to get rid of her," he mumbled, half to himself.

"And then what would you do?" I asked without turning my head.

"Aw, then there'd be nothing to it," he answered. "I'd just hint around that I was hep to his secret, and from then on The Power would be in *my* power. Yes, sir. I'd be leading him around like a tame bear."

"I can just see you doing that," I muttered sarcastically.

He ignored the interruption. "Yes, sir," he went on, sort of licking his chops, "I sure would know how to act then. First of all, I'd get him to tone down all this Jew-baiting stuff. In fact, I'd make him cut it out entirely. I'd follow the policy of those Mankind United boys. They don't even mention the Jews. They just talk about the Hidden Rulers, and that's smart, Clem." He nodded emphatically, and paused to gulp at his drink. "You bet that's smart," he continued after he'd put his glass down. "It's like leaving a blank for each sucker to fill in with his pet hate. The Hidden Rulers can be anything—Jews, Jesuits, Masons, Mormons, Communists, Fascists—any goddam thing you please. See the point?"

"Yeah," I answered, "but if you think he'd see it, you're crazy."

"But he'd *have* to see it!" Doc yelled. "After all, the only thing he wants, fundamentally, is power. He's got what we in the medical profession call delusions of grandoor. Know what I mean? He's just got to play Superman all the time. Well, that's okay with me. I'll let him play Superman all he pleases—so long as it's on my terms. And the way I'll have him tied, he won't have any choice. He'll know that I know all about his father."

"You *are* crazy," I said. "Don't you realize he'll deny that whole story."

"Sure," Doc answered blandly. "And I'll tell him I myself don't believe it either. But deep down he'll know I do, and that's all that'll be necessary. He'll always be scared to death maybe I'll give his secret away."

"Like hell he will!" I said, sitting up and pointing a finger. "You don't understand his case at all, Doc. The fact is, that poor screwball doesn't altogether know what the secret is! It's like his sister explained: he's *re*pressed the whole thing. He's buried it somewhere deep in the bottom drawer of his brain." I could see Doc wasn't following me, so I tried another tack. "Look," I said, still pointing with my finger, "why do you think he wants to kill all the Jews? Fundamentally because that's the only way he has of getting back at his own father. It's like when a man's sore at his wife, he'll take it out on his stenog. See what I mean?"

"But wait a minute," Doc yapped at me. "Didn't you just say he isn't even conscious who his father really is? If that's the case . . ."

"Yeah, yeah," I cut in, "I know that sounds like I'm contradicting myself. But I'm not. I've been thinking over all that psychological stuff his sister handed us, and I think I've got it clear now. What you've got to realize is that though he doesn't *know* his father was a Hebe, he *feels* it. The fact that he's buried the memory doesn't mean he's destroyed it. It's like when you've buried a corpse in a trunk down in the basement. You may not be able to see it, but you can still smell it. That's what made him tell you his sister was mixed up with a Hebe. He probably believes that himself, the way a crazy murderer will believe that the smell coming through the floorboards is from a dead cat or something. Get the idea?" Doc didn't answer, so I pushed on. "Now here's the next point. Although deep down he hates the Jews solely because he hates his father, on the surface he has to have a better reason. So what does he do? He says he hates them because they're a menace to the world. Their crime is that they want to run everything. But actually that's his own crime. *He* wants to run everything, and in his heart he knows that isn't right. So when he accuses the Jews of that, he isn't merely creating an excuse for hating them. He's also creating an excuse for not hating himself. See?" I could tell by the look on Doc's face that he didn't even begin to see, so I gave up. "What's the use?" I groaned, stretching out on the couch again. "The trouble with you is, you don't understand psychology."

That seemed to get him sore. "*I* don't understand psychology?" he ballered. "Christ Almighty, didn't I practice medicine for almost twenty years? You've got a helluva nerve, making a statement like that. Why, I know more psychology in a minute than you'll . . ."

"Horse radish!" I snorted. "Anyway, what's the use of arguing? The point is, there's still his sister to be considered. You'll never be able to get her out of the way. She's not that kind."

He had no comeback to that. He just heaved a sigh and started refilling his glass.

We remained like that for maybe twenty minutes, he in his chair with his feet on the bridge table, and me on the couch. Neither of us spoke. He kept on drinking, and I chain-smoked.

Finally he stirred uneasily. "Maybe we'd better hop over to the German House, after all," he said. "We'll tell 'em we had a flat tire, or something."

I turned and glared at him. "Are you nuts?" I demanded. "What the hell do we want to go over there for?"

"But there's still the rally tomorrow. We don't want to be left out of that. Don't forget there's going to be a collection."

I made a dirty sound with my lips. "Without J.C. to whip up the mob," I said, "you won't collect enough to put in a pig's eye."

He considered that a minute and then shook his head. "What

makes you so sure he won't be there?" he asked. I made a gesture to indicate I didn't consider the question worth answering. "Okay," he said, starting to reach for his wallet, "I'll lay a bet right now that he shows up as if nothing had happened. You just said yourself he'll never admit the truth about his father."

"Not if *you* tell it to him, he won't," I replied. "But coming from his sister, it'll be different. Just the shock of seeing her will split his mind wide open." I sat up suddenly and began pointing my finger again. "You know what I'll bet? I'll bet he goes right out and tries to kill himself. Yes, sir."

Doc turned white. "Christ!" he breathed. "I never thought of that! What d'you think we ought to do?"

"I know what I'm gonna do," I answered, getting to my feet. "I'm gonna start packing."

34

I must have been having a nightmare when the phone woke me up. I was gooseflesh all over, and at the same time I was running with sweat.

It was Doc calling. His voice sounded like he hadn't had such a good night either. "Whadye say?" he asked. "Didja think it over?"

"Think what over?" I growled.

"About coming along with me this morning."

I said a word you're not allowed to print, and hung up. Then I went back to bed.

A couple of minutes later there he was, rattling the doorknob. I repeated the bad word, but got up nevertheless and unlocked the door. The slob was wearing a bathrobe over his pajamas, and looked in terrible shape. There was pus in the corners of his eyes, and dried saliva on his lips.

He started to say something, but I wouldn't give him a chance. "Why the hell won't you lemme alone, Doc?" I whined. "I wanna sleep." It was true. He'd kept me up till way after two o'clock, jawing me deaf, dumb and blind—and here he was, routing me out again at eight. "I told you I'm through, didn't I? So lemme alone."

"Aw, is that the way to talk to a pal?" he pleaded, pushing his way into the room. "Listen, Clem. Don't let me down now. I've stuck by you often enough, haven't I? Well, why won't you stick by me for once?"

"But for crisake, whadye need me for?" I cried. "Hank'll be there, in case he goes berserk."

The guy ran a coated tongue over his lips. "No, that's just the trouble," he began to argue. "I'll have to send Hank away before I can get her in. See?"

I did, but still refused to be budged. "That's your worry," I said, "not mine. If you had any sense, you'd do what I'm doing—get the hell out of this mess right now."

"And give up everything I've worked so hard to develop?" he yammered. "Not without a fight, I won't! No, sir!"

"Okay," I shrugged, "if that's the way you feel about it, go ahead. But don't expect me to come along. I'm through. . . . Now don't start asking me again. I'm through, absolutely!"

Two hours later I was driving with him to pick up Miss Bauer at the Y.W.C.A. Don't ask me why I'd given in. There were sound reasons, as you will soon discover.

She was waiting on the sidewalk when we drove up, and I couldn't help marveling at the way she appeared. Her long face was chalky, and there was a strained look in her eyes, but otherwise she showed no signs of nervousness. She was wearing the same neat black hat and coat as yesterday, but I noticed she'd changed her dress. The one today had a high net collar that fitted tight around her scrawny neck. Also she was wearing a big cameo brooch that I hadn't seen on her before. It looked like it might have been her mother's.

I hopped out to give her my seat, but she shook her head and got into the rear compartment. The way she carried her little suitcase, all I could think of was a grim old visiting nurse starting out on her rounds.

Almost nothing was said as we drove along through the Sunday-quiet streets. The woman sat with her face toward the window, her gloved hands gripping the suitcase on her knees. When we finally reached the Citadel, Doc parked on the other side of the street and told us to stay in the car while he got rid of Hank. He'd already figured out a way to manage that, and it apparently worked. In a couple of minutes I saw the squarehead come out of the front door and march off down the block. He was wearing a Ranger's uniform, and I noticed a long flashlight poking out of his hip pocket. I knew what that was for, and had to laugh to myself. Hank was on his way to the Fillmore Stadium to search for any bombs that the warmongers might have planted under the speaker's stand.

Doc signaled us from the porch, and we crossed over and entered the house. "John's upstairs," he said to Miss Bauer in a low tone. "You don't want me to go along, do you?" She shook her head, and I caught the look of relief on Doc's face. Pointing to the room on the second floor, he watched her climb the stairs, cross the landing, and disappear through the door.

We listened a minute, heard nothing, and then he grabbed my arm. "Come on," he side-mouthed. "We've got work to do." Taking up the empty valise we'd brought with us, he led the way to his own office. First he opened the small safe in the closet, and handed me the cash-box, the tray of postage stamps, a couple of account books, and the mailing list. Next he unlocked his desk and began clearing out various papers and belongings, including a half-empty bottle of rye. I meanwhile put the cover on my portable and carried it out into the hallway.

I paused at the foot of the stairs, my ears pricked, but heard no sound from above. I was on the point of gumshoeing up to the landing when Doc appeared, carrying the valise. "Okay," he said. "Now let's see what we can find in Cleaver's desk."

I followed him into the other office and produced a key. It was the one I'd used in the days when the desk there had been mine. But the lock had evidently been changed, because when I put in the key, it wouldn't turn.

"Here, let me try," said Doc. I stepped out of his way, and he gave so hard a try that he snapped the key in two. "Hell!" he swore. "Now we'll have to jimmy the damn thing open!"

I said: "Aw, let's forget it! There's probably nothing in there anyway."

He wouldn't listen. Putting on an impatient scowl, he told me to run down to the basement and look for a chisel or something. I hesitated a second, but then turned to obey. I knew why Doc was so anxious to break into that desk. He wanted to get something to hold over Flanahan & Co. in case they tried to get tough later on. I, of course, wasn't worried on that score. I was all set to kiss the Crusade a final good-bye the minute I collected my half of the cash and stamps we'd just picked up. Nevertheless I felt I ought to stick by my partner.

Returning to the hallway, I opened the basement door, switched on the light, and started down the steps. But then of a sudden I became frozen. It was because of a bellow somewhere above me, and a crash like a piece of furniture had been knocked over. I listened a second, and then came bounding back up to the hallway.

Doc was already at the foot of the stairs, and I joined him there. The bellowing had stopped, and I could hear the woman's voice now. It was too faint, though, for me to catch the words. For maybe fifteen or twenty seconds the voice went on, and then there was another roar. It came from The Power, of course. "They're forged!" I heard him blast. "Take them away! I don't want to see them! They're all forged!" Then there was another crash. It sounded like he'd hurled her suitcase across the room.

Again I heard the woman's voice. It was still low and gentle, as if she was trying to reason with him. I strained to make out what she was saying, but couldn't. "Let's get closer," I whispered to Doc, starting to climb the stairs.

He caught my sleeve and pretty near tore it off. "You gone nuts?" he hissed. "We better beat it out to the car."

"And leave her here alone with him?" I cried under my breath. "He's liable . . ." I broke off because The Power was screaming again. His voice was even louder now, and I could hear him stamping his foot. "It's a lie!" he screamed. "It's a God-damned lie! You know it's a lie!" Apparently she tried to interrupt him, but he wouldn't give her a chance. "It's a lie!" he screamed, over and over again. "It's a lie! It's a lie! It's a lie! . . ."

I turned to look at Doc, but he'd already picked up the valise and was halfway to the front door. "For crisake, Doc!" I called after him hoarsely. "You can't do a thing like that! She may need help!"

"So what?" he whined. "If you want to act like a Marine, go ahead. I'm gonna wait in the car."

I looked at him with disgust. Somehow the sight of his funk made me feel brave as hell. "And you're the guy who's always calling me yellow!" I sneered.

That seemed to get him. He hesitated a second, then dropped the valise and started to come back. "Okay," he growled. "What d'you think we ought to do?"

I waved him to shut up so that I could hear what The Power was shouting about now. It was something concerning the Jews, and his voice was practically a screech. "No, don't try to deny it!" I heard him yell. "They put you up to this, didn't they? I know those devils! They'd do anything to destroy me! Anything, anything, anything! . . ." It was almost like a record when the needle gets caught in a groove. Then suddenly the needle appeared to start weaving all over the record. "They want to crush me just when—just when I'm about to—to—just when the world—I know you, Jane —they sent you—they'd do anything, anything, anything. . . ." The needle seemed caught again.

I began glaring around the hallway, searching for something. Finally I spotted the umbrella stand, near the door, and darted in that direction. J.C. kept his canes there, the ones he liked to take along when he went on his hikes. They were heavy canes with thick nobs on the end, and I grabbed the two that looked wickedest. "Here," I panted, handing one to Doc, "let's take these and go on upstairs."

He started shaking his head, but I shot him a glare that forced him to obey. I took the lead, and began climbing the steps like I wasn't in the least scared. Actually I could hardly keep my knees from folding under me. I had no idea what I was going to do when I got upstairs. All I knew was that I just had to get there right away. The Power seemed to be getting more and more frantic. He wasn't making any sense at all now—just yelling words and half-phrases that didn't connect. And he seemed to be throwing things around, books, lamps, chairs, all sorts of things.

Then of a sudden he shut up. It was just as if somebody had switched off a blaring radio. I was on the landing by that time, and the abrupt silence made me stop dead in my tracks. I turned to look at Doc, who was hanging on to the banister like he was ready to collapse. He sign-languaged for me to come back, but I scowled no. Then, getting a fresh grip on my club, I tiptoed across the landing and put my ear to the door.

Apparently they were out on the sleeping porch, because I could hear him groaning now, but from a distance. I turned the knob very quietly and peeked in, but all I saw was the drawn portieres. Now, though, I could make out what the poor nut was saying. "Why did you do it to me?" he was groaning. "Oh, my God, why did you do it?" Over and over again he kept repeating that, his voice sort of smothered, like he was holding his head in his hands.

Finally I heard the woman's voice again. "Don't, John," she pleaded with him. "There's no reason for you to cry. You'll be all right. Lie down, John." She sounded just like a mother talking to a sick kid, and for a minute I thought she was going to get him calm again. But it was only for a minute, because then, without any warning, he screamed, "Get out! Go on, get out! I'm The Power! They can't destroy The Power! Go on! Go back and tell those swine that sent you! They'll never destroy ME!"

He paused an instant, and I could hear him struggle to get his breath. "Go on!" he started screaming again. "Get out! Get out! GET OUT! . . ."

Suddenly his voice broke off, and I thought I heard him rush into the bathroom. There was a sound like he was opening the medicine-cabinet. Then all at once I felt myself turn to solid ice, because I heard the woman let out a terrible shriek.

"*No, no, John!*" she shrieked. "*Put that away! You wouldn't dare. . . .*"

That was all I heard, because in that instant the portieres parted, and there she was, flying toward me, with him after her.

He had an open razor in his hand.

I stepped back just in time, let her pass me, and then brought my club down square on his head. I didn't hit him hard, but the surprise of the blow must have stunned him, because he dropped right at my feet. I turned and stared at the woman. I was even more amazed than she was at what I had just done. Then Doc came rushing up, pushed me aside, and began feeling the head.

"Is he all right?" Miss Bauer asked in a trembling whisper.

Doc nodded and then looked up at me. "Gimme a hand," he said. "We better put him on that couch in there."

The guy didn't weigh much, but he was so long and limp that we had to practically drag him. Doc put a pillow under his head, and the woman ran to the bathroom to get a wet towel.

"Think we ought to call a doctor?" she asked after a minute.

"Nah, he's okay," said Doc. "He's coming to already. See?" The eyelids were actually twitching. "What we've got to do is get you out of here right away." She tried to protest, but he overruled her. "He'll be all right," Doc assured her, sounding very professional. "The best thing you can do for him now is to stay out of his sight."

I felt the same way, and between the two of us we finally managed to talk her into leaving. At the front door, though, she suddenly realized we meant to leave with her, and then she started arguing again. "Somebody's got to remain here," she cried. "He may need help when he comes to."

Doc threw me a wink and said out loud, "That's right. You better stay, Clem." Then, through the side of his mouth, he pig-Latined, "Atkay the usbay."

I got the point at once, and said, "Sure, Doc, if you think that's best." Then, handing him my typewriter—he already had the valise —I opened the door for them, and watched them go to the car.

35

I reached the hotel half an hour later, and found Doc slumped in a chair and drinking.

"Boy, that was a close call!" he said. "He might have carved up all three of us if you hadn't conked him in time." He gave his face

[232]

a quick wipe with the palm of his hand. "I've got to give you credit, Clem."

"I'd rather take the cash," I said. "How much was there altogether in that strong-box?"

He answered that he hadn't looked yet, but I wouldn't believe him. "That's straight," he insisted. "I haven't even opened the valise."

"Well, let's get busy then," I said. "I want to get the hell out of here before things start popping."

It turned out that we hadn't made away with nearly as much as I'd hoped. Including the stamps, the entire loot didn't count up to more than around sixty bucks. So there was a slight argument between us. I felt that Doc oughtn't to insist on taking half, seeing as how much harder up I was than he. We must have sparred for maybe fifteen minutes before we finally hit on a compromise. I got $40, and he kept the balance of the cash and all the stamps. Whereupon, tucking the dough in my wallet, I prepared to scram.

"I think you're making a mistake, Clem," Doc said as he poured me one last drink. "This racket isn't played out yet. Not by a hell of a long way."

I said I thought he was talking like a sap. "Long John's through now," I said. "He'll be just like a watch with a busted mainspring after what happened this morning."

"So what?" Doc shrugged.

"So this," I replied. "With that guy gone, the Crusade's dead. *You* know that."

"Sure I know it," he admitted. "But the suckers on that mailing list are still alive." He smiled and spread his hands. "Sit down, Clem, and let me explain what I've got in mind. . . . Aw, come on. It'll only take a minute." And thereupon, forcing me into a chair, he started giving me a song-and-dance about organizing a new movement with himself as leader, and me as the second in command. "We won't go after the riffraff any more," he said. "Just the nice middle-class folk—the kind those Mankind United boys appeal to. With all we know now about running this type of racket, we ought to be able to clean up, Clem."

I wasn't impressed, and said so, whereupon he got sort of peeved. I suppose it was because at heart he wasn't completely sold on the idea himself. We jawed back and forth for quite a while, both of us getting more and more heated. Finally I said, "Aw, what's the use of arguing, Doc? My mind's made up. You'll never convince me . . ." Then I broke off, because I saw him look toward the door suspiciously. I pricked up my ears, and started to tiptoe across the room. I was almost positive someone was listening at the keyhole.

I was just about to reach for the knob when the door flew open, and in rushed Cleaver with Flanahan and Kronkhite at his heels. The ape was wearing his uniform, and he'd evidently been drinking.

"What've you done with him?" he blasted, grabbing me by the lapels. "Come on, talk, you little runt, or I'll knock your teeth out!"

Instinctively I brought up my knee and tried to ram it in his groin. I must have missed though, or else I didn't ram hard enough, because the next thing I knew I was on the floor. He leaned down to hoist me back on my feet, slammed me up against the wall, and started slapping my face.

But Flanahan pulled him off. "You can do that later," the Mick said, talking through his teeth. "Throw him over there."

Cleaver gave me a shove, and I sprawled into the chair next to Doc's. Apparently my pal hadn't even stirred despite what he'd seen happen to me. He must have been too petrified.

Flanahan took a stand in front of us. His skinny little face was drawn and white, and his eyes glowed with a sort of cold fury. "Now then," he rapped out, "you'd better talk fast, both of you. Where is he?"

"If—if you mean J.C.," Doc stammered, "he must be at the Citadel. That's where we left him no more than an hour ago."

Kronkhite started yelling it was a "gottamn lie," but Flanahan flagged him to shut up. Turning to us he said, "He's not there now."

We could only shake our heads. "That's where we left him," Doc repeated. "Maybe . . ."

"Maybe nothing!" Cleaver butted in. "We're on to you two rats. You've shanghaied him, that's what you've done."

"You're crazy!" said Doc, pulling shakily at his shirt collar. "What would we want to do that for?"

"You know vot for!" Kronkhite barked. "You vunt to sabotash de rally!"

"Sure, that's it," said Cleaver. "You've been working against us all along." Doc started to deny it, but the ape wouldn't give him a chance. Turning to Flanahan, he held out his fists and begged, "Aw, let me work on 'em! It's the only way you'll ever get 'em to talk."

The Mick brushed him aside. Looking at us, he asked, "What became of you yesterday? Why didn't you show up at the German House?"

"Well, it was like this," Doc started to explain. "I had a flat tire, and by the time I could get it fixed . . ."

"Aw, cut it out, Doc!" I broke in. "We might as well tell 'em the truth." Then, turning to Flanahan, I said, "We decided to quit, that's all."

"Is that so?" he asked, sort of biting off the words. "And may I ask why?"

"Because we happened to find out something about The Power that we hadn't known before. That's what we went to see him about this morning."

"Yeah?" Cleaver snarled. "An' what was that?"

I suddenly realized I'd rather not be the one who broke the news. "You tell 'em," I said to Doc.

He hesitated a minute, evidently trying to figure out a way to break it to them gently. But they wouldn't give him time. "Come on," Cleaver yelled. "Quit stalling."

Doc wet his lips and set himself for the blast. "Okay," he said hoarsely. "Here it is: J.C.'s really a Jew himself!"

For a second they just stared, and then Kronkhite hurled himself at Doc. "You sonovabitch!" he screamed, trying to get his fingers around Doc's throat. "You say a ting like dot about your own Leader? I'll kill you, you sonovabitch!"

He looked like he really meant it, and I got so panicky I screamed out, "But it's true! His sister . . ." Suddenly something that felt like a rock hit me in the mouth. It was Cleaver's fist, and I kicked with all my might. This time I didn't miss, and the thug let out a howl that must have been heard ten blocks away. Then he was on me again, one knee holding my legs fast, and his fists flailing my head.

How long that kept up I can't tell you. All I know is that suddenly he wasn't hitting me any more, and I could hear the phone ringing in the bedroom. I let down my guard, opened an eye, and saw Flanahan dragging both his goons away from us. Then I heard him say to Doc, "Go answer that."

The poor slob could barely get to his feet, but he finally managed to reach the phone somehow. Flanahan followed him as far as the door. "Hullo?" I heard Doc croak. "Who? Yeah, he's here. Just a minute." Then, staggering back, he said to me, "It's Tom Duranty. He says it's important."

Flanahan asked, "Who's he?"

"One of the reporters," I managed to say through the handkerchief I was holding to my bleeding mouth. "He probably wants to ask something about the rally."

The Mick jerked his head for me to go. "Tell him there's been a delay," he ordered, "but the meeting'll start at two-thirty at the latest."

I started to cross the room, one eye on Cleaver, who was following me with his fists still clenched. Sagging to the edge of the bed, I picked up the receiver and put it to my right ear. The other one was too sore to be even touched. " 'Lo?" I mumbled, trying not to move my jaw more than necessary. "Whadye want?"

I listened a minute, and then almost dropped the phone.

"What's the matter?" Flanahan asked, coming close.

I motioned for him to wait, and went on listening. Then I said, "Hold on a second, Tom." I put a hand over the mouthpiece and turned to the others. "Well, now you've got your answer," I told them. "Duranty's phoning from the police station. J.C.'s been arrested."

Cleaver growled, "I don't believe it! Here, lemme talk to him." He grabbed the phone and barked, "That you, Duranty? . . . Cap'n Cleaver talkin'. What's this about . . ." I watched his ugly mouth fall open as he listened. "Kurryst!" he rattled in his throat; and then a second time, *"Kurryst!"*

Kronkhite couldn't stand the suspense any longer. "Vat iss it?" he hissed, tugging at Cleaver's tunic.

The ape started to elbow him away, but Flanahan snapped, "Come on, Doug. What's he saying?"

"It's true!" the Captain answered hoarsely, pressing the mouthpiece against his chest. "They picked him up on Pershing Square!"

Flanahan asked, "What for?"

Cleaver's lips started quivering, like he couldn't bring himself to utter the words. Finally he managed to croak, "For—for indecent exposure!"

"*What?*"

"That's it," the ape insisted. Turning back to the mouthpiece, he said, "Hey, Duranty, tell it all over again. . . . Yeah, of course I understood, but there's some'dy else here wants to get it." Then he tipped the receiver so that all of us could hear.

"Okay," the brassy voice came back over the wire. "They've just booked Power on a morals charge! The cops caught him doing a strip-tease right in the middle of Pershing Square! It seems he jumped upon a bench—Hey, can you hear me? . . ."

"Yeah," Cleaver spoke into the mouthpiece. "Go ahead."

". . . Well, as I was saying, he hopped on a bench, started tearing off all his clothes, and yelled, 'Look, I'm not a Jew! It's a lie! You can see I'm not a Jew!' He's still yelling that right now, down in his cell. You can hear him all over this building. They've got him in a strait-jacket . . ." Suddenly the voice dropped. "Hey, I think I better hang up."

I snatched the phone out of Cleaver's paw and shouted, "What's the matter now, Tom?"

"I just saw Keniston walk in," came the muffled answer. "He's got a couple of the boys from the FBI with him. Call you back later. G'bye!"

"No, Tom! Tom!" I yelled. "Don't hang up. Where are you? In a booth?"

"Yeah."

"Well, duck your head out and see what you can learn right away. I'll hang on here."

A minute later he was back on the phone. "Hey, Clem," he panted, "you guys better scram. It seems your nut has been raving about guns you've got stored away some place. I think they're gonna pull a raid."

I dropped the phone and jumped to my feet. "Did you hear that?" I blatted. "The cops are coming after all of us."

They hadn't heard it, but they believed me. I guess they couldn't help believing me, the way my voice sounded. Flanahan was the first to come to life. Turning to his cronies, he said, "Come on!" Then all three of them ran.

I went back into the parlor, expecting to find Doc there. He was gone, though. I stared around, wondering where he could have disappeared to, and then beat it to my own room down the corridor. The door was locked, so I knew I'd guessed right. "It's okay, Doc," I yelled. "Open up. They're gone already."

He'd evidently barricaded himself inside there, because I heard him start dragging furniture out of the way.

"What happened?" he asked, when he was finally able to let me in.

"I'll explain later," I said. "We've got to make a getaway. And fast."

36

We got away all right, and damn fast. We lit out for San Diego, figuring that was about the nearest place where we could hole-up safely. The town was swarming with strangers on account of all the new defense plants. We registered under pseudonames at a quiet little hotel near the beach, and laid low for six days.

Finally, though, Doc couldn't stand it any longer. By that time he'd become convinced that there hadn't been any raid after all, because there hadn't been even a hint of one in the news dispatches. We'd scanned every edition of the L.A. papers to find out, and had tuned in on newscasts four and five times a day.

There had been lots of publicity about the Crusade, but solely in connection with The Power. Monday's papers carried his picture taken in jail—he looked awful—and a long story giving a jumbled account of his history and crack-up. The story mentioned Doc's name, and also Cleaver's, but only in passing. There was no reference at all to Flanahan, or Kronkhite, or anyone else. On Tuesday there were interviews with Miss Bauer, and also with Reverend Keniston and half a dozen psychiatrists. All those people were agreed that the judge had done right in committing J.C. to a state institution for the insane.

Wednesday evening we caught a broadcast over KNX in which some commentator with an English accent gave what he called a "psychoanalytic interpretation" of the case. It was pretty involved, and full of Ph.D-mon words, so neither Doc nor I got much out of the spiel. The nub of it seemed to be that every son just naturally hates his father—an idea which seemed to me not alone silly but positively indecent.

On Thursday there was no reference whatsoever to the case. Nor on Friday. Then on Saturday, when we searched through the papers and again found nothing, Doc blew up. He'd been difficult right from the start, constantly yapping that we'd taken a powder for nothing. Only the fact that he was plastered most of the time enabled me to keep him under control. But now he was sober and impossible to manage. He simply insisted that we go right back to L.A.

I tried to reason with him, of course. I don't know why, but I just had a psychic feeling that it would be a terrible blunder for us to go back. So I repeated what I'd been saying all week long—namely, that the cops had probably kept the raid out of the news in order to trap us. For maybe the hundredth time I pleaded, "Don't you see, Doc? That's the way they'd naturally operate if they wanted to lure us back." But he couldn't see, or anyway wouldn't. In part it may have been because he was suffering from a brutal hangover, one he just couldn't get rid of no matter how much hair-of-the-dog he swallowed. But mostly, I think, it was because he'd sold himself on the idea that if he went back right away, he might still be able to salvage the Crusade.

We argued all afternoon long—we hadn't gotten up till around noon—and finally he threatened to go without me. He actually packed up and got into the car, ready to leave. So then I said, "Look, Doc. Let's at least phone my old landlady again." I'd already spoken to her earlier in the week, she being the only person we could think of whose phone we felt sure wasn't being tapped. But the call had been wasted, because she'd spent the entire three minutes trying to get me to explain where I was, and why I'd left, and what made me so insistent that she shouldn't tell anyone I'd phoned. Apparently she'd known nothing more than what had come out in the papers. But that had been on Wednesday, and this was Saturday. "You never can tell," I said to Doc, "maybe she's heard something by this time."

In spite of the mood he was in, he could still see that that was a reasonable suggestion, so he shut off the engine and said he'd give me ten minutes to put through the call. As it turned out, I didn't need more than five. At the end of that time I returned to him kind of guilty-eyed and said, "You win, Doc. The coast seems clear, all right."

I'd learned a good deal more than that from Mrs. Gunderson, but I figured there'd be time enough to tell him the rest after we reached L.A. He must have sensed, though, that I was holding something back, because we'd no sooner got under way than he began prying and pumping till I just had to come clean. "Doc," I said, wetting my lips, "it looks like those bastards have stolen a base on you."

He shot me a scared look. "You mean X.Y.Z.?" he asked.

"Yeah," I answered, trying to avoid his eyes. "They've called a big meeting for tomorrow night to raise hell about what's been done to Long John. The old girl says the town's plastered with throwaways announcing the affair. They're claiming the warmongers trumped up that whole story about his being a Hebe. And you and I are supposed to have been in on the plot. She says . . ." I broke off, alarmed at the way Doc was driving. He was hitting sixty-five, yet looking at me instead of the road. "For crisake," I yelled, "watch where you're going!"

But I was too late. Out of nowhere a great big tree suddenly rushed at us, and the next thing I knew I was in a heap under the dashboard. For a second I thought my neck was broken, because I couldn't move my head. It was just panic, though, because when I tried hard I managed to move it all right. Then I felt Doc heave me back onto the seat, and I started pawing over myself to see if I was still in one piece. Apparently I was. The only thing I'd actually broken was my pocket-comb. I guess I must have had it in my hand at the time of the crash.

After a couple of minutes I felt collected enough to get out and join Doc, who was prowling around the front of the car, eyeing the damage. He seemed ready to break into tears, and I could hardly blame him. He'd always been so proud of that car, nursing it like it was his baby, and now the entire front was a mess. The bumper was busted, one fender was bashed, both headlights were in splinters, and the right tire was flat.

"Jeez, Doc," I sympathized, "that's a dirty shame!" He wheeled around, and for a second I thought he was going to sock me. "For Pete's sake!" I yammered, jumping away. "You're not blaming *me*, are you? Was *I* driving the car?"

He didn't answer. Instead he just turned on his heel, and climbed back into the car. Stepping on the starter, he got the engine going again, and slowly backed away from the tree. Then, getting out again, he waddled to the rear of the car and started unlocking the spare-tire compartment.

It took us fully an hour to make the change, because what with him being so fat, and me all bruised, we were neither of us much good at the job. By the time it was finished, I had sweat almost leaking out of my shoes and was about ready to collapse. Doc seemed to be in the same condition, and when we dragged ourselves back into the car, I felt sure he'd take out the bottle in his grip and suggest we have a drink. He didn't, though. Apparently he still felt so sore at me that he was willing to torture himself rather than make one friendly gesture.

But he drove slower now; in fact, he practically crawled along. It wasn't from choice, however. Apparently something was haywire with the steering gear, because the wheel kept shimmying in his hands, and there was a funny scrape in the front hubs. He got out a couple of times and made passes at trying to locate the cause of the trouble. I didn't offer to help. I felt too miffed, and besides I knew I was just as dumb around a car as he was. The only thing I could have done was suggest getting hold of a mechanic, and I figured he had brains enough to think of that all by himself.

He did. He stopped at the first garage that was still open—it was nearly 8 o'clock by this time—and the guy in charge spotted what was wrong in a minute. He was an old geezer with a corduroy voice and tobacco juice drooling down his chin, but he seemed pretty smart at his job. He said the front axle was bent, and both front wheels were out of kilter. He thought it would take half a day at least to get everything trued up right.

When Doc heard that, he almost died. "Half a *day?*" he wailed. "My God, man, I can't spare even half an hour!"

"That's too bad," the guy remarked, shifting the plug in his cheek. "But it'll still take half a day. That is, if you want the job done up proper."

"But can't you fix it temporarily?" I butted in.

He thought for a minute, aimed a jet of juice at a puddle of oil, and finally allowed that he could try. "But I don't figure it'll help much," he warned.

And it didn't. He tinkered for all of two hours, but when we started driving again, the steering gear seemed as wobbly as before. Nevertheless Doc wouldn't turn back. Gritting his teeth and gripping the wheel, he drove straight ahead in spite of all the noise and shimmying. He even tried to make time. At twenty miles an hour the car weaved from side to side like it was drunk, yet he kept forcing it to go to twenty-five, and even thirty. And he was driving without headlights! All he had was the spotlight near the windshield to show the way. And in addition to all that, there was fog along a good deal of the road. It was so thick in some places, you could hardly see the white guide-lines.

How we got through at all, I still don't know. The only thing I can tell you is that we did, though not until well after 3 A.M. And by then, naturally, we were both so worn out that we could barely stagger to our rooms. We parted without a word. I guess if either of us had tried to say even good night, the other would have busted him in the jaw. That's how mean we felt.

Suddenly—it seemed no more than five minutes after I'd piled into bed—I felt noises sort of prodding me awake. A radio was blaring in the next room, and people were jabbering in the corridor. I growled something and pulled the covers over my head. Even that failed to drown out the noises, so I yelled, "Shut up! Can't you let a guy sleep?" That seemed to silence the voices outside my door, but the radio continued as before. For a minute I thought of calling downstairs to squawk about the disturbance. It was supposed to be against the hotel rules to turn on a radio before 9 A.M. But I didn't feel like crawling out of bed to get to the phone, so I just snuck deeper under the covers and made another try at getting back to sleep.

It was no go, however. I did manage to doze off a couple of times, but only to be kicked awake again by those damn noises. They kept getting louder and more confused, like not one but half a dozen radios had been turned on. And the jabbering had started up once more out in the corridor. Also it seemed to me I could hear newsboys yelling in the street below, but not the way they usually did on Sunday mornings, in a sort of sing-song. They were really yelling.

I opened an eye and groped for my watch on the chair next to the bed. But it wasn't there. That gave me a start, and I opened both eyes. "What the hell?" I growled, peering all around. Finally I discovered what was the matter. I'd been so tired on going to bed that I'd forgotten to take the watch off my wrist. I looked at the dial and was amazed to see it was already one o'clock. I decided I might as well get up.

I didn't have the makings of breakfast, and was glad of it. The way I felt, I needed some real coffee, not just colored bilge. So I got some clothes on as fast as I could, and then started for the restaurant on the lobby-floor. A couple of guys got out of the elevator just as I got in. They seemed in a hurry, and almost knocked me over.

Pedro, the Mexican bellboy, was running the elevator, and the minute he closed the door, he turned to me and said, "You been away, no, Meest Smullet?" Then, before I could even nod, he rushed on, "Jeezkryst, ain't it tarrible, what dey done? Dose leedle yaller bastards, I hope dey shoot 'em all up!"

I gave my face a wipe like I was trying to sweep away cobwebs. "What are you gassing about?" I asked.

He evidently thought I was trying to spoof him, but only for a second. Then he cried, "Whatsa matter? You no hear the news? De Japs, dey just bomb Hawaii!"

"Go on!" I snorted. "Somebody's been kidding you. The Japs have got more sense . . ."

"No, Meest Smullet!" he panted. "It's true! They are telling on the radio since two hour already!" He turned to bring the elevator to the floor level, and opened the door. "You ask anybody!" he cried, pointing to the people in the lobby.

I started to rush over to the radio by the cigar stand, but heard the clerk call me as I passed the desk. I thought he was going to ask where I'd been all week, and maybe remind me again about my bill, so I said, "Just a minute, Martin. I want to hear the news. It isn't true, is it?"

"You mean about Pearl Harbor?" he said. "Yeah, I guess that's true all right. But don't worry. I'll lay a bet we'll have those rats wiped off the map inside six months!" He paused and suddenly threw me a funny look. "And that includes those Nazi rats too."

I stood and thought a minute. Then, half to myself, I chuckled, "Well, I'll be damned!" I was thinking what a joke this was on Flanahan & Co. Here we were at war after all, and they couldn't blame any American warmongers for it.

"I guess," the clerk remarked, "there's a lot of guys who're going to be damned now."

I looked at him, suddenly worried by his tone and the expression on his face. I was about to ask what he meant, but turned around instead. I thought I'd just heard someone mention my name. It must have been Pedro, because I could see him pointing in my direction. He was talking to one of those guys who'd bumped into me on the fifth floor a couple of minutes ago. Then I saw the stranger nod, and start toward me. He was a good-looking fellow, neatly dressed, and at a glance I'd have cast him for a salesman.

"You're Clem Smullet, aren't you?" he asked in a quiet voice.

"That's right," I said.

"Would you mind stepping outside with me?" he went on. "There's something I've got to talk to you about."

I looked at the guy, trying to figure out why he somehow made me feel uneasy. Then, putting on a scowl, I growled, "Can't it wait? I haven't had my breakfast yet. What d'you want to talk to me about anyway?"

"I think I'd better tell you outside," he said, still in that same quiet voice. Then, taking my elbow, he started leading me through the lobby.

I didn't try to resist. I somehow sensed it wouldn't be wise. Besides, I could see the clerk was trying to listen. Once we were out on the sidewalk, though, I faced the stranger and snapped, "Okay, now what is it?"

He took a thin wallet out of his coat-pocket, and opened it so I could see the identification card inside. "My name's Kelly," he said. "I'm with the Federal Bureau of Investigation. We have some questions we'd like to ask you at our office."

I felt myself go weak all over. "What kind of questions?" I asked hoarsely. "I don't know anything! You can't arrest me. . . ."

"Now, don't get excited, Mr. Smullet," the guy said, starting to lead me to a car parked against the curb. "I'm not arresting you. I'm just taking you down to have a little talk with my chief."

He opened the door of the car, but I wouldn't get in. "I haven't had my breakfast yet," I tried to stall. "Can't you come back later?"

"I'm sorry," he said, curling his lip slightly, "but I've got quite a few more people to call on. This has turned out to be a very busy day for the Bureau. I think you'd better come along right now."

I opened my mouth to argue some more, but then shut it with a click. There, coming out of the hotel door, was the other guy who'd bumped into me in front of the elevator—and he was leading Doc! I shot a glare at the slob, and then turned and got into the car. "Okay," I growled to Kelly, "let's go. . . ."